THE DRAGON'S DAUGHTER AND THE WINTER MAGE

BY

JEFFE KENNEDY

Invisible Loner

Gendra—partblood daughter of an elite mossback soldier and the only shapeshifter to achieve the coveted dragon form—is anything but interesting. She's actually plain and awkward and … invisible. Every guy she meets either looks right through her or—worse—thinks of her as just a friend. Fortunately Gen is far too practical to wallow in self pity. Much.

A Search for True Love

But as Gen accompanies her oldest friends on a quest for Her Majesty High Queen Ursula, she can't help feeling bitter about her lonely fate as, two by two, they pair off with each other. As usual, everyone but odd-woman-out Gen seems to be finding the happiness in true love that has always eluded her. And Gen's pathetic attempts to come out of her shell have only met with social disaster.

Dragon's Daughter

Still, with magic rifts plaguing the Thirteen Kingdoms and a strange intelligence stalking them from an alter-realm, Gen has plenty to deal with—especially when she's cut off from the group, isolated and facing a lethal danger. It just figures that Gen is on her own, once again. But with no one coming to save her, she has only herself to rely upon.

And, perhaps, the help of a mysterious, stranded magician…

ACKNOWLEDGMENTS

A special hat tip to Serena Romero for suggesting the perfect nickname for Gendra.

Many thanks to Darynda Jones, who—once again—read this book literally as I was writing it, to the point of—once again!—vetting the final chapter the night before I sent it to the proofreader. Thanks also to Marcella Burnard for vetting my sailing lingo and action (any remaining errors are mine) and to and Emily Mah Tippetts for an early read.

Much love to Kelly Robson for messaging a good morning every day and reminding me that I can finish the book, because I always do. Another bottle of Gruet bubbly to Megan Mulry (as long as she shares) in thanks for all the lovely Sunday afternoons.

Thanks and love to Carien Ubink for All The Assisting and on-the-fly answers to my questions on what I may or may not have written in earlier books.

Love to David, who is there every day, and who makes everything possible.

Thank you for reading!

Credits
Proofreading: Pikko's House (www.pikkoshouse.com)
Cover: Ravven (www.ravven.com)

THE DRAGON'S DAUGHTER AND THE WINTER MAGE

BY

JEFFE KENNEDY

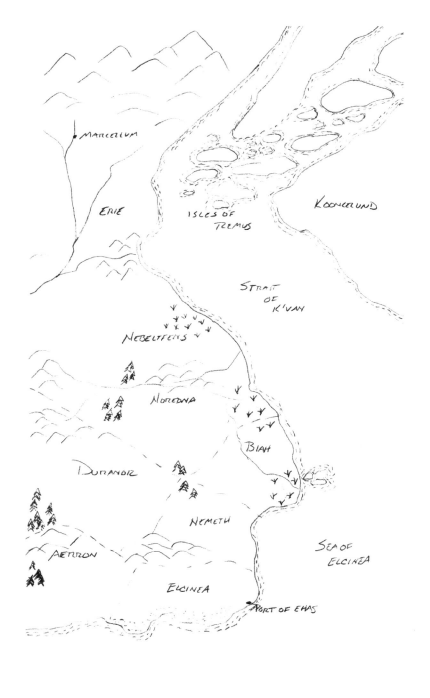

~ PROLOGUE ~

DRAGON FORM.

Dragon form.

Dragon *form*.

Dragon form.

Gen concentrated on images of the dragons she'd seen, including her own mother, turning them around in her mind with various kinds of emphasis, trying to get her skin to feel that shape. But how did being a dragon feel?

"Gen!" Lena shouted from down the beach. Her brown skin tanned to a shade as golden as her glorious hair, Lena jumped up and down, waving her arms as if Gen could somehow fail to see her. "You've practiced shapeshifting enough for one day!"

"Party at the falls!" Zeph, walking beside her and holding up a picnic basket, yelled also. Gen's cousin tossed back her glossy black hair, which curled wildly in the sea breeze and still somehow looked perfect.

"Go have fun with your friends." Gen's mother, Zynda, in human form and not a magnificent sapphire dragon at the moment, nudged her shoulder in that direction.

"I need to practice more," Gen insisted.

"Gendra," her mother said with rare exasperation. "You're

only seventeen. You have plenty of time."

"I'm not even close to getting dragon form," Gen pointed out, feeling mulish as she watched Rhy drop from the sky in raven form and divebomb Lena, who shrieked with laughter. Gen loved her friends, sure—and she was truly happy Rhy and Lena were in love—but watching them make starry eyes at each other got old after a while.

Zynda rolled her gorgeous eyes, long black hair whipping like a banner, looking effortlessly beautiful, just like Zeph. Really, Zeph could be Zynda's daughter instead of her niece, they looked so much alike. Even their names were similar. And Zeph had inherited all of the beauty, charisma, and sensual charm of the wild and magical Tala side of their heritage, while Gen took after her mossback father. She loved her father, but Marskal was the polar opposite of the romantic and exciting shapeshifter nature. Solid, serious, a man of the earth in personality and coloring, Marskal was dependable and stalwart in every way.

So was Gen. Alas.

She twisted her own boring brown hair into a rope, wishing she could be less dependable and more... well, exciting and romantic. Dragon form, now *that* would be something. And it would show everyone that Gen wasn't all boring brown mossback.

"Dragon form, seriously?" Zynda demanded. "Have you even listened to the stories I've told you, what I went through to attain dragon form? Even your uncle Zyr can't—"

"Can't attain dragon form," Gen said with her dutifully. "And he's been trying all these years, I know. But *you* are the one who named me 'dragon's daughter.'"

Zynda gave her a sharp look. "Gendra is more accurately translated as 'born of the dragon,' and I named you that because I became pregnant with you—against huge odds, particularly with a mossback lover—at the same time I attained dragon form. I wanted to celebrate that miracle, but it doesn't mean anything more than that."

A miraculous name for a dull girl, Gen thought glumly to herself. Still, she clung to the likelihood that if her mother had the shapeshifting talent to acquire dragon form, Gen could, too. Then she'd be something more than dull. "You got there, though, by practicing your shapeshifting. All the time, you've said," she replied stubbornly. "I can at least do that much."

"You can and you have," Zynda replied more gently. Prying her daughter's hands from her twisted rope of hair, she combed her fingers through it, arranging it around Gen's face, her expression fond now. "There. You look so pretty with your hair loose like this. My beautiful daughter."

Gen wrinkled her nose but didn't argue. After all, Zynda said the same about Marskal, confirming that love gave her questionable judgment.

"Dragon form," Zynda continued, "takes more than practice. It requires a sacrifice."

"I know that."

"It's one thing to know it and another to experience the agony of that choice. I don't wish that on you."

"But you don't regret it," Gen persisted.

Zynda looked thoughtful, and a little sad. "Me having dragon form has been good for the Tala, of course—which was the main reason I aspired to it, remember—and I don't regret that aspect of it. But I was lucky. I was willing to give up any chance at happiness to save my people, and I got to be happy anyway. The goddess Moranu bestowed a great favor on me."

"No surprise, as you were Her devout acolyte. You took on a holy quest for Her, so of course she bestowed a favor on you."

Zynda gave her a considering look. "That's an oversimplification, but suffice to say that Her favors are not guaranteed. Our lives and efforts aren't coin we pay to obtain something in return. Besides," she continued before Gen could argue, "if I got to pick my divine favors, if had to choose again between dragon form and your father, having you...." Her mouth twisted wryly. "I would choose differently."

"You don't mean that."

"I do mean it," Zynda insisted. "My life with Marskal and you—you are my real treasures."

Huh. Gen kind of doubted that. It sounded good in retrospect, but she'd heard the stories all her life, and everyone agreed that Zynda had been single-minded in pursuit of dragon form. Besides, Gen had no Marskal pining for her. Beautiful Rhy was head over heels in love with Lena; Astar would be the next high king, and a marriage of state awaited him. And Jak—when he was around—had eyes only for Stella. No one looked twice at Gen.

"You're young still," Zynda said earnestly, as if reading Gen's thoughts. "You have your whole life ahead of you, and you deserve to have fun, too. If dragon form is meant to be, you'll get there. Enjoy life while you can."

What's to enjoy? she nearly grumbled, but she swallowed the words and attempted a smile. "I enjoy shapeshifting. Refining my skills *is* fun."

"You're so like your father," Zynda said on a sigh. "Always thinking about work."

"You fell in love my father," Gen pointed out. "After you finally noticed he was alive."

Zynda raised her brows. "That was my flaw, not his. Once I paid attention, his many fine qualities shone brighter than the sun."

Gen nodded, fixing her smile in place. It wouldn't do any good to dwell on the fact that Marskal had been invisible to Zynda for ages, in love with her from afar, and dully reconciled to her never knowing it.

"*Gen!*" Zeph slipped an arm around Gen's waist from behind, startling her and taking advantage of her surprise by pressing enthusiastic kisses to Gen's cheek. "Didn't you hear us calling you?"

Gen extracted herself. "Yes, but I'm busy practicing."

"No, you're not," Zeph and Zynda said at the same time, then grinned at each other.

"I was just telling Gen that's enough practice for the day," Zynda said. "You all go have fun."

"Thank you, Auntie Zynda!" Zeph sang out. "We're taking a picnic to the diving cliffs. We even talked Willy and Nilly into coming."

Sure enough, Astar and Stella, the twins dubbed Willy and Nilly from their troublesome toddler years, were strolling toward them from the cliff city. Astar waved, the sun highlighting him in affectionate gold, Stella a darker, slighter form beside him. Zeph sighed dreamily. "I swear, Astar gets more beautiful every day. How is that fair?"

Gen could've told her life wasn't fair, but Rhy—back in human form—came galloping past just then, snorting like a horse, with Lena clinging to his back, laughing gaily. "I meant a *real* horse!" she protested, barely able to get the words out.

Rhy whinnied, quite realistically, and bucked as wildly as his human form allowed. Lena shrieked with laughter, falling to the sand, Rhy diving after to roll her over and over, tickling her into hysterics. "Stop!" she cried, batting his hands away, and he stole a kiss. She softened, then squealed. "Let me up, foul beast."

"As my lady wishes," Rhy declared, leaping up and leaving her in the sand. He bowed gallantly. Tall, rangy, and impossibly handsome, his black hair caught blue lights that matched his ocean-deep eyes. "Hello, Zynda, Gen. Beautiful day for a picnic."

"You're going to pay for that, Rhyian." Lena was sitting up, shaking sand from her cascading caramel hair, a shade that perfectly complemented her brown skin. Though Lena wasn't even a full year older than Gen, she'd developed an enviably lush figure ages ago, while Gen was only tall, skinny, and regrettably lanky.

"Will I?" Rhy spun on Lena, pretending to stalk her, then scooping her up in his arms, stealing another long, languorous kiss that had Lena winding her arms around his neck, her whole body sighing. "I'll pay any price, lovely Salena," he declared. "Anything you ask of me is yours."

"Young love can be so nauseating," Zeph commented, and Zynda snickered.

"You say that after you were just ogling Astar?" Gen demanded.

Zeph rolled her eyes. "I want into Astar's adorably tight and princely pants," she corrected. "Sex, not love."

"I think that's my cue to leave you all to it," Zynda said with smile.

"Sorry, Mom," Gen said, blushing hard, though Zeph only smiled wickedly.

"Nothing to be sorry for." Zynda patted Zeph's cheek. "Just be careful of flying too close to the sun, niece of mine." Suddenly condensing into a jewel-bright hummingbird, Zynda's First Form, she zipped off.

"What did she mean by that?" Zeph demanded.

"Mean by what?" Stella asked, her hand clasped in her twin's, her solemn gray eyes wide with concern.

"Nothing," Gen said hastily, hoping to avert an uncomfortable conversation. "My mom and I were just discussing what it takes to achieve dragon form."

As Gen had hoped, that thoroughly distracted Zeph, who spun to eye her sharply. "Any clues?" she demanded, as eager as Gen to unlock the key to dragon form.

Gen shook her head. "Her usual inscrutable nonsense."

Zeph huffed out an impatient breath, then returned her predatory attention to Astar. "Astar, darling," she purred, winding her arm through his and gently prying him away from Stella, "tell me you're going to dive off the cliff today. I'll be your coach."

"Not me, Zephyr," he protested, smiling broadly. "I can't be irresponsible like that."

"Just a teensy bit irresponsible?" she wheedled. "Live a little. Have some fun!"

"It's fun to watch you," he replied sunnily. "And Gen and Nilly."

Rhy galloped past again, this time in actual horse form, Lena perched atop the gleaming black stallion, her strong brown legs clasped to his side, her short skirt riding up as she lay low over his neck, whooping in joy. His black mane twined with her dark golden hair. They were stunning together.

Gen let out a wistful sigh, and Stella echoed it, giving her a rueful smile as they trailed after Astar and Zeph, who had their heads bent together in some intent conversation. "It makes you sad to see them together," Stella noted gently, without censure.

Not bothering to deny it to her empath friend, and not asking which "them" Stella meant, Gen just smiled. "I'm in a mood today is all."

"There's someone out there for you, Gen," Stella said, gaze fixed on the distance.

"Is that prophecy?" Gen asked, startled. Stella had never said anything like that to her before.

Casting her a chagrined glance, Stella shook her head. "I misspoke. I forget sometimes that someone might think I'm talking about the future when I'm making a simple observation. There's someone out there for everyone, so obviously there's someone for you. Take heart. You're young still."

"You sound like my mother."

"And your mother would know," Stella replied equably. "Look how long it took her to find and settle down with Marskal."

"That doesn't make me feel better," Gen grumbled, watching Rhy gallop into the surf, Lena shouting enthusiastically from his back, the water spray catching crystals of light.

"It's easy to envy them," Stella said in a quiet voice, "but don't be too quick to wish to trade lives. Rhy and Lena have a long and difficult road ahead."

"Now *that* sounded like prophecy."

Stella only smiled sorrowfully and said nothing more.

~ 1 ~

Seven Years Later

BATTLING MONSTERS AND worrying about magic rifts in the sky should be more worrisome than trying to keep the peace between two of her closest friends, Gen reflected. And yet, not so much.

"I swear to the three goddesses, Rhyian," Lena hissed, lips pressed white with anger, "if you don't quit following me, I'll—"

"It's not your castle, sweetheart," Rhy drawled, shoving his hands in his pockets and giving her an insolent smile that had Gen bracing herself for Lena's explosion. "You can't tell me where to go."

"Oh, I'll tell you where to go." Lena's tone dropped ominously, her weather magic intensifying in the air, like pressure plummeting before the onset of a storm.

"I'm interested in the library," he insisted, goading her. "I like books."

"Rhy, Lena." Gen tried to be soothing. "Let's not—"

"I doubt there's anyone lurking among the books hoping to be seduced by a faithless idiot," Lena snarled, completely ignoring Gen. "But I suppose hope springs eternal, doesn't it?

Stay away from me, Rhyian."

"I did," he snarled back, "for seven years. It didn't take."

"Try another seven," she spat. "Or how about forever. Does forever work for you?"

"Princess Salena Nakoa KauPo," Prince Wilhelm called. "Is there a problem?"

"If there is, it's not mine," she declared, and pointedly turned her back, stalking away. Gen let out a breath of relief that they'd avoided a worse argument. She'd come along on the post-breakfast tour of Castle Marcellum's library entirely to play referee between Rhy and Lena. Seven years of distance hadn't done much to resolve the heartbreak and bitter feelings between the once-lovers. Being thrown together again after all that time had unraveled the barely marginal détente they'd recently established. Lena would never get past Rhy's callous betrayal of her trust—not that Gen blamed her—and Rhy seemed to be unable to get that through his head, more determined to win her back than ever.

"She doesn't mean it," Rhy said, gazing after Lena, proving the point.

"It's lovely, Prince Wilhelm," Lena's voice drifted back to where Gen and Rhy still stood, barely inside the doors.

"I dare say, it's as well stocked as any you've seen, save the library in Nahanau, naturally," Wilhelm replied.

"Ah, but we of Nahanau know our library is a wonder of the world, one established by our wise ancestors. We can't take credit for it, nor do we expect any other library to compete."

"You are too generous, Your Highness."

"Please, call me Lena."

"Then you must call me Wim."

"You must call me Wim," Rhy mimicked in a foppish whine that sounded nothing like the prince, offering Gen his arm with an absurdly grand gesture. "I'll call him dinner if he keeps touching Lena like that."

"Down boy," Gen muttered back, taking his arm in case he lunged for their host. "Wilhelm is just looking to court a princess, since he doesn't run into many this far north. And you promised Jak you wouldn't kill the prince."

"No, I did not," Rhy corrected, patting Gen's hand where it rested on his black-velvet-clad forearm. "Besides, Jak would help me hide the body." He winked at her, so charming when he wasn't being an ass. "So would you."

Of course she would, but she had no intention of encouraging him. "If you kill the prince, we'll get kicked out of Castle Marcellum," she pointed out reasonably, "and I'm really happy to be warm again. I can't face the winter weather just yet, Rhy. Not so soon. I know we have to continue our mission, but give me another day to thaw. Please."

He followed her gaze to the wintry landscape outside the frosted windows. Though the day had dawned sunny, heavy clouds were gathering, wind blowing glittering snow up from drifts on the hills. "Good point," he conceded, then grinned at her, his deep-blue eyes breathtaking, black waves tumbling around his gorgeous face. "You're so practical, Gen. Why didn't I fall in love with you instead?"

Gen sucked in a breath at the sting of his casual teasing. Why indeed? Because she might as well be invisible with beautiful, sensual Lena in the room. Not to mention gorgeous Zeph, who'd naturally succeeded in her quest to make Astar fall in love with her. She was even off playing his consort, in meetings with the king and queen of Erie, as impossible as that change seemed for the flighty Zeph. And now Jak had finally gotten through to Stella, the pair of them probably off in bed together at that very moment.

And Gen was still alone, practically still a virgin, save for one embarrassingly horrible experience that didn't really count, except that she couldn't seem to rid herself of the galling memory and vague sense of illness surrounding it. *Quit dwelling,* she ordered herself.

"What did you make of Nilly actually *giggling* at breakfast like that?" Rhy asked, his mind clearly on Jak and Stella's newfound liaison, too, though his gaze lingered blackly on Wilhelm and Lena where they examined some tome he'd extracted from a shelf for her.

"That was a love giggle," Gen replied wistfully.

"Is that a real thing?" Rhy demanded with a wicked glint in his eyes. "I think you made that up."

Gen bit back pointing out that Lena used to giggle just like that with him, back when they were in love. She would never, however, deliberately hurt him like that. Rhy could be an ass, and he brooded enough to make her want to kick him, but he was also a friend. And ever since he'd been trapped in wolf form in an alter-realm without food or water, unable to shift, he'd been moodier than ever. Lena's light laugh wafted over to them.

"*That,*" Rhy snarled. "Was that a love giggle?"

"No," Gen replied in all seriousness. "That was a polite pretending-to-find-your-host-amusing chuckle."

Rhy cocked his head, his raven First Form's canniness in the gesture, his attention entirely on her for once. It was a heady feeling. Or it would be, if Gen thought she had the remotest chance of catching Rhy's interest. "How do you know?" he asked.

How do you not *know?* she wanted to ask in return. Rhy had known Lena all his life, knew her just as well as Gen did, better in some ways, and was head over heels in love with the woman. Shouldn't he understand Lena better than anyone? Though, maybe that was partly why their love hadn't survived. That and Rhy fucking everything up so horribly.

"I *listen*," she replied with some irritation, yanking her arm from his. "I pay attention to my friends."

"Hey, I pay attention to my friends, too," Rhy replied defensively. He leaned in, waggling his eyebrows. "I gave up the room to Jak so he could seduce our Nilly, didn't I? And when she was ready to bolt and screw it all up, I talked her into giving him a chance."

Arrested, Gen stared at Rhy. "Wait. You did?"

"See?" He drew himself up and stuck his hands in his pockets. "I can be a friend."

"To Jak," she specified, "so he could get laid."

"That's not fair," Rhy protested, but he was grinning. "I'm fully invested in our Nilly getting laid, too."

Despite herself, Gen laughed.

"I know *that* laugh," Rhy declared. "That's a you're-so-clever-and-entertaining, Rhy giggle."

"You *are* clever and entertaining," Gen agreed, adding ruefully, "even if you are an ass."

"Is that any way to talk to the guy who saved Jak and Stella's tender new love affair from being nipped in the bud?"

"So, what *did* you say to Nilly?" Gen asked, terribly curious. She hadn't known any of this. Where had she been? At the ball being a wallflower, probably.

Rhy shrugged, expression going moody as he gazed past Gen to Lena deep in conversation with the flirtatious prince. "I advised her to learn from my great cautionary tale. That giving in to fear can ruin what might be the only opportunity you have for happiness."

"Oh, Rhy," Gen murmured, her heart twisting for him. She regretted the uncharitable thought she'd nursed in being jealous of Rhy and Lena's giddy love affair back in the day. They'd been so deliriously happy together, and they were both so miserable apart. She should've appreciated it more when they were all together, one big, entangled group of friends. The split between Rhy and Lena had impacted all of them. As much as she'd been privately envious of the others pairing off, she missed even more what they'd all had back in the day. Going on this quest together had begun to rebuild some of that old camaraderie, but it would never be the same as it was back then. Back when they'd all been considerably more innocent. When they hadn't been worried about the world coming to a grisly end. "You'll have other chances," she told Rhy. "You'll find someone else."

His gaze returned to her face, neutral and unreadable now. "You mistake me, my old friend. I don't want anyone else. All I want is to get back what I had and carelessly destroyed. I know I'm the last one to figure this out, but I'm finally facing the truth. She's never going to forgive me."

Gen wanted to tell him he was wrong, but she couldn't. She'd listened to Lena's tearful confessions and angry diatribes enough to know that Lena would never, ever give Rhy another opportunity to stomp all over her heart. Rhy read the truth in her eyes, grimacing for it. "You're a good person, Gen," he said. "A good friend. At least you never lie to me."

"So, what can I show you, Prince Rhyian?" Wilhelm asked jovially, inserting himself into the conversation with the confidence of royalty. "Or you, Lady Gendra?" He tipped his head to indicate Lena, who sat at a table, head bent over an obviously ancient tome. "Princess Salena Nakoa KauPo is engrossed, as you can see."

"Thank you, Your Highness, but I'm not a lady," Gen replied. "I'm not nobility of any kind. Your Highness may call me Gen."

"Then call me Wim," he replied with an easy smile. Prince Wilhelm was young and solidly mossback, and not handsome exactly, but striking with his mother's ivory hair and lake-blue eyes. He was also pleasant company, when he wasn't focused on flirting with Lena. He didn't seem to notice the predatory glint in Rhy's eyes. "You also, Prince Rhyian."

"Not really a prince," Rhy reminded him with a flash of teeth. "Call me Rhy."

"I still don't quite understand how the Tala handle the line of succession," Wim said, his curious tone inviting Rhy to explain.

"No one does," Rhy mused grimly. "Largely because it makes no rational sense. What you get for letting animals rule themselves."

Gen narrowed her eyes at him in warning, but Rhy had shifted his focus fully to needling the young prince of Erie.

Wim considered Rhy, absorbing his words. "You refer, I'm sure, to the Tala being shapeshifters, but I seriously doubt that anyone—especially you, yourselves—would call the Tala animals."

"Don't be so sure," Rhy shot back, a growl in his voice.

Stepping forward ever so slightly, not quite putting herself between the two men, but close enough that she could if Rhy lost his temper, Gen smiled sweetly at Wim. "We don't think of ourselves as animals, it's true, but neither do we think of ourselves as entirely human." She threw a pointed look at Rhy. "In fact, some of us are less human than others, our First Forms dominating our natures, sometimes to the detriment of polite society."

Rhy simply bared his teeth at her, unbothered.

"I confess I'm wildly curious," Wim replied. "What is a First Form?"

"The form we shift into instinctively for the first time, often as infants," Gen explained.

Her Majesty High Queen Ursula had wanted them to keep their shapeshifting low profile on this journey, especially as they traveled to the less sophisticated, more distant realms of the Thirteen Kingdoms. That plan, however, had pretty much come apart at the Midway Inn when the alter-realm entity that they'd taken to simply calling "the intelligence," for lack of a better name, kidnapped some of the locals, forcing their group to resort to their most vicious—and startling—forms in order to effect a rescue. The sight of Zeph as a gryphon—or *gríobhth*, in the Tala language—had thoroughly shredded their cover as a group of frivolous young nobles touring the countryside. Of course, Astar taking dragon form back at Lake Sullivan to save Zeph's life had done that as well, just with far fewer witnesses.

It stuck in Gen's craw that Astar had somehow fallen into dragon form with none of the diligent practice and study Gen had put in over the years. *It's one thing to know it and another to experience the agony of that choice,* her mother had said long ago. It didn't take much guessing to figure out what Astar had been willing to sacrifice in that moment, with Zeph plummeting to her death. Gen allowed herself a dreamy, totally internal sigh for that truly romantic gesture.

"So, is it rude to inquire what your First Form is?" Wim asked her, clearly fascinated. Men rarely noticed Gen, but Wim focused on her with those pretty blue eyes, studying her with great interest. "You are a shapeshifter, yes?"

"Gen is the most talented shapeshifter of our generation," Rhy put in proudly, resting a hand on her shoulder. "As her mother is of hers."

"Zeph is just as talented," Gen temporized, blushing a little.

"You have more forms," Rhy insisted. "Plus your other skills are better."

"Only because I practice more."

"This is amazing," Wim commented, his eyes shining with

admiration. "It never occurred to me that shapeshifting requires practice. I guess I thought you just did it like, *poof*, naturally."

"If only," Rhy drawled.

"Our First Form works that way for most shapeshifters," Gen cut in smoothly. "And for many, it's their only form. Some acquire a few more."

"And then grind to a halt at that point, confined to those pitiful few," Rhy added.

Gen turned on him. "Do you really want to get in a conversation, here and now, about how your poor attitude and work ethic get in the way of you acquiring more forms?"

Rhy gave her an unamused smile. "Seems we just did. I think I'll see what Lena is reading so intently."

"Don't go and—"

"I can be civil," he snapped, sounding anything but.

"I thought you were facing up to things," she said quietly, meaningfully.

That gave him pause, and he raked a hand through the tousled black waves of his hair. "Right."

"Jak and Stella were going to practice with her magic," she reminded him. "Maybe you should go work with them. They said a shapeshifter would be helpful."

Rhy thrust his hands in his pockets, brooding gaze going to the oblivious Lena, then dropped his chin in a reluctant nod. "I'll do that." Without another word, he prowled out of the room.

"It seems Prince Rhyian—I mean, that Rhy doesn't like discussing this topic?" Wim ventured. "I apologize if I was too invasive."

Gen sighed. "Not at all, Wim," she replied, manufacturing a warm smile. "Rhy is still recovering from some of our more disturbing adventures. Please forgive us for being on edge."

Wim returned the smile, the genuine warmth in it lighting up his face. "You don't seem to be on edge at all. I find you most charming and delightful."

No one could blame her for preening a little at that, even though she couldn't claim to be traumatized at all, since she hadn't journeyed to an alter-realm. Of their group, only she hadn't gone to one of those uncanny and dangerous places— willingly or unwillingly—which made her feel vaguely ashamed. It didn't mean she was any less brave than the others... did it?

"So, you have many forms you've practiced?" Wim asked. "Is that what makes you the most talented shapeshifter of your generation?"

She felt herself blushing harder, kind of wishing Rhy hadn't said that. "Talent is an inherent thing. My mother and Zeph's father—they're twins—are very talented shapeshifters, able to take many forms. We both inherited that ability."

"But you work at it more."

"I'm naturally more inclined to study than Zeph," she allowed. More inclined to being alone while Zeph was forever surrounded by admirers.

Wim smiled sympathetically. "I can see how the crown prince's fiancée is a bit... flighty. Not serious and grounded, like you are. I bet your First Form is something substantial, like a horse."

"Zeph is committed to learning how to be the best high queen she can be," Gen replied, feeling she should defend Zeph, who really was trying. "And our First Forms aren't necessarily discernible from our human personalities. Mine is a hummingbird."

Wim's face went momentarily slack with astonishment, then lit with utter delight. "You're right—I would never have guessed. But now that I know, I can see it in you. Your eyes are so lovely, like jewels. I bet you're a beautiful hummingbird. We only have them here in the summer months, but I love them."

"I do too," she agreed with a like smile. "It's also my mother's First Form."

"So it runs in families?"

"Not necessarily. In fact, it's unusual that I have the same First Form that she does."

"And how many other forms can you take?"

"I haven't counted," she replied honestly. Zynda was famous for answering that question with a vague "several," which was outrageously misleading. Gen didn't have it in her to be that sneaky, which was probably why she'd never be as interesting as her wild and dramatic mother.

"So many as that, then." Wim grinned. "What a remarkable thing it must be to—"

A raven burst into the library at top speed, becoming Rhy so fast that he took a few steps from the momentum. He looked wildly at Lena, who'd knocked her chair over when she leapt to her feet in shock, then to Gen: "They're gone. Jak and Stella—they've been abducted."

~ 2 ~

WIM ACTED FASTER than Gen would've credited the lighthearted young prince, immediately calling for the guards before turning on Rhy. "It shouldn't be possible for someone to be abducted from this castle. It's a fortress. How did it happen?"

Gen looked helplessly to Rhy and Lena. They really needed Astar for this. Almost certainly the intelligence from the alter-realm was at work here. And that was an element of their extraordinary quest that Astar had carefully omitted from his explanations to the royals of Erie. Lena put a hand on Rhy's arm, calming him as only she really could, even now. "Just tell us what you saw, Rhy."

He focused on her, steadying. "I went to our room—the one Jak and I share—and the door was open. They weren't inside. No sign of either of them."

Wim relaxed, signaling to the inrushing guards to stand down. "Well, it may be no great mystery, then. They probably went elsewhere and forgot to close the door. Or a servant went in and left the door open." His smile faded as he took in their tense expressions. "What am I missing?"

"It smelled wrong," Rhy growled at him. "And their trail

led to the room, then vanished."

"Their... trail?" Wim asked faintly.

"Rhy would've checked that in his wolf form," Lena replied crisply, smoothly concealing the fact that, like many shapeshifters of the oldest blood, Rhy could use wolf senses in human form, too. "We need Astar and Zeph, likely the king and queen, too. Would you take us to where they're meeting?"

"They won't like being interrupted," Wim replied dubiously. "Especially if this is a false alarm."

"It isn't," Gen told him firmly before Rhy could throttle the young prince. "Rhy knows what he's talking about—and time could be of the essence."

"Come with me, then." Wim strode off, and they fell in behind him, the guards forming a phalanx behind.

"Can you identify if the portal is still open?" Rhy asked Lena.

"I can try." She didn't sound confident. "But I don't know where Jak's room is."

"I'll take you," Rhy said, then looked at Gen. "Bring the others. We may need Zeph."

Because Zeph's gríobhth form could withstand travel to the alter-realm better than the rest of them. "If the rift is still there, don't go through," she urged them.

"No worries about that," Lena replied grimly, the haunted shadows of her previous visit to the alter-realm stark in her drawn expression.

They peeled off, a few guards trailing after them. Gen caught up to Wim, who looked after Rhy and Lena with a frown. "They're going directly to the room to check for more clues," Gen explained.

"Leaving us to brave the lions. Wonderful," Wim replied unhappily.

"I'll take responsibility," Gen said, then wondered at herself. But no—Astar would want her to interrupt him, even if this did prove to be a false alarm. In fact, she'd happily accept any embarrassment or chastisement if they were wrong and Jak and Stella were off practicing somewhere. The alternative was far worse. They could be stuck in some alter-realm none of rest of them could get to. Or they could've emerged in midair in some other world, falling to their deaths. A sick feeling settled in her stomach, fear making a cold sweat drip down her spine.

Please, goddesses, look after them.

"IT'S NO FALSE alarm," Astar declared, pacing the room, his grizzly bear First Form heavy in his ponderous movements, the low growl of rage emanating from his human chest. "Stella isn't in this world. She's gone."

"Why didn't you feel her disappear?" Zeph asked, her hands knotted together as she anxiously watched Astar's pacing.

He shook his head, angry with himself. "I've been giving her privacy, like she asked me to. And since she's been with Jak, I..." He deflated. "I didn't *want* to know, and now I've failed her."

"Don't be ridiculous," Zeph snapped, going to him and punching his meaty arm. "Of course you stayed out of Nilly's sex life. That's not a failure."

"I don't think I understand much of what's going on here," King Cavan said to his queen, both of them perplexed.

"Twins," Gen explained, since clearly no one else was going to. Lena was trying to find the portal, Rhy hovering over her as if ready to yank her back should she misstep. "Astar and Stella have always had a deep bond. They're aware of each other almost telepathically. And Astar knows that Stella is no longer in our same… reality."

Queen Nix sucked in a breath, fixing Gen with an expression of dawning horror, while the king frowned still. "Explain," he demanded.

Wonderful. She was not supposed to be the diplomat here, but Astar was currently arguing with Zeph, probably about going after Jak and Stella. "Your Highnesses, remember how you explained that the Isles of Remus sometimes shift from one plane of existence to another? Queen Nix, you said that your homeland of the Isles are sometimes in this world, and you can travel back and forth freely. Other times you can't."

Queen Nix was still watching her with an odd expression. "As we had that conversation over breakfast not hours ago, I believe I do recall."

Gen plunged on doggedly. "On this quest, we've, ah, occasionally encountered a similar phenomenon, where various members of our party have been transported to what we're calling alter-realms."

She had their undivided attention, which wasn't comfortable at all. "That's why you weren't surprised by Nix's tales," the king noted. "And yet you didn't confide in us."

"That was my decision and my fault, King Cavan," Astar said, joining the conversation to Gen's great relief, and dragging along a flashing-eyed Zeph with an implacable grip on her hand. She glared daggers at him, which he ignored. "I was hoping this was information you wouldn't need to know."

Cavan set his jaw. "If my kingdom is going to be vanishing piecemeal into some alter-realm, then by Glorianna, I should *think* it's something I need to know."

"Cavan," Queen Nix said in quiet warning.

"What? This is our kingdom, Nix. Do you think Her Majesty would condone this young whelp deciding unilaterally that—"

"Cavan." The queen's voice whipped out like a lash, cutting off the king's tirade. "It was none of our business until now. Isn't that correct, Crown Prince Astar? You had no reason to believe these portals would trouble you here."

Astar nodded, then shook his head grimly. "I hoped they wouldn't. Stella had expressed the concern, however, that the intelligence causing these portals—that perhaps creates and controls these alter-realms—was deliberately stalking her."

"Why Stella?" Queen Nix asked, not questioning the statement, but as if keenly interested in the specifics.

"She's a sorceress?" Astar ventured.

"So is Salena," Rhy inserted.

"I'm not anywhere near Stella in skill or native ability," Lena protested. "She's studied with Queen Andromeda her entire life, and I just move weather around."

"You have amazing powers," Rhy insisted. "Don't sell yourself short."

"What, like you do?" she snapped. "You're sure one to be giving advice to—"

"Enough!" Astar's roar, more than a little bear, drowned out their argument and had them both staring in shock. Zeph rolled her eyes, and Gen nodded back at her.

"I apologize, Your Highness," Lena said meekly, dropping her gaze. "That isn't helping. But I also can't sense a rift here, and I can't open one on my own."

"Then how do we get to them?" Astar demanded. "I want solutions, people. Start *thinking*." He emphasized the word with an extra growl for Rhy.

"We could go back to Midway Inn," Gen suggested, squaring her shoulders when they all glared at her in varying degrees of astonishment and anger. "It's the last place we're certain of there being rifts. Numerous ones."

"Gen is right," Lena said, nodding slowly. "Failing that, we could go back to Lake Sullivan where we found the first rift."

"Or we can go forward, to the Isles of Remus," Zeph put in. "From what Queen Nix has told us, we'll find similar rifts there."

"We don't know that it's the same phenomenon there," Lena argued.

"We don't know that it isn't," Rhy pointed out.

"The one in the Isles has been going on much longer," Lena countered.

"How many alter-realms, portals, and rifts can there be?"

Rhy demanded.

"An infinite number, you numbskull!"

"Children," Astar growled.

"I'm just saying," Rhy protested, "that if we go to the Isles, we'd at least still be pursuing the quest."

"Rhy is correct there," Astar said slowly, nodding, Rhy looking surprised, then pleased. "Considering the timeline that Queen Andromeda foresaw, we don't have time to backtrack. That's the only reason we're even considering sailing to the Isles in winter. We have to get there soon, find King Isyn, and avert the major rift she saw would open, or it will indeed engulf our world."

Gen shivered at that stark image. It had been bad enough when Andi had described the catastrophe in vague prophetic terms. Now that they'd experienced the nightmarish alter-realms and the monsters they spawned, the prospect was truly chilling.

"And how are we supposed to get there?" Lena was arguing. "Jak was supposed to sail us."

Rhy threw up his hands. "There are other sailors in the world."

"We're talking about Jak and Stella," Lena nearly shrieked. "I know you're heartless, but even *you* can't be that cold."

"If I'm so cold, why did you kiss me so passionately on top of Castle Ordnung on the longest night?" he demanded.

"Temporary insanity," she ground out.

"Why didn't any of you tell me they're lovers?" Wim murmured in Gen's ear, and she sighed.

"They're not. Well, they were, but it came apart."

"Sure looks like they'd like to come together again." He snickered, then paled at Gen's expression. "I am *so* sorry. Such an inappropriate joke. I don't know what possessed me to say that to you. Please accept my apologies, Gen."

She could hardly fault him. The sexual tension between Rhy and Lena tended to roll out so thickly it was difficult to remain unaffected. Also, as Jak had pointed out several times, something about the alter-realm intelligence seemed to make the shapeshifters more impulsive, less rational. More *animal*, for want of a better word. She studied Wim's lake-blue eyes. Not Tala blue, but... "Are you sure you're not a shapeshifter?"

"I wish, but I think I'd know by now if I was. I am, however, very much my mother's son." He tipped his head toward Queen Nix. "If you know what I mean."

"I don't."

With a rueful smile, he shrugged. "Fair, because no one really does. I can see things no one else can. I do have an affinity for animals, like my mother does. My brother, Isyn, though, he's the one who can—"

Intertwined male and female screams ripped open the air, and two bodies fell from the ceiling, crashing in a heap just inside the doorway. The breath caught in Gen's throat at the sight and smell of blood covering Jak and Stella. They lay unmoving, wrapped around each other.

"*Nilly*," Astar gasped, falling to his knees.

"Are they... dead?" Lena asked in a cold, still voice.

"No," Rhy, Zeph, and Gen answered as one.

"Heartbeats are strong," Rhy added for Lena, who lacked their sharper shapeshifter senses.

"I'm sending for our healers," King Cavan said. "How else can we help?"

Zeph had fallen to her knees also, helping Astar examine the battered pair—not easy, as the two were tightly entwined and unresponsive—and Rhy was talking in a low voice to Lena, offering comfort by the look of it. So, once again, it fell to Gen to say something. "Healers would be wonderful, Your Highnesses—thank you." She tried to think. When Jak had nearly frozen to death, Gen had known what to do. Her father's family had land near Castle Ordnung, mostly fields for farming, but it also bordered the wildlands in the foothills of the mountains. Frostbite and deadly chill were regular perils of wintertime, and she knew a lot about treating those. Who knew what Jak and Stella had just gone through?

"Hot broth and fresh water would be welcome," she said. "Lots of blankets." Just in case. "Otherwise... can we just let you know as we figure this out?"

"Of course, Gen," Queen Nix said, taking Gen's hands and squeezing them. "And you don't need us hovering. Just send word. Wim, would you stay with them, see that they get what they need?"

"Absolutely," Wim replied, giving Gen a reassuring nod. "Whatever I can do."

"Fuck!" a man swore, adding a few more filthy sailor's curses, and Gen's heart relaxed to hear Jak being his usual self. King Cavan raised a brow, and Queen Nix paled.

"I think that's our cue to go," the king said, escorting his wife around the heap of bodies almost blocking the doorway.

"Is that anatomically possible?" she asked him as they left

the room.

Gen winced, thankfully not hearing the king's reply, and Wim caught her eye, tilting his head. "Well...*is* it anatomically possible?" he asked mischievously.

"How should I know?" she snapped, beyond embarrassed. "Ask Jak."

Wim grinned. "I think I'm going to have to."

"Gen, we could use a hand here," Zeph called, and Gen hastened over. "I don't *think* she's hurt, not physically."

"There's a lot of blood on her," Gen replied dubiously. Stella's rusty-black hair spilled over both of them, hiding her face.

"I think it's all Jak's," Zeph confided in a worried tone. "We need to stop his bleeding, but they won't let go of each other."

"Won't ever let go," Jak muttered, barely conscious. "I promised her I'd come for her."

"You did, Jak." Astar, on his other side, used a cloth tied around Jak's head to wipe blood out of his eyes—ineffectively, as the cloth was saturated already, a motley of fresh and old blood. "You can let go now."

"Never," Jak ground out, holding tighter. "You won't keep us apart, Willy. I won't let you. I'll kill you first."

Astar closed his eyes briefly in pain, and Zeph nudged his shoulder. "He doesn't mean it. He's out of his head."

"I shouldn't have tried to—"

"Time enough for guilt later," Zeph interrupted him. "Jak, sweetheart, we need to treat you. Nilly is right here, but you need to let her go."

"No!" Jak's hold on Stella tightened. "I love her and he can't have her. I promised."

Gen's heart squeezed at the romance of it all, even as Zeph muttered about Jak being a thickheaded idiot. The difference between Gen and her cousin, right there. "Too bad Stella is the only one with the trick of knocking people out," Gen said. "That would be the fastest and easiest route."

Astar cocked his head. "There are other ways. Rhy, buddy, come here and help."

"A chance to knock our friend senseless? Don't mind if I do." Despite his glib words, Rhy's face was serious and concerned as he crouched beside Jak. Lena came to Gen's other side, and they all looked at each other, nodding in mutual understanding. Rhy and Astar seized Jak, and even Jak's wiry athleticism was no match for their combined shapeshifter strength. Once they had Jak in an unbreakable grip, Zeph, Lena, and Gen eased Stella gently away from him.

Jak fought wildly, screaming for Stella, but Astar and Rhy pinned him to the floor. The girls rolled Stella onto her back, careful not to touch her skin more than necessary, so they wouldn't tax her sensitive empathic magic too much. Gen brushed the hair out of Stella's face, which was pale and wan, violet shadows under her eyes, but her breathing was steady. Lena and Zeph ran light fingers over Stella, examining her for injuries.

"I think she's unhurt," Zeph told Astar, after confirming nods from Lena and Gen.

"She's probably sleeping off whatever sorcery she did to get them out of there," Lena added, her usually lushly curved lips pressed into a flat line. Lena was haunted by her own trials in the alter-realm and, though physically healthy, suffered from the psychological wounds still. Stella had been working to heal her mentally and emotionally, too, but so much had been happening...

Jak was still thrashing, hurling threats, and cursing with vicious enthusiasm.

"We need to tie him down or something," Astar said.

"A good punch would knock him out," Rhy suggested.

"No," Gen countered crisply, before she realized she was going to. Rhy gave her a look of blank surprise at her vehemence. "Jak doesn't need a concussion on top of everything else."

"The healers are here," Wim announced. Gen had forgotten he was there. A triad of serene-looking people of indeterminate gender glided forward. One knelt at Jak's head and laid a slender hand on his forehead. Jak's dark eyes rolled up so the whites showed, and he sagged, unconscious.

The healer smiled. "If you would put him on the bed," they said, low and musical. Rhy and Astar carried Jak to the bed, Gen dashing ahead to pull down the covers.

Then Astar gathered up Stella, cradling her slight form in his big, bearish arms. "I can carry Nilly to the room she's sharing with you." Castle Marcellum wasn't big enough for them all to have their own rooms. As official betrotheds, Astar and Zeph had a room to share. Jak and Rhy had shared another. Gen didn't know where Rhy had slept after giving Jak and Stella the room for their new liaison. Probably outside somewhere in wolf form, where the cold wouldn't bother him too much. Gen, Lena, and Stella had shared, too, though Stella hadn't actually slept there.

"No," Gen said impulsively, and Zeph nodded in immediate agreement. "Put Stella in bed with Jak. It's big enough that she won't be in the way, and they'll both be easier for knowing the other is there."

Astar nodded reluctantly, still not quite able to get over putting his beloved twin in bed with a man, but he carried her over, laying her down gently. The healers had already stripped Jak of his bloodied and ragged clothing, and were sponging him clean while chanting in a low, warm buzz that was oddly comforting and stimulating at once.

"Moranu," Zeph breathed beside her, "what did Jak do to his *hands*?"

Gen looked, then hastily averted her gaze from Jak's leanly muscled gymnast's body, her cheeks heating. Maybe it was because she'd done such a piss-poor job of losing her virginity, but she couldn't act like the sight didn't affect her. She focused on his hands, the fingers bloodied stubs, the nails mostly missing. "Hopefully he'll be able to tell us," she murmured, stepping back.

Wim set a warm hand on the small of her back, and she glanced at him. "The broth and blankets are here." He smiled, searching her face. "Is there anything else I can do for you? Anything at all."

"Thank you, no." He was sweet. And... possibly flirting with her? "Actually, you could take Astar and Zeph to meet with the king and queen again. There's nothing they can do here. Lena and I can keep an eye on Stella."

Lena nodded, and Zeph sighed. "It's probably for the best," she said ruefully. "They had a lot to cover, and talking politics will at least distract Astar."

Wim glanced at Rhy leaning against a wall, brooding gaze on Jak's still form. "Shall I find an occupation for Rhy? Keep him busy?"

"That would be wonderful," Gen replied in a grateful gush.

Wim nodded and smiled, then picked up her hand to kiss it. "I'm sure your friends will be fine, but I'll check back with you. Otherwise… will I see you at dinner?"

"Maybe so," Gen temporized. Formal dinner seemed impossibly far away—and meaningless in the grand scheme. But she supposed they all needed to keep busy and fed. "Probably so," she corrected, adding a smile, in case he was flirting with her. If she wanted to erase Horrible Henk's lingering taint on her body, she'd have to try again with someone else. And Wim was nice.

He squeezed her hand. "I hope so." Releasing her hand, he strode away. "Your Highness Crown Prince Astar, if I may…"

"Quick," Zeph hissed, seizing Gen's arm and pulling her farther away from the others, "before I get dragged back to endless meetings, when did *that* happen?"

"When did *what* happen?" She probably wouldn't be able to get Zeph's claws out of her that easily, but it was worth a try.

Lena had followed closely, face alight with interest. "In the library, I think," she told Zeph. "I was reading a book and—"

"Of course you were," Zeph cut in, rolling her eyes in exasperation.

"And the charming Prince Wilhelm started his flirty flirting with Gen here."

"Excellent," Zeph cackled, the gleeful gríobhth in her voice. "You should take him to bed. Maybe tonight."

"That is *not* going to happen," Gen protested, despite her own thoughts in that direction. "Wim is in the market for a princess to marry, and I'm not royalty."

Zeph growled in frustration, and even Lena gave Gen a pitying look. "Would you please stop looking for true love and happily forever after in every person you meet?" Zeph demanded. "I thought we covered this."

"I tried that, and I was not happy with the results," Gen replied, sounding prim to her own ears. Better than revealing just how much that incident still haunted her.

"Because Henk was an ass," Lena assured her.

"Henk *was* an ass," Zeph agreed. "But you need to get back on that horse."

"Back on that ass?" Lena mused.

"A *different* horse," Zeph insisted. "You know I'm right. It's terrible that your first experience had to be so…"

"Lackluster?" Lena suggested.

"Disappointing," Zeph corrected.

"Painful, awkward, and just plain humiliating," Gen said, more strongly than she'd meant to.

Her friends both winced, gazing on her with sympathy.

"Zephyr," Astar said, coming over, "there's nothing I can do here, so I should go meet with the king and queen."

"That's an excellent plan," Zeph told him, as if it hadn't been her idea to begin with.

He smiled at her with affection, taking her hand and inter-lacing her fingers with his. "Do you want to stay here or...?"

"My place is with you," she replied firmly, then plastered on a brilliant, patently false smile. "Besides, I love meetings! They're like spending endless hours hunting small tasteless prey you never wanted to eat anyway."

Astar laughed. "Is it any wonder I love you so much?"

"None at all," she replied. "The wonder is you took so long to figure it out."

"True." His summer-sky-blue gaze went to the bed where the healers chanted and Stella lay sleeping.

"They're in good hands," Zeph told him.

"I know." Keeping her hand in his, Astar turned them to join Rhy in following Wim, who waved farewell, adding a special smile just for Gen.

~ 3 ~

"IF YOU DON'T want to bed Wim, maybe I should," Lena said, pretty much out of nowhere.

The healers had long since gone, leaving Jak clean, bandaged, and resting more or less peacefully. He occasionally muttered curses in his sleep, but he stopped thrashing and calling for Stella when Lena and Gen rolled them closer together. Once he had his body curled around Stella, Jak calmed considerably. Lena had fetched Stella's nightgown, and Gen had sponge-bathed her. Except for the bandages and the many bruises they both sported—though Jak won that contest easily—they looked normal.

It would just be nice if they'd wake up already.

Gen and Lena were sitting vigil in the otherwise empty room, having promised to immediately alert the others the moment Jak or Stella awakened. "I'm serious," Lena insisted, as if Gen had argued, "but only if you don't want him."

"I thought *you* weren't interested." Gen was actually sure Lena wasn't interested, but hearing her rationale could be entertaining.

Lena shrugged, wiggling her rear down into the cozy armchair, adjusting her lap blanket. "I'm just leery of giving him ideas, because you're right—our princeling is looking for a princess to marry, and I am not signing up for that job."

"I'm sure it's not *always* winter in Erie," Gen said with a wide smile, and the princess of tropical Nahanau glared at her.

"Not funny." Then she sighed. "I just want to go back to my weather research in Aerron. Is that so much to ask?"

"I'm sure Astar would give you leave to go, if you did ask." Especially given how much Lena still struggled with the aftereffects of the trauma she'd undergone.

"No." Lena sighed again. "Queen Andromeda said I'd be needed, and I'm not going to turn tail and run just because it gets difficult." She was thinking of Rhy, Gen knew, and how he'd apparently ditched them and the quest before unexpectedly turning up again.

"So, you want to bed Wim, so long as he doesn't get any funny ideas about marrying you and making you the queen of Erie?"

Lena gave her an owlish look, cupping her warmed wine in her hands. "When you put it that way, it sounds like a stupid idea."

"Then why are you contemplating it?"

Wriggling in the chair, Lena gazed on Jak and Stella, sleeping in each other's arms, sadness in her face. "I have got to do something to get Rhyian out of my system," she said quietly.

Ah. No surprises there. "And sleeping with someone else will do that?"

"Yes. No. I mean, I've had other lovers since Rhyian," Lena replied, sounding almost defensive. "Quite a few, in truth."

"How many?" Gen asked, fascinated enough to be rude.

Stella had been a virgin until Jak, and Zeph had been with so many lovers she had no idea where to begin counting. But Lena would know, and not only because she loved data so much.

"Twelve," she replied immediately, confirming Gen's assessment. "At least for full intercourse, as opposed to a little fooling around. Including Rhyian, naturally, who was my first," she added, lips curling unhappily. "I know a dozen isn't a lot compared to someone like Zeph, but…"

"It's a lot compared to my one," Gen pointed out. "Does Henk even count as one? Maybe he should be something like a half. Or a quarter."

Lena grimaced sympathetically. "Well, if you couldn't really feel if he'd put it in?"

Gen giggled. "I felt it all right, but it was just like *nudge, nudge, nudge, pain, poof, over.*"

"Is this what you girls always talk about?" Jak asked, startling them both. His dark eyes were open, sparkling with mischievous glee, though he hadn't stirred.

"It is rude to eavesdrop, Jakral Konyngrr," Gen retorted, though she couldn't summon any anger, she was so happy to hear him speak lucidly.

"Hey, you're the ones hanging out in my bedroom, gossiping while I'm trying to sleep." Carefully, without disturbing Stella, he levered up onto one elbow and started to rake his brown curls out of his face, then stared, bemused at his bandaged hand.

"It's not gossiping if it's about yourself," Lena informed him, also smiling with a wide and silly grin.

"Yeah, but you're talking about Horrible Henk. On behalf of my gender, Gen, I formally disown that ass as a member. *Nudge, nudge, nudge, pain, poof, over* is a disgrace to us all."

Her face hot, Gen glared accusingly at Lena. "How does he know that it was Henk?"

She raised an eyebrow. "I don't think it took a lot of guessing."

"Nope. Besides, I was eavesdropping for a while." Jak grinned, then glanced down at Stella, his grin fading into concern. "Is Stella all right?"

"We think she's recovering from expending magic," Lena replied, a question in her voice. "She certainly didn't use energy healing you."

"Oh, right." Jak grimaced. "She created a rift to portal us out of that tower. Probably took a lot out of her."

"Tower?" Gen repeated.

"The really tall one I climbed to get to her."

"That explains the hands," Lena said.

Jak climbed a freaking tower to rescue Stella. Gen's romantic heart turned over with a little dreamy sigh. "What happened?" she asked. "Where did you go?"

"If you don't mind, I think I'll take a page from Lena's book." Jak tossed her a little salute. "Let's wait until everyone is together so I can tell it only once." He scowled at the mitten of bandages on that hand. "These mitts have to go. No way I can throw a blade hampered like this." Looking for a free end, he nipped at it with his teeth.

"Don't you dare!" Lena's voice cracked out, startling everyone with her vehemence.

"Shh, lovely Lena," Jak said. "You'll wake Stella."

"An earthquake wouldn't wake her," Lena snapped.

"I feel like you shouldn't jinx us by suggesting stuff like that," Gen put in. All they needed was to contend with earthquakes, too.

"Well, Jak is keeping those bandages on until Stella can complete his healing, or I'll let Rhyian coldcock him to keep him subdued like he wanted to."

"Some friends you are," Jak grumbled, lying back and making a show of flopping his bandaged hand heavily on the bed. "At least Gen can pull out saber-cat form to protect us if that alter-realm intelligence comes roaring through a portal over the bed."

"Is that likely?" Gen asked. Maybe she should take saber-cat form as a precaution. She felt powerful in that form. Not like she would in dragon form, but she liked it best of all her forms, even if it did alarm people like Henk. The look of utter revulsion on his face when he'd seen her... *Monster.* That was a good reason not to shift unless it was necessary: she hadn't decided yet if she wanted to have sex with Wim, but she wouldn't be able to take it if his admiring smiles turn to horrorstricken hate.

Not again.

"If I were putting money on it," Jak was saying, propped up on his elbow again, "I'd bet that Stella killed the thing. But we're talking about Stella's life here, which means all wagers are off the table." He looked down at the sleeping Stella, then brushed his lips over the widow's peak of black hair on her pale forehead. "I'm taking no chances with her."

Even self-admittedly bitter Lena looked moved by that. She and Gen exchanged glances, both of them misty-eyed. Lena snapped out of it first, standing abruptly and dusting off her gown as if ridding herself of unwanted sentimentality. "I'll go fetch the others. They only agreed to leave on condition that we tell them immediately when you woke. We're already in arrears. I'll leave Lady Saber Cat to guard you."

"Just plain saber cat," Gen called after her, her skin itchy with irritation, for the first time understanding why Rhy bristled when people called him "prince." Being addressed with an honorific you didn't deserve—and couldn't live up to— chafed with surprisingly sharp spines.

"I really am sorry, Gen," Jak said, dark eyes somber, with no teasing sparkle. "You deserve better than someone like Henk. You should've had someone who could initiate you to the delights of sex who really cared about you, who valued what a wonderful, lovely woman you are."

Jak meant well, she knew, but his words stung. Clearly she *hadn't* had someone who cared about her like that. She took a breath to speak and swallowed it, finding she couldn't meet his direct gaze. "I'm not sure I'm comfortable discussing this with you, Jak."

"We're friends, aren't we?" He sounded a little hurt, so she made herself smile at him.

"Of course we are." But there had been times she'd hoped Jak would see her as more than a friend. Yes, he'd only ever had eyes for Stella, but Stella had ignored him so thoroughly, had been determined that her empath's sensitivity meant she'd never be able to take any lover, that Gen had sometimes entertained a painful fantasy that Jak would turn to her.

It had been a silly dream, one born of wistful loneliness. She'd entertained similar fantasies of Astar and Rhy, too. How surprised everyone would be if the golden crown prince or the dark and brooding son of the king and queen of Annfwn had fallen for *her*. Besides, all of them were such good men, staunch friends, all handsome and charming in their own ways.

All of them completely oblivious to her as anything but one of their buddies. The story of her life.

"You truly deserve better," Jak insisted. "You're, smart, gorgeous, talented. Any guy—or gal—would be lucky to have you. You might consider a gal for the next time. Women are usually more willing to go slow. They're more sensitive."

"Probably good advice." Her face had to be on fire. "But I'm afraid it's guys for me."

"It was worth a shot." He smiled ruefully. "Too bad I'm taken already. Otherwise I could have offered to—"

"Don't!" she burst out, clapping her hands over her ears, abruptly on the verge of tears.

"What did I say?" Jak asked, bewildered.

"Something obnoxious, no doubt," Stella said sleepily, smiling up at Jak as his gaze snapped to her, Gen completely forgotten. "Hi you," she murmured.

"My star," he breathed, cupping her cheek awkwardly with his mittened hand and sinking into a kiss. She melted under him, her fingers caressing the back of his neck.

Gen knew she should look away but couldn't make herself. All that restless longing in her snarled with desperate envy, not helped at all by Jak's almost-suggestion that he'd have been willing to take her to bed. Which was patently untrue, because if he'd been at all interested, he'd had years to make a move. Any kind of move. But no.

Why did everyone have *someone* but her? Even Rhy and Lena had loved each other for so long, with such consuming passion, that they were bound together. Lena might talk about getting him out of her system, but she clearly didn't really want to. And even with that, she'd still had eleven other lovers. *Eleven.* And Gen had *one* and it had to be Horrible Henk and she couldn't think about that without feeling vaguely nauseated. Even Jak pitied her for that one. Probably Astar and Rhy knew about it, too, also feeling sorry for their loveless buddy, Gen.

She tried to tear her gaze from Jak and Stella, who were sinking deep into the kiss and oblivious to all else. They were so beautiful together, like two halves made whole. The way love and intimacy should be. Graceful, sensuous, loving. Nothing like the jarring, awkward mess of her own experience.

"Some guard you are." Zeph's hand on Gen's shoulder had her nearly leaping out of her chair. "Or maybe you're just an excellent voyeur," Zeph added with a salacious brow waggle.

Gen was too choked on her own embarrassment, her face scalding, her heart about to crash out of her chest, to come up with any kind of rational response. Fortunately she was spared that—and prevented from launching into a furious tirade at Zeph—by everyone else piling onto the bed, embracing the invalids. Lena was yelling at everyone to be careful, but they were all too caught up to listen.

Finally Astar called the group to order, everyone automatically obeying him as their natural leader. Given the opportunity, she'd normally go flying or running to burn off some of this humiliation and agitation, but no way did she want to miss this story.

To busy herself and help restore her composure, Gen passed out water and wine, depending on who wanted which—though Jak's request for whiskey was resoundingly overruled. She passed around the tray of snacks, too, everyone thanking her absently, though Zeph eyed her as if she wanted to say something pointed. That was all Gen needed, another lecture from gorgeous, ridiculously popular Zeph, who would never understand how it felt to be overlooked.

"We were coming back to the room to practice weapons work," Jak began.

Zeph snorted. "Is that what you kids are calling it?"

"Zephyr," Astar said in a quelling tone, and she subsided, though a fair amount of gríobhth seethed in her aura. They were all upset, all showing it in different ways.

"We actually were," Stella said in her quiet way. She and Jak were sitting up in bed, pillows mounded behind them, holding hands as much as Jak's bandages allowed. "Jak was concerned that I be able to defend myself, given the possibility of something happening like... well, what happened."

"A rift?" Lena asked.

Stella nodded solemnly. "Jak held the door for me, and I fell in as soon as I stepped over the threshold."

"Why didn't you sense it?" Lena persisted.

"I'd like to know that, too," Jak put in. Of all of them, Stella was the best at sensing the presence of the rifts in reality that led to the alter-realms.

"I just *didn't*." Stella looked and sounded brittle as glass. "It didn't feel like the ones we've encountered before. I was falling before I realized anything."

"A trap," Rhy observed. "Like a pit put in place, knowing you'd step into it."

"It makes sense." Astar shook his golden head, letting out a long breath. "Jak already theorized that the alter-realm intelligence is somehow tracking us and laying booby traps, that it recognizes Nilly and knows how to target her."

"Even more, it wanted to acquire her," Jak put in grimly. Stella gazed unhappily at her lap as Jak related for the first time the story from the alter-realm they'd encountered at Midway Inn, how Stella had rescued him and how the intelligence had assumed a form like Jak's, confronting them and displaying an unsavory interest in Stella.

Everyone absorbed that unsettling information in silence. Astar lifted his head, staring hard at his twin. "You didn't tell me all of that."

"We didn't want you to worry," Stella replied evenly, her calm gray eyes holding his.

"It's my *job* to worry," Astar growled. "About you and about this team. You all are my responsibility, and *you* most of all, sister."

"Wrong," Jak said with firm conviction. "Stella is my responsibility most of all now. I've sworn it to her."

"Oh, for Moranu's sake." Stella tugged her hand from Jak's. "I'm my *own* responsibility."

"Then you fucked up," Astar spat at her, a rare temper

making him curse as he almost never did. "You could have gotten yourself *killed*."

"Do you think I somehow failed to notice that, Willy?" Magic gathered around Stella, shifting her dark hair so that red highlights glinted in the shadows like flickers of lightning in a distant storm, her eyes going silvery with it. "When I came to and saw I was locked in that cursed tower from my nightmares, I—" She broke off abruptly, everyone's eyes on her.

"What. Tower." Astar spaced out the words in a facsimile of patience that fooled no one. "What. Nightmares."

Stella pressed her lips together, looking both full of regret and mutinous. This had to be hard on her, being the focus of all these sharp-edged emotions, Astar hurling such strong feelings at her. Jak glanced at her, then set his jaw, meeting Astar's demanding gaze. "She didn't want to tell you. She didn't tell anyone, because that's Stella. She doesn't want anyone worrying about her."

"But she told you," Astar said flatly.

"Willy," Stella said in a warning tone that held a hiss of her feline First Form, "I love you, but don't you dare make this be about you."

"Tell me," Astar replied, unbending.

"All her life," Jak continued, after glancing at Stella for permission, "Stella has had visions—sometimes nightmares— about being locked in a tower in field of poppies." When Astar opened his mouth, Jak chopped his mittened hand through the air. "*Listen*. She was convinced she'd die there, all alone. She only told me because I demanded the answer. I had to know why she wouldn't let me love her. And that's why. Because she was certain she'd die alone."

Stella met his gaze then, everything about her softening. "But I didn't, because you came after me."

"And I always will," he averred, lifting her hand to kiss the back of it. "I don't care how far you go, I'll be right there with you."

Lena cleared her throat. "I'm really sorry you carried that burden alone, Nilly. I wish you'd felt like you could have confided in us."

"Exactly," Zeph said, less gently, her gríobhth tail invisible in her human form but lashing nonetheless. "All those times I said that you always took care of everyone else, that was an opportunity for you to lean on us."

"Don't chastise her," Astar said with considerable irritation.

Zeph's mouth fell open in dramatic astonishment. *"Excuse me?* Who's been roaring around like a wounded grizzly, demanding answers, telling her what she should and shouldn't do?"

"That's different," he replied stubbornly. "Stella is my sister."

"She's *my* lover," Jak shot back with narrowed eyes.

"And she's our friend," Gen snapped, exasperated with all of them. "Are we really going to compete over who loves Stella the most?" Jak and Astar both opened their mouths, and Gen stabbed a finger at them. *"Don't.* Really, just… don't."

"Gen is in a mood," Lena said as everyone stared at Gen.

"Maybe," Rhy said, "just *maybe,* everyone is worn out, stressed, traumatized, and exhausted on every level. We've been transported to nightmare worlds, stranded without help, injured, believed each other dead or worse. You know, people, it could be that we are all just hanging by a thread, and the real concern would be if we were behaving calmly and rationally."

A silence settled over them. "You know it's bad when Rhyian is the voice of reason," Lena commented.

"I love you, too, Salena," Rhy retorted, holding her gaze, neither of them looking angry in that moment. With a little catch in her heart, Gen knew Rhy absolutely meant it. And that Lena knew that also.

Astar cleared his throat, shaking his head minutely. "Setting aside recriminations and debates over our relative sanity as a group, what happened after Stella found herself in this tower from her nightmares?"

Stella visibly steeled herself to answer. "The intelligence was there with me. It had made itself look kind of like Jak, though it wasn't a close enough facsimile to fool me. Better than its giant gríobhth version of Zeph back at Gieneke, and better even than when Jak and I confronted it in the flat-grid alter-realm."

"So it's improving, refining its technique," Lena murmured.

"I think so. But maybe it's dead?" She looked hopefully at Jak.

"Maybe," he agreed, though it sounded like he highly doubted it. "When I saw Stella disappear into the rift as she stepped over the threshold, I threw myself after her before it could close—and it was a near thing, it sealed that fast. If I hadn't been right behind her..." He shook away that thought.

"But I ended up in this field of poppies with nothing in sight. I figured there should be a tower, given the poppies matched the rest of her vision, but I couldn't see one. Turns out it was invisible from the outside, at least to me."

"How did you find it, then?" Zeph asked, fascinated.

"Stella spoke in my head and guided me to her." Jak eyed Astar sideways. "We only recently discovered that she can."

Astar nodded, saying nothing. That news obviously bothered him, but he was controlling himself.

"So, I ran toward her, basically until I slammed into the Danu-cursed thing," Jak continued, rubbing the considerable bump on his forehead ruefully.

"Let me heal that for you," Stella said, shifting to reach for the wound.

"Later," he told her with a stern smile. "After I'm convinced you're fully rested. Anyway, once I found the tower with my face, I climbed it."

"But it was invisible," Lena said, frowning.

"Made it a challenge," Jak agreed cheerfully.

"You climbed an *invisible* tower for her," Gen whispered, not aware she'd said it aloud until Jak looked her way, then dipped his chin in acknowledgment.

"It had to be done." Jak shrugged. "It took a long time."

"All of this seems to have taken much longer than you were gone from here," Rhy inserted, gaze crawling moodily around the room. "It confirms something I noticed while trapped in wolf form in the flat-world alter-realm. Time moved more slowly there. I noticed the effects of being in wolf form for too long."

"It makes sense," Lena said, her gaze lingering on Rhy as if she'd like to comfort him, though she didn't move. "Everything is different in the alter-realms, the worlds themselves, the laws of magic and shapeshifting. Why would time be exempt?"

They were quiet, absorbing that. Astar shook himself, pointing at Jak. "Then what happened?"

"We confronted the intelligence, and Stella defeated it. While it was distracted, Stella crept up behind it and slammed her Silversteel daggers into its ears, and it melted."

"Silversteel seems to have that effect on the alter-realm creatures," Astar noted as they all murmured in impressed surprise.

"Do you want your sword back?" Jak asked. He looked around. "That is, if I made it back with the thing."

"Your weapons are all here, along with the clothes you were wearing," Gen informed them, wrinkling her nose at the remembered filth and odor. "We're having them cleaned."

"Nice to have staff," Jak remarked. "Our next digs might not be so comfortable."

"We're going on, then?" Astar asked. Everyone looked to him in considerable surprise.

"Do we have any choice?" Rhy queried in turn. His expression had gone brooding again, though he leaned against the wall near the window in apparent ease, his arms folded.

"Of course we have a choice," Astar retorted. "We can go back to Castle Ordnung and report on what we've found."

"We *have* gathered considerable data on the rifts," Lena commented thoughtfully.

Zeph looked around at the somber group, incredulous.

"And slink back with our tails between our legs, begging our mommies and daddies to save us from the big bad looming disaster that we still don't know what it is?"

"Not all of us have tails," Jak pointed out, but it lacked his usual fire. "I wouldn't mind having reinforcements, frankly." They sobered at that. Jak was the cheerful daredevil of the group. If he was having second thoughts... "But if the intelligence—are you sure we can't discuss a better name for it than that?—is dead, then that changes things."

"We don't need to name it if it's dead," Astar replied instantly. "Is it destroyed?"

Stella shook her head, garnering everyone's instant and focused attention. "The visions of the cataclysmic rift haven't changed. Unless the intelligence isn't related to that..."

"Then it isn't dead," Jak filled in grimly.

"And that means we can't lose this window of opportunity." Gen put in, feeling she needed to remind everyone, shore up their spirits. It was tempting. To go home, back to Annfwn, back to the tropical warmth and time spent doing little but practicing her shapeshifting. She could shift into a cold-hardy winged form and be home in a couple of days. It surprised Gen how much she longed to do just that. And yet... "If we go back, we won't make it to the Isles by spring. You all convinced me of that earlier. The Isles and King Isyn are the key to averting the catastrophic rift."

"I sure hope Isyn holds the solution," Stella said quietly, "because so far, Lena and I don't know what it is."

"Before we left," Zeph finally said into the fraught silence, "Dafne said something to me and Rhy. She said that we always think we want adventure until one throttles us, drags us out of our cozy nests, and guts us with its talons so we end up wishing for our boring lives again."

Lena cocked her head. "My mother said that?"

"There were fewer talons in Dafne's version," Rhy commented wryly, "but that was the gist of it. And I've been thinking about that, too." He inclined his head at Zeph. "Our parents didn't back down from the challenges they faced."

"Arguably they had no one else to turn to," Stella put in quietly, the first words she'd said in a while. She lifted her chin. "It might be easy for me to say, since I already faced my worst nightmare and survived, but I'm for going on."

"Sailing across the Strait of K'van in winter won't be smooth," Jak reminded them. "There's a reason no one does it."

"Has that changed since breakfast when we decided to go anyway?" Stella demanded, and he grimaced.

"No," he conceded. "But can we rest another day?" He sounded almost plaintive. As Jak was fully human, with no shapeshifter blood or magic in him, Gen could only imagine how beat up he felt.

"At least a day," Astar agreed, clapping his hands to his knees and standing. "Maybe a couple. We're pressed for time, but not that much. We might as well find out everything we can about these mysterious isles and the elusive King Isyn before we go chasing after them. Everyone rest, heal. If anyone needs to talk, well, I'd say come to me, but Stella is better at that kind of thing. Go talk to her."

He cocked a smile at his twin, and she returned it. For that moment, everything felt in harmony again.

~ 4 ~

THOUGH GEN KNEW it was part of keeping up appearances, it was odd to attend the formal dinner and ball that night, given the disorienting events and horrifying revelations of the day. That was another strange aspect of adventure—or maybe just of this one—they went from frenzied battles with monsters to kicking their heels at various parties, pretending to be frivolous nobles. A pretense that must be maintained still. Even though the royal family knew something of the group's real quest, the other guests and courtiers at Castle Marcellum didn't. As far as they were concerned, Gen and her friends were simply part of the crown prince's entourage, interested in nothing more than frolicking and sightseeing.

It was up to the able-bodied and -minded among them to keep up the façade, but it was getting more difficult all the time.

"If only these people knew the sights we've seen," Lena commented drily, echoing Gen's thoughts. Lena sipped her sparkling wine idly, eyeing the crowd with a regally bland expression. She had at least grown up in the court at her parents' palace in Nahanau and, as a bona fide princess, had been trained to deal with such events appropriately. Same with

Astar and Stella, though Stella and Jak had seized the excuse to stay in bed and sent their regrets. Stella hated crushes like this anyway, the bombardment of so many thoughts and emotions overwhelming to her empathic senses. Rhy, on the other side of the ballroom, pretending like he wasn't staring at Lena, slouched broodingly against a pillar, not bothering to be social at all. Not that it stopped the gorgeously dressed young women from eyeing him in giggling groups.

Zeph wasn't any better at court manners than Gen was, but at least her mother had drilled Dasnarian etiquette into Zeph's head. She appeared, however, to be gamely attempting to hone her skills. With her arm looped through Astar's, Zeph flitted about in a sapphire gown with slashes that revealed emerald silk below, dazzling everyone. Every once in a while, she gazed at Astar, clearly so besotted she was actually enjoying herself.

Gen would like to be enjoying herself. The first few balls she'd attended—including the incredibly glamorous one at Castle Ordnung on the night of the crystalline moon—she'd been so excited. Dressing up in the pretty gowns had been fun, being part of the whirl, wondering if she might meet her true love and dance all night...

Well, she'd gotten jaded awfully quickly. "At least we're not stuck at Midway Inn wondering if we'll get eaten or freeze to death first?" she replied, belatedly, to Lena's observation.

Lena flashed her a smile, the camaraderie of all they'd been through making them perfectly clear to each other. "Are you going to dance?" Lena asked.

"I suppose I should," Gen answered without much enthusiasm. "In keeping with our cover and all. Are you?"

"I'm torn between dancing with someone so I can enjoy watching Rhyian lose his shit or avoiding it entirely so I don't have to endure Rhyian losing his shit."

"Tough call," Gen observed, giving Rhy a little wave, his scowl deepening. "At least you *have* an option."

"Don't sound so glum." Lena elbowed her. "Prince Wilhelm is headed this way."

"Unless he asks you to dance, Princess Salena Nakoa Kau-Po."

"I bet he asks you. Double or nothing."

"Speaking of which"—it suddenly occurred to Gen—"who won the bet on Jak stealing Nilly's virginity?"

Lena grimaced. "Zeph, of course."

Gen snorted, laughing. "Of course."

"Laughing at me?" Wim asked with a smile warm enough to show he wasn't offended by the possibility.

"Girl talk," Lena assured him.

Wim waved over a server. "Your glasses need refreshing," he explained, swapping out their half-full ones for fresh, full flutes of the sparkling wine. "It's best drunk cold, to fully savor the pleasure of it." He smiled at Gen as he said that, Lena shifting to step on Gen's slippered foot meaningfully—and painfully enough that Gen nearly slopped her sip of wine. Wouldn't that make a great impression?

"You ladies haven't been dancing yet," Wim observed. "Is our music not to your taste?"

"We were simply waiting for the perfect partners," Lena simpered in a very un-Lena like way. Gen narrowed her eyes at her friend, who batted her lush lashes in return. Lena looked stunningly beautiful in her gown borrowed from Queen Nix. The bronze velvet brought out the golden highlights in her caramel hair, styled into sleek ringlets hanging from an elaborate crown of braids. The color complemented Lena's brown skin, emphasizing the deep blue of her eyes. And the low decolletage flattered her enviably rounded bosom, the tailored fit and full skirts making her narrow waist look tiny. No wonder Rhy couldn't keep his eyes off of her. Gen resigned herself to being the too-tall, small-breasted wallflower yet again, while Wim danced with her gorgeous friend.

"I'm willing to send a friend over to partner you, if you like, Princess." Wim gave her a friendly wink. "It's the least I can do, because I'm afraid I'm about to be unforgivably rude and steal Gen away for a dance."

"Go right ahead," Lena responded before Gen could, snatching Gen's flute from her hand. "Let me hold this for you."

The next thing Gen knew, she'd been whisked onto the ballroom floor, Wim's strong arms and graceful stepping whirling her into the foreign dance with ease.

"You look lovely tonight," Wim told her, holding her a bit away so he could look her over.

Involuntarily, Gen glanced down, only somewhat remembering what the borrowed dress looked like. Oh yes—it was the powder-blue silk. Not really her favorite color, but Gen was taller and narrower than Lena, so she'd left the fuller fitting gowns to her friend. Stella was the most petite of all of them, but she naturally hadn't needed a gown for tonight. The one Gen had found fit well for the most part, except that the castle seamstresses had needed to add a forearm's length of lace ruffle to the hem to make it long enough. Regrettably, though she wore flat slippers, she still towered over Wim, feeling gawky and more than a little foolish. And so much older—though Jak had pointed out that he and Wim were about the same age, which made him only a couple of years younger than Gen.

"Thank you," she replied, hearing the doubt in her own voice.

"It brings out the blue in your eyes," Wim told her confidently. "Tala blue, isn't that what they call it? The deeper the color, the more shapeshifting magic you have, I've heard."

"That's more or less true." Wim sure was interested in her shapeshifter nature. *Better than not interested in you at all.* "There are exceptions. Stella, for example, has deep gray eyes, like Queen Andromeda, which is an indication of their magic as sorceresses. I'm just a plain shapeshifter."

"Nothing plain about you," he replied warmly. "Tell me, what's the largest animal form you can take?"

Gen fervently wished she could just say "dragon" and watch his mouth fall open. As it was, however, she hesitated to answer. It felt a little weird. No wonder her mother had gotten in the habit of saying "several" and shutting down further questions.

"Probably a polar bear," she said, then regretted it when Wim goggled.

"You can become a freaking polar bear?" He gasped. "I've never even seen one."

"Good form for cold weather," she offered, for lack of anything else to say. The saber cat might be bigger, but it was also considered mythical, which upset mossbacks, and it depended on if you were figuring by length or body mass anyway. Truly, it was kind of a dumb question. "That's if you're talking land animals," she felt compelled to add. "If we count aquatic, a blue whale would be my largest."

"A whale," he echoed in astonishment.

What was *wrong* with her? She was dancing with a handsome prince at a ball—pretty much the literal answer to her wishes—and she was going into the weed on land versus aquatic forms. She needed to get her head together and enjoy the moment. Get back on the horse. Or the ass, as it were.

"So, you and Marjolein might rule jointly?" she asked, seizing on the inspiration as Wim's twin sister danced by with a handsome dark-skinned man.

Wim grimaced after his sister, who noticed and stuck her tongue out at him over the man's shoulder. "It looks that way," he agreed glumly, then brightened. "Though she's not so bad. Smart. The main problem is if she marries before we take the throne of Erie. Any royal family worth their salt will want their son on the throne, not me."

"The same isn't true if you marry first?" No matter how much time Gen spent with her father's mossback family, politics of the Thirteen Kingdoms made little sense to her.

"Oh, it is," he assured her. "It's just that Marjolein has a lot more options than I do. Unmarried princes tend to be more diligent about hunting for available princesses who can bring them thrones rather than the reverse."

Gen considered mentioning Berendina, granddaughter of King Groningen and ambitious princess from Jorrit. She'd made the trip from her home in the hinterlands to Castle Elderhorst in order to pursue Astar, and she'd certainly been diligent in her bid for the high throne via marriage. She might be willing to settle for the throne of Erie, now that Astar was thoroughly taken. But none of them had much liked the imperious, predatory woman—which was saying something for a group of shapeshifters who enjoyed taking the forms of predators—and Gen wouldn't wish her on anyone, much less Wim, who she did like.

"You'll find someone," she reassured him, fully aware of how little she liked receiving that very same empty promise.

"Maybe I already have," he replied warmly, leaning in to brush her temple with his lips.

She was no good at flirting, unclear on whether she should clarify or assume he did mean her. Her mother would flirt and evade; her father would insist on clarification. As she so often did, Gen went with her father's stolid mossback soldier ways. "Do you mean me?" she asked bluntly.

Wim laughed a little. "It wouldn't be very romantic of me to kiss you and be talking about someone else."

True, but... "That didn't answer my question."

"Fair enough. I like that you're plain-spoken. Genuine, no games. Yes, I mean you, Gen."

She gazed back at him uneasily. "I'm no princess, remember? Just a partblood shapeshifter."

"There's no 'just' about it. I think you're fascinating. Besides, can't we just spend some time together, without there being thrones and politics involved?"

"That pretty much describes my usual life." Except for the spending time together part. But she'd wanted this, right? Flirting: she could do it. "I'd like that, Wim."

"Me too." Moving the hand on her back a bit lower to settle intimately on the upper curve of her bottom, he snugged her in closer, pressing a kiss under her ear. "You know what I'd really like?"

"What?" she asked breathlessly.

"I'd like to take you to bed," he murmured, "to discover the delights of that marvelous shapeshifter body. Want to get out of here?" he asked, saving her a reply to that startling declaration.

"Yes," she made herself answer, before she declined out of nerves. And before she said something sarcastic like how polar bear sex was off the table. Lena could say that without sounding too snarky. So could Zeph, though she probably wouldn't mean it. *Ugh,* she groaned internally as Wim smiled, took her hand, and led her off the dance floor. *What am I doing?*

You are getting back on the horse, she answered her more timid self sternly.

Yes, but what if he turns out to be an ass?

Zeph was right about that much—Gen really needed to get over herself.

Wim threaded his way through the crowd, drawing her along and occasionally glancing back to grin at her. They passed Lena, who gave her a big, toothy smile and a thumbs-up. *Ugh.* Gen attempted to grin back, but it felt kind of wobbly. Once free of the crush, Wim tucked Gen's hand in the crook of his elbow, leading her up a grand staircase. They passed other guests, all bowing to Wim and eyeing her speculatively, whispering to each other after they'd passed. Unfortunately, out of the noise of the ballroom, Gen's keen shapeshifter ears picked out their words easily.

That's one of those Tala people.

Are you sure? I thought they all had black hair and brooding good looks like that Prince Rhyian. Hers is mud brown.

Not very pretty, is she? Not like Crown Prince Astar's fiancée.

No doubt why she's trying for our *prince.*

Freakishly tall and rather plain.

That dress is wearing her. *Puffed sleeves—really? Those sleeves are three times the size of her bosom!*

Did you see how she added a foot of lace to the hem? Tacky.

Gen kept the smile fixed to her face, nodding as Wim—completely oblivious—pointed out paintings of his ancestors to her. Those snide remarks shouldn't sting so much. They weren't saying anything she didn't already know. Even among her father's mossback family, the women bemoaned their mud-brown hair. And Gen had always known she wasn't pretty. She also should have gone with a simpler gown. Wearing something that sparkly on her long, lanky body was like dressing up one of her grandmother's hogs in sequined satin. And the neckline flounce did little to conceal the sagging material over her too-small breasts. She should have gone with one of her cached ballgowns, even if everyone had already seen all of them.

"These are my chambers," Wim said, breaking into her increasingly glum thoughts. He nodded as the guards bowed, guiding her through the doors they opened. She took in the graciously appointed outer room decorated in browns, burgundies, and golds. Masculine and warm, comfortable and comforting. Surprisingly, she felt at ease in the space, as she didn't always in mossback rooms. Big windows looked out on the wintry night sky, and a fire crackled in a large fireplace, reading chairs set before it.

"I took the liberty of having an iced carafe sent up for us," Wim said, handing her a full flute of more of the sparkling wine.

"Your chambers are very nice," she said, figuring that was the polite thing to say.

Wim looked around, too, a line between his brows. "They belonged to my brother," he confided. "After Isyn left, Marjie and I wagered on who would get them. I won, obviously, and it's driving her crazy that I haven't had them redecorated."

"Why haven't you?"

Wim grinned. "Because she had all these grand plans, and it's driving her crazy that I'm not 'appreciating what I got.'"

Gen laughed, because she figured she was supposed to, then wandered away, examining the bookshelves. "These aren't your books, then?"

"No." Wim stepped up beside her, sounding vague. "I mean, why did Isyn keep so many in here when there's a huge library downstairs?"

"So he could access them easily," Gen replied, surprised that he could be so insensible.

"I don't know why he'd want to. He'd read them all already."

"All the more reason," she insisted, shaking her head when Wim only gave her a puzzled frown. An emerald-green cover caught her eye, sitting out as it was by itself, clearly well-thumbed. "May I?"

"Sure. It's not like Isyn would know or care. He's long gone."

Setting her glass aside, she examined the well-worn book. *Tales of the Fae.* A rose in full bloom, exotic and magical in style, was etched in gold on the cover under the intricately scrolled title. It wasn't a book she'd seen or heard of before, though Lena would almost certainly recognize it. Oddly disappointed, she found that it seemed to be written in a language other than Common Tongue. The Tala weren't much into reading and writing—their written language quite spare, in fact—but Gen had learned Common Tongue along with her mossback cousins. This... she could pick out a word here or there, but not read it easily. With a sigh, she started to put it back, surprised at her own reluctance to part with it.

"Keep it," Wim said. "A memento of tonight." Moving up behind her, he settled his hands on her waist, nudging aside one of the curls the maidservant had carefully styled so he could kiss the side of her neck.

She held still, wanting to enjoy the caress, but his lips felt weirdly cool. And wet. "Should you be giving away your brother's books?" she asked lightly.

"Like I said," Wim murmured against her skin, pressing kisses down to her shoulder, which he bared by tugging down her puffed sleeve, "it's not like he'll know, even if he did care."

"I'm surprised he didn't take his books with him when he

went to be king of the Isles."

Wim shrugged, tugging down her other sleeve to kiss that shoulder. "There was some question of whether he could take anything physical with him, so he erred on the side of leaving his valuables behind rather than lose them between realms." He spun her to face him. "And why are we talking about my brother?"

She held onto the book still, keeping it between them like a shield over her breasts, but she produced a smile. "I don't know."

He plucked the book from her hands and tucked it into a deep pocket in her voluminous skirts. "There. My gift to you." Pressing her back against the shelves, he angled his head and kissed her. He was more gentle than Henk had been, though he introduced his tongue rather startlingly fast. Trying to play along, she returned the kiss, placing her hands awkwardly on his shoulders. Wim pulled back, giving her a slight frown. "You're not a virgin, are you?"

"No," she answered emphatically, and quite honestly.

"I've heard the Tala are freer than we are," he replied, pressing his body against hers. "That you all have sex with anyone, all kinds of ways and partners." His hand came up to cup her breast, and she had to work not to flinch away. Why wasn't she enjoying this more?

"That's true for some," she agreed, able to talk because he was busy working the bodice of her dress down, apparently done with the kissing effort. "But, as I mentioned, I'm a partblood. My father is—well, was, though he's still active in many ways—a lieutenant of the High Queen's personal guard, and he's not a shapeshifter. All of his family lives near Castle Ordnung, on extensive lands that they farm. They're all pretty much farmers, except for the hunters and trappers. And I have a few cousins who work at the castle in various capacities."

Wim closed his mouth over the nipple he'd bared and she squeaked. "Mmm," he murmured, rubbing her other nipple between his finger and thumb. "Petite and delicious."

She stared steadfastly across the room as Wim messed about with her breasts, resigned to the "petite" remark, wondering about the "delicious" comment. Didn't a nipple taste pretty much like... a nipple? Not that she should be thinking about that. Shouldn't she be overwhelmed with desire or something? Somehow she was doing this all wrong. Surely she shouldn't be... bored.

There was, however, an interesting painting on the far wall of a misty island shoreline. The longer she looked at it, the more it seemed she made out shapes in the shadows. Animal shapes? There was a feline slinking behind a tree, a snowy owl roosting in the limbs above. A flock of birds shimmered and disappeared, the waves seeming to churn against distant rocks, an orca breaching in the farther sea. It seemed like a work of art you might see something new in every time.

"Gen, are you with me?" Wim had stopped kissing her breasts and inserted his face into her field of vision. He let out a sigh. "You are *not* enjoying this."

"I, ah, what?" she stammered. *Good going, Gendra. Congratulations: you are officially terrible at sex.* "Not at all! No, I was just, um, savoring the, um, lovely kisses. Shall we get in bed?"

His mouth quirked in a wry smile, and he tugged her bodice up again, covering her petite breasts. "I don't think so. Not when you don't want to be here."

She opened and closed her mouth again, feeling like a foolish fish. "I do want to be here, Wim. I like you." He'd been so much more considerate than Henk. And now she'd blown it.

"I like you, too." His smile turned rueful, and he kissed her cheek. "But sometimes the passion isn't there. I don't want you to go through with this just to please me."

"That's not what I was…" She trailed off, because that was far too accurate. "The truth is, I'm no good at sex," she confided in a mortified whisper. "But I'm trying to learn."

He canted his head, regarding her with an odd expression. "I doubt that's true."

"I *am* trying to learn," she insisted. Oh, Moranu, how had she screwed this up so badly?

"I mean," he said, cracking a real grin, "that I doubt you're no good at it. The right partner can make all the difference. Clearly it's not me."

Ouch. "I'm sorry, Wim."

He shrugged. "So it goes. Though it's just my luck: four gorgeous women turn up at my castle in the middle of winter, and not one of them is interested in me."

"There are extenuating circumstances," she offered weakly.

"There always are. Anyway, let me escort you back to the ball, so you can at least have *some* fun tonight."

Double ouch. "Actually, I think I'll just go back to my room. I'm more tired than I realized."

He nodded sympathetically. "You all have been through a lot. I'll escort you back to your room, then."

"You don't have to," she assured him. "I can find my way."

"I'm sure you can, but it would look bad to the others if I sent you out to walk back by yourself." When she looked blankly at him, he waved a hand at the greater castle. "I don't know if you noticed, but there are always people watching and gossiping."

"I noticed." She decided not to say more than that. She really should know better than to let overheard comments like that get under her skin.

"Ah." He smiled mirthlessly. "So, if you don't mind, I'd prefer to preserve the fiction that we had a glorious evening together. For the sake of my reputation, too."

"Glorious, but brief," she pointed out, charmed despite her chagrin over the entire failed enterprise.

"Well, no help for that."

"There is," she declared firmly, taking up her flute of wine. "I see you have a game board to play kiauo. Shall we?"

"Is that what that thing is?" Wim studied the multitiered boards embedded with lovely spiraling tiles. "It's Isyn's, of course. I thought maybe it was some kind of weird art piece. He goes in for that stuff." He waved a hand at the painting Gen had admired.

"Kiauo is a strategy game from Nahanau," she explained, extracting the game pieces from a sliding drawer in the base. "Lena is obviously much better at it than I am—partly because her parents are masters of the game—but I can at least teach you."

"All right." He rubbed his hands together. "And then I can teach Marjie, but only enough so that I can make sure to win every time. That'll get her."

Gen had to laugh. "You should be nicer to your sister."

"Aww." He thrust out his lip in a mock pout. "Where's the fun in that?" He watched Gen set up the board. "So, about Lena and Rhy…" Gen glanced at him sideways, and he held up his hands in mock surrender, grinning innocently. "*You* aren't interested in me, so I figured it's not wrong to ask."

"Fair enough," Gen said, finding it didn't smart at all. "It's complicated between Lena and Rhy. I can tell her that you and I decided to be just friends, but if I were you, I wouldn't get in the middle of that mess."

Wim considered that thoughtfully. "That kind of complicated, huh?"

"You have no idea."

~ 5 ~

THEY SET OUT for the coast a few days later. True to his word, Astar waited for everyone to feel rested and somewhat normal again. Gen spent many cozy hours with Wim playing kiauo. He picked up the strategy rapidly and soon graduated to playing Lena. During those hours, Gen went flying with Zeph and Stella, pushing Stella to build up her endurance again. Even though Stella hadn't experienced much physical injury from her trip to the tower alter-realm, facing her lifelong nightmare had been a blow to her confidence.

Gen also took her turn playing living target for Stella's fledgling offensive magic, until she tired of having her feathers burnt. Sure, she could heal as she shifted, but that was draining—and they were all under strict orders from Astar to be building their strength. Besides, their sweet and quiet Nilly had discovered a hitherto unknown streak of savagery, hurling fireballs with accuracy even shapeshifter speed couldn't duck— and those things *hurt*. Even Jak conceded that Stella had come a long way.

In the end, Wim and Marjie ended up accompanying them to the coast, making the journey into a bit of a festive parade. Though the weather remained wintry, the lowlands between

Castle Marcellum and the coast were buffered from the sharp winds of the steppes. And towns were frequent, boasting comfortable inns with excellent food. Being the off season, the inns had enough space for all who wished to have their own rooms. The privacy was nice, though Gen missed the late-night gossip sessions with her friends.

Having Wim and Marjie along reminded Gen of the excursion from Castle Elderhorst to Lake Sullivan, when Henk and Berendina had accompanied them—and subsequently abandoned them after Henk witnessed Gen's transformation into the saber cat. Even now, the look on his face flashed into her mind with crystal clarity, twisting her gut. The sheer revulsion made her feel heartsick. And she hadn't liked Henk that much by that point, post disappointing bedding. Still, she'd supposed they'd try again, and that maybe their relationship would grow. But no.

The resemblance to that ill-fated outing—which had ended with Lena falling into an alter-realm and Zeph nearly dying in the process of rescuing her—stopped there. Wim was good company, and Gen enjoyed his friendship now that she wasn't worried about love and sex. Zeph probably had a point that Gen was sabotaging herself by continually looking for true love. Everything was certainly easier and more fun when she wasn't. Marjie proved to be a pleasant companion, too, especially as she relaxed more away from Castle Marcellum and her responsibilities there. She'd also begun spending more time with Rhy. A lot of time, in fact, the two of them often in conversation.

When Gen tentatively asked Lena if that bothered her at

all, Lena declared that Rhyian had always done exactly as he pleased and would doubtless continue to do so. And that was that. If Lena seemed to be devoting more attention to Wim after that, well, Gen wouldn't judge.

Jak and Stella rode in the carriage mostly, completely wrapped up in each other. And, while Zeph and Astar were out and about in company more, they were also taking advantage of the more leisurely journey to enjoy their blossoming love affair. The end result was that Gen spent a fair amount of time alone—trying hard not to wallow in self-pity over it—and on the wing, usually as a snowy owl, acting as a scout for the party with her sharp eyes and excellent camouflage.

They hadn't encountered any more rifts or attacks by creatures from the alter-realms as they had before. The spirit horse Falada, who'd been Queen Nix's companion, and who only Stella could see, had accompanied them as promised. Stella said that Falada was on the lookout for anything strange, too, and would alert them. But no one questioned Gen's choice to continue to act as scout. The solitary hours with nothing between her and the vast silence of the sky soothed some of the agitation in her heart. When she was worn out, she sometimes imagined they were all happier to be rid of her, the odd person out in their otherwise merry crew, but she could usually set those dark thoughts aside.

And so they reached the small fishing village of Aduard without incident. Gen supposed she'd been subconsciously expecting something like home, as Wim and Marjolein had said Aduard was situated at the base of some cliffs on the rocky coast, with a semicircular protected harbor. It had sounded like the cliff city at Annfwn, and a wave of homesickness washed over her in her disappointment at seeing Aduard.

It wasn't ugly—but it also entirely lacked the lush beauty of Annfwn. Not gleaming white like in Annfwn, the rocks forming the cliffs were a granite so dark they looked black jutting against the obstinate overcast. The Strait of K'van spread out in more shades of gray to the horizon, choppy with white caps, nothing like the gentle turquoise sea of home. It was winter, so she couldn't expect the vines, fruits, and flowers of Annfwn, but the place also lacked much snow to speak of, leaving it looking wet and barren to her eyes. A pervasive mist made the whole place feel muffled and quiet.

"Not anything like home, is it?" Stella said, coming up beside Gen on the point where they'd stopped to take in the view, such as it was. As a company of Castle Marcellum servants and retainers had also accompanied their entourage, they kept up the façade of being on a sightseeing tour.

"You thought it might be, too?" Gen replied with some relief that it wasn't just her.

Stella sighed a little. "I shouldn't have. Obviously not all cliffs and seaside cities are the same. And I knew it wouldn't be *warm*, but still…"

"I guess it's normal to miss home."

Nodding, Stella looked over at her, wide gray eyes somber as the sea and sky, seeing *through* Gen. "That's not why you're so sad, though," she observed.

"No? Do tell," Gen replied lightly, though not enough to soften the edge in her voice. Being friends with an empath sounded good until you realized you had no secrets from them.

Stella simply gazed at her, the smooth oval of her face pale in its frame of mist-beaded dark hair, her lips curved in a sympathetic smile. "You have friends, Gen."

"I know that." Because she sounded testy, Gen blew out a breath and tried again. "I appreciate that, Nilly, I really do. I'm just starting to feel like I'll be alone for the rest of my life."

"I can sympathize with that feeling," Stella replied quietly, and Gen immediately felt bad.

"I'm sorry. I didn't mean that my situation is anything like yours. There's no way for me to compare my bad luck in love with you having a vision of dying alone in a tower in that alter-realm."

Stella shrugged a little. "We all have problems, and they are all important to us. There's no scaling of one person's troubles being greater or lesser than another's. When it's your hill to climb, it's steep and requires effort. Knowing someone else's hill is steeper doesn't make yours any less exhausting."

"I'm trying to decide if that makes me feel any better," Gen mused.

"It should. It's not healthy to dismiss what's bothering you as irrelevant," Stella chided gently.

"I'm not." But a sigh escaped her, dolorous and self-pitying.

"Do you want to talk about it?"

"I really don't," Gen answered after a moment. "I appreciate the offer, Nilly, but I'm tired of hearing myself talk about it. I'm tired of thinking about my hill, steep or otherwise."

"I understand that, too." Farther down the cliffside, Jak was walking on his hands along a narrow stone wall bordering the drop, a dagger in his teeth. Balancing on one hand, he plucked the dagger from his teeth and threw it, nailing a bore in a nearby tree gnarled by the ocean winds. Wim and Marjie applauded, both handing over coin as Jak returned to his feet. Stella shook her head. "That man."

As if he heard her, Jak caught Stella's eye and swept her a deep bow, pocketing the coins deftly.

"It's really nice to see you together," Gen told her, realizing she probably hadn't said so. "I'm happy for you both."

Stella regarded her gravely. "Thank you. You're sweet to say so, as I know it can't be easy for you, seeing us all pair off like this."

"I'm not jealous," Gen assured her, then grimaced. "Well, I'm envious in principle, because I want that, too, but not jealous of you having Jak. You two are perfect together."

Stella smiled, a full and radiant expression that brightened her solemn face, a light giggle of pure happiness escaping her. "We are, aren't we? I never would have guessed I could experience this kind of partnership with someone."

"Enviable, indeed," Gen acknowledged, her heart feeling lighter for no good reason. It felt good, though, to be happy for Jak and Stella. If anyone deserved true love, it was Stella. "And not everyone is really paired off—there's always Rhy and Lena. I doubt either of them is serious about the flirtations with the Erie twins."

"No, they aren't." Stella looked into the distance, a line between her brows. "They'll have to figure it out, though, or suffer greater consequences than any of us will be able to endure." The shiver of prophecy echoed in her voice, chill with vague alarm. Stella glanced at Gen, once again looking *through* her, eyes gone silver. "You too, dragon's daughter. Your fire will be sorely needed to melt the ice. Don't let the fear hold you back."

Gen didn't have to ask if that was prophecy. Rhy always said prophetic words were easily identifiable because they made no helpful sense. "I will, ah, keep that in mind."

Stella blinked, the silver fading into storm gray again. "Marjie says the inn down in Aduard makes the best cioppino she's ever tasted. I plan to eat hearty tonight, as Jak says the voyage might be so rough we won't be able to stomach much."

"Lots of cioppino it is, then," Gen agreed. "And a whole lot of wine."

THE SHIP DIDN'T look like much, but Jak hummed with approval, so it must have been suitable for their purposes. They all gathered on the dock in the morning drizzle, saying their goodbyes, waiting for Jak to complete his inspection, the small sailboat bumping against the wood with the surging of the irritated sea. The dock itself bobbed, too, but with a different rhythm, and the truly excellent cioppino of the night before curled uneasily, deep in Gen's gut. She'd sailed before, of course. Sailing tournaments were a time-honored tradition in Annfwn. But those seas were far kinder, and the boats sleek and trim. "I think I'm going to be doing a lot of swimming," she muttered to herself. Probably her orca form would be fine in this water, and with it being just their group, she wouldn't have to worry about revolting their new friends by taking the form of something huge and dangerous.

"Astar says no shifting," Zeph corrected, a sullen look on her gorgeous face as she also eyed the ship dubiously. "He wants us to stay together."

"That's only fair," Lena pointed out, she and Stella edging closer. "Since not all of us can shapeshift."

"And not all of us have forms that can survive this arctic hell they call a strait," Rhy agreed sourly.

"So if we drown, we all drown together," Jak declared cheerfully as he jumped onto the dock and put his arm around Stella and drew her close against his side. "Worthy of a Dasnarian romantic ballad."

"Only Dasnarians think death is romantic," Zeph countered, making a face. "It's the worst quality of the race. You wouldn't believe some of the stories my mother tells, expecting us to somehow appreciate them. Some would depress me for days."

"Did she tell you the one about the young newlyweds who went looking for their lost kitten?" Jak asked.

"Oh, Moranu, yes!" Zeph dug her fingers into her hair, clutching her skull. "I wish I could erase that one from my brain."

"Don't tell us," Stella said hastily.

"I would never," Jak promised solemnly, giving her a kiss.

"Because I love you and I would never inflict that story on any of you. Not even Rhy." Jak grinned wickedly. "Though I could hold that in reserve, in case you piss me off again, bro."

"Your story wouldn't bother me," Rhy replied coolly, "as I have no heart. At least, so I'm reliably informed."

Lena rolled her eyes but didn't respond—thankfully.

"Now I'm wondering if the kitten lived," Gen remarked.

"Me too," Lena said with a worried frown.

Zeph and Jak exchanged glances. "You really don't want to know," Zeph said, a shadow in her brilliant sapphire eyes.

"What don't I want to know?" Astar asked, having finished a final conversation with Wim and Marjie.

"Nothing to worry your pretty head about," Zeph told him with a saucy smile.

"Oh, good." He grinned at her. "Danu knows my pretty head is full enough as it is. All right, everyone, Zeph told you that there will be no shapeshifting? No swimming or flying excursions. You may consider that a royal command."

"Can I ask why?" Gen asked plaintively. So much for her plan to escape seasickness.

"Because we don't know what we'll encounter," Astar explained. "You heard Queen Nix—the Isles have a reputation for fading in and out of our realm. It may not be the exact same phenomenon as the rifts that lead to the alter-realms, it's true." He nodded at Lena, who met his gaze thoughtfully. "But the possibility remains that the two phenomena are linked in some way." Astar tipped his head at Rhy, who gave no indication of noticing. "If we go anywhere," Astar concluded, "we go together."

Jak sang a brief line in Dasnarian that no doubt referred to drowning together, probably with innocent kittens.

"Any other questions?" Astar asked.

"What if the boat breaks apart?" Rhy asked as he slouched against a post.

"Jak, is the boat going to break apart?" Astar asked.

"Nope." Jak grinned and tossed off a Dasnarian salute with his free hand. "Not unless we slam into an immovable object, that is."

Rhy flashed an accusing look at Astar.

"Fine," Astar conceded. "If you are facing imminent death, you may shapeshift to save yourself—and we'll hope that you live a long life with the guilt of having abandoned us to this distinctly dismal watery grave."

"I'm sure I could get over the guilt," Rhy commented with a thin smile.

"Because you'd need a heart to even care to begin with," Lena muttered, and he glared at her.

"It's a small ship, and we might be on it a few days, searching for King Isyn or a hospitable island," Astar said, giving them all a meaningful look. "Let's attempt to get along, as we have no choice but to be in each other's laps."

"You are always welcome in *my* lap," Jak murmured to Stella, and she giggled.

"There will be no sex on board," Astar declared, the looks on Jak and Stella's faces almost comical.

"What?" Zeph demanded, clearly outraged.

"It's a small ship," Astar repeated, giving her a serious stare. "We will be considerate of each other."

Gen glanced at Rhy, who shrugged and smiled, unperturbed. Lena was ignoring all of them, and the others nodded, unhappy but resigned.

"Anything else?" Astar looked at each of them in turn, and they all shook their heads. "Gen, do we understand each other on the shapeshifting?"

Why did he single her out? She wasn't the only one unhappy about the no-shapeshifting rule. "I will abide by Willy's new moratorium," she replied with a bow.

Rhy snickered, expression lightening with amusement at her reference to Astar's previous, unpopular, and now discarded rule on no romantic relationships within the group.

"May it go where the old moratorium went," Rhy added.

"Hmm." Jak cocked his head thoughtfully, dark eyes sparkling. "I'm pretty sure it went up Willy's—"

"Don't say it." Astar stabbed a finger at Jak, but he was laughing. "All right, the sooner we set sail, the sooner we can be on dry land again. Nilly, is Falada on board?"

Stella nodded, her gray gaze tracking over what looked like nothing to Gen. "I think we're as ready as we'll ever be."

They all turned to wave to Wim and Marjolein, who'd stayed back on the solid part of the dock—which should've warned Gen right there. Taking turns, they ascended the narrow gangplank, Jak going first so he could designate their stations for being abovedeck and their associated responsibilities. Astar hung back, catching Gen's arm.

"Truly, Gendra," he asked quietly, "will you be all right with that rule? I know it will be hardest on you."

She bit back the caustic reply that had sprung to her lips.

"It's no great hardship," she answered honestly. Not such a steep hill as all that. "I can go a few days without shapeshifting, and your reasoning is good."

He smiled slightly. "I've heard so many stories about Zynda. Marskal always says your mother can't go a few hours without needing to stretch her wings or fins. I know you've been circumspect around the Erie folks, and I appreciate your discretion, especially as it's clear you have a lot of your mother in you."

Gen really didn't think so. She was nothing like her wild-spirited mother, who'd fallen in love so inadvisably with a stolid mossback soldier. "I'm much more like my dad," she confided. "Nothing very interesting about me."

Astar gave her an odd look. "That is not how I would ever describe Marskal. Just because he banks his fire doesn't mean it's not fierce. In fact, he burns all the hotter for keeping it contained. I understand why they named you born of the dragon."

"What is it like?" she asked before she could stop herself. "Taking dragon form. What did it feel like?"

"I really don't remember a lot." He frowned, thinking back. "I was so focused on saving Zeph—and Lena—that I didn't even realize what form I'd taken. But it was powerful. Fiery," he added, with a part smile. "When you get the form, you'll enjoy it."

"I don't know that I ever will." She was immediately sorry she'd said that; she sounded so plaintive.

But Astar grinned, clapping her on the shoulder. "I believe you will. If anyone can do it, you can. And *you* will be able to do it more than once."

She smiled back, surprisingly moved. *"You* did it when you needed to most, and without ever practicing, but thank you for your confidence. And Astar?" she added impulsively as he started to turn away. He faced her again, his summer-sky blue eyes intent, gold curls tossing around his noble brow. "I think you'll be a really good high king," she told him. "You're a good leader. Wise and forward-thinking. I'm sorry I questioned you."

He tugged one of her long curls, just as he had when they were kids. "You have royal dispensation to question me anytime you think it necessary, Gen. Any king would be lucky to have someone as quick-witted as you are to point out their flaws."

Maybe it was because she was already emotional, but that surprising statement made her weepy for no good reason at all. She opened her mouth to argue, then thought better of it and blinked the tears away. "Thank you."

"Hey, you two," Jak called, one booted foot propped on the gunwale. "No lollygagging will be tolerated on my ship. Get yourselves up here."

"We're not on your ship yet," Gen pointed out, tempted to stick her tongue out at him, which had been her go-to response to Jak's mischief when she was ten.

He grinned, dark eyes sharp. "If you want to be on it—and not get tossed overboard—you'll step lively."

"I don't care if you toss me overboard," she argued, though she obediently trudged up the gangplank. Slowly. "I'll just—" She broke off, realizing that she wouldn't be allowed to shapeshift.

"Exactly." Jak rubbed his hands together. "Your ass belongs to me now, mossback."

"You are not funny."

"But I *am* in charge." He still smiled, but steel underlaid it. "My ship, my kingdom. The captain of the ship outranks everyone on it," he reminded them. "That includes you, Willy," he added as Astar stepped on board.

"It's apparently true," Lena called from her perch on an upper deck, near the big wheel for steering. "I found it in a Dasnarian sailing manual."

"Would I lie?" Jak inquired jauntily.

"Cheerfully and without remorse," Astar retorted with an easy smile, then he snapped to attention and saluted. "Permission to come aboard, Captain Konyngrr?"

"Granted. Stow the gangplank, Willy. Gen, come with me. Step lively."

"I had no idea you could be such a tyrant," Gen muttered.

"I did," Stella said as they passed her, her tone sultry and her slight smile full of smug mystery.

Jak winked at her, and the too-familiar envy stabbed at Gen. She let it go with a blown-out breath, actually grateful she needed to pay attention to Jak's instructions on her new responsibilities. He left her to memorize the lines and ties he'd explained, and went to place Astar on the wheel, as the most muscular of all of them.

"All right, crew," Jak shouted, waiting for everyone to pay attention. "All joking aside, I mean it when I say I expect you all to obey my commands and obey them immediately. It could mean the difference between us sailing or sinking. You're a raw crew, but you're all smart, capable people. If you need help, yell out my name. Don't use it otherwise. I'll get to you as quick as I can. Don't leave your stations without permission for *any* reason. Lena, you are the sole exception. Do your weather magic in any way that might smooth our passage. Move around if you need to—just keep your eyes open, because stuff moves around fast sometimes. Just remember, your new motto is: One hand for you; one hand for the boat. *Always* be holding onto something, so you don't go overboard. That goes for all of you."

They all nodded, and Jak continued. "The rest of you, just focus on *your* job, and not what anyone else is doing. Let me do the thinking. This is going to be a miserable crossing, but we can do this. You can do it."

"I can't decide if I'm inspired or terrified," Rhy drawled.

Jak tossed him a little salute. "Both work for me, as long as you obey orders."

~ 6 ~

IT WAS A miserable crossing. Even though they had packed away their winter furs and donned oiled canvas outer gear, Gen was soon soaked to the skin and colder than she'd ever been in her entire life. That was what came of not being able to shapeshift. Much as she resented the stricture and how truly awful she felt, she began to understand Astar's reasoning. Some people being able to shapeshift when others couldn't set them apart in a critical way when they all needed to work together as one.

And after a while, no one joked anymore about Jak's insistence on absolute obedience. They were all in a small boat together, being tossed about on a stormy sea. Those metaphors might be overused, but they also captured something important: In that vastness of churning gray sky and water, they had only each other, all parts of a whole.

The first few hours were chaos. Nothing like five people learning totally new skills under pressure. And if she'd thought the water at Aduard had been rough, it was nothing compared to the waves they hit around the time they lost sight of land. Gen nearly panicked and gave up several different times—and only Jak barking at her to pay attention and do her job kept her from flying or swimming away. Not that she'd abandon her friends. Or, rather, she wouldn't if she thought it through. The pressure, though, was killing her, and her inner hummingbird wanted nothing more than to fly away from it all.

Even normally unshakable Stella dissolved into tears at one point—and Jak treated her no differently than he did anyone else. Rhy had his jaw set in grim determination, and Zeph looked purely furious as only a drenched cat could. Astar hung onto the wheel, face red with the effort of holding them on the course Jak set. All the while, Jak leapt about with indefatigable agility, surefooted and alert, clearly in his element. Gen would hate him for it, except he worked harder than any of them.

Lena did her best to steer the worst of the crosswise gusts around them, but her dusky skin had paled with exhaustion to the point of being as gray as the rest of the world around them. Stella had briefly argued with Jak about using the Star of Annfwn to supplement Lena's weather magic, but he'd told her in no uncertain terms that she had a more important job to do and that if she took her attention away from her set of sails, it would be dereliction of duty. That had led to the tears, which Jak ignored, striding away to yell at someone else. Gen no longer felt so envious.

After the first few hours, though, they began to work together better. She was getting progressively more tired, sure, but she'd grown kind of numb to it—and to the miserable chill. In fact, she felt overwarm during moments of intense activity, uncertain if the water rolling down her face was rain, seawater, or sweat. The roll of the wind and waves, and Jak's orders in response, resolved finally into a rhythm. The first time she anticipated Jak's order, moving to shorten a line even as he turned to shout at her to do it, he grinned and gave her a thumbs-up.

The feeling of accomplishment was almost as good as attaining dragon form.

By the time Jak shouted his sighting of land, everyone had grown at least accustomed to their tasks, if not proficient. They sailed their little ship into a sheltered harbor, the wind and water blessedly settling into tamer patterns as the small island rose up around them, a comforting hummock of rock frosted with greenery. Had Gen thought this landscape was ugly? It sure looked beautiful to her now, serene, mists coiling gently around the peak that disappeared into the low clouds.

Lena plopped down beside Gen, decidedly ashen. Rhy frowned in her direction before quickly looking away again. "How are you holding up?" Gen asked her.

"Frankly I wish I'd been given sails to manage. I think it would've been easier than trying to wrangle this tangled mass of weather."

Gen held out one palm, showing Lena the angry blisters that had grown, popped, bled, and grown again. "Not necessarily," she said, rolling her stiff shoulders. "I think I nearly wrenched my arms out of their sockets half a dozen times."

"No chatter," Jak snapped, jogging past. "We're not anchored yet, and we don't know these waters. Pay attention now. Gossip later."

Lena stuck her tongue out at Jak's back, and Gen had to swallow a giggle. No wonder they'd been friends for so long.

At last, Jak declared himself satisfied, telling Astar he could leave the wheel and lower the anchor. Astar slowly peeled his fingers from the wheel, his hands stiff and chapped bright red, and he moved ponderously, Gen's abused body throbbing in sympathy. The boat bobbed some in the cove they'd found, but compared to what they'd been through, it felt glassy calm. Lena eyed the distance to shore. "I have a bad feeling we're sleeping on the boat tonight," she murmured to Gen under her breath.

"Everyone, tie off your lines if you haven't done so already," Jak ordered. "Make sure your stations are tidy. Then join me here on the deck."

They were all moving slowly, but they also obeyed without grumbling, soon gathering around a table Jak had set up. "I think we're here," he said without preamble, pointing to a small island on the map. "It's marked as having no facilities, no population, so we'll sleep on the boat tonight."

Gen groaned but restrained the protest that leapt to her lips. She also didn't point out that a shapeshifter on the wing could determine exactly where they were on the chart. A shapeshifter on the wing could disappear, too, and never be seen again.

Jak glanced around at all of them. "Miracle of miracles. And here I thought nothing would shut you lot up."

"We're tired," Rhy said shortly.

"Can we expedite this meeting, Captain Konyngrr," Stella asked in a cool voice, "so we can eat something and get the sleep you've promised?"

Jak eyed her. "Yes. We'll sleep in shifts. There's four bunks below. That makes four asleep at a time, staggering by twos. Of the remaining three, two are on watch, one fore, one aft. The one not sleeping or on duty will spend the time eating and exercising."

"Exercising!" Zeph burst out. "Not a one of us needs a workout after today."

"If you don't exercise tonight," Jak replied evenly, "you won't be able to move tomorrow. Trust me. Keep it light, but work those muscles and ligaments. Enjoy your brief walk in my mossback boots."

Zeph fumed but said nothing more. Gen sympathized, as she'd love nothing more than to shift and return to a human body that didn't ache in every pore.

"If there's no further discussion, Gen, break out the rations. Rhy, you help her and get the water cask. Lena, Stella, Astar, and Zeph, you're first in the bunks. After two hours, I'll wake Stella and Zeph, and we'll rotate every two hours from there."

"I need to heal everyone first," Stella said quietly.

"No healing," Jak replied.

"But people's *hands* are—" she began.

He shook his head. "If you heal them tonight, they'll only blister again tomorrow, and you'll lose progress on the calluses you're building," Jak said. "This was only the first day, people. We've got at least two more, and that's just until we can start looking for Isyn. Healing for debilitating injuries only."

Stella jammed her fists on her hips. "It's just as well that Willy forbade sex, because I wouldn't let you come near me, Jakral Konyngrr. I may never sleep with you again, you ass." With that, she stomped away, heading for the hatch leading below.

"Do you want your rations?" Gen called after her.

"I'm too *tired* to eat!" Stella yelled back, voice wobbly.

Jak watched her go, a flash of regret in his eyes, but he didn't follow her.

"I'll talk to her," Astar said quietly.

Jak nodded. "Eat first or sleep first—up to each of you. Gen, why are you still standing there?"

IN THE MORNING, they all resumed their stations and sailed away from their sanctuary. When the first gust of wind hit the little boat as they left the shelter of the island, it shuddered in every plank of wood and snap of canvas, Gen's bones aching with every jarring motion. She'd gotten eight hours of sleep, but breaking it up into two chunks at a time left her feeling as if she'd barely slept at all. Jak had slept even less, only two hours total, so far as Gen could tell. When she mentioned it to him, he asked if she was questioning the captain, so she backed off.

Still, it seemed Jak spent most of the night working diligently on something with his hands as he paced the deck, sharp eyes looking out for trouble. When they took their stations in the morning, he handed out fur-lined leather gloves he'd cobbled together from a ruined jacket of his, commenting that at least it was good for something.

Stella almost refused hers, but Jak pulled her aside, saying something quietly to her. She wasn't happy, stalking away from him with spine rigid, but she yanked on the gloves.

"I tried talking to Nilly," Astar murmured to Gen, "but she told me to keep my nose out of it."

"Good advice."

"That's what Zeph said, too." He watched Stella settle into her station to check her lines. "But I'd hate for this love affair to fizzle so soon."

"I'm surprised at you, Willy."

"Why, because I didn't want them to get together in the first place?"

Gen laughed a little. "No, that you have so little faith in the strength of their attachment. This is a bump. They'll get over it."

Astar gave her a curious look. "That's what Zeph said, too," he repeated. "Did you two consult?"

"No." Gen patted him on the cheek. "We're just wise."

"Why aren't you all at your assigned stations?" Jak barked.

Gen rolled her eyes. "Who knew Jak would be such a tyrant?"

"He's worried," Astar murmured. "It's a lot of responsibility, captaining us through this crossing, with so much that could go wrong. I feel for the guy."

Gen felt for Jak, too, but several hours into a sail that was every bit as rough as the day before, if not worse, she turned her misery into fury at Jak for putting them through this. It wasn't rational, but when he barked a correction at her one time too many, she snarled back, beyond tempted to hurl herself overboard for a refreshing swim. Jak saw it in her, dark eyes snapping. "Going to turn tail and run?" he sneered at her. "You're barely doing what the greenest Dasnarian sailor does before he's eleven."

"Youth is a beautiful thing," she snapped back, but she sharpened up, promising herself to do better. She recognized Jak's technique, of course. Her father was a soldier who trained soldiers. And she hadn't missed that Jak made sure that Stella and Lena got the most and first sleep the night before.

"Look alive, people," Jak shouted to them all from the prow, agile body moving with the pitching boat, rain and seawater lashing him, dark hair plastered to his skull. "We're all cold, wet, and tired. You're also learning your tasks well enough that you don't have to think about every little thing. This is when people make mistakes. But look around you—there's no room for mistakes. No one to save us if we fuck up. So we have to be sharper than ever."

They made it through that day with only a few errors, working far better as a sailing team, and collapsing into even the alternating sleep schedule was welcome. They talked little, simply eating and then sleeping or taking up watch or repairs under Jak's eagle eye.

It was on the afternoon of the third day that the mistake happened.

They were tacking against the wind, making for an island that should be populated, and everyone was excited about the possibility of sleeping a full night in an actual bed with a warm meal in their bellies. Gen's skin itched to shift, too, a craving that came even before food at that point. She couldn't remember the last time she'd gone so long without shapeshifting. By the look on the other shapeshifters' faces, they felt the need, too. Gen was daydreaming a little about which form she'd take—maybe they could all go flying or running, as she'd had a bellyful of ocean at that point—and Lena was picking her way over a loose coil of rope, moving aft at Jak's instruction, so she could attempt to shift the wind more in their favor.

A sideways surge of water tipped the boat precariously, Lena losing her footing as she lurched with the sudden tilt of the deck.

"Lena, watch out!" Rhy shouted.

At the same moment, a stray gust of wind caught the sail Rhy was handling, the rope spinning through his fingers, the boom snapping around behind him and *thonking* him on the head with a crack audible over wind and water. With the sail flapping empty, the boat skewed sharply, pitching suddenly in the other direction—and throwing Lena overboard.

It all happened so fast that Gen found herself blinking at the place where Lena had been as if the problem was her eyesight.

"Nooooo!" Rhy howled, abandoning his station. Jak was on him in a flash, using the surprise to smash the stronger shapeshifter back into his seat.

"Man your sail!" Jak shouted in his face.

"I'm going after her!" Rhy shouted back, struggling against Jak's leverage—and stranglehold.

"No!" Jak shouted. "We lose this sail, we're *all* dead. Everyone stay on task. Lena is a strong swimmer, and Gen is going after her."

It took Gen a moment to process that, a large part of her brain still grappling with Lena's sudden disappearance. Then Jak was hauling her to her feet. "I've got your station. Orca form. Go!"

She was obeying—Jak's burred order reminding her of her dad in the best way—before she processed what a good idea it was. As she flung herself into the raging sea, she shifted, the pleasure of it almost orgasmic after so long in human form. Of course orca was the best choice for these waters. Even in the dim light and tumultuous waves, she could use echolocation to find Lena, and she'd have the strength to pull her a long way if necessary. In the sudden quiet of below the surface, she marveled that Jak had clearly thought ahead to that eventuality to have a solution so readily at hand. Something that she herself should have done.

Swimming a circle, she sent out a series of clicks, listening for anything she could learn from the echoes that bounced back. She hadn't spent enough time in orca form to develop any real expertise on the finer points. That was a funny aspect of shapeshifting—much of a given animal's abilities were instinctive, which was fortunate or flying would kill a lot of young shapeshifters—but much was learned, too. Just as animals refined their skills as they matured and over the course of their adult lives, only time in a given form allowed a shapeshifter to get really good at some of the more esoteric skills.

So she was probably like a bumbling calf sending out her bursts of clicks and sorting what her orca brain told her the echoes meant—but she found Lena surprisingly easily. Her friend was thrashing in the turbulent water, fighting her rain slicker but staying afloat. Lucky that Lena was a such a strong swimmer, having spent her childhood bodysurfing in the seas of Nahanau.

Gen made for her, hoping Lena would understand that she was a rescuer, not a killer whale on the hunt for a tasty snack. Orcas didn't eat humans, of course, but not all humans remembered that, especially when confronted with one in the water. She breached next to Lena, who—thankfully—gave a cry of relief and lunged for Gen's dorsal fin, levering herself onto Gen's back. Cheers in the distance indicated they'd been spotted.

Swimming carefully so as not to dislodge her rider, Gen made for the boat, which pitched alarmingly in the rough sea. How were they getting Lena back aboard? Her friend didn't have much strength, her teeth chattering as she shivered against Gen's whale body. Then Gen spotted a figure scaling a rope ladder down the side of the boat, clinging with athletic grace and sure knowledge of his place on even a wildly pitching sailing ship. Jak, naturally.

Gen swam up as close as she could, scraping against the ship uncomfortably, doing her best to keep in place in the churning water. Not at all easy without more practice than she'd had. Then Lena's weight disappeared from her back, and Jak's triumphant shout signaled success. Gen swam a circle to double check, confirming that Jak had a soaked Lena between him and the side of the boat, Astar leaning over the edge to pull her up.

Jak turned back to Gen and gave a hand signal for her to

get back aboard. She briefly debated the best way to do that. A seabird that could leap from water to air would be the best bet, but she wasn't sure if any of her avian forms would handle this weather well. Maybe mermaid so she could swim to the rope ladder, grab on, then shift to a good climbing form like monkey. Swimming closer to the ladder, she went to shift... and couldn't.

She couldn't move at all.

Everything went black, icy cold.

Then nothing.

~ 7 ~

WHATEVER THEY'D CAUGHT in their nets, it was huge. The nets strained, the folk calling to each other in excitement as they worked to haul it in. Isyn squinted at the wintry sky, gauging how much time—and how much weather magery remained to him—before the blizzard broke through his control and overwhelmed them. The white fog of thick snowfall obscured the most distant isles, sweeping in on the ones in the middle distance. Only the small area around them on the frozen sea and the narrow aisle back to land remained clear.

He had maybe an hour of magic left in him, probably less. And he didn't want to be out on the ice when it gave out.

"Whatever we've netted, my king, it's too big to bring through the hole," Jasperina reported, wiping the ice crystals from her long lashes. "We've got to enlarge it. You need to melt more."

"No time, and I don't have it in me," Isyn replied, even as the folk not working the net set to chopping at the edges of the hole in the thick ice with hatchets. He raised his voice. "Leave it. Dump the catch. We're going home."

A chorus of dismay howled over the ice to him. Jasperina

stared at him, flabbergasted. "But, my king, it's a *big* one! We could feed everyone for a week with it. Maybe longer. A feast!"

A group shout went up as the folk holding the net went skidding over the ice, pitons ringing as they dug in their spiked boot heels for purchase to keep from being dragged into the black open hole in the gray ice. The black water churned from the creature's struggle, sending gouts of spray to splash along the edges of the fishing hole, making the surface slick in the moments before it froze. "We'll be lucky if whatever it is doesn't eat *us*," he noted.

"We'll kill it before we haul it out, my king," Jasperina explained. Indeed, Gizena, a tall woman with deadly aim, stepped up to the hole, aiming her harpoon at whatever thrashed below.

"No harpoons!" His command rang across the ice, Gizena looking up and bowing in acknowledgment, stepped clear of the action again.

"My king, we're not bringing it out of there alive," Jasperina said, her disapproval clear.

"We're also not killing it only to leave it to rot because we can't get it out of the cursed hole because it's too small," he replied, levering to his feet, his thigh aching. Leaning heavily on his staff, he tested his footing on the ice. All he needed was to fall on his ass in front of everyone, legs splayed like a newborn fawn. The break in his thigh bone was healing, but oh so slowly. While it did, he mostly sat in the big chair like a fool and tossed out commands instead of being useful.

Jasperina hovered anxiously at his side. "Should you be standing, my king? Let me call the bearers to carry you closer if you need to see."

He ignored her, digging the sharp point embedded into the end of the staff into the ice, securing it before he took a cautious step off the rug his chair sat upon. Then another. "Let it go!" he called out to the folk on the net. "We have a decent catch as it is."

"We can't, King Isyn," the foreman on the net shouted back. "It's entangled. We haul it out or we lose the net."

The nets took two weeks for a team of twenty to weave, not to mention that just one net required a staggering amount of spun alpaca wool. They couldn't glean more from their small herd without jeopardizing the alpacas' warmth. Their winter stores were running lean since the last attack, and there was no longer any game to be had on the island, with the enduring winter lasting so very long. Ice fishing was all they had to keep everyone fed. They couldn't afford to lose two weeks of fishing.

Making his painstaking—and pained—progress, he called back to the foreman. "Can you cut it?"

The foreman jerked his chin at Gizena, who shouldered her harpoon strap and took his place on the net, keeping the lot of them from being dragged in. He jogged to meet Isyn, enviably steady on the ice with his short, broad stature and robust health. "We can cut the net, my king," he said, puffing, face chapped from the bitter wind. "But we'll still lose most of the net, and no guarantee that whatever is caught in it will live. It's well and truly fouled. We can't free it of the net without bringing it up, and if we bring it up we might as well eat it." He grinned, shrugging. "No sense wasting all this effort."

"What do you think it is?"

"Big." The foreman's grin widened. "Maybe an orca. We haven't sighted any whales in these waters since the ice sealed over so thick all winter, but the old folks tell how it's good eating, whale blubber."

"Would keep a lot of kids warm, my king," Jasperina added, ruthlessly working on Isyn's soft heart.

"Aren't orcas also intelligent?" Isyn asked.

"Not intelligent enough to avoid our net," the foreman cracked, then sobered. "That's the way of things, my king. Kill or be killed. Them or us."

Isyn knew it. Or rather, he understood that philosophy, though he didn't agree with it. Still, life in the Winter Isles was a hard one, and he wouldn't quibble with what the folk had been doing here for generations to survive long before he crashed through the portal to be crowned their king. Isyn eyed the considerable haul of fish they'd already netted, checked the advent of the storm again. Ever closer. Dangerous. His control was slipping. And he didn't want the whale killed.

"We don't have time to enlarge the hole enough to bring up a killer whale, if we even have the strength to pull it out of the water."

"You make the hole big enough, my king"—the foreman touched the side of his nose knowingly—"I guarantee my people will pull it out."

And there it was: Isyn's entire reason for being there, his sole qualification to be king and the only reason the folk had let him live at all. The reason they tolerated his commands and interference: because they needed his magic. Shouts went up as the creature in the net thrashed, nearly pulling one side of the net—and three of the folk—to their icy doom. There was no happy outcome here.

"Clear the cutters from the edge," he instructed on a sigh, drawing his magic back from the oncoming storm to focus it on the ice. "But be ready to move fast. You're going to have to haul it back. No time to butcher it here."

The foreman hooted, then bowed and jogged off again, calling orders that had the ice choppers packing up their gear and cheering.

"It's the right decision, my king," Jasperina said.

Isyn nearly bit out that he didn't need anyone to tell him the rightness or wrongness of his decisions, but it wasn't true— and had no effect regardless. He didn't feel good about most of his decisions, no matter what his people said about them. Summoning the magic that leapt readily at his command now that he wasn't holding back an entire storm front, Isyn coiled his mage senses into the edge of the ice, asking it to warm and melt. Slowly. They didn't need for the ice to destabilize and dump them all in the lethally cold water.

The net crew had retreated to the far side of the hole while he worked, but now, as the rim melted and enlarged the gaping eye of black water, they began to spread out again. Chanting a work song, they reeled in the net, hand over hand, working as one.

"Will you sit, my king?" Jasperina asked, sounding anxious. She'd sounded anxious ever since the attack and his grievous wounding.

"I'll stay," he gritted out, watching the churning water

with interest. He'd never seen one of the famed orcas. He also found himself torn between avid curiosity to see the creature and bitter regret that he'd finally see one only to watch it be killed and butchered. With his magical senses still wound into the ice, and thus with the water melting back into the sea, the whale's beingness made itself known.

Intelligent, yes—and afraid. Panicked, even.

Isyn's heart went out to the poor thing. He couldn't bear it. "Is the hole big enough?" he asked, needing to pull his magical senses back. A stronger man would stay with the creature through its violent demise, but it had been a long time since he'd felt strong. He couldn't save himself, much less this whale.

"Not quite big enough," Jasperina answered, having shouted the query back and forth. "Just a bit more."

Isyn concentrated on widening the hole further, going a bit faster.

"Help me. Nilly! Lena! Can you hear me? Help, oh, help. They'll kill me."

Isyn shook his head of the buzzing voice. Now he was imagining the whale calling for help. The folk chanted louder, accelerating the beat, hauling in earnest, gloved fists clenched in the net. *Heave. Ho. Heave. Ho.* A glimpse of fin in the water had them shouting in excitement. *Heave. Heave. Ho. Heave. Heave. Ho.*

It was larger than Isyn had imagined, huge compared to the folk. The white belly showed stark against the glossy black dorsal side. And it shrieked in his head, fighting the net, sobbing in fury and despair. Gizena, relieved of her station on the net, aimed her harpoon at the small eye highlighted by white, like a court lady's meticulously applied makeup.

"No no no no no," the whale spat mentally, thrashing in the net and depriving Gizena of her target. *"Help! They're going to kill me. And it just fucking figures that I'll die alone."*

Unable to extricate himself from the doomed whale's thoughts—and amused despite everything at the wryness of them—Isyn decided he would be a monster if he didn't attempt to offer some comfort in her last moments. *"It's all right,"* he thought at her, not at all sure when he decided the whale was female. Something about the tenor of her mental voice. *"I'm with you. You're not alone."*

She latched onto his thoughts with surprising tenacity, seeming not at all surprised by a voice in her head. *I don't know who you are, but please help me. I'm a person. Please!*

Did all creatures think of themselves as people? Perhaps so. *It will be over in a moment,* he soothed. Gizena had repositioned herself, taking aim. It would be a quick death, at least.

No! she snarled, a feline growl in it that sounded oddly un-whalelike. *You will save me, sorcerer."*

"I'm no sorcerer. Only a mage."

He could almost feel her rolling her eyes. *"Does it seriously matter? I feel your magic and you know you can talk to me. Let me go."*

"I can't," he replied sadly. *"I have starving people to feed."* And not much power to affect the whale's fate. But he signaled to Jasperina. "Tell Gizena to hold fire until we're sure the hole will be big enough."

Jasperina looked sour but relayed the order.

"Let me go, and I'll help feed them," she replied immediately. *"I promise."*

"How?" But wasn't this how the tales went? The fae creature promising wealth and fortune, a lifetime of wishes. His favorite book had a story like that, a prince rescuing a fish that promised to make him king of all he surveyed. He should've brought that book with him instead of leaving it back in Erie. It would've been a comfort in his exile.

"I don't know how exactly," the whale answered, surprising him that she didn't make any wild promises. *"I'm no fae fish who can magically make you into a king."*

That startled him. Did she know that same tale somehow? Or—more likely—she'd plucked it from his thoughts. *"I'm already a king, and it's done me no good."*

"You're the king of this place?"

"In the land of the blind, the one-eyed man is king," he replied wryly.

"Hmm. Well, I'm much bigger and better than a fish, and look how much good it's done me."

He couldn't really be having a telepathic conversation with a whale about faerie tales. Could he? *"How do you know that story?"*

"I read it in a book. Tales of the Fae. *Do you know it?"* The whale sounded increasingly desperate.

"I once did," he replied, entirely bemused. Perhaps he was finally losing his mind. Really, the surprise was only that it hadn't happened before.

Heave. Heave. Heave. Ho. Heave. Heave. Heave. Ho. The net drew taut, the whale thrashing in all her glossy, vivid glory, a stark black and white in the endlessly gray landscape. Gizena stalked closer, poised for the kill, the whale no longer able to turn her vulnerable eye away.

"The hole is big enough now, my king!" Jasperina reported breathlessly.

"Would a whale know about a book??" she demanded. *"I'm a person! A shapeshifter."*

"So shapeshift."

"I can't. Don't you think I would have if I could? Help me, Moranu curse you, idiot king!"

Moranu? A whale couldn't know about a goddess, much less a book. Gizena armed the harpoon. Isyn wound his magic into the ropes of the net, offering a mental apology to the hours of bloody-fingered labor that had gone into weaving it and spinning the wool, so painstakingly collected and used for this purpose instead of a hundred others. Finding a spot where the whale's weight pressed most heavily, he frayed the fibers of the rope.

With a crack, the net suddenly split, folk falling back as the whale fell into the water with a mighty *sploosh*. The harpoon went wild, *thunking* into whale flesh. She gave a mental cry but dove deep, the harpoon embedded in her side. Above the ice, all was in an uproar. People shouting in disappointment and astonishment. Those able to hauled in the net, pointing to the frayed fibers, exclaiming.

"Guess it was too big for our net," Jasperina commented in dull disappointment. "So much for a feast."

"We hauled in plenty of fish," Isyn reassured her, signaling to the foreman that they needed to load up. That last trick with the net had drained him, and he'd need every bit of magery he had left to keep the path home free of the oncoming storm. The folk glumly loaded up the sleds with the few fish trapped in the remnants of the net, supplementing their previous meager catch. And Isyn sat heavily in his chair, guilt and remorse wracking him on two fronts. *"Whale, are you there?"*

No answer. Of course there wasn't. Because whales weren't telepathic, and they weren't fae creatures to offer wishes to broken and lonely kings. He was a sentimental fool who'd deprived his people of desperately needed food. He hadn't even extracted any useful promises from his magic fish.

"Never seen a net split like that," the foreman said, stalking up and shaking his head. "We nearly had it, too, my king. Biggest, healthiest whale I ever seen. Don't know how it got here, but I doubt we'll see its like again."

Both he and Jasperina looked at Isyn. Neither were so insolent as to look accusing, but the doubt was there. "At least you retrieved the net," Isyn pointed out wearily. "It will take less time to repair than weave a new one. If it can be mended in time, we can return here tomorrow."

"Tomorrow? Are you sure, my king?" Jasperina asked, hope in her voice and eyes. "You won't be too wearied?"

Normally he didn't like to agree to the ice-fishing excursions more than weekly. The cold made his leg bone ache to the point that he couldn't walk on it for days. But it was the least he could do, given that he'd ruined their chances at a whale feast. Maybe his magic fish would somehow deliver on her reckless promise. "Tomorrow," he answered firmly.

That cheered everyone, and they set off across the ice to

shore, everyone chatting merrily about the chances of netting the whale again, Isyn deep in silent thought.

THAT NIGHT, HE dreamed of a woman like no other. He was in his personal library, back at Castle Marcellum, sitting by the fire, a glass of good brandy at his elbow, and *Tales of the Fae* open on his lap. It was a familiar dream, no doubt born of homesickness and a longing for all he'd left behind. The folk had no books, and the tales they told by their fires were all bloodthirsty stories of hunting triumphs or cautionary tales of tragedy. Magic and miracles weren't part of their cultural repertoire.

It would be a comforting dream except that he could never quite make his eyes focus on the page. Or, when he could make out the letters, they formed nonsense words, as if written in a language he didn't know.

"It's N'Andanan," the woman said, and he glanced up to see her standing at his shoulder. She had long hair, richly waving, the color of fertile earth and the trunks of trees in the deep forest. Her face glowed with calm intelligence, a restfulness to her oval face, strength in her firm jaw. Her eyes caught his attention the most, however. They were an extraordinary deep blue verging on violet, an indigo shade he hadn't seen since he left Erie so long ago.

Unsurprised by her sudden appearance, as is the way of

dreams, he pointed at the book. "It's written in N'And…"

"N'Andanan," she repeated, enunciating the oddly lilted word, walking around his chair to hold her hands out to the fire. The light shone through her filmy gown—far too silky and thin for the Winter Isles, even indoors—revealing a long, trim figure in keeping with her height. "An ancient language that not many people have encountered, so I'm not surprised you don't know it."

"Do you?" he asked.

She glanced over her shoulder with a wry smile. "Enough to recognize it—it shares quite a bit with the Tala written language, such as it is—but I don't know enough to read it. Though I have a friend who can." She frowned, puzzled. "I should know her name. Why don't I remember her name?"

"Because this is a dream?" he suggested.

"It's your dream, not mine."

"But you are in it with me."

"A good point. Though that's a puzzle, too." She scanned the room. "Where is this?"

"The Winter Isles."

"That explains why I'm so cold." She put a hand to her side, fresh blood suddenly staining the white silk. "I'm hurt."

"Let me help you." He tried to stand, but his leg wouldn't cooperate. Even in his dreams, it plagued him.

She shook her head, the firelight showing brighter through her ethereal form. "I have a feeling you already helped me as much as you can. The rest is up to me." She wrinkled her nose, a surprisingly girlish expression. "I wish I knew why I always end up alone," she added wistfully.

"You're not alone," he pointed out. "You're with me."

She held up the bloodied hand, both it and the blood going transparent. "Not anymore."

And she was gone.

THEY SET OUT for the ice-fishing hole the next morning, as soon as Isyn was able to clear the storm from the area. It would be welcome to have some sunshine, but it took too much out of him to fight the entrenched storms to that extent. So he settled for something less than a blizzard, the looming gray clouds making the endless field of fresh snow look dim and shadowed. The sleds whisked over the snow, sending up powdery sprays that would sparkle in better light.

The ice hole hadn't completely frozen over during the night, but the arctic temperatures had done their work, ice encroaching in concentric circles, growing over all but a smallish disc of black water, the ice a relentless foe ever determined to reclaim its territory. A shout went up from the vanguard, excitement that spray from the whale's blowhole had been sighted. Several more of the folk carried harpoons today, in the hopes of maximizing their chances of killing the orca. Isyn hadn't been able to think up a good reason to tell them not to.

He was deeply torn, having hoped that the whale would be long gone and safe from being killed—and being glad to be reassured she still lived. *"Are you there, whale?"* he called mentally.

"Where else would I go?" she replied drolly.

"Far from here and the harpoons of my people."

"Yes, well, there aren't exactly a lot of breaks in the ice around here, and a girl has to breathe once in a while."

Oh. That made sense. *"We're here now, so I advise you to stay away as long as possible."*

"I heard you coming, and now I'm down deep. That's why I stayed at the surface as long as I did, filling my lungs and getting nicely oxygenated."

"How long can you stay down deep?"

"How long are you people going to be fishing today?" she countered.

"Hard to say." Though he could try to influence that. *"They're excited to try for you again, but the more fish they catch, the faster we'll be done. We can only carry so many on the sleds."*

She sighed mentally. *"I should be able to last that long. At least in water this cold I don't burn oxygen all that fast."*

Reassured that she would be safe from them for a while, he waved a hand at Jasperina's importuning and sent his magic into the thinner ice that had grown over the hole, melting it from the center out. And judiciously keeping it too small to pull his whale woman through. *"You sound very intelligent."*

"I have smart friends. At least, I'm pretty sure I do."

"You don't know?"

"Whales have big brains, fortunately for me, but they still don't think—or remember—like a human brain does. The longer I stay in whale form, the more of my human self I'll lose." Though her

mental words were matter of fact, an overwhelming sorrow wound around them. Pitch-dark, freezing water swirled around her. *"It's nice to have someone to talk to, though. It was a long night."* She sounded so wistful that his heart broke a little for her.

"Was that you who visited my dream?" he asked on impulse. Around him in the outside world, the surface world, the folk shouted, mustering nets and other tools, setting him down in his chair to observe, well away from the hole of ice so he could keep the weather at bay.

"Was it?" She sounded surprised now. *"Do you have white hair and a broken leg?"*

"That would be me." The sum total of who he'd become. *"And in human form, you are a lovely young woman with long brown hair and striking indigo eyes."*

She snorted, a very unwhalelike sound, and he could picture that charmingly girlish nose wrinkle. *"A flattering description,"* she replied. *"Clearly I look better in dreams than reality."*

He doubted that very much. She seemed likely to be the sort who underestimated herself. But he also knew that mere words wouldn't change her mind. *"You're hurt,"* he said instead, focusing on the most pressing issue.

"Fucking harpoon got me," she grumbled. *"Jak would tear me a new one for not dodging fast enough."*

"Who is Jak?" he asked, an uncomfortable curl of jealousy surprising him. He had no business being jealous of anyone, let alone her. Still, in the brief span of their acquaintance, he'd come to think of her as his alone. His fae shapeshifter, who

existed only in his mind and dreams, leapt from the pages of his favorite book. Maybe he *was* losing his mind, the final disintegration he'd been waiting for, if not patiently, then at least with resignation.

"Jak is… one of my friends?" She didn't sound certain at all. *"It's not clear. Whale brain is having an effect. I feel immense affection for him, and I'm certain he will be annoyed I didn't dodge fast enough, but I can't picture his face."*

"I don't understand why, if you could shapeshift into whale form, you can't shift back to human."

"It's a weird effect of the alter-realms, I know that much. They prevent us from shapeshifting. I don't know why, or the specifics, but I do know that others experienced the same problem. Believe me, I've been trying, if only to heal myself."

"Are you badly injured?"

"It's painful, and the blood loss slows me down," she confided. *"Fortunately, there don't seem to be any sharks in these waters."*

A stab of fear for her went through him. *"I didn't think of that."*

"I could fight them off for a while, but if I weaken any more… Well, I'll keep trying to shift."

"I wouldn't advise shifting into human form underwater," he commented drily.

She laughed, a rich musical sound. *"My brain isn't that far gone. But you've put your finger on the problem. Shifting into human form wouldn't be the smartest plan in that artic tundra of a frozen sea up there either. I'd have to be something like a polar bear, and that's an even smaller brain."*

"You can do that?"

"Polar bear? Yes, and a number of other forms. When I'm not in

an arctic alter-realm, that is."

"What do you mean by 'alter-realm'?"

"Ah—it probably feels like just a regular realm to you. To me it's a place I've arrived at via a kind of portal in space, possibly time. I'm on a quest to find out why these rifts are appearing, and why stuff from other places is coming through to mine. And to stop something bad from happening," she added after a moment.

For the first time in decades, he felt the prick of hope. Giddy anticipation rose up, and he regarded it warily. Hope could be a trap. He'd learned that well enough. *"Tala,"* he murmured, in part to himself. *"In my dream, you said you knew the Tala language, and you're a shapeshifter."*

"From Annfwn," she agreed, bright curiosity flaring. *"Do you know my realm, then?"*

He had to take a deep breath, waving off a concerned Jasperina, not pressing a hand to his thundering heart only by dint of will. *"Yes,"* he made himself think the words at her slowly, a measured pace to counter his desperate hope, braced for how the death of it—yet again—might finally kill him. *"I was a man of your world, long ago. A prince. A foolish one."*

~ 8 ~

"WHAT HAPPENED?" SHE asked quietly, sympathy curling warm around him. He wouldn't have to explain to her how hard his exile had been. She already understood.

"*It's a long story,*" he offered with a sigh.

"*We have time,*" she pointed out. "*And it helps me to have a person to talk to. It makes me think about more than fish and breathing.*"

"*True.*" The folk shouted with glee, hauling up the net they'd cast into the hole. His heart clenched, thinking for a flash of a moment that they'd caught her. But no—she'd have said so. Instead they were pulling in a full net of large, healthy fish. Far larger and fatter than they'd seen in years. "*Are you doing something?*"

"*Scaring up the big fish that lurk at the bottom and driving them into your nets.*"

"*Isn't that using up more oxygen?*"

"*It's a trade-off. I figure the sooner you fill your sleds with nice, big fish that aren't me, the sooner you all will leave and I can breathe at leisure again. Though I don't want you to leave.*"

"*Unfortunately I must. I don't have much in the way of independence.*"

"*The broken leg?*" she asked with that natural, genuine sympathy of hers. She didn't pity him, he could sense that from her, but she empathized in a way that made him feel, for the first time in what felt like forever, that he wasn't alone.

"That, and other complications." The ravages of old age were brutal, and not something a bright young thing like her would understand.

"Like falling into an alter-realm and being crowned king there of a people not like you."

He paused, rather astonished that she'd understood so much about his life so quickly. *"You're sharper than you think, to discern so much."*

"I can also hear a great deal of your thoughts that you don't articulate," she admitted. *"You're quite a powerful mind mage. Were you one in our world, too?"*

"Not so much. I had some talent back home, but I'm far more powerful in the Winter Isles, for whatever reason."

"Magic works differently in the alter-realms. Thus my inability to shapeshift. Still, it must be nice to at least be powerful in this place. Better to be a mage-king than a stableboy, yes?"

"Some days I'm not sure. The magic has its price."

"The leg?"

"Among other things."

"I have a friend who could heal you," she mused.

"This Jak again?"

"No… I don't think so, anyway. Regardless, it's a moot point for now. Tell me your story. Driving fish into the nets isn't all that diverting."

"Much appreciated, however." The folk had pulled up another net full of deep-sea fish, happily butchering some so as to make more room in the sleds, tossing the offal back into the

water, though the chum was hardly needed. Blood spattered over the ice, making for a scarlet contrast. At least it wasn't hers. *"And I'm realizing the story isn't so long as simply tiresome."*

"I'm a captive audience!" she noted cheerfully, and he could picture the lively sparkle in those deep indigo eyes. If only he'd met her when he was a young man, then perhaps… but there was no sense wishing after the past. It was gone, never to be retrieved.

"I left home with ambition, believing I could be a king, but of a different land," he said, thinking back to that long-ago voyage. *"Hubris is the downfall of many a would-be hero."*

"Heroism is overrated," she commented wryly. *"If I've learned nothing else from this quest, it's been that."*

"What are you questing for?"

"This is your turn to tell stories," she reminded him. *"Besides which, I find I can't quite remember. Maybe I was looking for you,"* she added impishly.

If only.

"I just know that I feel bitter about the whole heroism thing," she continued more soberly.

"I can agree there. I set sail into the Isles of Remus—do you know them?"

"They sound familiar. Maybe I was there, before I came here. I remember a boat."

"That would make sense. You could have fallen through the same portal I did. I was on the deck of my ship, a grand sailing vessel, using what little magic I possessed to search for the isle that should've been there but wasn't."

"Oh! I remember this part. The Isles fade in and out of the differ-

ent realities and have done so for centuries."

"Yes, I had this idea that I could find the isle my grandmother had ruled and somehow coax it back into connection with our realm. After her death, it had vanished, and I saw myself as some sort of golden king who would retrieve those people, isolated and lost." He had to laugh at his past self, so full of glorious purpose and little sense.

"Elements of this tale seem familiar," she commented, her mind-voice vague.

"Perhaps I've gone down in history as a great cautionary tale."

"Perhaps," but she didn't sound convinced. *"So, you were on the deck of your ship, searching for the Isle of Forgotten Treasure and..."*

"Nice touch."

"Thank you. I amused myself with it. And?"

"And..." He paused for dramatic effect. *"I fell overboard."*

She giggled. He'd be offended if it wasn't such a delightful sound—and if he didn't richly deserve it. *"I know. Very unprincely and unheroic. I was studying a sea chart and got absorbed... and next thing I knew, I was in the water. And the people who fished me out weren't mine."*

"How terrifying," she commented, her mental voice earnest and sincere. *"At least I knew about the alter-realms and could guess what had happened. Though the net was a shock and a stroke of bad luck."*

"I am sorry about that."

She mentally shrugged. *"Bad timing. Or good timing, as I met you. At least you can talk to me, tell me where I am."*

"Does knowing you're in the Winter Isles mean anything to

you?" he asked, intrigued. It hadn't to him, but perhaps something had been learned of them in the time he'd been gone.

"No," she conceded. *"But there's whale brain to consider. Still, I guess it's just nice to put a name to the place. Did the name mean anything to you?"*

"Not at all. I didn't speak the same language as the people here. It took months to learn to communicate."

"Ouch."

He smiled, utterly charmed by her.

"Did you need something, my king?" Jasperina asked hopefully. She hadn't much liked being sent away.

"I'm fine," he replied. "Don't hover." She went off again, dragging her spiked boots.

"So, how did you go from half-drowned foreigner to king?"

"I could do magic, a kind they needed. They recognized it before I did, using me for various rituals and ceremonies. By the time I understood what was going on, they'd made me king, and I was... entrenched."

"You sound almost more like a captive than anything else," she said, after a pause.

"There is some truth to that." He swallowed the urge to sigh. *"But I am king of all I survey—even if there's not much to see."*

"Is your world very small, then?"

"It seems to be. We can't travel past the ice."

"And it's winter all the time?"

He'd laugh at how horrified she sounded, if the truth weren't so stark. He remembered a few of the tales of Annfwn, how it was a tropical paradise, unparalleled in beauty and verdancy. As a young man, he'd fancied traveling there, after he was king. And now he was king, but a captive one, as she'd so perceptively noted. *"There apparently used to be a summer season, long before I arrived. The folk don't keep extensive records, but it seems only in the last century has it been fully winter. The situation has grown gradually worse, compounded by some recent strange attacks."*

"What kinds of attacks?"

"Odd creatures appearing to slaughter livestock, even a child in one village. Like nothing we've ever seen, some with tentacles, others furry with sharp teeth. They arrive in hordes and attack with mindless fury. We end up killing them all. That's how I broke my thigh bone—fighting a tentacle monster. It stripped me of my sword and threw me into a wall."

"You were fighting it alone, with only a sword?"

She sounded so incredulous it stung his pride. He apparently had some left. *"I'm not that old, and I am a trained warrior. This may not be the land I intended to claim, but these are my people, and it's incumbent on me to protect them."*

"I didn't mean it to sound like that," she replied contritely. *"I just have a bad feeling about those tentacle creatures, and it bothered me deeply to imagine you fighting one alone. I think it has to do with my quest, with what I'm supposed to be doing."* Her mental voice had gone strained, rife with frustration, a sense of her great tail churning black water. *"I need to get back."*

"I realize this may be a silly question, but I have to ask—have you looked for the portal back?"

"Have you?" she asked in turn.

"It would require me to dive into the freezing sea," he noted sourly. *"And yes, I did try, for years, when I was younger. But my*

people… they stopped me from trying, afraid I'd do myself harm."

"I'm sorry…" She paused. *"It's funny, I feel so close to you, but I've just realized I don't know your name. Did you tell it to me already and my whale brain forgot?"*

"No," he reassured her, hating that he'd given her a moment of anxiety. *"It's Isyn."*

"I know that name… Don't I?"

"I don't think we've ever met." More's the pity. *"And I fell through the portal into this world more than fifty years ago, long before you were born."*

"That's a very long time to be exiled among a strange people," she replied, a heaviness to her thoughts that made him think she was pondering a similarly long future for herself.

"You haven't told me your name," he suggested gently.

"Oh! It's…" She was quiet for far too long.

"Are you all right?"

"Physically, yes. But I don't remember my own name."

He sat with her in silence for a bit, absorbing that. *"Perhaps I should give you one."*

"Oh, I would like that! And then you can remember it for me."

How heartbreaking. Certainly a cure for feeling sorry for himself. He thought of her loveliness, the magical quality to her grace, like a faerie princess. And how she was trapped, as if enchanted, her human side falling into dreaming. *"I shall call you Briar Rose."*

"Like the princess in the story."

"Yes, just like her."

"My king," Jasperina said, interrupting the rapport so that he frowned at her. "We've got a full haul, but no sign of the orca."

Relief swept through him. He wouldn't have to attempt to forbid them from killing such a rich source of food. "We should go, then," he said. "I weary of holding the weather at bay."

"Perhaps," she tendered, "we could return tomorrow? If we approach quietly, we might surprise the orca as it comes up for air."

"Not going to happen, sweetheart," Briar Rose thought caustically, and Isyn had to smother a laugh.

"I'll see how I feel tomorrow," he promised, planning to feel very bad indeed. If he envisioned his Rose's whale body splayed on the ice, painting the gray scarlet and crimson, that made him convincingly ill.

"Yes, my king!" Jasperina trudged off happily to spread the word. Thankfully, the crew began packing things up with only a little grumbling.

"You can hear her through me?" he asked her.

"Mostly I just get your thoughts in response to what you hear. As I said, you're a powerful mind mage."

"Seems like you're the powerful one, to know all my thoughts."

"Not all of them, I'm sure. And I could never do this before. I knew a sorceress, the greatest in the realm, and she could speak inside my head like you do, but it was all her. She could talk to anyone, even speak through their mouths."

"You remember that much," he pointed out. *"Surely that's a good sign."*

"I'm sure it is," she replied, but here her sincerity failed. She was clearly saying it to please him.

"Ready to be moved, my king?" Jasperina asked, the bearers already lifting the platform to carry him to the sled. He might've chosen to walk, if she'd actually waited for his agreement, as he hated for Briar Rose to see him carried about like an invalid. A beautiful young woman, a magical Tala shapeshifter, stepped out of the storybooks to enter his life like a dream come true, and he was nothing more than a crippled old man.

"Your mind is vibrant and fascinating," she said, a sharp reminder that she could hear his unspoken thoughts, too. *"I wouldn't have said anything,"* she added hastily, *"but I didn't want you to go a moment longer thinking that I agree with that vision of yourself. Bodies don't matter. Every shapeshifter knows that."*

"Then why do you deny your own beauty?"

"I'm comfortable in my skin. Which happens to be a lovely, thick black-and-white dermal layer lined with luscious fat that I'm grateful you're helping me keep intact. Thank you, Isyn. Truly."

The sleds lurched into motion, the hiss of the runners rising in pitch as they gained momentum, the folk pulling them going from a laboring walk to an easier jog. *"I won't let them hurt you any more than we already have,"* he promised. *"We won't be back tomorrow, so you needn't worry."*

"Thank you. I don't suppose you could come visit me on your own?"

She sounded so bereft, so forlorn that he rubbed his forehead, trying to think. *"I don't see how, but I'll try."*

"Does your head pain you, my king?" Jasperina asked solicitously.

"Yes," he lied, laying the groundwork for claiming illness

the following day. "I have overextended, I'm afraid."

"You *have* seemed distracted today, my king." She peered at him in concern. "We'll put you to bed immediately, with some warm broth."

Oh joy.

Briar Rose snickered at his dismay. *"To be fair, a warm bed and a bowl of hot broth sounds really good to me right now. Also, I make an excellent bone broth. Don't ask me how I know. I just do."*

"I have no doubt of it. But should you feel cold? I didn't think orcas did in these climes."

"It could be the blood loss? Or just the human, emotional side of me imagining it. That's one positive of me eventually losing human thinking. When I'm fully a whale, I won't mind it anymore."

It sounded like a dismal fate to him. *"How long will it take? Before you forget you were ever human?"*

"I'm not sure. Every shapeshifter is different, and obviously, the ones who lose themselves aren't able to report on the experience. It helps if you don't eat or sleep in that form, I know that much—our teachers pound that into our heads so we'll remember whatever form we're in—but I really can't go without eating or sleeping for much longer."

It was a long night, she'd said. He could only imagine—and he fervently wished he knew of a way to help her.

"I wish you could, too," she replied to his thought. *"I think some sorcerers can trigger shifts; I have that idea in the back of my mind. Maybe you could figure out how?"*

"I'll work on it. And I'll find a way to visit you. Will you be all right?"

"Sure, I'll be just fine," she replied brightly. *"I'll probably find that portal and swim back home. Don't you worry about me."*

"I wish you could take me with you," he said on impulse, immediately regretting it.

"I would if I could. But there are two problems: If I find a rift, it will almost certainly be because I'm going through it already. And even if I could detect it in time to wait for you to join me, I don't think you could survive the cold water long enough to make it through."

"Both excellent points." He should've known better than to entertain hope. The frozen island loomed ahead.

"My friends will be looking for me," she said suddenly, after a morose pause. *"I feel it in my bones. When they arrive, I'll have them rescue you, too."*

"That's a nice story," he agreed, smiling wistfully. *"Why can I still hear your mind-voice so well?"*

"I've been swimming beneath you, but I have to stop now—this near to shore, the ice is solid."

"Maybe I'll see you in my dreams tonight."

"Maybe."

But it was the kind of "maybe" that people use when they mean they doubt it but don't want to say so.

SHE DIDN'T VISIT his dreams, though he did dream *of* her. At least he thought it was her, swimming in endless circles, keeping herself awake in the lightless, freezing waters. She was growing weak and miserably hungry. She surfaced periodically, breaking the crust of ice filling in the fishing hole to breathe.

And he sat upright in bed, the horrifying reality hitting him with a numbing agony very much like when that tentacle monster had thrown him into the wall. *We haven't sighted any whales in these waters since the ice sealed over so thick all winter.* Because the whales needed to breathe. And once that fishing hole froze over thick again—which it would without his magical assistance—she would suffocate and die.

He couldn't let it happen. He also couldn't return to the hole without assistance, and if he went, the harpoons and butchers would come along. So much for the power and glory of being king of all he surveyed; he couldn't save one whale without being questioned. Couldn't go somewhere on his own.

Well, that was going to change. If Briar Rose could keep herself awake, so could he. Grabbing the staff waiting for him beside the bed, he levered himself to his feet, awkward with the splinted leg. After teetering a moment, dizzy from the rush of pain and the change in body position, he began pacing, grimly forcing himself to walk from one side of the room to the other. As the movement woke up his brain, he began reviewing all he knew of magic from the many books he'd read in his youth, his mother's stories, and his own experience.

By the time dawn broke, the weak sun lightening the sky from black to dark gray, he had a plan.

~ 9 ~

S HE WAS GETTING seriously tired of this shit. Swimming, swimming, swimming. *Don't sleep. Don't eat the yummy fish.* Swim, swim, swim. Her side ached where the harpoon had lodged, its barbs preventing it from falling out, though she'd broken off the longer shaft on a submerged rock outcropping. Swim, swim, swim.

Swim swan, over the sea, swim swan, swim…

What was that? Oh, yes—she'd learned that along with her cousins in lessons on reading Common Tongue. She could picture them in a classroom, sitting with her, their brown hair all alike, along with other kids, all taking turns reading aloud. Why could she remember *that* and not her own name?

It doesn't matter, just keep swimming. Don't sleep. Don't eat the yummy fish.

But why not?

She knew she'd had a reason, but she couldn't remember it. The fish looked very yummy indeed, and she was *so* hungry. And weak. She really didn't feel good at all. So cold. So tired. She was also supposed to be looking for something, but she didn't know what anymore. It was lonely in the dark. Shouldn't there be other whales? But she'd sounded and sounded, to no reply. All alone.

"Briar Rose?"

A voice in her head... how odd. Not another whale sounding. Perhaps her thoughts circling loudly, banging against the inside of her own skull. *So tired.*

"Briar Rose!" the voice called more loudly. *"Are you there? Please answer me."*

Hmm. This was very odd. The voice seemed to be familiar, but not her own. Could it be a trap? She had a niggling feeling that something had been trying to stalk her, some powerful being. And then there were the hunters who'd shot her with the harpoon. This could be one of them. Best not to answer, and perhaps it would go away. She kind of liked the name, though. Like a faerie princess.

*"**Briar Rose**, answer me. I feel you down there. You're tired and hurting and hungry. I'm here to help you."*

"I don't know who you are," she replied reluctantly as it seemed it wouldn't leave her alone until she did.

"I'm Isyn, your friend." The voice was filled with relief. *"I was worried that you* couldn't *answer."*

She decided not to say anything to that. She wasn't even entirely sure what that meant, except for this feeling that she should remember more than she did.

"I think I can help you," the Isyn voice said. *"But you'll have to surface at the fishing hole."*

Oh ho! Now the creature's strategy came clear. *"I don't wish to be murdered today, thank you very much,"* she replied tartly.

A ghost of a mental laugh caressed her. *"You're still you. I promise not to hurt you. I'm alone. There are no hunters. Come up and see? If I'm lying, you can swim away."*

Grudgingly, and admittedly curious, she swam upward. She knew the hole the Isyn thing meant, as it was the only place to get air. Was that what she'd been looking for, more places to breathe? It didn't sound right.

Above, it was brighter, daylight filtering down through the hole. She couldn't see much past the rim, but there was nothing wrong with her hearing. Listening, she detected no sounds but of the Isyn thing. No stomping boots digging into the ice, no fresh blood swirling down from their discards.

"Briar Rose?"

"I see you tell the truth."

The Isyn blew out a long breath. *"Then here is where I need you to trust me. I'm putting a net in the water."*

"No!" The memory of panic and pain flooded her. *"No nets!"*

"I promise, I promise, I promise, Briar Rose—it's only to help you. To keep you from drowning."

She had to laugh at that. *"Silly Isyn creature, whales can't drown."*

"You can if you can't breathe, which is what will happen if the ice seals over."

Going quiet at that, she wondered how the Isyn knew about the ice and breathing. Over and over, she'd had to break the forming ice with her head, cutting and bruising herself. *"I don't understand how a net helps me breathe,"* she finally said.

"Because you weren't always a whale. You're a human, too. I can help you be human again, but then I'll have to pull you out of the

water quickly. I need the net's help."

"This is a very odd tale."

The Isyn's mental laugh was dry, and she found herself liking it. *"Believe me, I am in absolute agreement there. Let me show you the net. You'll see that it's not anywhere big or strong enough to hold you as a whale. It's only for your human self."*

"Show me the net." Just in case, she swam a distance away. A puny web of ropes fell into the water, shimmering golden with the light from above. "Pretty."

"Thank you. I wanted you to like it."

"Why?"

"Because I didn't want you to be afraid of it. So you would swim into it."

"I don't think so."

"Briar Rose, please, you have to. Just try. You can always swim away again."

She was torn. Part of her believed it and in fact wanted to try this game that appealed to some sense of fancy in her. A more powerful instinct remembered the hunters and warned her away. Fancy or instinct? She wished she had other whales to confer with. Always alone…

That was what decided her. She was tired of only fish for company, of being alone in the dark water. The Isyn at least amused her. It had made a pretty net for her. *"I'll try,"* she finally allowed.

ISYN WENT DIZZY with relief. Well, that and no sleep on top of prodigious magic use. Weaving the golden net hadn't been easy, but Briar Rose was already so far gone into the whale mind that he was glad he hadn't waited even hours longer. Besides which, by now Jasperina and his other keepers might have penetrated the illusion he'd left to cover his absence.

The orca moved in the water below, her black shape a quicksilver shadow. Still wary—and who could blame her? He stayed silent, listening for her, but not giving in to the urge to prod her along. A brush of the net should do it. The trick would be hauling the human woman out of the water before she succumbed to the cold.

So he lay flat on the ice, hoping the leverage would be enough. At least he had plenty of upper body strength still. He was much better when he wasn't teetering on one leg.

She passed by again, closer now. *Come on, Briar Rose,* he silently urged, keeping the thought close and quiet. *Trust me. I'll help you. I promise.*

Though it obviously made no difference, he held his breath and remained still, as if coaxing prey into his net. She passed by a third time, shallower still, nosing the net as she did.

And he poured his remaining magic through, heightening and deepening the enchantment he'd worked into the golden threads, praying to Moranu, the goddess of shapeshifters, to aid them both. Briar Rose's whale body convulsed in the water, a strangled human scream tearing from the orca's throat, disconcerting and heartrending. This was no awakening with a kiss. "Hold on, Briar Rose!" he shouted. "Stay with me!"

He scraped the bottom of his soul for all the magery in

him, giving it to her as her form flickered through a hundred shapes, so fast it rattled his own sense of self and reality. *"Human,"* he urged. *"You know the way, Briar Rose. Wake yourself."*

And there she was, a human woman, the one from his dreams, barely conscious, barely clinging to the net. "Briar Rose! Hold on. I've got you."

He didn't have her, not at all, but this was the make-or-break moment. Steeling himself against the icy water, he plunged his arms down, seizing her by one slender wrist and hauling her out with all the strength he had. It was a near thing, with her sodden weight plus the net pulling him down. Fortunately, he'd learned more than a few things from ice fishing, and he'd used water to freeze his clothing to the ice, providing something of an anchor.

Also, he'd expected her to be naked—because a whale wasn't dressed, after all—but she wore quite a lot of clothing, including an oiled canvas coat he recognized as being of Erie make. He gritted his teeth, holding on with all his might, at least able to release the magic drain now. She looked up at him, indigo eyes huge in her pale face, and his heart lurched. Something clicked inside, and he felt like he'd been waiting for her all his life.

And it was too fucking late for him. Ah, the bitter irony.

"Don't let go," she told him, teeth chattering.

"Never," he vowed, and pulled.

It took some doing, but between them, they managed it, both drenched by the end of it, their clothing and the entangling net freezing rigid and bonding to the ice as they lay on it in an exhausted sprawl. "We can't stay here," he muttered, unable to summon the will to move. "I brought you dry clothes. You need to change into them."

She lifted her head, wrinkling her nose as her long hair, frozen to the ice, pulled. "I can do one better." She disappeared, an incongruous small jewel-bright hummingbird in her place—a fantasy of a bird he hadn't seen since his youth—and then she was there again, dry and bundled in furs. "Let's get *you* into those warm clothes instead." She pushed to her feet with surprising vigor, no longer pale, eyes bright as she surveyed the barren landscape. "How does the sled move?"

"It moved with my magic," he told her. "And I've got nothing left. I'm afraid you'll have to walk."

"I may have a solution for moving the sled, but we need to get you in it. I'm strong, but I don't think I can carry you. You'll have to work with me." She crouched to help him sit up, the fabric of his coat hissing as she ripped it from the ice with surprising strength. She paused, holding his gaze. "Thank you," she said, with her simple earnestness that gave resonance to every word she spoke. "You literally saved my life and my sanity."

He smiled back at her, this kindred soul, feeling the warmth of real emotion for the first time in forever. "You're welcome. And you have to leave me here."

Her answering smile dropped like a rock, disappearing into the black hole of frozen sea. "I am *not* doing that."

"I planned it this way," he told her, trying to drum up a reassuring smile. "I'm old and done for. Freezing is a gentle way to go, and I'm not afraid of death." In truth, he was far more afraid of continuing to live as he had been.

"You are hardly on your deathbed," she replied crisply. "And I realize we barely know one another, but I am not the kind of person who leaves anyone behind, least of all a good person who risked his life to save mine."

"I'll only hold you back," he insisted, searching for a way to convince her. "I used up everything in me with this conjuring, and it was worth it. Far better than saving myself for more of this life I've been leading. I can't walk, and you can't carry me, but you can make it to land and survive."

"Isyn, I have no intention of—" Her lovely eyes went wide. "Isyn. I know who you are now. I just came from Castle Marcellum, where I met your parents, and Wim and Marjie."

He grappled with that information, confused—and wondered if her brain addling might be affecting her still. But... she knew his siblings' names, and their nicknames. "Which of them ended up on the throne?" he asked, which wasn't the most important question at the moment, but it was what he could grasp. It was hard to imagine them as old as he when they remained forever in their early twenties in his mind.

"They haven't decided yet. They might rule together. Let's get you in the sled."

"No, leave me."

"Not going to happen. You can die *in* the sled if you're so determined to."

He huffed out a laugh and put his arm around her as she slipped her shoulder under him to support the bad side. Fighting her would be foolishness. And she *was* strong. Tall and steady. She had a gentle touch, too, taking small steps to lead him to the sled. She smelled good, like tropical flowers and warm sunshine, her tumbling hair silky against his hand, her long, lean body hot against his side. The urge to kiss her nearly overwhelmed him. He needed to distract himself from her intoxicating effect. "How can there be no one on the throne of Erie?" he wondered aloud.

"Your parents, King Cavan and Queen Nix, are still alive," she answered. "It's only been a few months since you left after all."

He stumbled—nearly falling on his face on the ice—but she deftly caught him, her full breast pressing into his chest. "Careful, there," she warned. "A fall is the last thing you need."

That sounded like something you'd say to your grandpa. Which was probably how he seemed to her. Not moving, he held on to her as he stared into the distance, trying to understand. "Briar Rose, I left Erie almost fifty years ago."

She didn't say anything right away, so he risked a glance at her. Was that pity in her gorgeous eyes?

"I know that sounds hard to believe, but—"

"No," she interrupted. "Keep moving. It's not hard to believe at all. You're in an alter-realm, and time moves differently from one to the next. We've guessed that it happens, but this is the most extreme example so far. I promise you, Isyn—in our world, you've only been gone a few months."

A few months. He'd lived a lifetime in that time. The knowledge ground him down, the sheer futility of it all. A life wasted on ice and dead fish. "I wish you would just leave me here to die."

"Are you always this morose—or is it just the bad news?"

"You're direct."

"Yes, pretty much always. Sorry."

"Don't be. I prefer direct. And having been trapped in this place has not been conducive to optimism," he remarked, bearing down on the pain. Nearly to the sled.

"Well, you've been rescued now," she informed him cheerfully, easing him into the sled. "Things are looking up."

"Did I miss a dramatic rescue?"

"I feel like I need a more intense word than 'morose.' Gloomy?"

Why she made him want to laugh, he didn't know, but she looked delighted that she had. Tucking the fur blankets around him that he'd brought for her, she gave him a warm smile. "My friends will absolutely be coming soon. One is a sorceress who's been perfecting opening portals into the alter-realms. They'll find us, and we can go home. Is there a harness for this thing?"

Bemused, he opened the compartment in the console with the ropes the folk looped around their chests so they could lean into pulling the sleds. "You're strong," he said doubtfully, "but I doubt you're strong enough to pull the sled with me in it by yourself. You should leave—"

"If you tell me to leave you here to die one more time, I'm going to smack you." She looked at him expectantly, and the words died on his lips. Had he ever met anyone like her? No, he absolutely hadn't. And it killed him that it was too late.

"Good," she said, satisfied. Briefly, she caressed his cheek, then looked abashed. "You can be forgiven for a bit of fatalism. Decades in this place would drive anyone to despair. And you've forgotten I'm a shapeshifter. Once I shift, drop the harness over my head and chest, would you?"

Maybe all of this was a dream, and he was asleep in his bed. Just another version of the whale woman's visitation. Going along with it, he nodded.

She stood there and blinked at him. If her face hadn't suddenly crumpled into an expression of profound despair, he wouldn't have realized anything had happened. Or, rather, hadn't happened. "Oh, Rose," he said. "You can't shift now?"

"Of course I can't," she bit out, then gave him a weak smile to show she wasn't angry at him. "I'm an idiot. Just because you were able to force me to shift out of orca form didn't restore my shapeshifting ability. Apparently I had just enough left in me to shift to dry clothes, but that was all your magery." Though her smile remained, sorrow haunted her eyes. "I suppose it's human form for me."

"Well, then," he said, moving to throw off the blankets, "we'll walk."

"With that leg? Think again. I can pull this sled."

"I know you're strong, but you have that injury from the harpoon."

"Oh, I healed that when I shifted."

He took a moment to absorb that. "That's a useful ability."

"Yes"—she wrinkled her nose—"except I'm going to have to learn to go without the trick. Nevertheless, I'm fine to pull the sled."

"It still seems like too much."

"Not much choice, is there? At least the physical effort will warm me up." She took the ropes from him and wrapped them around herself. They didn't fit well on her long, tall body, but with some impressive knotwork, she made them work. "Your people aren't very tall, are they?"

"Ah, no." He realized she might be in for a surprise. "I should warn you that—"

"I'm resilient," she promised with a jaunty wink. "And cold. You can tell me later." She put her back into it and began trudging along, pulling the sled slowly.

By the time he'd have an opportunity to tell her about the folk, she'd have seen them for herself, and there'd be nothing more to say. Ah well. With no choice but to be taken there, Isyn sat back and wondered what the reaction of the folk would be to their new guest. Exhaustion catching up with him, he fought to stay awake. But the rhythmic tread of her steps, the soothing hiss of the sled runners over ice, and the lovely warmth of the furs soon lulled him, and he slipped into darkness.

~ 10 ~

THE HARD WORK of pulling the sled helped distract Gen from worrying *too* much. She'd put on a good show for Isyn, but she was worried. Worried for herself, worried for Isyn, and seriously concerned about their chances for rescue. Fifty years he'd spent in this iced-over landscape. On the plus side, at least this alter-realm hadn't killed him right away like the tentacle-beast forest would have, nor had he starved like would happen in the sterile flat-world alter-realm. But the downside was living a lifetime in a few months.

She could see glimpses of Wim's youthful vitality in Isyn. He resembled his brother in some ways, but his lined and weathered face had aged well past even Nix's and Cavan's. What would happen if they did get him home? He'd be decades older than his own parents, and like a grandfather to his siblings.

And that was *if* they got home. In all this time, he'd never found another portal, nor had this island magically sifted back to rejoin their home reality, or whatever these isles did. She might be stuck here forever with him. The others would be looking for her, she knew that, but would they be able to find her? One portal could lead to any number of alter-realms, they knew that much. Lena theorized that the person passing through affected which place they ended up in. Stella had been working on controlling that outcome, but she'd hardly had time. Gen hated to think of them circling that stormy sea, putting themselves in peril searching for her. She should hope that they hadn't lingered there searching for her, and instead had sailed onward in order to save themselves, but she didn't have it in her to be that generous. She *wanted* them to save her.

Please come rescue us. Moranu, if you can hear me, please guide them to us.

Given the disparities in time between the alter-realms, it might still be only moments since she disappeared through the underwater rift. She'd been in this alter-realm for at least two days—she guessed, anyway, as whale brains didn't track time all that well, it could've been longer—so what would that be in her home realm? A one-quarter to fifty proportion would be... she had no idea. Lena could do the math in her head, but that had never been Gen's forte, even if she hadn't had her brains recently scrambled by staying in orca form for far too long.

It was difficult to discern what long-term impacts it would have on her. Isyn didn't know her as anything but what she'd been as a whale and now as a woman still mostly whale in her mind. She should be grateful that the way his magery had triggered her shapeshifting had also allowed her to return to human form healed and in the furry clothing she'd cached. She'd been able to direct that much of the shift; she just couldn't do it on her own.

And that... that was something she simply couldn't think about. The loss of shapeshifting twisted like a knife in her heart, and a lifetime loomed ahead of her, sterile and empty as this frozen sea. Had she really spent so much time and energy fretting about finding true love? Now she had no friends, no family, and no refuge in shapeshifting. Isyn would be company for a while, but... despite her teasing, she didn't think he was being simply morose. He'd been, what, in his late twenties when he came though the portal? That put him nearly eighty now, and not a healthy eighty either. Perhaps it was the leg injury, but he seemed to be less than vigorous.

Too bad, because he was the first man in a long time— maybe ever—who'd made her think that maybe...

But no. No sense in dwelling on that either.

Despite the arctic temperatures, sweat dripped down her back with the effort of pulling the sled. She might've healed herself in the shift to human form, but that didn't replace the food and rest she'd missed while in orca form. Fortunately land loomed ahead, promising both. She wouldn't be able to go much longer.

The irony of it all settled over her like a cloud of depression. Her mother had been stuck in hummingbird form after the dragon nearly killed her. Well, Kiraka *had* killed Zynda, immolating her human form into a pile of ash, and the goddess Moranu had intervened, giving her a second chance at life, but it saved a lot of questions to simply say "nearly killed her." Still, was Gen somehow doomed to follow in her mother's footsteps? No, the similarities weren't that exact. Especially given that Zynda had had Marskal to save her. Loyal, steadfast, heroic Marskal who'd taken Zynda in hummingbird form back down the volcano and nursed her back to life.

And she'd finally fallen in love with him in return. It was such a romantic story, one Gen had sighed over often as a girl, listening to her parents tell the tale. Marskal had been so afraid of losing Zynda that he'd hold her hand in telling the story, as if to assure himself of her continued presence.

In keeping with Gen's decidedly *un*romantic life, her rescuer was a man older than Gen's own grandfather, and not in good health. Nor was she recuperating in tropical Nahanau, listening to the sea and tempted to suckle flowers to ease her hunger, being fed honey by a man secretly in love with her for years. Oh no, she got to be in the land of eternal winter, craving a bellyful of raw fish, and towing a sled with her now-unconscious rescuer who might expire at any moment.

It all just figured.

Maybe, though… Just maybe she'd find her true love here in the Winter Isles. They were near enough to shore for her to see figures moving about. A double line of them appeared to be trotting swiftly in their direction, no doubt intent on recovering their absentee king. Something odd going on there, that he'd gone alone to rescue her, leaving his folk behind.

Perhaps among these people, Gen would find the one she'd been searching for. Her tale could have a romantic ending still. A big, burly warrior might be among those coming toward them even now. Taller than her, with muscles bulging from years of chopping ice and hauling nets, he'd be wearing leather boots and a long fur-lined cloak. He'd have rough hands and an artist's soul, and he'd have been waiting too, all this time, finding no one to tempt his heart among the sparse people of the Winter Isles. Until Gen, a foreign woman from another world, appeared before him.

Enjoying the fantasy, she embroidered on it lavishly, embracing the distraction of the daydream. He'd take one look at her, her winter warrior, and be struck dumb by her beauty. *(Shut up, it's a fantasy.)* And he'd fall immediately in love, sweeping her into his arms so he could carry her to a warm fire where he'd feed her raw fish—*Ugh, no!*—warm broth with his own hands before he swore his undying love.

Her eyes watering from the biting wind, she squinted at the people hurrying toward them. She could've sworn they should've been much closer by now, but they weren't much bigger. By the time the understanding penetrated her starvation-fogged, sleep-deprived brain, Isyn's subjects were upon them. The warrior at the lead—complete with blue eyes, long fur-lined cloak, and... furry face?—scowled at her and shouted something she didn't understand in a high-pitched, chittering voice. He also stood no higher than her waist.

I specifically pictured taller than me, she thought fiercely at Moranu. But no, he and all of his compatriots were small, square-bodied, and were covered in gray fur. Now Gen fully understood the depths of Isyn's loneliness. Not only had Isyn spent a lifetime here among a people not his own, he hadn't even been among humans.

The lead warrior shouted at her again, waving a staff capped with a metal head that was an axe blade on one side, a thick knob on the other. Gen eyed it warily and held up her hands in a peaceable gesture. "I'm a friend," she said, knowing they wouldn't understand, but hoping the tone would convey intent. Dafne always swore by that. "I've brought your king back to you." She gestured to the unconscious Isyn. "See? All is well."

Except for the unconscious part, but hopefully they wouldn't blame her for that. Several of the furry folk went to examine Isyn, chattering with what she hoped was concern. Gen wanted to look but kept a wary eye on her challenger and his threatening staff. He was still shouting at her.

"I don't understand," she replied, smiling gently, trying to radiate sincerity and lack of threat. It would be super convenient, however, to be able to take saber-cat form at the moment, and just *be* a threat. More of the furry folk had come to untie the sled ropes from her, taking them and the sled away from her and towing Isyn with it. She started to follow, but the furry warrior blocked her with his staff. "Look, buddy," she said, putting her hands on her hips. She was way too tired and hungry to put up with this. In orca form, she'd eat him in one bite—and she was still orca enough to contemplate attempting it now. "Don't mess with me. I've had a really bad couple of days."

He snarled something in return and swung the staff at her head. She ducked—Jak would be proud!—swiping out with a hand that, shit, had no claws, so she ended up kind of slapping at him like a little kid might. And something hard slammed into the other side of her head.

As she hit the ice and blackness overtook her, she imagined Jak shaking his head in disgust. *Fuck my life.*

She wasn't sure if that was him who'd said it or her.

SHE AWOKE IN a soft, warm bed, in a small dark room, lit only by a blazing fire in a stone alcove—and for a moment she thought she was in Castle Marcellum in Erie. Or no, perhaps at Castle Elderhorst where she'd had her own room. No… Castle Ordnung? It was cold and damp, so definitely not home. She shook her head in confusion, the sharp pain making her head swim and nausea well up.

"Try not to move."

A man with ivory hair and deep green eyes leaned over her, smoothing her hair back from her forehead, his face shadowed. "Wim?" she asked, her voice creaky.

He breathed a laugh. "I once looked much like my younger brother, but no longer. I'm only Isyn. How are you feeling, Briar Rose? I'd wake you with a kiss, but no faerie princess wants a kiss from the likes of me, and I suspect some soup would do more to restore you." He gave her a crooked, self-deprecating smile. "I do have some warm soup here if you're up to eating."

Hungry as she was, the intensifying nausea made eating a bad idea. She shook her head, something she instantly regretted as the starry blackness tried to reclaim her.

"I'm very sorry about the head. The folk can be quite… enthusiastic in my defense." He grimaced, the charming self-deprecation turning darker. "I apologize that I failed to protect you from them."

She prodded her aching skull gingerly, finding it bandaged and recalling how her not-so-fantasy warrior had clubbed her with his staff. Probably she was lucky he hadn't split her head open. Jak's chiding that she needed to learn to fight without claws came back vividly. Where were her friends now? Were they out of their minds with worry, searching frantically for her, or had they already resigned themselves to her death? Or maybe it had been only minutes there since she'd disappeared, and no one had even noticed. The continuing saga of her life.

"The good news is your skull isn't cracked," Isyn continued. "It's a head wound, and you bled a lot, and you'll have a headache for a while, but you'll recover soon."

No magical healing. No shapeshifting to heal. Her head throbbed, and she'd have to just live with it. Better and better.

"Briar Rose?" Isyn frowned, studying her, the change in angle illuminating his face. He did resemble Wim, but a harder, more mature version, the bones of his face conveying a strength of character, his skin weathered, eyes a shadowed green full of concern for her. *Briar Rose,* he called her. *A faerie princess.* "Are you able to speak?"

"Yes," she answered on a sigh. "But my name is Gendra. Gen, for short."

He smiled wistfully. "Born of the dragon."

"Very good. Not many people get that."

"I used to read a lot. Now I pass the time by remembering stories I once read. Were you? Born of a dragon, I mean."

"In a manner of speaking. My mother is a talented shapeshifter who is able to take dragon form. Around the same time she finally managed to do that, she became pregnant with me, so…"

"Ah, a good name, then." He tilted his head thoughtfully. "I know that tale. She helped with the final battle against Deyrr."

"Yes, and my father, too. Both heroes."

"And their daughter following in their footsteps, performing heroic deeds."

"Hardly. Getting knocked unconscious by a waist-high furry creature won't go down in the history books well."

He laughed, green eyes catching the firelight like sunshine through summer leaves, and she caught a glimpse of what he'd been like as a young man.

"It will be no comfort, but if my experience is any indication, it's unlikely anyone will ever know our tales." That sobered them both. "I should have warned you the folk aren't human," he added. "I'm sure that came as a shock to you."

"I can only imagine how lonely it's been for you here."

"Yes. And it's an incredible pleasure to have a conversation with another person again." His gaze lingered on her face. "I only wish…"

When he didn't finish, she took his hand in hers. His was rough from work and weather. "What, Isyn? Surely you've wished for many things over the years."

"A hundred thousand of them," he replied, cupping her hand in both of his. "And all of them futile, as wishes always are."

"And this one?"

His smile turned rueful. "Selfishly, I wish you had fallen in my sea decades ago."

Oh. Her heart turned over, settling into a seeping pool of regret. Had things been only a bit different, had they been sent on this quest only months ago, she might've arrived in the Winter Isles when Isyn was still a young man. When they might have...

"But," he continued with forced cheer, "I would not have wished this life upon you, not for any reason, much less a selfish one. You look steadier now. Ready to try some soup? I think you'll feel better for some nourishment."

Recalling her fantasy of the warrior feeding her broth by the fire, she winced at her foolishness. Apparently she would never learn. "I think that would be lovely," she answered, giving Isyn a smile.

He helped her to sit up, his arm strong around her, his scent a pleasant blend of fur, leather, and spicy smoke. Taking up a bowl, he ladled soup from a brazier with a low flame, passing it carefully to her. "Do you need help, or..."

Feeling the blush heat her cheeks—maybe she'd get lucky and it was a fever, not embarrassment over her torrid fantasies—she took the bowl from him. It was made of a heavy rough-fired clay, large enough she had to cup it in both hands. "I think I can do it myself." The scent of the rich broth hit her, and she nearly groaned. "Fish stew." At least it wasn't raw fish? The still strongly orca side of her instincts didn't care either way.

"I'm afraid we pretty much live off the sea here," he replied, settling himself back to lean against the post at the foot of the bed, his bad leg outstretched. "That's why the folk were so excited for whale meat, and blubber. It's no excuse, of course, but—"

"I understand." And she did. Since there was no spoon, she tipped the bowl to her lips and sipped. It was decidedly fishy, naturally, but flavorful, and it hit her stomach with satisfying warmth, her starved body singing praises for the nourishment.

"For the first twenty or so years here, I dreamed of having a steak," Isyn remarked. "Then I longed for *anything* but fish. I even began to crave things I never liked before, like broccoli and salad greens."

"You don't have vegetables?"

"No growing season to speak of. Seaweed is our only green. The folk tell tales that it wasn't always this way. There used to be open water in the summers, enough of a warm season to grow food, to hunt whales and seals, trade with people from other lands. Then it changed. Their world grew much smaller and froze over."

"As if walls went up to isolate their realm," she mused, considering the strangeness of the other alter-realms they knew of. Lena had commented at length about how none of them seemed to have sustainable ecologies, all them more like a small slice of a place, rather than a complete one.

"Or as if someone—or something—somehow cut them out of their world and set them apart," Isyn said, watching her, the green glint of his eyes reminding her of something. "Over the years, I've considered how that could have come to be."

"Have you ever encountered an... intelligence?" Her stomach growled, demanding more, and she quickly swallowed more soup.

"A what?"

"Something *else*. Something... strange."

Isyn's eyes lit with humor, and he leaned forward, intrigued. "Something... *else*. *Something... strange*," he echoed, dropping his voice dramatically, like a storyteller might. Then he laughed. "I can't think of anything strange. As often as I dreamed of steaks and broccoli dropping out of the sky, it sadly has never happened. Only a talking orca."

She laughed with him, enjoying his wry and intelligent humor. "Sorry, I'm being unclear. My friends and I, we've encountered an intelligence in the alter-realms. And you mentioned the attacks, monsters coming through the rifts."

His expression altered as he comprehended her point. "You think this intelligence sealed off the Winter Isles and made it into one of its alter-realms."

"It makes sense, in a way," she offered. "At least, it's one possible explanation."

"An intelligence."

"I know it's not a good term. Jak has been campaigning to change it, but we haven't come up with anything better yet."

"Ah, you mentioned Jak before." Was it her imagination or did Isyn look displeased? "Is he your lover? Husband?"

"*Jak?*" she repeated incredulously and then laughed. "No. Even if he weren't madly in love with Stella, Jak and I... well, we're not a good fit." As she said the words, the truth of them resonated. Her dreams of Jak noticing her—or of Astar or Rhy suddenly noticing her as a woman—they were all fantasies born of a deep longing for what she couldn't have, not unlike Isyn dreaming of steaks and broccoli falling from the sky. She'd been craving love, looking for it in every man she met, trying to wedge them into that empty space in her life. That had been Zeph's point all along. *Stop evaluating every person you meet for true-love potential.* Finally Gen understood how backward she'd been about it. Instead of meeting people and discovering whether love bloomed between them, she'd been running around trying to trim people to fit into her idea of love.

And it just figured she'd have this epiphany when she was stuck in an alter-realm with only one other human being—a man who, if he did want her, would only be interested because he hadn't seen another person in fifty years—and a bunch of fur-covered, waist-high creatures with non-human brains. Moranu sure had a way of driving the point home. *All right, then, Goddess,* she thought. *I'll stop trying to force every man I meet into the mold of true love.* Perhaps if she held up her end, the goddess would help her get home. *Her favors are not guaranteed,* Zynda's warning echoed in Gen's mind.

"Who is Stella?" Isyn queried with a frown, breaking into her thoughts. "Is she the sorceress you mentioned? Not Princess Stella of Avonlidgh, apprentice to Queen Andromeda of Annfwn, twin sister of Crown Prince Astar, heir to the high throne of the Thirteen Kingdoms?" As he built upon Stella's resume, Isyn's voice rose in pitch along with his patent astonishment.

"The one and the same," Gen replied drily.

"You were traveling with Princess Stella," he marveled. "You didn't mention what exalted company you were keeping."

Funny to look at it that way, though Gen was so accustomed to her friends that she forgot their larger-than-life reputations. "I didn't mention a lot," she replied, a bit more tartly than she meant to. Sometimes it got tiresome being interesting only for the company you kept. "Largely because my whale brain wasn't terribly interested in retaining memories of human names."

"I apologize," Isyn said immediately, scrubbing a hand over his face. "My manners have clearly grown rusty over the years. I'm surprised to discover your friends and family are people I know of from legend and by reputation, but that's no excuse. Forgive a mannerless old man?"

"Forgiven," she replied with a warm smile. "But you are far from an old man. In the interests of avoiding further surprises, I should mention that my other companions included Crown Prince Astar; Princess Salena Nakoa KauPo of Nahanau; Rhyian, son of the king and queen of Annfwn; along with Zephyr, another shapeshifter; and Jak, who is half-Dasnarian and all human."

"But he's the one whose name you did remember," Isyn noted so blandly that she really wondered if, absurd as it sounded, he might truly be jealous.

~ II ~

B RIAR ROSE—GENDRA—GAZED BACK at him thoughtfully with her wide eyes, the indigo a nearly purple-black in the firelight. She looked so lovely, like the princess from the faerie tale, with her oval face framed by the tumbling glory of her glossy chestnut curls, the firelight glowing lovingly over the smooth skin of her long arms and casting tantalizing shadows in the hints of her bosom in the simple slip he'd had the folk put her to bed in. Her gown and cloak had blood on them, so he'd tasked Jasperina to having them cleaned.

It had seemed wrong to undress her himself, so he'd supervised from the other side of the small room, making sure they didn't hurt her further. The longing to touch her, far from dissipating, was only building. It didn't help that he *liked* her so much. And the fact that she was in his own bed, nearly naked, and so unbearably beautiful… Well, it was enough to make an old man forget himself. And how awful was that? The ancient dodder barely able to move from lusting after the fresh-skinned and sweet-natured young woman.

"I remembered Jak because he was teaching me bladework," she was saying, reminding him he should be paying attention to her words and not fantasizing over something that could never be. "He learned from his mother, who was one of Her Majesty's Hawks. He wanted us all to learn self-defense, particularly us shapeshifters, as we'd discovered we couldn't shift out of whatever form we entered an alter-realm in. He thought we relied too much on being able to shift into a form with fangs or claws. And, it turns out, he was absolutely right, or your lead warrior guy would never have gotten the drop on me. Even as an orca, I should've been thinking about dodging that harpoon. Jak would have—so yes, my friend who wanted to teach me to defend myself better so I wouldn't end up in exactly the circumstances I have was looming large in my mind." She finished with a defiant flash of her incredible eyes, chin set in determination, empty soup bowl clenched in her hands far too tightly.

"I apologize again," he said on a sigh, raking his hair back from his face. He was far too tired to be having any kind of conversation, clearly. "Would you like more soup?"

"Yes, please," she replied meekly, handing him the bowl. "Or, wait—your leg—let me get it."

"I can get it," he said mildly, pushing to his feet. "It's good for me to move around, and you shouldn't yet with that concussion."

She leaned her head back on the pillow. "Thank you. The food does help. And it's my turn to apologize. I didn't mean to subject you to a tirade."

He handed her the bowl, steadying it until she'd wrapped her hands firmly around it. "It wasn't a tirade, and I deserved the set-down." Unable to resist the impulse, he caressed her cheek, her skin seductively warm and soft. Not a grandfatherly gesture at all, so he made himself step away, pacing to the fire and adding a log, though it didn't really need it.

"Should you really be walking on that leg?" she asked dubiously.

"If I don't use it, I'll lose it." He'd said it far too snappishly, his greatest fear fueling the emotion behind his words. Then he'd be entirely at the mercy of his supposed subjects. More than he already was. "Tell me more about this intelligence," he said, making an effort to sound more civilized. A lifetime amid the folk had clearly made him unfit for polite company.

"There's not a *lot* to tell," Gendra replied easily, taking the peace offering. "Lena—Princess Salena—was the first one to notice it, after we were attacked at Gieneke. Do you recall the place?"

"At the confluence of the Phoenix and Grace Rivers, where they join to form the River Danu, yes?"

"I'm impressed you remember that, after all this time."

He was, too, frankly. "I did study the geography and political landscape of the Thirteen Kingdoms in my youth. I thought I'd be adding the Isles of Remus to Her Majesty's realm and learned accordingly."

She made a small sound of sympathy, which grated. He didn't want her pity. *What do you want from her?* a taunting voice whispered. That answer was all too starkly clear. He wanted to press her into the bed and hold her against his skin. He wanted to hear her moans and cries of delight, taste her sweetness and sink into her heat.

All things he could never have.

"Well, Her Majesty had sent us on a quest following the

strange eclipse of the crystalline moon during the Feast of Moranu, and—"

He held up a hand to stop her, his attention at last captured by something that wasn't this intense craving for his faerie princess. "An eclipse? On the longest night?"

"Yes. Why—did something happen here, too?"

"It did." Wanting to go back and sit on the bed with her, he instead stretched an arm along the fireplace mantel, using it for support to take some weight off his throbbing leg. "Not that anyone here observes the Feast of Moranu, but I've kept track of the calendar all these years." Something in her expression as she gazed at him, eyes large and glistening over the rim of the bowl made him hurry on. "That's how I know exactly how long I've been here. On the rare clear nights, I track the stars and make calculations."

"And observe the feast days," she inserted in a quiet voice.

He shrugged off the surprising sentiment at having someone else understand. "It made me feel connected to home."

"Of course it did. I—" She broke off, expression going abstract with thought. "The stars are the same?"

"Yes. And the phases of the moon…" He trailed off, following her line of thought.

"And you used them to track the passage of time, but the time here isn't the time there, and yet the eclipse happened on the same night. It doesn't make sense!" She pinched the arched bridge of her nose. "Trying to calculate time slippage is giving me a headache."

"That could be the head wound," he noted drily, and she dropped her hand with a huff of a laugh of agreement.

"All right, time slippage aside, the eclipse that shouldn't have happened also gave Queen Andromeda violent premonitions of a world-ending disaster. Ah, I should mention…" She looked abashed, wrinkling her nose at herself so charmingly that all he wanted was to kiss her lush mouth until she moaned with pleasure.

Get a grip, he instructed himself. "Mention what?"

"Our eventual destination were the Isles of Remus, because Andi—Queen Andromeda, that is—saw this area, or that area, depending on the overlap of the alter-realms, which also gives me a headache to think about so I won't, as being the epicenter of the disaster." She creaked out a tentative smile. "I am realizing that information would be of vital importance to you, and I should've mentioned it before now."

A curious storm of anger, regret, fear, and the fierce need to protect his kingdom that never was flooded him. "What happens to my isles?" he asked softly, so he wouldn't shout or scream or rage at the goddesses for stranding him here to slowly fall apart while his people—the people who truly needed him—suffered.

Gendra's face creased with regret, and she set her bowl aside, sliding out from under the covers. He caught a glimpse of long golden-skinned legs before her slip fell to cover them. "You shouldn't get up…" he started to say, but she shushed him.

"You've been alone for a long time," she murmured, coming to him. "Take some comfort when it's offered to you." And she slipped up against him, sliding her arms around his waist in an embrace, leaning her cheek against his, and hugging herself close. She was very nearly as tall as he was, he realized in an abstract way, as the sheer enormity of human contact thundered through him.

He folded his arms around her slim, strong body, the reflexive reaction turning urgent and needy. Holding her against him felt like a hot fire after a day on the ice, like a draught of water after a raging fever, like… like touching another human being after fifty years without. Emotion welled up, choking him, and his eyes dampened with tears. He didn't want her to know, so he leashed the unexpected sentimentality tightly down. Surely nothing was more unpleasant than having a crippled old man sobbing on you. But he couldn't make himself let go of her. Instead, he clung tightly, burying his face in the glory of her hair. *You've been alone for a long time. Maybe too long.* Maybe he'd lost his mind somewhere in the dull tread of years.

"I should have been there," he choked out. "I was meant to be their king, and if I hadn't gotten lost, maybe I'd have been there to prevent this destruction."

"Isyn." Though he tried to stop her, she pulled back, framing his face in her hands, gazing into his with soft compassion, not commenting on his unmanly tears. "You're forgetting something very important. It hasn't happened yet."

"What?"

"Listen to me closely. In my timeline, it hasn't happened yet. Queen Andromeda saw it in a vision, with foresight. Yes, you'd disappeared, and the Isles had fallen out of contact, but there were no disasters yet. Your parents were concerned, but not overly so. They said the elapsed time wasn't unusual. Her

Majesty sent us to prevent the calamity from occurring. We were, in fact, searching for *you* so you could help us."

He couldn't help returning her half smile. "And you did, in fact, find me."

"Yes, I did." Her eyes went vague with thought. "I wonder if that means something, since I more or less fell right into your arms."

With her words, they both became suddenly aware of the intimacy of their position, their bodies pressed together from thigh to breast, close enough to kiss if he only closed the breath of distance—and they sprang apart, like guilty teenagers caught by their parents. Well, he did. She was no doubt repelled by unpleasant groping from a man old enough to be her grandfather. Great-grandfather, perhaps. Huffing an embarrassed laugh, he raked a hand through his hair, scraping it back from his eyes. When had he last attempted to trim the stuff? Clearly far too long ago. "It only means something if we escape this frozen prison."

"Are you a prisoner here, Isyn?" she asked quietly. "I mean by more than the nature of the alter-realm," she clarified when he didn't reply. "You alluded to this before. It seems the folk control a great deal of your life. For a king, you don't seem to have much power."

"Noticed that, did you?" He was tired and his leg ached, so he sat, pointing at the bed. "You should get back in bed. It's too soon for you to be up."

She nodded, not arguing, and climbed back under the covers. He watched the fire, so as to keep from devouring her lithe form with his ravenous gaze. "Finish telling me about this intelligence, would you? You'll learn the dreary mundania of my world soon enough."

"All right," she conceded. "It's a long story, and I think I'm going to fall asleep again soon, so I'll try to sum up. At Gieneke, we encountered a monster ravaging the town. A giant made of local stone. It was tearing people and animals into pieces and mashing them back together, only all wrong, like a child playing." He winced at the image but didn't interrupt. "When it caught sight of Zeph in her First Form— which is an gríobhth, or a gryphon in Common Tongue—it transformed itself into that shape."

"So, it's a shapeshifter, too."

She shook her head, glossy curls sliding over her enticingly bare shoulders. "Not in the same way. It's more like a chameleon, seeing an intriguing shape and taking it on. It became a gríobhth roughly, but still made of stone and not detailed. And it couldn't fly, fortunately, or we'd never have defeated it."

"How did you?"

"Lena and Stella combined their magic—Lena is a weather mage, like King Nakoa KauPo—and that's when Lena noticed the presence of an alien sort of intelligence animating the creature. And Stella, who is also an empath, I think that's common knowledge?"

He nodded. He'd heard as much, though not in any definite way.

"She took the intelligence's emotions and hurled them back at it, which wounded it, but also unfortunately attracted its interest. It became fascinated with her and jealous of her love affair with Jak. It tried to abduct her and assume the form of Jak. It's gotten better, though not enough to be convincing. They killed it, this time with Silversteel, and escaped."

"So the intelligence was destroyed."

"That would be nice, but we doubt it. Stella has some foresight, and she says the futures that she can glimpse haven't shifted. That's why we continued on to the Isles of Remus in search of you. And…" She spread her hands, indicating the stone chamber. "Here we are. Or here I am anyway."

Yes, here she was—trapped in this icy prison of an alter-realm with him. Even if her friends managed to find her, it could be decades from now. The slow grind of anger burned under his skin. "I can't believe my parents agreed to assist you with a winter crossing in the first place," he ground out. "And then encouraging this ridiculous fantasy that you'd be able to find your way to me, something impossible without a guide, even under the best of circumstances, let alone knowing I'd disappeared."

"Remember that they think you've only been temporarily misplaced, not lost forever," she cautioned, seeming unperturbed by his harsh tone. "Besides which, Her Majesty the high queen had charged us with going. And we did have a guide," she added. "Falada, the fae spirit horse."

That jolted him as hard as being, oh say, thrown against a wall by a tentacle monster. "My mother sent Falada with you?" he asked incredulously, then with even more shock. "You can *see* her?"

"Not me," Gendra assured him. "I haven't got a lick of magic in me, but—"

"Other than shapeshifting."

"Other than shapeshifting," she agreed, "which doesn't count."

"Why not?"

She paused, realigning her thoughts, apparently surprised by the question. Tilting her head, she considered him. "Because it's not me doing something. It just... happens."

"But you mentioned your mother acquiring dragon form, so there's clearly some sort of effort or practice involved."

"Lots and *lots* of practice," she assured him. "I only have as many forms as I do because I practiced so much growing up."

"See? You *are* doing something. And you're good at what you do because of diligent practice. It's an admirable trait."

"I don't know about that." She looked wistful, a little lost. "I didn't have anything else to do."

"Why not?" He shouldn't be badgering her with so many personal questions, but she intrigued him so. He wanted to know everything about her.

Her nose wrinkled—just a bit—and she gave him a long, bemused look. "Why do you ask?"

Hmm. Good question. He needed a good reason besides this growing obsession with everything to do with her. "Understanding you and how your shapeshifting works could be important to figuring our way of here," he improvised.

And didn't fool her for a moment. "Up until this point, you've sounded fatalistic about our chances of escaping this place."

"I didn't know about Falada then," he replied, which was true, if not the whole reason. But what could he say? *I'm fascinated by you, and the obsession is only growing. I think you might be the woman I'd waited for, and it's killing me to finally meet you now and know it's too late.* "And you dodged the question."

She shrugged, just a little, a twitch of irritation. "I've never been a very social person. I'm sure you understand why."

"No? You're a beautiful, vivacious, and intelligent woman. I'd think you'd be at the center of every social whirl."

She laughed, a hearty sound with a bitter edge. "No, that would be Zeph. But I've resolved not to dwell on those things, and *you* distracted me from the actual topic of conversation." She shook her finger at him, eyes dancing. "Stella is the one who can see Falada, which I suppose is a sorceress thing. And apparently Falada volunteered to come along, however that works, and agreed to guide us to you."

Falada. She'd known of his predicament and had come to save him, as he'd dreamed for so long that she would. Another heartfelt wish finally granted—and again, far too late.

Gendra yawned hugely, clapping a hand over her mouth, her jaw cracking nonetheless. "I apologize," she said as soon as she could.

"Not at all. It's me who should apologize." Pushing painfully to his feet, he took a few stiff steps, teetering embarrassingly, before his hip would cooperate. Bone breaks and arthritis did not play nicely together, though he should be grateful he could walk at all. Old people got laid up for the rest of their lives from injuries like his. Sobering when the bright side of that equation was that the rest of his life wouldn't be all that long.

Are you always this morose? Yes. Yes, apparently he was.

"Let me help you," he said, adjusting the pillows for her and tucking the covers up under her chin. She blinked sleepily at him, a childlike innocence in her lovely eyes—though his feelings toward her were anything but paternal. "Sleep well," he said, beyond tempted to kiss her. Once upon a time, he would have. And he'd have crawled under the covers with her, tempting her to make sweet love with him.

Such an ironic twist of fate, that he'd once had any woman he fancied. The ladies of the court at Castle Marcellum had been more than eager to join him for a night of pleasure, sometimes several at once. Then he'd been stuck here, having not touched a woman in all these long, lonely decades. And now he... simply couldn't.

Gendra frowned at him. "This is your bed, isn't it?"

"I'm afraid you'd have found all the other sleeping arrangements far too small to be comfortable," he answered wryly. "But don't give it a thought. You need your rest."

"So do you. You were exhausted after saving me, and you need plenty of rest to heal that bone break. Have you even slept at all?"

"I've slept some." In the chair, quite uncomfortably. "I had to extract you from the protective fury of the folk. They were quite alarmed at your sudden appearance, and it took some doing to settle them down and have you installed in here."

"Oh." She chewed her lip. "I didn't think of that. I'm so sorry for the trouble I've caused."

"The trouble you caused by being unfairly attacked and wounded?" He tsked at her. "How terribly thoughtless, indeed."

She smiled weakly. "I suppose I'm being silly. But… please come sleep in the bed with me. I've been sharing with the other girls on the journey, and it's not as if—" She broke off, blushing intensely enough to be discernible in the dim light.

No, not as if anything sexual would occur with an oldster like him. He didn't blame her, but the bitterness lodged in his throat. "All right," he conceded, the prospect of lying down suddenly more than he could refuse.

She scooted over, making room for him so he didn't have to go around to the other side. Sitting heavily, he eased his way under the furs, aware that the delicious warmth he settled into had come from her luscious body. Her scent lingered, too, on the pillow. Tropical flowers and seaside sunshine. It reminded him of his long-lost youth, of summer trips to the beach, and kissing girls with skin heated by the sun.

~ 12 ~

GEN AWOKE WITH a pounding headache, aches in every muscle, and a briny taste in her mouth. Had she succumbed and eaten the yummy fish? She'd certainly slept, which was terrible, though she couldn't remember exactly why it was wrong...

Oh, right, because she could be stuck in orca form forever. But she wasn't cold anymore. She was toasty warm, cuddled up against another body. Someone tall and strong, her arm draped over his muscular chest, her leg intertwined with his hairy ones. Decidedly masculine.

Isyn. The surreal midnight conversation from the night before came rushing back, including her talking him into sharing the bed with her. It wasn't as if he'd be tempted to seduce her. She probably looked and smelled terrible and, let's face it, men weren't exactly falling over themselves to bed her. Not even a man who'd been forcibly celibate for decades, as evidenced by Isyn's clear disinterest in her. When she'd embraced him the night before, he nearly thrust her away from him in his eagerness to distance himself.

He was so beautiful, though, lying on his back, face peaceful in sleep, the thin sunlight filtering in highlighting his elegant profile, and bringing out the warm tones in his ivory hair. Wim had that same color hair, which they'd clearly gotten from their mother, Nix. Gen had assumed at first that Isyn's hair was white with age, but the golden undertones indicated otherwise. Absent of pain, stress, and exhaustion, his face looked far less lined. He might've been stuck in this alter-realm for decades, but he had retained a robust strength.

Moving slowly and carefully, she eased her entangled limbs from his, holding her breath and hoping he wouldn't waken and be repulsed by her groping him during the night. And after he'd risked his life to save hers, too. She'd very nearly succeeded detaching herself, when a hard grip suddenly vised on her wrist, making her squeak in reflexive alarm.

Isyn's head turned and eyes opened, the green brighter in the light of day, sharp with suspicion, his face hard and angry—then softening with recognition. "Briar Rose," he breathed.

"Gendra," she corrected gently, feeling as pinned by that intense gaze as the surprisingly strong grip on her wrist.

"Gendra." He made her name into such an intimate caress that she trembled—which, unfortunately, with their bodies pressed together, he immediately felt. "You don't have to be afraid of me," he said, tensing. Then, as if abruptly aware of his grip on her, he released her and yanked his hand away as if he'd burned himself. "I apologize," he said, as rigid as his body. "I didn't mean to, that is, I—"

She scrambled back, swiftly putting space between them now that she didn't have to worry about waking him. "No, it's my fault. Somehow as I slept, I must've..." She couldn't finish that sentence. Sitting up, she regretted that, too, her head swimming with nauseating effect. Putting a hand to her head, she groaned. *Please don't puke on Isyn,* she urged herself.

"Don't move so fast," he bit out. "You have a head injury."

"I noticed," she snapped in return, then flopped back on the bed. "I forgot," she admitted, "though you'd think the pounding headache would've been a clue. Not being able to heal myself really burns my tail."

He laughed. "A shapeshifter metaphor, no doubt." Still moving stiffly, he edged out from under the covers, sat up, and massaged his thigh muscle for a moment before turning his back to her and pushing to his feet. He'd slept in his clothes, but they were soft, thinner garments, possibly woven from some sort of wool, probably for wearing under other clothing—and they clung to his fine physique. He stretched, joints popping. He might be aged, but his body hadn't lost its condition, his waist narrow and shoulders wide, his ass—displayed at nearly eye level, so was she not supposed to look?—taut and firm.

When he groaned, she felt guilty for ogling him, determinedly lifting her gaze to the back of his head. "Does your leg pain you?"

He glanced over his shoulder, expression rueful as he gathered his long ivory hair into a queue and tied it with a cord from the table beside the bed. "My everything pains me, but the leg aches particularly in the morning."

"I can sympathize there. Why does my body ache all over, though?"

"You pulled me for leagues in the sled, remember?" His smile looked almost affectionate. "I doubt you were in condition to be a draft horse."

"I do so much better when I can be an actual draft horse," she grumbled.

"I can just imagine. You lie still and I'll call for food." Taking up his staff and leaning on it for support, he crossed to the soup urn, put a hand on it, and grunted. "We definitely need something brought up. The flame went out, and I don't think either of us wants cold, congealed fish soup for breakfast." He unbolted the door and hobbled out, closing it again behind him.

Gen was pretty sure she didn't want even hot fish soup for breakfast—but not even the lingering orca in her was tempted to eat those leftovers. Besides, it was probably *very* cold, congealed fish soup, as the air temperature in the room was decidedly crisp. Gen was just as happy to snuggle back under the furs, where it was cozy and comfortable. Though she did have to pee quite urgently, so that would have to be taken care of, and soon.

With Isyn out of the room, she scooted just a bit toward where he'd lain, running her hand over the impression from his big body under cover of the blankets, inhaling his scent. He'd never know, and she wanted to remember this. Scent memory was the strongest. If she survived this experience, she wanted to be able to comfort herself on lonely nights by evoking this moment and how she'd felt waking beside him. Comforted. Cared for. Not alone.

The chamber door banged open, and a red-furred, grumpy-looking member of the folk stomped in. They pointed at her and chittered something long and complex. Before Gen could try to frame a reply, Isyn limped back in, clucking and chitting a reply. Moranu! No wonder he'd taken the better part of a year to learn their language. Truly it was a marvel he'd learned to speak it at all. The red-furred folk spun on him, speaking even faster, overlapping and interrupting him. Isyn continued evenly, showing no sign of backing down on whatever they argued about.

Finally the creature of the folk threw up their hands and stomped out again, talking to themselves the whole way. Isyn gave Gen a wry smile, green eyes bright and amused. "That's Jasperina. She's protective of me and is not yet convinced that you aren't another of the creatures from the other alter-realms sent to murder me."

"She's not entirely off target there," Gen pointed out. "Except for the murder part."

"Lucky for me, or I'd be a killer-whale snack by now."

"Orcas don't eat people," she told him primly. "And I wasn't *that* far gone."

Another of the folk came in carrying a tray with steaming mugs, eyeing Gen curiously. Isyn said something that sounded like a thank-you, gesturing for them to set the tray down. "Here, let me help you prop yourself up so you can drink." He limped to the bed, leaning on the staff.

"I can move under my own power," she protested. "I just need to take it slowly."

"Gendra, let me—"

"And I must answer the call of nature," she admitted, hoping she wasn't blushing. A normal, natural thing—just not something she'd discussed with a man, ever.

"Ah." He looked as chagrined as she felt. "Thoughtless of me. Let me show you the way."

"You sit and have your tea or whatever it is. I'm sure I can find it."

"Are we going to be forever urging each other to be still and rest?" he asked, humor quirking his lips. He had a fine mouth, sensitive and firm at once.

"It's either that or we don't get out of bed," she quipped, then blushed in earnest. *What is wrong with you, Gen?* Afraid that any attempt to explain herself would only dig her in deeper, she fled—quite gingerly after her head gave a sharp throb—for the facilities, such as they might be.

They were not much. Plus, the chute seemed to open to the outside far below and produced a seriously strong updraft of freezing air. Fully awake and alert after that bottom-chilling experience, she scurried—gingerly, curse it—back to Isyn's bedchamber, which now felt delightfully warm by comparison. It also helped that two more folk had arrived, one stacking firewood into the empty bin and the other stoking the fire into a cheerful blaze.

At Isyn's raised brow, she tucked herself back under the furs, delighted to find the bed still warm, and arranged herself into a sitting position to accept the steaming mug he handed her. It was made of the same rough-fired, ugly clay as the bowl had been, with no handle, but it fit well into the cup of her palms. And the hot liquid inside—paradise.

Isyn had been watching her, and he chuckled at her gasp of surprise. "Chaife. It's the one good thing about this place."

Whatever chaife was made from, it tasted like nothing Gen

had ever encountered before. Very sweet, almost creamy, with a spicy edge somewhere between pepper and cinnamon, with a finishing flavor that reminded her of Jak's good whiskey.

"The only good thing?" she asked Isyn, who sipped from his own mug in his chair by the fire. He only had one of everything, which made her sad. No one ever sat with him by the fire or kept him company on long, dark evenings.

By comparison, her life had been rich and full of important friendships, and she was ashamed that she'd ever complained about loneliness. *This* life was true loneliness, every bit as terrible as Stella's tower. Perhaps more so, that he was surrounded by others who were so very different.

"I shouldn't say the *one* good thing," Isyn answered, his gaze going past her. "I mean, I was able to survive, which it sounds like, from your description of the other alter-realms, I wouldn't have in one of those. And the folk aren't terrible companions. Just different. Somewhat single-minded."

"How did you explain my presence?"

"I said you arrived as I did, from my own land and people, and they're mostly satisfied. With a few salient exceptions." He grimaced for Jasperina's behavior. "Once you feel better, I'll take you on a tour and introduce you to everyone. They'll soon grow accustomed to your presence."

She considered that, trying to put the prospect in a positive light, rather than succumbing to the cloud of gloom waiting to descend over her. Surely Stella and the others would find them. Eventually. Had even a day elapsed in their home realm? Feeling a bit more clear-headed with rest and nourishment— the folk serving them had also brought a creamy cheese with smoked fish that was quite good, though she longed for toasted bread to accompany it—she tried the math again. If Isyn had been here approximately fifty years and had been gone from their world for a few months—call it a quarter of a year to make it more or less even—then she could multiply everything by two hundred and get close, right?

So, one hour at home was two hundred hours in the Winter Isles. Two hundred hours was eight days, and she'd been here at least half that long, maybe longer, so it could have been just an hour or less back on the little sailing ship. But the math got a lot more depressing after that because if it took them a full day to find her... It didn't bear thinking about.

"Gendra?" Isyn asked, cocking his head in concern as he studied her. "Are you feeling worse?"

Definitely, she was. Much worse. "Not at all," she lied. "I'm looking forward to that tour."

She might as well settle in.

THE TOUR DIDN'T take long. The island where Isyn and his people lived was the larger one amidst their small cluster, but that wasn't saying much. Isyn said one could circumnavigate it at a brisk walk in about three hours. Which, he confessed with a distant look, he'd done many times over the years, just for something to do.

Gen's skin already itched with the need to shapeshift, and

the low-grade craving to swim or fly would only worsen, only this time there was no end in sight. Would she go mad eventually with the need to shift? Stories implied that had happened to the old high queen, Salena, who'd been exiled from Annfwn in the days when magic hadn't penetrated past the barrier. So far from the ancient Heart of Annfwn, she'd been unable to shapeshift and had slowly deteriorated, losing her health and sanity.

Not something pleasant to dwell upon. Nor was the endless vista of frozen sea that formed the rest of the small world of the Winter Isles. They stood out on a rocky promontory, enjoying a break in the overcast in the late afternoon. The sun seemed far away, the light thin and weak, but it did warm her skin, if infinitesimally. After napping for a good part of the day, she felt substantially better. She'd donned her furry cloak and the other winter clothing she'd worn across the steppes of Erie, glad that she'd at least had the subconscious wit to shift back to human form wearing her cold-weather gear.

That moment of pure instinct, when she'd been soaked to the bone and freezing, and she'd grabbed her First Form and come back warmly dressed, seemed impossibly long ago, and equally beyond her now. The inability to shift felt so odd, like reaching for something familiar only to find it missing. It wasn't fear blocking her, like her mother had talked about, or an external magical force, like the sorceress's hold that had trapped her uncle Zyr in gríobhth form. It was just not... *there*. Something about the alter-realm's very nature put her other forms out of reach. Just as they couldn't physically leave the place, except via the rifts. Hmm.

"What happens if you just keep going across the ice?" she asked.

Isyn laughed without music or humor, gaze hard on the horizon. "If you go far enough to be out of sight of these islands, very soon afterward you find yourself coming toward them again."

She gazed at him in cold horror, thinking it wasn't her imagination that the lines on his face seemed carved more deeply than usual. "That's awful."

He tore his gaze down to hers, mouth twisting in wry agreement, though his eyes held only bleakness. "The very definition of madness, yes?"

The thought was so close to her own that she shivered.

"Cold?" he asked with quick concern. "Let's go back inside."

"No, I mean, yes, I'm a little cold, but…" She turned to face him, the yawning pit of despair making her bold as nothing else seemed to. "Could I just hold onto you for a moment?"

His smile turned genuine, and he opened his arms and cloak to her. "Anytime you like, Briar Rose."

She wasn't sure if she was comforting him or herself, but she snuggled in against him, winding her arms around his waist and her cheek against his. He wrapped her in his cloak, holding her with gentlemanly looseness. The scent and feel of another human being in all this vast, alien landscape helped to calm her, grounding that dizzying sense of vertigo. "I can't imagine how you stayed so sane all these years without this," she murmured. How much longer would he live? If she was stuck here forever, how soon before she wouldn't have even this companionship?

"It's not so terrible," he whispered against her hair. "The folk are good people and competent at survival. And perhaps your group of heroes—not to mention Falada—will find you soon."

She tipped her head back, unwilling to let go of him, searching his deep green eyes. They had a dark gray border, like a ring of shale around a forest pool she'd seen once. His handsome bones shone through the weathered skin, the sterling integrity of his character apparent in the lines radiating from the corners of his eyes, even the set of his chin. What a truly strong mind he must have that he hadn't succumbed to madness or despair trapped in this place. "They'll find *us* soon," she corrected.

He smiled sadly. "My rose, I—"

"No defeatism," she instructed firmly, placing a finger over his lips to stop the words. He tensed, his lips surprisingly soft against the pad of her finger, framed by the faint ivory bristle of a few hairs the old-fashioned straight razor he'd used had missed. His breath whispered warm against her skin, his eyes lighting with a fire that made her wonder what it would be like to kiss this man. This was no boy like Wim, no dissolute charmer like Henk. Isyn was a man, matured and hardened in the fiercest crucible. His gaze caught and held hers, his lips moving under her touch, slightly pursing in... a brush of a kiss?

Her breath caught hard in her chest with longing, wanting it to be true, that he was thinking of kissing her. And if he did, she knew in her bones that she wouldn't have to think about trying to like it. She wouldn't be able to think at all. It would be dazzling and passionate and scintillating in all the ways she'd ever dreamed of, and—

He cleared his throat, gaze lifting from hers to fasten on the distance again. Suddenly and brutally aware of the intimacy of their position, she yanked her fingers away and stepped back. It was unfair and needy of her to keep clinging to him. That was something else to know about him, that a man like him might be tempted by her by virtue of long isolation, but being wanted because there was no one else? Not exactly a wonderful prospect. Of course, give her a few months and she doubted she'd have any pride left. She'd be begging Isyn to notice her, which was pretty much a given for her life. "I apologize," she whispered. "I didn't mean to—"

"You didn't." His blazing green gaze bored into hers again. "Gendra, you're a beautiful young woman, but I don't want—"

Instead of clapping her hands over her ears as she dearly wished she could, she interrupted. "I believe you promised to show me the alpacas?" she asked brightly. She couldn't bear to listen to him explain how he didn't want her. How she was such a good person but his heart was given elsewhere. Oh, Moranu, what if it was? Isyn had been sailing to the Isles of Remus to claim a kingdom—and perhaps a bride? Someone he'd longed for all these years, staying true in his heart. So romantic, but for once the romance didn't elicit a dreamy internal sigh from her. Instead she wanted to rail at the uncaring sky and shake her fists at her stupid fate.

Isyn inclined his head formally, eyes softening with relief. He was clearly just as happy not to have to explain himself.

"The alpacas are indeed the pinnacle of the tour," he replied with a cheerful smile she was pretty sure he faked for her benefit, so she wouldn't feel so miserable.

She refrained from commenting that it didn't take much to be the pinnacle of the tour of the Winter Isles. Even talking about them in the plural was overstating the case, as only the one was big enough to sustain a population. Side by side, they strolled back to the wooden fortress that was home to the folk. It crawled in varying levels over the sloping hillside, long covered corridors snaking out to attached buildings that were equally sprawling. Isyn had explained that there had once been a village arranged in a circle around a central plaza, but the persistent winter had caused them to cover everything over. At least wood was plentiful, the evergreen forest thickly covering most of the islands.

The alpacas lived in a large barn, steamy with their collective warmth and smelling not unpleasantly of the woody materials they ate. Isyn explained that the creatures could subsist on twigs and bark that the folk stripped from the timber they harvested, along with the evergreen needles. In the past, the alpacas had grazed on grass, but it had been years since any had grown on the Winter Isles. It was a good thing the ruminants could live on the harsh diet, as they in turn provided milk, cheese, and wool for the folk.

Gen had never tried an alpaca form—they weren't good for speed, strength, or giving rides, which were the main reasons to take an otherwise pretty boring, grazing herbivore body. These were more interesting animals than she'd imagined, however, with keen, intelligent gazes and fierce dispositions.

Though Isyn warned her to be careful of their teeth—and spitting!—she couldn't stay away, edging closer when he turned to gesture at the feed storage bins. She was interested, but his detailed explanations gave her the uneasy feeling that he was grooming her to take over as ruler of this tiny kingdom. The man had a fatalistic streak and seemed determined to die, which only made her heart ache.

So, instead, she sidled over to a deep-brown alpaca, studying it closely, lulling it into perhaps letting her feel its woolly coat. Stretching out her senses, she tried to consciously access that intuitive part of her that recognized another form and delivered it to her. She hadn't tried to so consciously assess and assume a form since her last spate of attempting dragon form—long before this quest began. That same sense of groping in the dark for something that should be there and wasn't resulted from her efforts. But... something there, glimmering beyond sense, lured her with distant promise...

"Gendra—no!"

~ 13 ~

"So, the lofts are designed to allow air circulation in order to prevent mold." Sensing that Gendra wasn't listening, Isyn stopped blathering on. He didn't blame her for losing interest in his decidedly pedantic recitation of how to manage their imperiled community. The details would put anyone to sleep. Still, he couldn't shake the feeling that he could die at any moment—from another attack or from his aging heart simply giving up the fight—and that would leave Gendra responsible for all of this. The folk simply didn't think in terms of long-term planning.

Also, he could admit to himself that he was doing everything in his power not to think about that near kiss. Briar Rose in the flesh was so lovely, so caring—and so very tempting. Having someone to *talk* to, who understood him was a kind of rapture he hadn't known to value when he had it. As a younger, far more arrogant man, he'd have scoffed if someone suggested that he needed something like compassion to thrive. Having Gendra sympathize with his emotional pain... Well, he'd never admit it to anyone, but it felt like sunlight warming the frozen hollows of his heart, and he wanted nothing more than to taste her soft lips, to drink from her, to drown in her.

Which he *would not do.*

Bad enough that she was trapped here with him, unable to shapeshift—he'd seen the sorrow and horror in her face as she contemplated a life stuck in one skin—unable to go home. He wouldn't compound her situation by taking even more from her, no matter how much he longed to do so. Very carefully curling his fingers into his palms, to remind himself not to touch her, he glanced over his shoulder to see where she'd gotten to.

"Gendra!" he gasped, seeing the alpaca's blunt teeth snap close to her creamy cheek. "No—" He lunged to put himself between them.

Gendra and the alpaca turned as one to blink at his extraordinary actions, their expressions oddly similar with their lustrous, long-lashed eyes. Then the normally irascible alpaca actually leaned its cheek against hers, for all the world looking like an affectionate lover.

Apparently his Briar Rose's faerie princess magic worked on everyone, man and beast alike. Lowering, to find himself jealous of an alpaca.

"Are you all right, Isyn?" Gendra asked, concern deepening the indigo of her eyes. "Does your leg pain you or do you need to—"

"I'm fine," he bit out, cutting off her kind words. He didn't want kindness from her. Better for her to spurn him so he could fight this debilitating longing for her. "I was trying to stop you from getting foolishly injured."

She and the alpaca gave a long, slow blink, considering that—and she turned to study the alpaca at the same moment that it cocked its head to look at her. It was uncanny. "I won't get hurt," Gendra assured him, scratching a spot between the alpaca's ears that had the beast lowering its lids in obvious pleasure. "The Tala love animals."

"Then I'm delighted to provide alpacas for you to make friends with."

"Thank you." Gendra patted the alpaca affectionately and came to him. "Why are you so angry?"

He opened his mouth to deny it, then realized he was. Boilingly angry. And sexually frustrated. A man his age shouldn't feel such need, but it was as if all the passion he hadn't spent in all those long, lonely years was rising up, a volcanic and molten need threatening to erupt and destroy everything—her trust most of all.

"Isyn?" She laid a hand on his forearm, over his shirt, but it might as well have been bare skin the way her touch scalded him.

He jerked away. "Don't touch me."

Her eyes flared with hurt, and she yanked her hand back, too. "I apologize."

He ground his teeth. "And *don't* apologize."

Her lips firmed, jaw tightening as she lifted it, the sternness in her gaze reminding him with pointed vividness that she was the daughter of an elite soldier and a woman who'd attained dragon form against all odds. If Gendra could spit fire at him, Isyn had no doubt she would have at that moment.

He almost wished she would. Then he could die on the spot and be done with both this painful existence and the even more excruciating hope she'd brought into it.

"Perhaps you will tell me, Your Highness, exactly what you *would* like me to do," she invited silkily.

A flurry of inappropriate replies flooded his brain and tongue. But for his thin thread of control, he'd have her naked and on her back in the dirt, with him thrusting into her as she screamed his name and the folk and alpacas looked on with placid interest. Well, a thread of control and the fact that he couldn't do it regardless. His broken thigh bone wouldn't allow it. Who knew? After all this time, he might not be able to sustain an erection. Or, given how hard he was at his lurid thoughts, he'd spend embarrassingly quickly. And why was he analyzing the possible humiliating scenarios that would never happen? What was wrong with him?

You've lost your mind is what's wrong. You're no longer fit for human company.

Snapping his fingers, he summoned the always-lurking Jasperina. "Take our guest back to my chambers. Arrange for her to have a hot bath and food." To Gendra, he added, "I have other things to do besides play tour guide." And he strode off before she could reply. That is, he hobbled stiffly off, which just figured that he couldn't even have a tantrum effectively.

THE WORST PART was, he couldn't exactly avoid his enchanting guest. Not when she was ensconced in the only rooms that fit a person their size. He'd call it an oversight that, in all the passing years of making improvements to their living conditions, it had never occurred to him to build a second set of human-sized rooms, but it reflected how absolutely he'd given up hope of anyone of his own kind arriving as he had.

So, he ended up slinking back—more clumsily even than usual, as being on his leg for so long was making it ache enough that he wanted to simply cut the cursed thing off and be done with it—unsure of what kind of face to put on his earlier boorish behavior.

Maybe she'd be asleep, though that would be simply another in a long list of his foolish hopes, as she'd eventually wake up and she'd still be in the only room—and bed—that fit either of them. He also highly doubted that she'd be the sort to pretend nothing had happened. She seemed more like the kind of person to calmly call him on his erratic behavior—and then compassionately interrogate him as to the roots of it. Still, if she was asleep, that would give him at least a bit more time.

She wasn't asleep. When he eased into the room, she was seated on a footstool by the fire, wearing only her silky slip, the light silhouetting her long, gently curved figure. With her head bent, she had the chestnut waterfall of her hair fanned to the flames, her eyes closed in soft pleasure as she ran a comb through the gleaming waves. Hearing him, she opened her deep indigo eyes and smiled at him, a sweet curve of closed lips.

And he finished falling in love with her.

He knew it because his heart dropped into place, and everything came into focus. It wasn't that she was the only woman of his kind he'd encountered in fifty years of loneliness, and likely the only one he ever would. And it wasn't madness driving him. People could argue for those points and draw those most logical conclusions, but he knew the truth.

Gendra was the one he'd hoped to find. The woman he'd traveled to the Isles of Remus to discover, because a seer had told him he'd find the love of his life there.

And he *had* found her. Gendra. Dragon born.

The seer hadn't mentioned the part about him finding her too late.

Had he been a younger man, he'd have followed his impulse and strode to her, sweeping her into his arms and kissing her with all the passion in him. But his aged and injured self wasn't striding anywhere, and if he tried anything like that they'd only end up in a pile on the floor, and not in a sexy way. So, beyond awkward, he hovered in the doorway.

"Did you get everything taken care of?" she asked.

For a moment, he had no idea what she meant. Then he recalled his feeble excuse from earlier and grimaced at himself. "I didn't have anything to do," he confessed, shifting to take his weight off the aching leg.

"Ah." She nodded understandingly. "I wasn't sure if you'd come back."

"It's the one thing you can be sure of," he replied wryly. "There's nowhere else to go."

"There is that." She pointed her comb at his empty chair. "Why don't you sit and rest your leg." Not a question, though she framed it as such. "I can see it's hurting you, so don't bother to deny it."

"You could have sat in the chair," he grumbled, but decided falling over would hurt his pride more than admitting weakness. Leaning heavily on his staff, he scrape-clomped over to the chair and sat in it with a groan of relief that he couldn't have suppressed if ten alpacas were laughing at him.

"I could have," she agreed easily, and said nothing more.

"You don't have to walk on eggshells around me." The clear irritation in his voice made that patently untrue, but she only gazed at him, blue eyes deep and calm enough to swim in, like a violet sea at sunset.

"Thank you for arranging for the hot bath," she replied, as if fitting an answer to a question he hadn't asked. "It felt really good to get warm and clean. The water is still reasonably hot, and I *think* I asked them to heat up more. The gesturing method only goes so far."

Despite himself, he laughed a little, ruefully, remembering his long months of getting by with only gestures and many, many errors of understanding. "At least you have me to translate for you until I can teach you the language so you can be self-sufficient."

She combed her hair thoughtfully. "You go back and forth, you know, between talking like we'll be rescued and then like you'll be dead and I'll carry on caring for the folk in your place."

That was an accurate summarization of his thoughts. "It's likely I'm not entirely sane," he explained.

She cocked her head, considering. "I doubt that's it."

Jasperina tromped in then, giving Gendra a suspicious glare, leading a parade of several more folk with buckets of hot water. Launching into the expected tirade, Jasperina expressed her disapproval of heating water, Gendra, and bathing in general, all equally villainous in her estimation. The fur-covered folk had never quite understood his reluctance to be licked clean the way they groomed each other. He'd heated and carried the water himself until this injury. After all, who would care but him? Now he realized he likely looked and smelled quite vile.

He didn't bother to argue with Jasperina, simply telling her to leave the buckets, that he'd handle the rest. Sniffing in disdain, she left. "Looks like you got your point across successfully," he noted to the curiously watching Gendra.

"Jasperina disapproves?"

She was certainly perceptive. "I don't bathe often, so she doubted your authority and judgment."

"The tub is plenty big enough to take your bulk."

"Yes." He looked at the carefully notched and fitted assem-bly of wooden lathes that he'd painstakingly soaked and warped to make a curved tub, then oiled with fats to make waterproof, as if he hadn't seen it before. It had taken him months to build and had been absolutely worth the effort. "I used to soak in it much more often, but that was mostly before Jasperina's time." At her questioning look, he added, "The folk are not that long-lived. Fifteen years is pretty typical, and she's young."

Gendra's pretty mouth twisted in sympathy. "So, on top of everything, you've also watched many friends and companions die over the years."

It was true, though he hadn't thought about that either in a while.

"I thought it would be good for you to soak at least that leg," she said into the strained silence. "Though it wouldn't hurt to soak all of you. The improved circulation is needed for healing. Afterward, I can take a look at you, see what I can do."

Oh, that was not going to happen. He could just see himself stretched out on the bed, barely draped, his cock straining like a lecherous old man's while sweet Gendra valiantly tried to ignore it. "That won't be necessary," he informed her brusquely.

"Isyn," she replied with measured patience. "Your body is out of alignment. I'll venture that half your pain or more is from you twisting your hips and back to take weight off your broken leg and protect it from further injury."

"So you're suddenly an expert in healing, too?" He'd gone past brusque into churlish and yet couldn't seem to stop himself.

"I'm no expert, but I know some things, particularly about warriors recovering from injury. We aren't aware of it consciously, but we contort our bodies to protect the wound, going to great lengths to fend off any more pain—which can result in all sorts of other problems."

That made too much sense. "Sounds only natural," he grumbled.

"It is natural. That doesn't mean it's not a problem. Fortunately I know quite a few massage techniques that should help with the pain and put your body back into alignment, so it will heal better on its own. My uncle Harlan taught me some Dasnarian techniques for such things."

He paused. "Your 'Uncle Harlan' is Prince Harlan, I assume. High Queen Ursula's husband." Her faint blush gave the answer away. "Exalted company, indeed," he muttered, not at all sure why that pissed him off even more.

She stood, the firelight silhouetting her long, lovely body—including the tempting triangle at the apex of her slim thighs. Fortunately, as he was incapable of tearing his riveted gaze away, she moved away from the fire to replace his comb among his few things. Then she turned, folding her arms, which unfortunately drew his gaze to the thin material drawn tight over her breasts and the shadows of her darker nipples. He was actually sweating.

"Isyn," she said, again using that extra-patient tone. "You saved my life, so I'd like to do at least this much for you in return. It's ridiculous to be stubborn when you could use my help."

"I did manage to survive all these years before you arrived," he bit out, forcing himself to stare at the fire instead of her glowing beauty.

Then she was before him, crouching down, her hands resting lightly on his knees. "Look, I'm sorry. I apologize for what happened out on the rocks earlier. It was wrong and invasive of me to ask to touch you. I'm so sorry that I made you uncomfortable. I'm awkward that way, but I promise I won't do that again." As if suddenly realizing she had her hands on him, she snatched them away. "I mean, I promise to try. The Tala are physical people. More so than I ever realized before this... experience," she finished, her voice rough, her eyes lustrous now with... tears? "Maybe it was being in orca form for so long, but I find myself needing—" She broke off, knotting her hands together and staring at them. "I would leave you alone, Isyn, I truly would, but I have nowhere to go. And I feel so terribly alone. I thought I was lonely before this, but I had no idea what—" Her breath caught on a sob.

Oh, Briar Rose. Before he could stop himself, he'd threaded his hands into her glorious hair, momentarily distracted by the sheer silken texture, the sensual weight of it before tipping her face up to his. "Don't cry, my rose," he murmured, brushing her tears away with his thumbs. "I can't bear it. My own pain is nothing, but yours might break me."

Her tears spilled over, wetting his hands, and she gazed up at him with perfect trust and utter loveliness. "I don't mean to be a burden, I truly don't. I just need..." She trailed off on a whisper, closing her eyes against some pain. "I don't know what."

He knew, though. *Needed. Craved. Wanted.* Of course she did. He knew exactly how she felt because he did, too. At last he had company in his exile, and at least she had him. He wouldn't let his perverse desire for her contaminate what could be a good thing between them. People needed human contact. He could be like a father to her. Or grandfather. Probably even great—*no, stop thinking about that.*

Leashing himself with ruthless control, he bent to kiss her forehead, then each damp cheek. She softened under the caresses, lifting her hands to lightly grasp his wrists, lips parting as her breath shuddered out, calming under his touch much as the irascible alpaca had gentled to hers. *Tala love animals. Tala are a physical people.* She was so extraordinary, so magical, that he hadn't thought of her in terms of needing comfort. "I'm sorry I was cruel," he murmured to her.

She nodded slightly, eyes still closed, tears welling out from under the fan of dark lashes like lace against the delicate, shadowed skin under her eyes. She'd been through multiple ordeals and had yet to recover. Moved by the tears, unbearably guilty that he'd caused them, he brushed kisses over her fragile eyelids, tasting salt. She sighed, a flutter of breath, her fingers clasping his wrists, moving in a light reply. "Thank you." Opening her eyes, she gazed at him, the ocean at dusk. "But you weren't cruel. I can be pushy, I know."

All of these little crumbs of information she dropped. He found himself wanting to follow each trail, to gobble up everything there was to know about her until he'd traveled every path to her heart and memorized them all. He still cupped her face in his hands, the strong bones and smooth skin, expression alight with her personality. Lips parted as she searched his face in turn.

He should let her go. They were much too close. This had already raced past grandfatherly to…

Something broke inside. All of it snapped. The leashed control. The sane assessment. All rationality.

With a groan of bone-deep longing, he closed the distance between them and tasted her lips. Sweet and hot, with salt from her tears. She gasped against his mouth, stiffening in surprise, and he tried to pull back. But she tightened her grip on his wrists, holding him in place as she rose up to meet the kiss, returning it with a febrile passion that vanquished the last chains of sober thought.

As her lips parted, drinking him in, he submerged in her

delicious warmth. She glowed around him, shifting with light and shadow. Her inherent shapeshifter magic, he realized, enveloping his mage senses with an overwhelming array of sensory delight. Kissing her reminded him of those sharp delights of youth, the exquisite blue of an autumn sky against scarlet-gold leaves. That first plunge into cool water on a hot day. The scent of flowers bending heavy petaled heads in the summer heat, bees buzzing sweet as honey on the tongue. The strum of music on a quiet evening, making his heart swell with yearning, wishing for someone to be there, not knowing who it could be, but feeling as if he summoned her across time and distance. And now she was in his arms, long, lithe, pressed against him and thrumming with the same desire. *His.*

Lifting her into his arms, he stood to carry her to the bed—

And promptly fell over, Gendra shrieking as they tumbled together onto the throw rug.

Her startled squeal turned to laughter before she gulped it down and gently disentangled herself from him and the rug. "Oh, Isyn—I shouldn't laugh. I'm sorry. Are you hurt?"

She bent over him, running her hands down his splinted leg. "I don't think you jostled it too badly, but how does it feel?"

Like a hot brand searing him from ankle to neck, which was nothing compared to the fierce burn of utter humiliation. What had he been thinking? *Obviously, you weren't.*

Setting his jaw and gritting his teeth, he focused on the low ceiling, cursing his foolishness up one side and down the other. "Just once," he muttered under his breath so she couldn't hear, "I'd love it if the first thing she asks me isn't about my deteriorating health."

"What do you mean by that?" she asked sharply, looming into his field of vision. Her cloak of hair spilled down around them both, the fire glowing through it and lighting it up like embers catching flame.

"I said it hurts but I think I'm fine," he answered testily, staring past her.

She grasped his jaw in one hand, with that surprisingly strong grip, and made him look at her. "You said that just once you'd love it if I didn't ask you about your deteriorating health before anything else." Cocking her head meaningfully, she tapped her temple with her other hand. "Shapeshifters have exceptionally keen senses, including hearing. I bet you didn't know that."

He hadn't known that, but felt he should have. "Can I get up?" he asked, pointedly staring at the ceiling.

"Sure," she answered easily. "As soon as you explain what you meant by that."

"I'd think it would be obvious."

She released his jaw but moved that hand firmly to the center of his chest, making it clear she'd hold him down, if necessary. "It's funny," she said conversationally, shifting to a more comfortable seated position. "All these years away from court, and yet you can still pull out this coldly arrogant royal tone that's meant to put me in my place."

He glanced at her—a mistake, as she looked more alluring than ever, her lips full from his kisses, cheeks flushed and eyes alight. She didn't look disgusted or mortally offended. She looked... His obviously addled brain didn't know how to interpret it. "Clearly it doesn't work on you."

She considered that, drawing up one knee and leaning her elbow against it, her cheek in her palm. With the hand on his chest, poised to stop him should he make any attempt to escape, she traced idle circles. "You like to tease me about keeping exalted company," she finally replied, "but it's true. Prince Harlan isn't really my uncle, but I did grow up running around Castle Ordnung thinking of him that way, and High Queen Ursula as my aunt. Astar and Stella are two of my best friends, and I've been witness to *him* pulling the crown prince attitude many times. Lena—well, she hardly puts on royal airs ever, nor does Stella—but they both can. Their parents may be kings and queens and scary sorceresses, but they're also family." Her indigo gaze drilled into his. "You don't scare me, Isyn."

With a sigh, he lifted a hand and laid it over hers, only in part in an attempt to stop her slow caresses. "I don't want to scare you. But I *am* trying to hold you at arm's length." He laughed at himself without humor. "Recent events notwithstanding."

She nodded, but with her head still leaning against her hand, it came across kind of sideways, indefinite. "And I threw myself at you. Again. Almost immediately after promising I wouldn't."

He frowned at her. "That's not how I remember it happening. I took advantage of you. After promising you and myself that I wouldn't touch you that way."

She sat up straighter. "Because you think of me as a friend."

He squeezed the hand he held. "I want to be friends. I hope we can be friends."

"But only as a *friend*," she clarified, stressing the word. "Not as... anything else."

"Yes, only as a friend." He'd tried to make it sound reassuring, but she frowned, distressed still.

"But, just now, you kissed me like maybe you're attracted to me," she ventured, sounding hesitant.

Maybe attracted to her. He'd laugh at how little that weak wording did to encompass the enormity of his yearning for her, except it hurt too much. He made himself let go of her hand. "I apologize for that. It was an accident."

"No," she replied, slowly and firmly. "When you tried to pick me up and fell, *that* was an accident."

He winced. "Don't remind me."

"You forgot yourself in the heat of the moment." She shrugged that off as irrelevant, going back to tracing circles with her nimble fingers. "But you didn't—*oops*—slip and fall into passionately kissing me for a *very* long time."

At his age, he couldn't possibly be blushing, but his face felt hot, and he couldn't quite meet her eye. "I warned you that it's likely I'm not entirely sane."

"That's an excuse."

Her even reply shamed him. "No, you're right. That was an unforgivable attempt to escape responsibility. I lost control of myself. I want to promise it won't happen again, but I wouldn't blame you if you don't trust me."

She was quiet for a long moment. "It was a really good kiss."

Huffing out a breath, he stared hard at the ceiling, acutely aware of her hand searing hot on his chest, tracing those maddening circles, giving him salacious fantasies of other ways she might touch him. It *had* been a really good kiss. Epic, really. Unlike anything he'd experienced before. After that single—albeit extended—taste, he already felt as if he was starving for another. He couldn't seem to think about anything else.

"You know, it's interesting," she mused. "I kissed your brother."

~ 14 ~

T HAT GOT HIS attention. "What?"

"Your brother, Wilhelm. Wim."

"I know who my brother is," he snapped, irritation rising at the image of his Briar Rose swooning in Wim's bandy arms. Though he'd likely filled out since Isyn last saw the brat. "Is there a reason you're telling me this?" *Now. While I'm incapacitated, lying like a helpless turtle on my back and wishing for this humiliation to end.*

"I was going to have sex with him," she confided thoughtfully.

He groaned and let go of her hand, slapping his over his eyes as if that would help him unsee that image. "Please don't tell me anything else about this," he begged her.

"I think it's important for you to know." She tugged his hand from his eyes, waiting until he opened them. "I was *going* to have sex with him, and he was kissing me, but my head wasn't in it. I kept trying to enjoy it, but—and I know this is terrible to say—I was sort of bored. And I think he sensed that because he started kissing my neck and then my breasts and—"

Isyn's pained groan came out like a snarl, and Gendra gave him a curious glance but didn't relent. "I was making an effort to go with it and all, figuring I'd catch up and start feeling the passion I was supposed to at some point. And then this painting across the room attracted my eye. A misty island shoreline and ocean, a forest filled with animal shapes."

"I painted that." The words burst out of him with the shock of recognition. He'd left that painting, and so much else, far behind in the dim past, and it was disorienting to think of her looking at it only days ago.

"Ah." The sound came out like a dreamy sigh, and her soft gaze fastened on him admiringly. "I wondered if you had. I loved that painting, Isyn."

"I can't believe Wim put it in his rooms," he admitted, faintly pleased. Wim had never seemed to care much about his art.

"Um, I think we were in *your* rooms."

The pleasure swiftly drained into rising irritation. "Do tell."

"Well, I know we were. Your former rooms," she corrected. "Wim said that he and Marjie wagered for who would get them, he won, and he hadn't redecorated because it annoyed her so much."

Despite himself, he laughed. He had no reason to disbelieve her, but that sounded exactly like the terrible twins. And to be fair, he'd left Erie with only vague ideas of returning. Castle Marcellum wasn't so big that they could simply let the rooms sit empty.

Gendra smiled widely. "A real laugh. That's lovely to hear from you."

"Can I get up now?"

Her fingers dug into him lightly, almost like the pinprick of claws from an affectionate feline holding your hand in place for additional petting. "Would you indulge me and listen to my story?"

"Do I have to be on my back on the floor?"

"No," she conceded. "Not if it hurts you. I know you don't want me to ask about that."

"I'm not in pain," he said. Then, as she raised a dubious brow, he added, "no more than I would be sitting up."

"If you don't mind, it's easier for me to talk about it this way. You're less intimidating."

Moved, he put his hand over hers again. "I thought I didn't scare you."

"I may have overstated." She blushed lightly. "But this isn't easy for me to say, and I don't want to chicken out."

He squeezed her hand, feeling that surely she'd have to sense all the love for her pounding through the heart under her hand. "Tell me."

"Well, and now it occurs to me that there's not much more to tell. Wim was kissing my breasts, and I was looking at the painting—and I realized that looking at the painting was much more exciting than his kissing me."

"My poor brother," Isyn murmured. How the lovely Gendra's disinterest must have stung.

"He was a gentleman about it," she assured him. "I taught him to play kiauo instead."

"On my set, no doubt."

"Sorry."

"No need to be." It amused him, in truth, to imagine Wim, deprived of bedding Gendra and forced to play kiauo instead, a game he'd always loathed. "But you play kiauo?"

"Passably, but that's not the point of my story." She looked shy, not quite meeting his gaze but turning her hand to hold his. "Isyn, I think just looking at your painting touched me in a way that all of Wim's caresses simply couldn't. And when you kissed me just now, it was... everything. I wasn't bored in the slightest. In fact, I couldn't seem to assemble any thoughts at all. I was barely aware that you'd picked me up until we fell."

Ah, yes. Isyn the great romantic. Seducer of innocents. Slayer of throw rugs. "I obviously wasn't thinking either."

"Were you..." She studied their joined hands as if they held the answer to a critical question. She took a breath and blew it out. "I am not good at this."

"That's all right, I—"

"Were you going to carry me to the bed and make love to me?" she interrupted in a rush, then blushed furiously, wrenched her hand from his, and clapped both of hers over her face. "Oh, please be kind with your answer."

Utterly charmed by her artless honesty and laid bare himself by her bald question, he internally kicked himself. He also levered himself to a sitting position while the opportunity lasted to reclaim some small morsel of his dignity.

"I, ah, did have an impulse that direction," he confessed, unable to see her face, or much of her at all, cloaked as she was in her long veil of shining chestnut hair. He reached out to stroke a soothing hand over it, but the visceral memory of how touching her affected him had him rethinking the wisdom of that. "As you noted, I was carried away in the impulse of the moment. I've been..." He let out a long sorrow-filled breath, studying his hands. When had they become so gnarled? They'd become his grandfather's hands. "Too much away from civilization. I behaved like an unmannered beast, and I'm truly sorry."

Somewhere in that mess of words, he'd said the right thing, because she lifted her head to gaze at him, not tearfully as he'd expected, but eyes sharp and discerning. "Why are you sorry?"

"For offending you."

"But I'm not offended. *I* am not sorry you kissed me or that you wanted to make love to me. I'd have initiated those things myself, except I don't have much experience that way."

Wonderful. She truly *was* an innocent. The virgin awaiting true love's kiss. "Briar Rose," he said helplessly, giving in and stroking a hand down her cascading hair, a caress she leaned into, her lovely eyes wide and hopeful. "You can't mean that."

Those lovely eyes narrowed with annoyance and wary suspicion. "I think I know my own mind, Isyn."

He held up his hands in a gesture of peacemaking. If he could stand, he would—but his staff was too far to reach, and he didn't see himself asking for her help at the moment. "I am far too old for you. We both know that."

Her lips parted in surprise. In this light, the deep blue of her eyes took on that violet glimmer. With a sudden and fierce desire, he realized he wanted to paint her. An exhilarating impulse he hadn't experienced in decades—quickly followed by the crushing reality that he had no supplies. He couldn't even sketch her effectively. Or could he?

"But I *don't* know that," she said, momentarily confusing

him.

"I am an old man," he argued, feeling foolish at having to point out an obvious and uncomfortable truth.

"Oh, you are not." She actually rolled her eyes at him.

"Look at me." He held out his hands. "I'm gnarled, bent, and aching. I can't even walk on my own."

She took his hands, holding them firmly in her sweetly soft grip. "Weathered. You work outdoors, ice fishing in harsh conditions, people get weather-beaten. And you're injured. Weren't you swinging a sword just weeks ago?"

"Months," he corrected. "This bone is taking forever to heal."

"Not surprising, as it's the biggest bone in the body," she informed him crisply. "And I'm going to help you with the bent-up and aching part. Stop being so stubborn. I wonder if the extra bath water is even still hot?"

Uncoiling to a crouch with elastic grace, she held out her arms as if to embrace him. "Let me help you up."

He eyed her slender form dubiously. "I could crush you."

"Not likely." Her eyes sparkled with mischief. "Shapeshifters are unusually strong, too. Quit stalling. On your feet, soldier."

"You're bossy all of a sudden," he griped as she easily levered him upright.

"Another of my personality flaws," she agreed cheerfully. She fit so neatly against him, as she helped him hobble the short distance to the tub, as if she'd been made for him. Maybe she had been, before his fate took a nosedive into this arctic prison of a life. "Did I mention my father used to be in command of the high queen's personal guard?"

"You didn't, but I understand so much more about you now," he commented drily.

"It's not hot." She frowned as she dribbled long fingers in the water. "But it's warm. I'll ask for more."

"No." He put a hand on her to stop her decisive move to the door. "They'd only have carry buckets out again. And Jasperina will be difficult about it."

She eyed him dubiously. "But you're the king here."

"By default, and it's complicated."

"The one-eyed man and the land of the blind."

"You remembered." He'd wondered how much of their mental conversations she'd recall. So far it seemed like most of them.

"Hmm. I want to hear more about that. For now we'll see about the water once you soak a bit. I reserve the right to heat it up if you're too cool, cranky Jasperina or no. Let's get you undressed and into the water. Steady yourself on the rim here." She hummed a tune he didn't know as she busied herself with the laces of his shirt.

"You sure are bubbly."

"Which is it—bubbly or bossy?"

"You can be both at once," he decided.

She giggled, another sign of bubbliness, and laid a hand on his cheek. "I'm happy, Isyn. I really like you, and you like me."

"That's not what I—" She tugged his shirt off, muffling his protest, then dove for the laces of his pants.

He stopped her. "I'll do that. You turn around."

"I'll see everything when I help you into the tub," she

scoffed. "The Tala aren't all that concerned with modesty."

"The Erieans are," he countered. "I'm asking you to respect that."

"I'll close my eyes," she said, giving him a sidelong look before she did. She clearly didn't buy his flimsy excuse. As well she shouldn't, as that was a bald-faced lie, but he also didn't want her seeing his achingly persistent erection. She had enough ideas already, and he still hadn't decided how to dissuade her. If he was in possession of any integrity at all, how would he handle this? By refusing to take advantage of an innocent, that's how. By being a gentleman and keeping his hands—and lips—off of her. *Too late for that.*

Wrestling off his woolen pants, he got them off over his feet, then edged his good hip onto the rim of the tub. True to her word, she kept her eyes closed, but her supportive hands on his bare skin nearly drove him mad. "I can do it," he bit out, swinging his good leg into the water and, using that and his arms braced on the side of the tub, lowered himself into the warm water.

"Is it hot enough?" Gendra had pulled up the stool to sit behind him, knotting his hair with deft expertise to keep it out of the way. She set her hands on his shoulders and—quite expertly—located the knots of tension, working some kind of magic with her fingers.

"It feels good," he temporized. "I haven't had a bath in a long time. I probably stink."

He felt her shrug. "The Tala aren't concerned with such things."

An exasperated laugh escaped him. "What *are* the Tala

concerned with?"

"Sorry," she answered sheepishly. "My mom says that a lot to tease my dad, and I guess I'm falling into that habit. I'm a little nervous."

She was an interesting combination that way, alternately shy and bold, skittish and seductive. "I'm sorry you're nervous around me now," he offered, hesitating before again promising not to touch her. He wasn't quite sure where they'd left things between them.

"I was nervous before now," she said candidly. "I suppose I should say I tend to be nervous around men I'm attracted to."

There she went, from bashful to outspoken with nothing between. He had no words. "Gendra, obviously you're a beautiful, charming woman, but I'm not attracted to you in that—"

"See? That proves it. No other man has ever thought I'm beautiful or charming." She said it so matter-of-factly that it hurt his heart. What was wrong with the men she'd met so far? "Don't bother protesting that you don't want me, also. It's too late for that. You also already admitted that you wanted— albeit in the rush of passion—to take me to bed and make love to me."

He nearly corrected her there, as none of the fiercely sexual fantasies plaguing him looked much like "making love." But then, he was also fully and helplessly in love with her, so there was that. He ended up saying nothing, feeling himself melt under her touch.

"I'm not asking for true love here," she added, so wistfully that he knew that's exactly what she wanted. "But I want to experience sex with a man who actually likes me. Besides, it would be a good way to pass the time here while we await rescue."

Imagining spending days and nights savoring the lovely Gendra nearly stopped his heart. Of course, indulging in that could very likely result in his heart actually giving out. A caution right there. And yet, what she'd said bothered him too much for him to leave it alone. "You haven't gone to bed with a man who liked you?" he asked. "I don't understand how that happens."

"Well, in all honesty, there's only been the one, since Wim and I ended up playing kiauo instead, which tells you something," she added with grim humor.

Not a complete innocent, then, but not far from it.

"I had high hopes that losing my virginity would make later... sessions... go better," she mused, tone thoughtful, "but in some ways it only made things worse."

"What happened?" he asked quietly.

She didn't answer immediately. He waited her out. "Why do you want to know?"

"If you want to discuss the possibility of sex between us, which you seem determined to do—though I don't think it's a good idea—then we should be able to have an open conversation about it."

"Oh." She was quiet a moment, deftly working sore points along his spine that made him want to moan in ecstasy as they released. "Discussing this with you doesn't feel very romantic."

"Romance is overrated."

"Is it? I suppose I wouldn't know. It always looks lovely

from the outside." There was that wistfulness again.

"Honesty is one form of intimacy," he told her, relenting, wanting to give her some measure of happiness. "And that can be romantic in its own way."

"I never thought about it like that. But then, I've never talked about sex with a man. Well, except for Jak, and that's because he's nosy."

Isyn was beginning to dislike this Jak. He was opening his mouth to ask about that when Gendra continued thoughtfully. "Zeph talks about sex easily, and so does Lena. Nilly doesn't so much—but she was a virgin, too, until recently—and they got even her to describe Jak's member."

He nearly choked. "Nilly?" he asked, sidestepping that one for the moment.

"Sorry—what we call Stella. Astar and Stella were ornery, shapeshifting toddlers that everyone called Willy and Nilly for a very long time. It still sticks."

Imagine, calling the heir to the high throne and the likely next queen of Annfwn by their toddler nicknames.

"Anyway," Gendra returned to her topic with enthusiasm, "there had been a lot of rumors and hearsay about Jak being unusually well endowed, so when Nilly—Stella—actually found out, well, we all wanted to know."

He didn't want to know. He certainly wasn't going to ask. He definitely hated this Jak.

"My point is," she continued, thankfully leaving the topic behind, "that it's not easy for me to talk about that stuff."

"If you can't talk about it with me, then doing it with me is a worse idea."

She was quiet a moment, digging into a knotted muscle with enough strength for him to interpret it as a bit of punishment for his observation. "You're right," she finally admitted on a sigh. "With Henk, I kind of went about it the same way I did with Wim, thinking that if I could just get through it all, then I'd feel better about things and begin to enjoy it. But I never did, and unlike Wim—who really is a good man with integrity, I can see how he's like you that way—Henk, he…" Her hands went lax and listless. Maybe he imagined they chilled.

"Unlike Wim," Isyn finished for her, glad his little brother had demonstrated that much awareness and basic decency, "this Henk didn't stop."

"No." She whispered the word, a vast icy ocean of turmoil beneath it. "But I also didn't tell him to stop. So, it's not his fault."

"Gendra, that's not how it works." He really disliked that she was behind him, that he couldn't see her face. He put a hand over her listless one on his shoulder, but she pulled it away.

"You're cold," she declared, "and getting a chill is the last thing you need. So either I summon cranky Jasperina to bring more hot water or you're getting out."

Back to bossy, which he was beginning to discover was her favored gambit for avoiding emotional vulnerability. "I'm getting out," he told her.

"Let me—"

"This one I've got. Fetch my walking staff, would you?" Bracing his hands on the rim of the tub, he levered himself upright, pivoting to sit on the side of the tub. Gendra draped a soft alpaca wool blanket around him, handing him his staff.

"Impressive upper body strength," she commented.

"I'm not completely decrepit."

"You're the one trying to make the case that you're an old man." She sounded more confident again, less like a vulnerable waif, so he didn't comment. "Lie on the bed, please, face up."

"Maybe now isn't—"

"I've warmed some oil for the healing massage. Yes, it's fish oil, but it will feel really nice," she wheedled. "Don't you feel better from what I've been able to do so far?"

He did. And, oddly enough, he didn't want to disappoint her. Bubbly, bossy Briar Rose was far preferable to her sad and lost waifish side. The latter made him want to cuddle her up and hold her close, which simply couldn't happen. He might not find it in himself to be a Wim—he wanted her too fiercely—but he could at least refuse to be a Henk.

Following her direction, he lay on the bed, pulling the covers over himself. She fetched her supplies, seating herself on the stool she brought over, rearranging a table closer to hold the oil, which she'd warmed over the brazier that normally heated soups and teas. A clever adaptation.

Her expression clinical, she adjusted the blankets, folding them so they covered his groin and the far side of his body, adding a few furs to cover his chest and shoulders. Those almost violet eyes flicked up to his face, assessing, no hint of either sensuality or vulnerability in them. This was Gendra in her element: nurturing and calmly efficient. "Are you cold at all?"

"No," he replied honestly enough. If anything, he burned, but he wouldn't tell her that. Gritting his teeth, he stared steadfastly at the ceiling. "Get it over with."

~ 15 ~

HONESTLY, THE WAY the man behaved, you'd think she'd announced she planned to amputate the limb. In truth, now that she finally had a chance to examine him without the splint and associated wrapping, it did not look very good. Not surprising, given the almost total lack of medical care in this place, but still distressing to see how much muscle atrophy had set in. Isyn's upper body remained strong—she hadn't exaggerated when she'd called it impressive—his shoulder, chest, and arm muscles displaying the bulk and definition that came from a lifetime of hard work.

He was also scarred in so many places and ways that she shuddered to think of all he'd endured. With his natural pale coloring exacerbated by living in the Winter Isles, where overcast seemed to be the norm, the white lines of scars didn't show up until subjected to close scrutiny. But now that she could look closely, they stitched and riddled his skin, a tale of suffering carved in a cicatrice design.

In contrast, the skin around the broken leg screamed in startling scarlets and purples. The ridged scar tissue billowed and folded, centering around a point mid-thigh, where she suspected there might be festering. That was not good. "The bone broke the skin?" she asked, gently skimming her fingers over the barely healing skin. He flinched, and she wished fervently that she had Stella's gift of healing. Well, she had what Harlan had taught her, and that was still something.

"Yes," he bit out. "Or so I'm told," he added, relenting. "I wasn't conscious for that part. I remember the snap of the break, the pain like nothing else, and waking up with the bone splinted and the wound you see now."

"Is this painful?" Obviously it was, as he flinched reflexively, his muscles twitching no matter how gently she prodded.

But he understood what she was asking. "Nothing I can't bear."

"Just tell me if it gets to be too much. It will feel so much better when I'm done, I promise."

He nodded, not replying, staring at the ceiling as if he could burn a hole through it with his gaze, seeming to ignore her completely as she examined the leg. Not only was it not good; it was bad. The upper leg muscles had atrophied from the long convalescence, as expected, but so had the lower leg, looking decidedly withered. In addition, he'd lost muscle mass around the hip on that side. Inflammation burned against her fingertips here and there, confirming a deep-tissue chronic infection, and she suspected nerve damage on top of that. Worst of all, the bone hadn't been set properly. No wonder it hadn't healed well. Frankly it was a wonder Isyn could move about on it at all. Someone with less ferocious will wouldn't be.

That will of his had been a blessing and curse. For the first time she understood his conviction that his days were numbered.

Even if this injury didn't kill him, he'd never be able to recover this leg. She wished she hadn't allowed the thought of amputation into her mind earlier, because the more she examined him, the more likely it seemed that cutting off the leg might be the only option to save his life. How could she possibly tell him that, though?

"That bad?" he asked, his voice a sarcastic rasp, his green gaze now resting fully on her face, seeing too much.

"It was a bad break, for sure," she replied with all the cheer she could muster.

He shook his head on the pillow, gaze fixed on her. "You, my lovely Briar Rose, are a terrible liar. That's not an insult, by the way. It speaks well of you that everything you think and feel shows on your face—and by your face, I can see it's bad. You might as well tell me the full truth."

Pouring some warm oil into her palm, she rubbed her hands together and began to work on the hip. If she could stimulate blood flow and healing to that big joint, that could help considerably.

"You've lived a hard life here," she observed. "So many scars."

"Gendra." He said her name flatly, his expression set into icy lines.

He looked so beautiful, his ivory hair spilling over the pillow, his contoured face elegant in its clean lines, the intensity of his green gaze like a hot summer afternoon. She longed to taste his pale skin, touch her lips to every scar, to feel those long, clever fingers against her skin. How could she break his heart with the truth? How could she not, because it was true that she'd never been any good at prevaricating, even when it mattered most.

"The bone wasn't set correctly," she told him, holding his gaze until he closed his eyes in pained acknowledgment and nodded.

"I think I knew and didn't want to face it," he said quietly. "The folk don't understand human bodies. They mean well, but…"

She nodded, too, though he couldn't see her.

"Can you break it and reset it?" he asked.

Could she? "I don't know. I wouldn't know where to begin. How I wish Stella were here."

"Magical healing would be a miracle at this point," he observed quietly, gaze on her again. "What happens if we don't break and reset the bone—it heals crooked?"

If it heals at all. "Let's give it a few days of this therapy and see." She suggested that option almost desperately, unwilling to discuss the possibility of amputation right then—if she could even do *that*—or the even more depressing likelihood that this would kill him no matter what they did.

His gaze lingered on her face, perhaps reading there all the thoughts she hadn't voiced aloud. "The massage does feel good," he said, lifting a hand to trail his fingertips along her arm. "Thank you for persisting in the face of my curmudgeon-ly behavior."

"I'm just glad I can do something to repay you for saving my life."

"It was clearly self-serving," he replied softly, sending a

susurrus of warmth through her. "I couldn't bear to lose your company."

The man's moods shifted like coastal weather. As Gen worked her way down his thigh, she did her best to ignore how good even the slightest flirtation from him felt. That kiss had turned her inside out, sweeping her away as she'd always imagined a kiss could do. She also determinedly ignored the proximity of his barely clad groin, the sprinkle of ivory hairs silvery on his pale skin, marking a path toward his member, which strained hard against the draping wool. She shouldn't feel this desire to put her lips there also, not with him unwell, but nothing seemed to deter her suddenly awakened libido.

The fact that he was erect and had remained that way meant he wanted her, she was fairly certain, thinking back over Zeph's ribald descriptions, the jokes with Lena. Men tended to be soft, hard, or somewhere in between, but they weren't hard if they were tired. Or uninterested. Or drunk. Lena had gone on at length about that last one.

With a pang, she missed her friends suddenly and viciously. What she wouldn't give to ask for their advice. Certainly having Stella's healing would be everything, but Lena's steadying acerbity would be the boost she needed. And Astar's solid leadership, along with Jak's wit. Even Zeph's irreverence and Rhy's brooding would be welcome. Lena would be studying the weather and finding a way to make the sun shine, if only for a little while. And Stella would heal Isyn.

She could picture them so vividly they almost seemed to be in the room. All of them, together again. Plus Isyn, of course.

"That's a nice smile," Isyn observed, still stroking her arm. She wondered if he was aware of it, but she reveled in his wanting to touch her, so she didn't call attention to it.

"Thinking of my friends," she replied. "You would like them."

His expression hardened. "But would they like me?"

"Of course. Why wouldn't they?"

He shifted restlessly under her hands, and she readjusted, moving farther away from the angry wound. "Did they like Henk?"

The question startled a laugh out of her. "Not at all, and not a one of them," she admitted with chagrin. "Which, in retrospect, should have told me everything."

"Why did *you* like him?"

That was an interesting question to consider. "He was handsome and charming enough. A good dancer." She tried to think of something else, but those few days at Castle Elder-horst felt like a lifetime ago.

"Not a rousing endorsement," Isyn commented.

"True." She sighed. "To be honest, I think I liked him mainly because he paid attention to me. I know that sounds pathetic."

Isyn frowned, puzzled. "Surely he was but one of dozens vying for your attention."

She laughed, barely pulling it back from that bitter-spinster hysterical cackle. "You, dear mage, have been too long among the folk of the Winter Isles. Having a titled gentleman pay attention to plain, awkward, too-tall and gangly me was head-turning. I cop to that. I wanted to find true love so badly that

I…" Hating that the thought of Henk and the disappointment of that interlude with him choked off her voice, she stopped speaking rather than fight it. Instead she focused on the ligaments around the knee, drawn tight from lack of extension and normal use.

Isyn's fingers clasped her arm. "That you went to bed with him, an inexperienced virgin, and he took advantage of you."

Oh, wow, that stung. Swallowing back the tears, she nodded. "I didn't want to be an inexperienced virgin any longer," she told him, mustering the determination she'd felt then. "I wanted to, well, get it over with." She glanced up at him with a wry smile, finding him watching her with rapt attention. Listening to her. Though she supposed he was a captive audience.

"Did he hurt you?" Isyn asked evenly, but the calm was deceptive, anger boiling beneath.

"That's the first question Stella asked, too," she replied with a pang of nostalgia. "And she sounded exactly the same, like if I said yes she'd hunt him down and gut him for me."

Isyn smiled ruefully down at his leg. "I would do that for you, if I could."

"Well, we're safe from that because he didn't hurt me. Not really," she amended, wary of the truth showing on her face. The penetration had been somewhat painful, but at least quickly over—and a minor twinge compared to the intangible pain. "Not the physical part."

"What part did hurt?" He slid his hand down her arm, coaxing her from her work on his knee to enfold her oiled fingers in his. "You can tell me."

She hadn't told anyone this, but oddly she did want to tell Isyn. "You know how I said that I liked him because he paid attention to me, because he seemed to see me?" Isyn nodded gravely, something shadowed in his gaze. "Well, there I was, naked, under him, our bodies as close as two people can be, and he's, you know, looking down at me and... pumping into me." She wasn't even blushing, recounting this part, too cold and miserably sick inside. Isyn squeezed her fingers lightly, a reminder and a reassurance. "And I looked at his face—and he wasn't seeing *me* at all." Her voice crumbled a little, like the small piece of herself that had broken off in that moment. "I might as well have been anyone, or not there at all. I felt more... invisible than ever."

"Oh, Briar Rose," Isyn murmured, sorrow in his face.

Awkward, and vaguely ashamed, she withdrew her hand, focusing on his leg, which was supposed to be the point. Healing Isyn was exponentially more important than her imagined hurts and slights. "Anyway," she said, making an effort to sound perkier. "I can recognize my own foolishness. I knew what I was getting into, knew that Henk didn't love me." Moranu take her that her voice wobbled a bit on that. Apparently recognizing a reality wasn't the same as feeling it in your heart. "Which is even sillier because I didn't want *Henk* to love me. I can see now that even *I* didn't like Henk all that much. Sorry." She winced at herself when Isyn grunted in pain at her too-vigorous assault of the tight ligaments in his lower leg. Working out one's inner angst didn't go well with tending to someone else. "So, I don't know why I expected... more."

"I think it's reasonable to have expected more," Isyn said

quietly. "Don't we all want to be loved?"

"Yes, but even I understand that love and sex aren't the same thing. Zeph has had sex with practically everyone, but she's only ever loved Astar. They're not the same to her."

"Are you a great deal like this Zeph?"

She had to laugh, glancing wryly at him. "Not in the least. We're first cousins, close enough to be siblings—my mother is her father's twin—but we couldn't be more different, and... oh."

"Exactly," he commented, a rueful note in his voice. "Why don't you come lie beside me for a moment?" He patted the bed beside him.

"I'm sorry I was rough," she replied, hesitating. "I'll be more careful."

"It's not that. Well, maybe it's partly that." He made a face. "I could use a break, and I think you could do with some comforting. Some simple human contact."

The offer made her choke up a little. "I don't want to hurt you."

With a wry twist of his lips, he dragged the blankets and furs away from his other side. "Come lie against my good side, then. Just for a moment," he coaxed.

Because she wanted, needed, what he offered, she nodded and crawled carefully over him, nestling under the arm he opened for her, cuddling against his side and allowing him to draw the furs over them both, as if she were a child to be tucked in. It soothed something raw inside her that she hadn't realized had been bleeding still. Pressing her nose against his warm skin, she inhaled his scent, adding it to her memories for the nights ahead when she would have no one to hold her.

He twitched, laughing. "Your nose is cold."

"Sorry."

"Don't be. Cold nose, warm heart."

Now she laughed, tipping her head back to look at him. "I don't think that's a thing."

Touching her nose gently with a fingertip, he smiled. "It is now." Their gazes tangled and, caught, held for a long breathless moment. He broke it first, adjusting his arm under her to relax her against his side and turning his head to look up at the ceiling. "What did you say to him after?"

Ugh. Despite the delicious warmth of his body, the soft furs covering them, that creeping, nauseating chill coiled in her belly. Because Isyn didn't seem to mind, and it made her feel better, she dared to put her arm around him, too, draping it over his narrow waist and resting her hand on his muscled chest. "I didn't say anything," she admitted.

"What, once the deed was done, you never spoke again?" he teased.

"Well, obviously we did, but not about anything important." He'd told her how great it was. She'd made appropriate happy noises. And they'd gone to sleep. In the morning, she'd gone on as if nothing had changed, pretending to like him as much as ever, even when she truly wanted to get as far away from him as possible.

"I acted like everything was fine," she admitted, wondering why that felt as shameful as anything else. "I tacitly agreed that the sex had been great. I didn't say so, but also didn't say otherwise. I smiled and flirted with him, same as I had been. I didn't even tell my friends I'd slept with him until much later. I don't know why."

"Sometimes it's easier that way," he noted, turning his head to kiss her forehead. It felt like a benediction, traveling through her to warm and soothe the cold, sickly raw places. "We learn not to dwell on pain, so it's not so distracting. We just soldier on, pretending that we're fine."

"That makes sense, though it's not the healthiest approach in the long run," she added, feeling she should mention this to him, as his determination to ignore his own pain had likely done him lasting harm.

He chuckled mirthlessly. "I can vouch for that." He nuzzled her hair, just at the border where it met her skin, his breath wafting sweetly over her skin, and she closed her eyes to savor it. Whatever he was willing to share with her, she'd take with gratitude. "Why do you smell like tropical flowers?" he asked. "I know you washed with fish oil soap. You should smell like that now."

"It's Annfwn, I think," she answered, the sense of home wrapping vividly around her, the nostalgia both welcome and agonizing. "It's magic, you know, everything about the place. Weatherwise, it should be like the bordering kingdoms of the Thirteen, but it's not. It's tropical and lush and lovely, all because of the magic that was concentrated there for so long."

"Magic that makes her children capable of shapeshifting."

"In part. So it's as if the magic that gives us flesh is the same that makes the flowers bloom."

"What a lovely way to think of it."

"Annfwn is a lovely place."

"Tell me about it."

That was easier, so she painted the picture for him, telling him about the shining white cliffs that faced the clear turquoise sea, the shimmering sands and how people made their homes in cliffs—those who didn't prefer to live away from the city in the forests, rivers, and wilder climes, according to the pull of their innate animals. She told him about the fruit trees and the flowering vines, the games children played sliding down tunnels to the beach, and the long, winding road that snaked back and forth, climbing to the meadows atop the cliffs and the snow-capped mountains rising behind.

"I always wanted to visit Annfwn," he said on a wistful sigh as she wound down. "One of many regrets."

"You still could. I'll take you there."

He rolled his head to look at her, his smile sad. "I think we both know I'm never leaving this place."

"No, I don't know that!"

His arm tightened around her when she moved restlessly in her desire to refute his gloomy outlook. "I saw your face, Rose," he said softly, remorselessly. "When I asked you about breaking and resetting the bone in my leg. You don't think there's any point because you know I can't survive this wound."

She searched for a way to lie to him, to compose her face into an earnest expression of hope that he might believe. Watching her, he smiled widely, eyes sparkling a lighter green with amusement. "Amazing. I can actually see you trying to figure out how to trick me into believing a hopeful prognosis."

"I wish I were less transparent," she muttered unhappily.

"I don't." He kissed her forehead again. "I love that you're so honest that it shines through your every word, expression, and gesture. You're incapable of being anything but your authentic self, and that's an admirable quality."

She gazed at him, deeply moved. "That might be the nicest thing anyone has ever said to me."

Caressing her cheek with a light finger, he held her gaze, *seeing* her, something unspoken traveling between them. "I wish I'd met you a long time ago," he whispered.

"You've met me now."

"When it's too late."

"As long as we're alive, everything is possible."

A line formed between his brows. "That feels… true."

"It is true." She poured all that earnest belief in her into the words, pressing against him so he'd feel her presence. "We have each other right now, and we're alive. So everything is possible."

He smiled a little, the curve of his lips fading quickly as his expression intensified, green eyes going dark and intent. "My Briar Rose…" The fingers caressing her cheek curled under her jaw, and she waited, breathless with anticipation. Excruciatingly slowly, he lowered his mouth toward hers, until only a whisper of distance separated them. Then his lips touched hers, a sensation sweet as nectar from honey blossoms. She sighed into him with her entire body, melting into him where their bare skin touched. He drank in her moan and answered it with a deep hum of desire and need.

Emboldened, she caressed his chest as he kissed her, tracing the lines of carved muscle, finding the lighter tracery of scars and the softer skin that moved with pleasure under her touch. The desire rose between them, hot and fulminous, and she learned him breath by breath, lips joined, mouths moving together. This was a kiss that couldn't be ignored, Isyn filling her mind and senses. Her own body thrummed with desire, yes, but more important was the sheer delight of touching him, of being close to him. Not unlike the healing massage in a way, she discovered him, finding each place that heightened his need, that made him hum in answering desire. Making love to him, she realized, fed and succored that raw and needy part of her.

Exploring him, savoring every bit of his enticing body, the unblemished skin and the ridges of scars alike, her seeking hands found their way to his groin, the silvery hairs there a silky path leading the way.

"Gendra," he murmured against her mouth, his hand buried in her hair, fingers combing through it as he kissed and kissed her. "We should stop."

"Because you don't want this?"

"I want this." His fingers tightened in her hair. "I shouldn't want it, but I'm finding I can't resist you."

"Then don't resist me." She slid her hand closer to his erect cock.

He groaned, hips encouraging her. "You don't have to."

"But I want to," she murmured back. "Do you mind?"

He breathed a laugh. "At this moment, I want nothing more than your hand on me, but I don't want to push you."

"I want this." When he hesitated, drawing back to study her face, she added. "Truly. I promise."

He nodded slightly, kissing her deeply. She traced her way along the clean line of his hip to the point of his pelvis, finding the root of his erect cock and encircling it with a ring of her clasping fingers. He groaned, body moving in an urgent wave that broke into an inarticulate gasp.

Not knowing exactly what to do—and not wanting to think about Zeph's detailed advice, as Isyn was right: she and her cousin were nothing alike, and it was time for her to stop comparing herself—she proceeded as she had been. Learning the shape and size of him, the length and girth, the softness of his skin and the turgid solidity beneath, she discovered what he liked, moving with him as he pressed through her encircling grip, sensing the increasing tension in him from the way his lips moved over hers, how his grip tightened in her hair, and the sheer waves of need shimmering back and forth between them.

She was giving him this. Her touch made him moan and gasp. The intimacy and power filled her with iridescent delight.

Then he went rigid, all of him tightening like a bowstring and then releasing with a thunderous crash. He tore his mouth from hers, throwing his head back in a taut arch, the cords standing out in a rictus of release, a strangled cry tearing from him akin to a wolf's howl, calling on a cold night. His hands, though, they tightened on her in a fierce grip as he rolled onto his side, thrusting his cock through her grip and into the compressed closeness between them, his seed spilling over her fingers to slide between their bellies as they moved against each other, her panting breaths as harsh as his.

Finally, the vising need released him, all of Isyn going

boneless in a full-bodied easing that flooded her as well. His head fell deep into the pillow, his hands at last relinquishing their fierce grip, as if he no longer needed to hold on to her for his very life. Feeling her way still, she soothed him with light caresses, gazing upon his clear face, at peace for the first time since she'd met him, suffused with calm and so beautiful with it.

She stored that away, too, memorizing how he looked in this moment. No matter what came after, she'd remember him like this, his ivory hair spilling around him, his body entangled with hers. Their hearts, pounding hard in a slowing rhythm, exactly matched.

She also wouldn't let this be all there was. *Because we're alive, everything is possible,* she reminded herself.

With a shuddering breath of a laugh, Isyn stirred, his eyes opening, the green of sun-dappled leaves, warming her like the sun she'd left behind. His smile took a wistful turn. "That was miraculous, but are you all right?"

Her heart, already so taut, so filled with unnamable emotion, burst with heat and light. This was love. This was what she'd been seeking, and she'd been looking for entirely the wrong thing. "I'm wonderful," she answered.

"You are," he agreed warmly, "but how do you feel?"

She laughed, the delight purring through her and reflected in his answering smile as he snuggled her even closer, dipping his mouth to catch hers in a lingering kiss. "Do you need a cloth to clean your hand?" he asked as he drew away, then fastening his lips to the underside of her jaw, kissing her there where the softer skin surprisingly hummed to life at the caress.

"Or do the Tala not care for such things?"

She really didn't. All she cared about was staying this close to him, for him to kiss her like this always and always. *Everything is possible.* "I don't want anything that involves you moving away from me," she answered, then winced a little at her excruciating honesty. Too needy? Probably.

But thankfully he only chuckled, warm and dark. "I absolutely sympathize with that sentiment, Briar Rose." He licked along her throat, and she shivered at the extraordinary sensation. "I feel like I've been starving," he murmured, "and I've barely tasted the feast."

His hand curved around her waist, sliding up her ribs over her thin slip, hovering just below her breast. Pulling back enough to see her face, he studied her very seriously. "I'd like to touch you. Would that be all right?"

~ 16 ~

WORDLESSLY, PRETTY MUCH unable to summon any thought at all, she nodded. He nodded slightly also, mirroring her, his rapt gaze holding hers as he slowly moved his hand to gently cup her breast. She moaned, feeling all of herself give a sigh of relief at the feel of him. His hand was big and her breasts small, so he held all of her in the palm of his hand. "Isyn..." she sighed, torn between wanting to press herself into his touch and bracing for a careless observation about her lack of bounty.

"You are so unutterably beautiful," he murmured, his thumb traveling lightly over her nipple, gaze on her face, carefully observing her reaction.

"I know I'm not," she replied, feeling there should be honesty between them. "You don't have to feel you need to say so."

He raised a brow in question, and she gasped as he rolled her nipple lightly between thumb and forefinger, the sensation indescribably delicious, suffusing her with a sweet desire that felt unlike anything she'd ever experienced. "If I were a poet, I'd make myself mad attempting to compose sonnets to do justice to how you look at this moment."

"Just as well you're not a poet, then," she teased, surprised to find she could find humor while engaged in sex play. Somehow it hadn't occurred to her that there could be teasing and laughter, too.

"As my sanity is already in question?" he replied, answering laughter in his voice, dipping his head to trail kisses along her collarbones. "Tell me if you need me to stop."

"Never stop," she commanded fervently, hoping that he'd be able to forge through any last-moment hesitation she displayed despite herself.

"Or pause, then," he replied on a soft laugh. "This is all for you. Only what gives you pleasure. No pretending for my sake."

She didn't think she had the wherewithal to pretend anything, simply receiving the simple, sweet susurrus of his lips on her skin, his body against hers. "I think I've been waiting all my life for this," she breathed, the realization almost too huge to bear.

"I think I have, too." He spoke the words against the hollow at the base of her throat, so she couldn't see his face, but a note of regret wove through them.

"We have now," she reminded him. "And this is everything."

"Yes." Lifting his head, he kissed her lips, toying with the tie at the neckline of her slip. "May I?" he asked, watching her closely.

She nodded, licking suddenly dry lips. He noticed. "We can stop here."

"No," she said, a bit too vehemently. "Please don't stop.

I'm only..."

He waited, then raised a brow, still toying idly with the lace, the light tug rippling through her awareness. "Tell me," he coaxed. "You know you can tell me anything."

She could, which was also everything. Could more than one thing be everything? There needed to be another word for the totality of all these feelings and realizations. She took a breath. "This, all of this, feels so good that... I'm afraid of it *changing*."

"Changing?"

"No longer feeling this good."

He nodded gravely, holding her gaze. "Protecting the wound, yes?"

She released a breath. *Oh.* "That is uncannily perceptive, yes."

"You were the one to teach me," he commented. "It's a useful metaphor. Shall we stop?"

What if this was all they'd have? Tomorrow everything could change, and they'd be torn apart again. "I don't want to stop," she whispered, testing the words aloud. "But... can we go slowly?"

"As slow as you like, Briar Rose," he murmured, kissing her with excruciating sweetness. "Just remember, the moment it changes from anything less than wonderful, then I stop and we go back to find what does feel good. All right?"

"All right." If she hadn't already fallen head over heels in love with him, she would have right then. Was it possible to fall in love over and over again? Perhaps so. No one had ever said anything like that, not that she'd heard or read, but the prospect of reveling in that ecstatic tumble over a lifetime with Isyn felt like that infinite possibility. *As long as we're alive...* Well they were alive now, and she intended to make sure they stayed that way. And she wasn't missing a moment of this, especially not out of fear of what the stupid Henks of the world had made her feel.

Thinking of Henk, though, reminded her of his comments about her disappointing figure. She put a hand over his on the laces at the neckline of her slip. "Not this, though, not yet?" She tendered the request, braced for his disappointment, but he smiled, immediately complying and sliding his hand down her back.

"How about I stay over the gown?" he murmured, pressing kisses along her jawline.

"Is that enough for you, for now?" she asked, breathless from the build of nerves and the relief of his easy accommodation—and from the way those kisses thrilled through her body, now that she was no longer worrying about what would come next.

"Briar Rose," he breathed. "It's already enough. This is more than I dared to hope for. So much so that I wonder if I'm dreaming all of this."

"Then I'm dreaming it, too."

"A shared dream," he murmured, brushing his lips hypnotically over hers. "Our own alter-realm, where only you and I exist."

To her surprise, that sounded lovely, the image resonating on a deep level. In the shadowed nest of furs, in the small room locked away from the dangers of the world, it was as if only

Isyn and she existed, entwined in trust and… love? This could indeed be love.

Breath gusting out of her, she wound her fingers through his hair, combing them through the tangled silken skeins of ivory, spreading them over her as he kissed her. Freed of the worry of how this might turn sour, she yielded to his kisses and caresses, trusting him to take care of her. His hands skimmed over her, leaving shimmering enchantment behind, his lips finding delicate, hidden spots that made her shiver, licking and nibbling her into mindless ecstasy. She moved under him, wanting all of him, her core aching and empty, needing him to fill it. Restless with the urgent need, she tried to open her thighs, not quite succeeding, pinned as she was between him and the furs. Isyn lifted his head, gaze smoldering. "Gendra?"

"I want you inside me." She bit her lip, vague apprehension pouncing, the odious sense of Henk thrusting into her while his eyes stared into nothing dissolving some of the delicious warmth Isyn had filled her with. No, she was done with that.

Of course, Isyn noticed her reticence. "I don't think that's what you really want yet."

"But—"

He kissed her, gently and sweetly. "We have time." His full lips twisted in wry humor. "We have nothing *but* time."

A whimper of protest escaped her at the prospect of remaining unfulfilled. She'd never been this excited, this needy. How could she sleep? Perhaps she could sneak off to the privy to finish herself off, but the prospect of that pale imitation of what she felt with him combined with the dank chill of that hole was hardly appealing.

Isyn trailed his hand down the narrowing of her waist and over the flare of her hip. "Perhaps I could touch you, as you did me?"

Mute at the tantalizing thought, she nodded. If his caresses on the rest of her felt rapturously intense, how would this be? Unbearably intimate—though she supposed that wanting him inside her would've been even more so, which spoke to his good sense in hesitating there. Zeph had always argued that Gen had gone about things backward, and she could see that now. Because Isyn still waited on her answer, tracing soothing circles on her belly as he watched her face, as if listening to her thoughts, she found words. "I would like that. No one has ever touched me there before."

He let out a hushed breath of sound. "How did this Henk manage to get his miserable excuse for a dick inside you without touching you?"

He sounded so indignant and incredulous that she giggled. "There were quite a few errant proddings."

Groaning, he rubbed his face with the hand he'd been leaning on, his other flat on her belly, a comforting weight. "On behalf of my gender, I apologize."

She stroked his cheek, tucking a wild lock of hair behind his ear so she could better see his beautiful face. "Funny—Jak said much the same thing. Only he disowned Henk on behalf of your gender."

"Fitting," Isyn acknowledged with a nod. "Perhaps I'll hate Jak a little less now."

Hate Jak? "But why would you hate him? In truth, you and Jak would probably get along famously."

Isyn turned his head, kissing her fingers, eyes on hers. "Because he has your admiration, and I am not so noble that I can set aside the jealousy."

How astonishing to contemplate that Isyn might be jealous. Perhaps she shouldn't have told him so much about her friends. Speaking too frankly had always been an issue for her. But Isyn's jealousy also pleased her, which probably didn't speak well of her own character. Still, it made her feel powerful in a way she'd never felt with a man before. *Wanted.*

"You are the only one who means anything to me, Isyn," she confessed on a whisper, taking the risk of coming too close to saying aloud that she loved him. He wouldn't want to hear that from her, not so soon. She'd only sound desperate and needy. But she did need him to know that only he mattered, wanted him to feel the truth of that.

Reaching down, she covered his hand with hers and drew it down her thigh to the hem of her rucked-up slip, until he met with bare skin. "Don't do this just to prove that to me," he cautioned, his fingers caressing her skin as if of their own accord. He held her tightly with his other arm, his expression fierce with like wanting.

"I'm not," she promised. She parted her legs, lifting her hands to drape over her head in sensual abandon. Holding his rapt gaze, she smiled, sensuous and powerful as never before. "Touch me, please."

GENDRA LAY SPREAD out beneath him like a goddess made flesh, like an ideal woman stepped out of his adolescent wet dreams to grace his decades-empty bed. Her hair spread in chestnut waves beneath her, catching gold and russet flames and framing her gilded skin where it showed, the sheer slip hinting at her figure with dips and shadows, so long and gracefully slender. And always, those magnetic eyes drew him, the violet cast of the blue reminding him of something long forgotten, a kind of nostalgia for something he'd lost without realizing it.

As magical as this interlude had been, the exquisite release she'd brought him to, he felt the weight of responsibility. She possessed such a trusting heart, her artlessness giving her a kind of naïve innocence that he raged that she had been treated carelessly by these other men. Gendra deserved to be treasured and worshiped, and it had fallen to him, with his rough and clumsy hands, to show her how it could be between lovers.

She deserved better than him. Except he had no intention of giving her up.

So he kissed her, lingeringly, the way she liked, measuring the hum of her body in response, her thigh silky smooth under his hand. Gradually he drew up her slip, taking his time, savoring the gradual change in texture to her inner thigh, where the skin became satin as shadows, plush in its concealment from the world. He'd never felt anything softer than the skin of a woman's thigh just below her sex, the satin of the jewel box framing the most precious of all places.

Gendra moved restlessly under his explorations, opening to him, the heat from her aroused sex radiating through the small distance, the slickness of her arousal inviting him. With a groan, he tangled his fingers in her silky curls, imagining them to be the same rich chestnut as her hair. He wanted to see her, savor every line and curve of her, but he could also understand how this would be easier, safer, the shrouding shadows and firelight like a comforting embrace. The shared dream.

With slow caresses, he eased his fingertips over her plump lips, the hiss of her breath against his lips encouraging him to do more. Parting them, the slick heat making it easy, he elicited a startled moan from her, the purring desire exactly what he hoped for. Lifting his head, he watched her face as he stroked her, learning the layers of her inner petals. Lucky for him that her expressions revealed everything.

He loved to look at her, eyes heavy lidded and sensually gleaming, the violet shaded indigo glimmering through the dark lace of her lashes, her gorgeous lips parted as if in mid-kiss.

He also needed to look at her, to be sure of her reactions to him. And so she would know that he was with her, that she was the center of his world. He might not be a young and vital lover, but he could give her all of his attention—something he'd have been too impetuous and selfish to offer when he possessed a youthful body.

In return, she gazed at him in wonder, fingers tangled in the hair at his temple, hips moving in a gentle rocking with his slow caresses. Every woman was different, he recalled, the memories of youth returning in a joyful flood, rather than tainted with the bitterness of what he'd lost. Like every painting demanded something different from him, every woman liked to be touched in a different way, in different places, at different speeds. He found Gendra's rhythm as if he'd been born to it, leading her through the intimate waltz as if they both heard the same music.

When she climaxed, her pleasure rippled through him as well, her cries of completion a song he'd been searching for. So he drank them in with his kisses, inhaling her and breathing his joy in her back in a living cycle. Tangling, combining, and recombining. Together, at least for now.

While we're alive, everything is possible.

SOME TIME LATER, Gendra shifted, turning into him, snuggling her charmingly cold nose into the nook of his throat and shoulder. His hand and arm had long since gone numb from him leaning on them, but that was a small price to pay for the luxury of having her so lusciously available to his touch. Taking advantage of her change in position, he tugged her slip back into place, then smoothed his free hand over the outside of it, up the back of her long, slim thigh, cupping her tight little bottom. All of her fit so neatly with him. It felt like fate, if he believed in such things.

He hadn't forgotten the age differential. In any other place and time, he could never have lured the nubile young Gendra to his bed. Well, he could have in his own youth, perhaps. He'd have done as Wim had, seducing the exotic and lovely shapeshifting visitor. With the arrogance of his station and youthful belief in his prowess—likely misplaced—he, too, might have charmed the Tala woman with the intent of seduction.

And he might have treated her just as badly, scarring her fragile and innocent heart in the same way as the others. The thought made him shudder for his past self.

And, in the wisdom of age, he'd have known better how to treat a gift like her, but he wouldn't have dared. No, he wouldn't have indulged himself. But here, in this place and time, in the timelessness of the Winter Isles, she could be his for a little while. And he could give her everything there was in him to give.

She pulled back slightly, opening her luminous eyes still heavy lidded with pleasure. "I know I'm not supposed to ask what you're thinking about, but you seem to be contemplating something important."

He caressed her soft cheek, tracing the line of her cheekbone from the delicate skin under her eye to her temple and along the shell of her ear. All of her so perfectly made. "Why aren't you supposed to ask me what I'm thinking?"

She shrugged a little. "Men don't like it?"

"Only men who have no thoughts in their heads don't like it. They're ashamed to admit their empty-headedness."

Giggling, she stroked a hand over his shoulder. "You could

never be that man. Your head is so full of thoughts, it's a wonder you keep it upright."

He let his head loll on his neck, as if too heavy to keep up any longer, dropping his hand and letting his head thump into the pillow. A good excuse to change position. As a bonus, it encouraged the laughing Gendra to lever up to lean over him. He feathered a hand through her long locks, guiding them to drape over his skin in a silken tease. "I'm thinking…" he said slowly, "that I'm only wise enough to appreciate you now, when I'm too decrepit to treat you as you deserve—but that in my vigorous youth, I would've been too callow. It's a conundrum."

She smiled, softly and enigmatically, running fingertips along the delineations of his collarbones and chest. "Maybe it's fate that we met now. The will of the Three."

That echoed his thoughts too precisely for comfort. "But to what purpose? There's no sense in trapping you here with me."

"A good question," she mused. "But it's an interesting coincidence otherwise, that you alone of all on your ship fell through the rift to this place. And I alone of my group did the same. I feel connected to you, Isyn, as if we fit together. As if you are the one I've been looking for." She blushed, averting her eyes. "I know that's a lot to say and far too soon, but I feel like it's important."

His heart squeezing so hard he almost couldn't breathe, he took her hand, lacing her fingers with his. "It is too soon," he agreed, tightening his grip when she would've pulled away in embarrassment. "But I feel the same. I'd never tell you this otherwise, but I'm totally and completely in love with you, Briar Rose. I have been since the moment you first spoke in my mind."

Her face crumpled, eyes luminous with tears, and for a heart-struck moment, he feared he'd royally fucked up by imposing an old man's sentimentality on her. "I'm sorry," he hastened to say. "I don't want you to feel pressured by—"

She stopped him with a kiss, deep and full of longing. "Never apologize for that," she whispered when she broke the kiss, cupping his cheek. "For loving me or for saying so. Because I am head over heels in love with you, Isyn. I fell in love when you caught me in your net, and I keep falling in love with you. Every new thing I learn about you makes me love you even more. You are the one for me."

"Well, if I'm not, I won't live all that much longer," he joked. "So I won't take up too much of your time, and you can find someone else."

"Don't *say* that," she told him fiercely, a predatory fire in her eyes. "You'd better plan to live a very long time, because there will never be anyone else for me."

"Don't *you* say that," he pleaded, aghast at what he'd done to her. "You have a long life ahead of you."

"In the Winter Isles, among the folk?" She tsked. "Not much to look forward to."

"Your friends will rescue you." They had to. "They have Falada to guide them. They'll find you, eventually."

She scoffed lightly, giving him a rueful smile. "It's the 'eventually' that worries me. They haven't shown up yet, and it's been at least an hour there by my measure. That means they weren't able to follow immediately. It could take them days or weeks to track me, which means years and decades here."

Years and decades in which he might be long since committed to burial beneath the ice of the arctic sea, food for the fishes. "Then we need to escape."

She cocked her head, curious, cautious, but not arguing. "What are you thinking?"

"I don't know," he confessed. "But we know those portals are the way out. They continue to exist. We both came through the one in the ocean, at vastly different times. It must still be there."

"I never found it." She was considering the idea, though.

"Did you always remember to look, though?" He remembered her conversation when she was the orca, nothing near as sharp as her mind was now.

"Not always," she admitted. "I was cold and tired—and injured by that harpoon."

"I'm sorry about that."

"Don't be. Saving my life more than made up for it." She looked thoughtful. "How did you force me to shapeshift back to human form anyway?"

"I wove magic into the net. Remember the old fairy tales where the fisherman uses a magic net to catch a mermaid wife?" He ran a hand down her arm, love for her blossoming inside so he felt twenty again. "I thought, why not try? So I netted me a magical shapeshifter and lured her into my bed."

Her lips curved in a generous, sensual smile, and she leaned down to kiss him. He'd never tire of kissing her, of sinking into her floral scent, savoring the slide of her skin against his. "And now you've captured me," she purred. "Do you have my sealskin hidden under the bed so you can keep me with you always?"

He shuddered at that. "Those stories are kind of horrible, now that I think about it."

"True. But they gave you the necessary key. You were able to trigger my shapeshifting when I couldn't. There's precedence for that, other magics that have controlled shapeshifting externally. There has to be a reason that shapeshifting doesn't work in the alter-realms. We've visited three of them—four, counting this one—and that's a consistent element of all of them."

"Because this intelligence you spoke of controls that magic somehow?"

Her eyes darkened, nearly black in the low light of the dying fire. He should get up and put more logs on, but he felt too lax and lazy, snuggled with his enchanting lover under the furs. And his leg barely throbbed, he realized, the chronic ache that had plagued him having ebbed somewhat. The eroding pain would no doubt return in the morning, but for the moment he'd relish the sweet release.

"The intelligence uses magic of its own," she mused, "taking on various forms, maybe controlling the rifts and travel between realms. The rules of magic change in the alter-realms in other ways, some kinds suppressed, others enhanced. Were you this powerful of a mage before you arrived in the Winter Isles? It seems like you said before that you weren't."

"Exactly. I had some magic. Enough that I could see Falada

and communicate with her after a fashion. Small things, visions, an affinity for knowing the weather. A fortunate quality of having sunshine when I wanted fair days." He grinned at the memory, a wide smile she returned. "I was very popular for picnics and excursions to the beach. But nothing like what I can do here. My abilities have continued to grow over time, too."

"Interesting." She firmed her lips, thinking. "I'd love for you to consult with Stella and Lena. I'm putting another log on the fire."

"I can do that," he protested belatedly, moving to stop her.

"I'm already up." She gave him a saucy smile, stretching, the filmy slip falling around her long, lovely body, the sheer material catching on her rosy nipples. Unlike his impatient youthful self, he was fully willing to wait to see her fully naked, to draw out the anticipation in little hints and glimpses. Speaking of which, there was an enticing sight as she bent over to add logs to the fire, the slip clinging to her small, taut bottom, dipping into the cleft between. He'd love to lift her gown and expose that bottom and all the delights awaiting in that shadowy cleft, to run his hands over those smooth globes, perhaps gently bite her so she squealed and then subsided into those breathy moans…

"…anything like that. Isyn?"

"Hmm?" He realized she'd asked him a question that had not made it to his brain.

She put her hands on her hips, shaking back her long hair and frowning. "You're tired. I think you're falling asleep."

"On the contrary." He held out a hand to her so she'd

come back to bed. "I was distracted by my beautiful lover. The sight of your gorgeous bottom made me momentarily senseless."

Taking his hand, she squeezed it, then climbed over him to snuggle back into her spot. The place at his side that should be forever hers. "That's very sweet of you to say, but you don't have to flatter me."

"It's not flattery if it's a simple observation," he noted, kissing the tip of her nose. "What were you asking me?"

"I was saying that I wonder what you could do with access to the Star of Annfwn, and if you've ever used a focusing artifact like that?"

"The Star of Annfwn?" he echoed. He'd been distracted indeed not to hear her first mention of the famous jewel. "Stella has the Star?" At Gendra's confirming nod, he whistled long and low. "So Queen Andromeda has officially made her niece heir of Annfwn."

"I wouldn't say officially, as no one but us knows that Nilly has it. Andi thought we'd need it on this mission. And we have. It's been useful for Stella to control the rifts. Since you can focus your magic with objects also, like making the net, I'm wondering if you could do something similar to locate and open the rifts."

"Deep in the freezing water."

"Well, there are logistics to consider."

"Like whether this decrepit human would drown or freeze first."

"If we worked fast, we could avoid either eventuality."

"Allowing me to survive to freeze or drown on the other

side of the rift."

"It's not nearly as cold there, and if we can nail down the logistics, then you could survive the other side as well."

"You're relentlessly optimistic."

"An excellent balance for your unrelenting gloom."

He laughed, pulling her under him for a long, deep kiss. She tasted of flowers, too, of sunshine and life. No matter what plan they came up with, it would at least get her home, and that was all that mattered. "Am I that bad?"

"You have good reason," she replied, confirming it without saying so.

"I resolve to do better." Skimming his hand over her slip, he cupped that bottom he'd been admiring. "Things have been looking up lately."

She sighed, pressing close to him. "You really should sleep."

"So should you," he agreed reluctantly. He had to remind himself she was still recovering, though she was healing at a remarkable rate. Something to do with her inherent magic, an idea that niggled at him, so he set it carefully aside to allow that seed to sprout and bear fruit.

"But this is nice," she purred, settling into a comfortable sleeping position.

"This is more than nice."

"Yes," she agreed sleepily. "This is everything."

Yes, *she* was everything. As long as they were alive.

~ 17 ~

"IT'S MUCH EASIER to get up in the morning when you live in a tropical paradise," Gendra observed, eyeing him from the pile of furs almost completely covering her in the bed he'd reluctantly forsaken. But the fire was catching now, chasing the chill that had settled in while they slept.

He chuckled, oddly enough feeling better than he had in years, even before the leg break. "I can only imagine," he replied wryly.

"When you come to Annfwn with me, you'll discover for yourself."

"We're not going anywhere if you refuse to get out of bed," he noted. With the brown furs nearly the same color as the spill of her hair, and only one baleful blue eye showing in the pale morning light, she reminded him of a wild creature gazing from the shadows of the forest. He suddenly and urgently wanted to survive to see her shapeshift into some of her many forms. All of them remarkable. All quintessentially her. "You're still magic," he said, the seed he'd slept on having sprouted.

"Magically determined never to leave this bed?" she replied doubtfully, then wormed a hand out to waggle her fingers at him. "Come back here and keep me warm."

"Absolutely not." He sat stiffly on the stool and began levering himself into his leather pants.

"Mean." She pushed the covers back enough to demonstrate her pout.

Oh, how he'd love to kiss those sultry lips into a smile—or to panting pleas. "If I get back into bed with my tempting lover," he explained, determinedly tucking his rigid cock away, "we won't leave it again for hours."

"You say that like it's a bad thing."

"It wouldn't get us any closer to finding a rift so we can escape. And that is the focus of our day."

"Fine," she huffed, pushing back the covers. She caught him looking and stretched her arms over her head, smiling in sultry invitation. "There's time to change your mind."

Suppressing a groan, he firmly tore his gaze away and snagged his shirt. "If you don't get out of bed on your own, Briar Rose, I'll wake you by dumping you in this now considerably chilly bathwater."

She sat up with an outraged squeak. "You would not!"

"Traditional treatment for witches and temptresses," he replied, shaking his head sadly.

"I am neither." Throwing the covers back fully, she dangled her long, lovely legs over the side of the bed and pushed her tangled mass of hair away from her face. "Ugh. Mother talked about this when she couldn't shapeshift, that one of the things she missed most was being able to just shift clean with her hair combed."

"An enviable trick," he agreed, hobbling over to retrieve

his comb and tossing it to her. "For now, you'll have to do it like us lesser humans."

"You'd think a mage could make me a magic hairbrush," she called after him as he headed out the door to brave the freezing privy.

When he returned, she'd dressed in her gown and had woven her hair into a single long braid down her back. She looked as fresh and lovely as a spring morning after a soft rain, a nostalgia that hit him hard and vividly. He'd love to lay her down in a meadow and make love to her on a bed of new blossoms.

"What did you mean," she asked without preamble, and startling him from his romantic fantasy, "when you said I'm still magic?"

His practical woman. "Breakfast is on its way," he said. "Meanwhile, some chaife to tide you over."

"Thank you!" She pounced on the mug he held out. "Where's yours?"

"It's coming. I couldn't carry two at once."

She came to him, laying a hand on his cheek and bestowing a sweet, lingering kiss on him, one that tasted of cinnamon laced with honeysuckle. "You are a wonderful man, Isyn," she murmured.

"Because I brought you chaife? This bodes well for our future together if that's all it takes to make you happy," he teased, but she didn't laugh.

"You're thoughtful, and you put my needs ahead of your own. Most men that I've met don't do that."

"Then you've been meeting the wrong men."

"Don't I know it." Then she flashed a smile, patting his cheek and moving away. "Also, it makes me very happy that you're talking about us having a future together. You can keep doing that."

He had, hadn't he? Hmm. "How's your head feeling?"

Pausing, she looked surprised, lifting a hand to prod the spot. "It feels fine," she answered with some surprise. "I'd actually forgotten about it."

He nodded, theory confirmed. "That's part of why I mean you're still magic. You might not be able to shapeshift out of human form, but you're healing much faster than any human could. Also, you pointed out to me yesterday that shapeshifters have sharper senses and unusual strength—and you still have those things."

She gazed back at him with wide-eyed amazement. "You're absolutely right. Why didn't that occur to me?"

He shrugged, opening the door for a parade of folk bearing food. No Jasperina, who was likely unhappy with him. "You're accustomed to being spectacularly gifted, so you don't realize how inherently magical you are, just by being."

She didn't reply, so he glanced over at her. Her blue eyes were luminous with unshed tears as she stared at him, an odd expression on her face. "What's wrong?" He went to her and pulled her into a one-armed embrace. "What did I say?"

"You're just so wonderful," she whispered, rubbing her cheek against his. "No one has ever said such nice things to me."

"Apparently they're all idiots, then," he said, stroking the smooth coils of her braid and tugging it lightly so she'd turn her head to meet his seeking kiss. "Let's eat and plot how we can combine your magic and mine to get us back home." Or, at least to get her back home, which he'd do if it killed him. Which it very well might.

"I'M REALLY NOT sure how far I swam before I found the fishing hole," Gendra said, not for the first time, chewing on her lip as she worried, her cheeks pink from the wind. He'd found a shadow-fox fur hat for her, the white fur framing her chestnut hair and oval face charmingly. With a hint of blue at the base—the shadowy undertone that gave the shadow fox its name—it brought out her startlingly deep-blue eyes. Isyn felt himself tumble a little more in love every time he looked at her.

The folk were pulling them along in the sled, happy to be going fishing. Isyn hadn't mentioned it to Gendra, but he'd heavily implied to the folk that they might be able to land the orca today. "I know," he replied patiently, "but it's a place to start. And it's the best excuse to get the folk to bring us out here without making them suspicious."

"What will we do if this fishing hole is too far from the rift, though?"

"I'll think up a reason for us to create a new one. The ice over the old one is thinner is all, which makes chopping through easier, but we make new fishing holes all the time."

She nodded, gaze fixed on the distance. "I really wish I'd

paid attention to the location of the rift I came through. It couldn't have been far from that fishing hole. I ran into the net so soon. It was unforgivably careless of me."

"Understandable," he corrected. "You were lost and disoriented."

"And panicking with that net around me." Her face set into chill lines.

He had his arm around her already, so he squeezed her shoulders, tucking the fur blanket more snugly over her lap, as if that could somehow keep her safe. "I can't imagine how terrifying that was."

"Well, the whale brain helped," she replied philosophically. "Animals don't worry about the future as much as we do. The needs are more immediate, with no dread for the potential consequences. There's a restfulness in that."

"Something I could stand to learn," he reflected, studying her lovely profile, the play of color in her face, roses, winter white, chestnut, and deepest ocean blue. "Would you let me draw you?"

She glanced at him, startled. "What does that have to do with fishing holes, searching for rifts, or whale brains?"

"Nothing at all," he admitted. "You're just distractingly beautiful. I would paint you, but we have no paints here. I could scrounge up something to draw you with, however."

"I'd like that," she replied shyly. "What inspired the painting of yours I saw back at Castle Marcellum? It reminded me of shapeshifters, but you said you haven't known any but me."

"A dream I had." A strand of glossy brown hair had escaped her hat and braid to whip against her cheek, and he tucked it away for her. "Maybe it was a dream about you."

"I wish I'd known to dream about you."

"I don't, for surely it would've been a nightmare."

"Isyn, I want you to know that even if we can't find a way home, I'll be happy here with you. I can get used to eternal winter and eating nothing but fish, as long as I can be with you."

"I won't live forever, though," he cautioned her, ignoring the sweet warmth her words stirred in him. "Even if this leg doesn't kill me, I'm old and—"

"You're not *that* old," she interrupted stubbornly.

"I'm on the downhill side of my life," he insisted.

"That sounds even worse."

"It doesn't make it less true. Gendra, we have to be realistic here. If you have a chance to get home, then I want you to take it."

"I'm not leaving without you." She stared off across the ice again, jaw set in obstinate determination. He loved her for it. He despaired because of it.

"I can't bear to think of you living here among the folk, all alone, for the rest of your life, with no human companionship. It's not a fate I'd wish on my worst enemy, much less the most precious person in the world to me."

She looked at him then, pink lips parted, indigo eyes full of emotion. "How can you ask me to leave you when you say things that make me love you even more?"

He leaned in and kissed her. Her lips were cold with heat beneath, honeysuckle blooming under the snow. "I'm asking because you love me, and because I love you. Because all that matters to me is that you go on to live a long and happy life."

"There's nothing for me without you," she whispered, on the verge of tears again.

He kissed her again. "There's everything."

THEY SPENT A cold and fruitless day at the fishing hole. Well, not entirely fruitless, as the folk brought up a good haul of fish. Not nearly as bountiful, however, as the one when Gendra had chased deep-sea fish into their nets. The foreman and Jasperina glumly agreed that the orca must be gone. Probably dead and no good to anyone.

Isyn kept Gendra as close as possible.

"So, tomorrow we look elsewhere?" she asked as they made it back to his room. She was walking at a solicitous pace, eyeing his halting steps but not asking about the leg. A day on the ice had undone all of her healing work from the night before, the thing aching as if the bone itself had frozen solid. It was likely his imagination, but now that he knew the bone had been set incorrectly, he fancied that he could feel the splintered pieces grinding unevenly together. Not a pleasant image.

"Yes. I have some idea of where I came through, so I've already suggested to the folk that we try fishing tomorrow in that area. They're all too young to remember that's where I was pulled out of the ocean, so they won't be suspicious." Not *too* suspicious, anyway. The folk had already noted the changes in his behavior, and the folk didn't like change. Having Gendra among them was pushing things already. Having him change routine only worsened their unease.

She handed him a mug of hot fish broth. "Drink this. You look pale."

"I *am* pale," he replied irritably. "By nature, and it comes of not seeing the sun for fifty years."

"Cranky, too," she observed equably. "How much pain are you in?"

"It's nothing for you to concern yourself with."

"A lot," she decided. "You're having a hot bath." Ignoring his protest, she opened the door to have a one-sided hand-waving conversation with the folk bringing up firewood. "It's not good for you to be out on the ice all day," she informed him on her return.

"It's for a good cause." The only cause.

"It makes no sense to find the rift if it kills you."

"We agreed that getting you home takes highest priority."

"No—you made a unilateral decision and are attempting to shove it down my throat."

He could almost imagine a lashing tail to accompany her sharp tone. "And here I thought you were so sweet," he grumbled.

"I can't imagine what gave you that massive misconception." She strode over and laid a hand on his forehead before he could duck her touch. "You have a fever. Mild but definite."

"Then a hot bath is the worst thing for me," he reasoned.

"Wrong. How many stubborn mossbacks have *you* nursed through exposure and other injuries resulting from hard mountain living? None, I'm betting, Your Highness."

She had him there. Jasperina arrived with a parade of other folk carrying buckets of hot water to fill the big tub yet again, giving him a long side-eye which she slid onto Gendra with marked distaste. Gendra, busy with assembling her supplies and warming the oil, carried on obliviously. But Isyn took the look for the warning it was—and fought the deep alarm it stirred in him.

If he died while Gendra was still trapped here, she wouldn't fare well with the folk. They'd likely decide to eat her rather than have the burden of serving her. Literally. She had no magery to improve their lives, so they'd fill their bellies with her instead. Even with her supernatural strength, she'd be no match for their numbers if they decided to overpower her. Also, she still had to sleep sometimes, and she wouldn't have him to magically ward the room.

The hot bath did feel good, he had to admit, despite the high price in the goodwill of the folk, and he sank into it with a sigh of pained delight as the heat penetrated his chilled bones. Gendra settled on the stool behind him. "Tonight I'm going to wash your hair," she informed him.

"So the Tala *do* care about hair things?" he asked, trying to sound less cranky.

"The Tala traditionally wear their hair long and loose, so yes, I suppose we do," she mused. "But mostly I think you'll feel better for it. More yourself. Dunk."

He had let many trappings of civilization fall away in his half-existence. So he obediently dunked, gasping a little as he rose again at the shock of heat over his scalp. Gendra set to scrubbing his scalp, another sheer pleasure that sent waves of relaxation all through him.

"Isyn?" she asked very quietly. "Have you set your wards in place?"

He opened his eyes in some surprise. "I didn't know you knew I was doing that. Yes, I have."

"I've been around magic workers. I might be a shapeshifter, not a sorceress, but I can recognize magic when I smell it."

He wondered if she realized that not everyone could. Even among shapeshifters, he doubted that was a common skill. "I thought some Tala are wizards and magicians."

"True," she admitted. "My mother can work some spells, but I can't. Too much mossback in me. I'm lucky I can even shapeshift."

"And yet you're sensitive to magic." He felt her shrug through her hands, the restless unhappiness in it that she revealed only when dwelling on her past, so he let it go. "Why did you ask about the wards?"

"I wanted to ask—why are you afraid of the folk?"

Ah. And there it was. He should've known she'd pick up on the many clues. Probably she'd noticed before now but had waited to ask. "Remember how you noted that it sounded like I was as much captive as king?"

"Yes." She drew out the word enough that it hissed with her displeasure. A tigress ready to defend him.

"There's a great deal of truth to it. When the folk pulled me from the water, they were planning to..." No sense protecting her from the ugly truth. "Kill and eat me."

Her hands stilled on his scalp. A bare pause, but noticeable.

"Cannibalism is a vile practice."

"The folk aren't human, so is it really cannibalism?" he returned lightly.

"Then whatever word we should have for killing and eating a thinking being." Her tight voice reminded him that the folk would've been happy to eat her orca self, too. "Rinse, please."

Did the more polite request indicate that she was more relaxed or more rattled? Could be both, he supposed. He dunked to rinse his soapy hair, leaning forward so she could wring out the sopping mass of it before draping it over the rim of the tub. "Clearly you survived," she commented neutrally, setting to work with the comb. "What happened?"

"I was fighting them off—losing badly, as they had the numbers and I was half drowned—when, in a desperation move, I tried to charm them as I would an animal. That's really my mother's gift, but I have a little of it. Well, the folk recognized the magic immediately and took me captive instead. It was a long few months there while I tried to find magic tricks useful enough to keep them from deciding I'd be more useful as dinner."

"I'm sorry," she said quietly. "How awful for you."

It had been awful. The grinding low-key terror and grueling loneliness enough to bring him to despair any number of times. "But I was, more useful, that is. My magery has provided more meals over the long term than a single week of fine dining."

"Not funny, Isyn."

Oh well, he'd tried. "In return, they taught me how to

survive here. Everything I know I owe to them, so I suppose the debt is mutual. My point is, however, that they won't want to let me go."

He felt her nod thoughtfully. "King of all you survey—only so long as you serve the will of the people," she observed.

"Not unlike every monarch, truly."

"Only the consequences are a bit more dire. Are you ready to get out?"

He was, so he lifted himself from the tub, taking the staff to lean on and drying himself as she tested the temperature of her massage oil. "Gendra," he said, waiting for her to look up. She did, indigo eyes sober. "If something happens to me…"

"Then I'm likely to become supper," she supplied. "And unlike you, I don't have enough meat on me to even feed them for a week."

"I feel like it's my turn to tell you it's not funny."

"Yes, well—gallows humor and all." Her lashes dropped as her gazed stroked over him. "On a happier note, I'd like to take a moment to tell you how very beautiful you are."

He glanced at his nakedness, a bit taken aback. In the seriousness of the conversation and his comfort at being alone with her, he'd forgotten. "Scarred, bent, and broken," he corrected.

"Scarred, yes," she breathed, coming to him and sliding oil-warmed hands up his back and pressing herself against him, his body rousing to her proximity. "Battered and with the odd bone bent out of shape, sure. But never broken." She kissed him, a delight that he only had to turn his head slightly to meet her lips. "Stalwart, enduring, stunning. I love you, Isyn."

"And I love you," he whispered against her lips, feeling them curve into a smile.

"And that is the most remarkable thing of all," she marveled, then tugged a lock of his hair. "You should lie down, but I didn't think about your hair getting the bed wet when I decided to wash it."

"Aha. Fate is working in my favor. I'll sit by the fire so I can let it dry while I draw you."

She blushed, wrinkling her nose charmingly. "I thought you didn't have supplies."

"I asked one of the folk to find me some possibilities." He gestured to the pile of scraped bark and charcoal bits he'd noted when they returned. "I won't be able to capture all the colors of you, but I can at least come close."

With both hands, he combed his fingers through the silken mass of her hair, turning her face from side to side to observe the play of candle and firelight on the strong bones, deciding how he'd draw them so her earnest, loving, and practical nature would shine through. Her eyes stayed fixed on his as he turned her head. There was guardedness in her, too, like a cat deciding whether to claw or purr. "Briar Rose," he murmured. "Would you indulge me in this? I want to have at least a drawing of you, so I can remember."

The wariness turned to irritated exasperation. "I'm not doing anything for you as long as you're talking like I'd ever leave you behind."

He held up his hands in grinning surrender. "Deal."

She huffed out a breath. "That was not meant as part of a negotiation."

"Too late," he replied cheerfully, tucking the staff in the crook of his arm so he could pull on his pants. "Turn around," he told her, once he was covered enough that his erection wouldn't be bouncing in the wind.

"Why?"

"So I can undress you." He reached for her laces.

She put her hands over his. "You didn't say anything about drawing me naked."

"Didn't I?" he asked innocently. "I thought that was a given."

"No, Isyn. That is *not* a given."

Relenting, he cupped her face in his hands, studying the depths of her eyes. "You don't have to. I didn't mean for you to feel pushed into something."

Something soft and shy moved in those lustrous eyes. "You're not. I'm just... I'm—I don't know *what* I am."

Wounded, was what she was. Isyn kissed her, lingering over it until she melted under his touch. "I'll draw you in your gown, then."

She wrapped her fingers around his wrists as he moved to pull away. "No," she whispered. "I want this. No more waiting and wondering." Working efficiently, she loosened the laces at the front of her gown, then turned her back, lifting her hair so he could get the rest. "It's much easier," she commented, nerves in her voice and posture, "when I can shapeshift. I can just shift to another form and come back naked."

"What becomes of your clothing then?"

"I can kind of cache my clothes, and accessories, too. Anything I'm wearing when I shift, within reason. In fact, I have quite a few gowns, fighting leathers, and so forth saved. It would be nice to access them." The gown fell in a puddle at her feet, and she stood in only the sheer slip she'd been wearing to sleep in.

"I'd wondered how you went from wearing soaked oilskin to a dry fur-lined cloak."

"I'm glad I had the wit to do so, in my addled state." She turned, holding her hands over her thinly clad breasts, self-conscious in a way she hadn't been before.

He smoothed his hands down her lovely, long body, shaping the lean curves through the silky material, savoring and soothing her. "I could draw you like this," he murmured, easing her closer for a kiss. She opened for him, softly, trustingly.

"No, I'm being silly," she whispered against his lips. "I know I have no reason to be shy. I just... You should know that I'm not voluptuous. I mean, I'm sure you figured that out already. I just hope you won't be too disappointed. Even if I could still shapeshift, I can't change my human body. We are what we're born with and grow into."

Fuck that Henk, he thought viciously. "Briar Rose, you are a miracle. You are perfectly you."

She smiled tremulously, but came to a decision, swiftly untying the laces at the neckline of her slip and swiping it off her shoulders to follow the gown. He was too close to get a good look at her, so he swept a hand down her long elegant back, savoring the expanse of satin skin, the sweet dip of her spine, holding her gaze and trying to read the glimmer in her eyes. Praying to the capricious spirits of the Isles that he'd find the right words. He didn't know *what* to say, so he simply asked the question burning in his mind.

"May I look at you?" he whispered.

~ 18 ~

WITH ISYN'S DEEP forest gaze burning hot into hers, even without him looking at her unclothed body, Gen felt more than naked. She felt as if she'd peeled off her very skin, leaving herself exposed, vulnerable, rawly open to even a hint of dissatisfaction in his eyes. All she seemed to be able to think about were Henk's offhand comments about her lack of womanly curves, saying how he'd thought a shapeshifter would be able to make her own body more appealing. How wasn't that what every woman wanted, after all, especially if she was the sort apt to take lovers freely. When she'd started to explain that shapeshifting didn't work that way, he'd been so clearly disinterested that she'd stopped talking.

Even the much kinder Wim had remarked on her small breasts. *Tiny, but delicious.* Like she was a dessert served in miserly portions. When Wim had commented, it had been irritating but little more than that. Now, however... If Isyn showed similar, even gentle scorn, it might break her. This was the agonizing side of loving so swiftly and deeply. She trusted Isyn with her heart, but she was so afraid that he'd be disappointed, no matter what he claimed.

"May I look at you?" he whispered.

She nodded, mostly because she was determined to see this through. *Get it over with.* Isyn wanted to look on her naked body, to draw her, and likely make love to her after—and she would give him that and more. If she couldn't enjoy sex with this man she loved more than her own life, especially in these new days of the bloom of first discovery, then... well, then she would know, yes? And once she knew, then she could decide how to proceed. Reconnaissance first, then strategy. That had always been her father's advice—much as he'd cringe knowing how she planned to apply it.

Besides, if she ever got home and had to recount this tale, which her friends would drag out of her with the relentless determination of a mule team, Zeph would never let her live it down if Gen had to admit she chickened out. Also, if she didn't look good to a man who hadn't seen a woman in fifty years, then she needed to rethink some things. Forget dragon form—maybe she did need to figure out how to shapeshift her own body. Or give up men completely.

That actually sounded like a decent option, as she couldn't imagine being with anyone but Isyn like this.

So, she stepped back, far enough for Isyn to see all of her, dropping her hands and straightening her shoulders to show off what little she had to best advantage, resisting the urge to pull her veil of hair around her. *No hiding.*

She couldn't bear to see his face, to witness a crease of disenchantment, and she thought he'd be kind enough not to comment, so she looked past him at the featureless stone wall, what she hoped was a welcoming smile pasted on her lips. The moment stretched on, however, and she shifted, uncomfortable, feeling on the verge of tears. Maybe this had been a terrible idea.

"My Briar Rose..." Isyn murmured. "You take my breath away. I have no words for the glory of your beauty. I *must* draw you."

She risked a glance at his face, to check for lies or flattery, but his rapt expression told her everything she needed to know. With his wet hair darkened and hanging heavy, it set off the paleness of his skin, the glitter of his eyes—hopefully not fever—and caught the firelight with ivory gleams on the drying wisps. He studied her, gaze traveling slowly over her naked limbs, absorbed as if memorizing every line.

"Would you turn around for me?" he asked softly, gaze still on her body.

She did, turning a slow circle, finding she liked the sensation of his close regard.

"So beautiful," he murmured, almost as if to himself, which felt even more honest. "Again, but lift your hair?"

Relaxing, warmed by his obvious admiration, perhaps feeling a little bit beautiful and sensual, she slowly piled her long tresses high on her head, pivoting slowly for him as she did.

"Oh, yes," he breathed. "Now lie on the bed," he instructed with more confidence, a fervor of excitement in his voice.

Oddly thrilled by the intimacy of the moment, no longer anxious, but filled with a welcome sensual languor, she did as he urged, going to the bed and throwing back the soft furs, stretching herself out. Isyn fetched his drawing supplies with alacrity, moving more easily in his excitement and with his attention focused elsewhere, dragging the stool into place and setting his things down. Then he came to her, hands hovering over her like hummingbirds, contained energy buzzing.

"May I?" he asked hoarsely.

She nodded, words somehow beyond her.

"On your side, please. Like this." He adjusted her deftly, almost impersonally—if not for the burning desire in his eyes. Tucking one of her arms under her head so she pillowed her cheek on her bent elbow, he draped her other arm just below her breasts. Then he extended the leg she lay on, drawing up the other so her bent knee rested on the bed in front of her groin. Grunting with satisfaction, he began arranging her hair, draping long locks of it to trail over and around her naked limbs. She marveled at the intent, absorbed expression on his face, how he seemed at peace in a way he hadn't been since she met him. How badly she wanted him to be pleased with her. How urgently she wanted him to keep touching her.

"Are you comfortable?" he asked.

"Yes, so much that I could fall asleep like this."

"Please don't. I need you to be looking at me, just as you are right now, thinking whatever it is you're thinking."

"All right." She flushed a little, shivering as he ran a hand over the round of her hip. When he caressed her that way, she felt she actually *had* curves.

"Are you cold?"

"Not too much."

He went and added a few logs to the fire, glanced back at her, then added another. Smiling wickedly, he lowered himself to the stool and shook back his hair. "All the better to see you," he teased. "Now don't move."

She found she didn't mind his intent gaze after a while, relaxing under the intensity of his artist's eye, imagining the strokes of the charcoal against the scraped bark were his hands and mouth tracing the lines of her body. He worked swiftly, a light in his face that gave a hint of how he must have been before time and trials wore him down into sorrow. Time ticked slowly by, the touch of his eyes like a palpable caress, the scratch of charcoal a touch she could nearly feel against her skin, heating and arousing. Need bloomed in her, hot and demanding, and she had to fight to remain still, arousal heating and slicking her sex so she wanted to restlessly rub her thighs together. To distract herself, she reviewed the memory of Isyn touching her there the night before, his deft and clever fingers so intimate and knowing, playing her body with the same artistry as he displayed in his intent study of her.

"You can move now," he said, startling her out of her reverie.

Relieved to be able to release some of her internal tension in movement, she stretched, long and languid—trembling at how his eyes followed along.

"Do you want to see how I see you?" he asked quietly.

Did she? She didn't know. "If you'd like to show me," she temporized. "I'm sure the drawing is wonderful."

He breathed a laugh, shaking his head. "Less flattering my pride and more truth, please."

It would be cowardice not to look. "All right."

He levered himself to his feet, gesturing for her to stay where she was. "It's funny—I'm beginning to think you say 'all right' when you're not convinced but want to please me."

That was probably not incorrect—and not an easy observation to swallow. Gen knew she liked to please people. Her mother was forever chiding her for it. *Don't worry about what other people want. What do you want?*

Isyn lowered himself to sit on the bed beside her, holding the drawing. She glanced at it nervously. "Do you trust me?"

"I do," she answered, realizing she meant it.

"Then look." He handed her the drawing.

She stared at the image, recognizing herself and yet not comprehending how he could see her this way. That was her body, certainly, long and skinny, but her knobby shoulders and elbows had somehow been rendered to be sylphlike, her small breasts made delicately lovely, the curve of her hips and gangly legs almost elegant. And her eyes... they dominated her face, lushly lashed and full of simmering knowledge. He'd also given a savage glint to her eyes that was oddly familiar, though she'd never seen it in the mirror. With a start of wonder, she placed that look: Her mother had it, especially when she hadn't gotten to shift as much as she wanted to, as if the wilderness gleamed in her eyes, looking to emerge and prowl by its wild lonesome.

"I'm not sure I got the eyes right," Isyn murmured, studying them as she returned her gaze to his. "I suspect I could spend a lifetime trying to capture them." He feathered fingertips over her cheek, smoky with the scent of charcoal. "I'd wish for blue pigment, but I doubt that exact shade of indigo exists anywhere but here." Tracing the line of her brow, he smiled, almost sadly. "Not that I have a lifetime to spend."

She caught his hand, their fingers lacing together. "None of us knows if we'll live past the next day, past the next hour or minute. You don't need a lifetime. You have life right now, which means everything is possible."

"A good thing to remember, my earnest optimist." He lowered his head, kissing her gently, jumping when she gasped. "Did I hurt you?"

"No." Releasing his hand, she tunneled hers into his still slightly damp hair, drawing him down and coaxing him into hotter, more passionate kisses. She gasped as his big, rough hand cupped her bare breast, her nipples, already taut with arousal, tightening almost painfully, and his glance flicked up to her face.

"No?"

"Yes," she said firmly. "It's just… intense."

"Intense," he murmured, easing her to lie on her back and propping himself on one elbow. His expression was reverent as he trailed his fingers around and over her breasts, teasing her nipples lightly. She shivered from the billowing heat, not cold at all. "I'm trying very hard not to be jealous that my annoying little brother kissed you here first."

"Then you should erase his kisses with yours."

His brows lifted in a wicked arch, eyes sparkling lambent green. "What an excellent suggestion." And he bent his head, placing a kiss on each trembling nipple. He proceeded to lavish them with kisses, teasing and arousing, until she strained with need, pulling him to her. Groaning deep in his throat, he followed, the strain of bracing himself over her only part of the reason for the bunched tension in his shoulder and chest muscles as she ran her hands over them.

"Gendra," he murmured in gentle protest, "I don't want you to—"

"*I* want you to," she insisted. In a bold move that would likely shock her more staid self later, once she was away from the seductive shadows of the firelight and an artist-warrior's hands, she captured his hand and guided it down to the juncture of her thighs, spreading her legs and flattening his palm against her melting sex. "I want *you*," she added breathlessly.

He stroked his fingers lightly through her folds, and she shuddered so hard at the gripping need that she had to hold on to him. "You're so wet," he said hoarsely, curling his fingers into her so her hips rose in plaintive need.

"Because you've been teasing me all this time," she breathed, holding his gaze, feeling boldly sensual with this man who saw her as beautiful, who saw *her*. Perhaps more clearly than anyone ever had. "Every stroke of your drawing felt like your hands on my body. Touch me, Isyn. Touch me everywhere. I want all of it."

He slipped a finger inside her, eyes darkening as she moaned, pressing her sex against his palm. "Are you sure?"

"Yes," she said, too quickly, because he arched a dubious brow.

"I think I'll keep checking back on that," he mused, sitting up some so he could stroke his other hand down her straining body. "There's a great deal I can do to please you without going there."

"I want you inside me," she begged, not sure how to convince him.

"I *am* inside you." He pressed the finger filling her passage upward, the sensation extraordinary, making her gasp with the unexpected pleasure. "Feel me inside you," he purred, his face shadowed amid the fall of firelit ivory hair.

"That's not what I mean," she managed to say. "And you know it."

"Oh, I know it," he agreed too easily, smiling as he added his thumb to pleasure her from without as his finger pressed up from within, extracting a garbled cry from her as she convulsed. "I don't plan to disappoint you."

"Good," she nearly snarled, "because then I might have to kill you and eat you—and then what good would you be to me?"

Laughing a dark, sensual chuckle that accompanied a wicked smile, he added another finger, stretching her vulva with keen pressure. "I can't wait until I see you with actual claws. You're very tight, Briar Rose."

"I don't care." She dug her blunt human nails into his shoulders. "Please, Isyn."

"Patience," he murmured, dipping his head to capture her nipple in his mouth, making her arch in offering, working his fingers deeper inside her. "We're doing this slowly. No *getting it over with*." He nipped her taut and sensitized nipple with his teeth, extracting a sharp cry from her. "I'm not letting you push me into doing that to you." His mouth closed over her stinging nipple again, salving and stimulating, pulling more of her aching breast into his warm heat, making her squirm in mindless need.

"You wouldn't be," she whimpered.

"I know I wouldn't." Releasing her breast, he stared into her face, the shadows making him look dangerous, a predatory shimmer in him that weakened her knees, the vulnerability of having his hand intimately stroking her somehow delicious. "I see you, Gendra," he murmured. "I love you, Gendra. All of this is for you."

Never taking his eyes from hers, he curled his fingers inside her, her hips arching with the intensity of the core-deep ecstasy, only to meet the heel of his hand pressing down on her pearl of pleasure with acute, keen delight. With his free hand, he cupped her breast, lightly pinching her nipple between thumb and forefinger, and she thrashed under his tender, devious manipulation, feeling as if she might become un-moored without his strong arms to hold on to.

"Please," she sobbed.

"Yes," he murmured. "Let go, my magical rose. You can let go with me. I love you. I've got you."

She felt it, too, as if that golden net still wrapped around her, holding her safe from the hostile sea. He'd taken her captive, and she belonged to him as surely as if her skin remained in his possession, along with her heart, along with her body, which sang for him. "Isyn!" she screamed his name, holding on to him as she came apart, thoughts reeling in all directions, her sex plunging hard against his firm grip, her anchor in the black and stormy seas.

His mouth fastened onto hers, drinking in the mewling cries, his body hard on hers, pinning her and holding her through the convulsions. Then, even as she began to quiet, reaching to draw her scattered thoughts back from the depths they'd vanished to, he renewed the stroking, kissing his way down her neck.

She moaned, low and long. "I don't know if I can…"

"I know. Trust me." And he bit down at the juncture of her neck and shoulder, not hard, but firm—an unbelievably erotic sensation, as if lightning had struck, and she cried out, feeling her fluids gush over his hand. Isyn laughed, dark and delighted. "Those other men were fools."

Before she could ask what he meant, he was urging her to her knees, laying back so she straddled him. "Your pants," she said, trying to scoot back.

"Not yet." Grasping her hips, he moved her forward until she nearly met the stone wall.

"What are you…?" She choked out a gasp when he dragged his tongue through her slick folds.

"Feasting," he replied. "I advise you to hold on."

She had nothing but the stone wall, but her fingers found what purchase they could in the desperate pleasure he wreaked on her body. With his fingers again inside her and his devastatingly clever lips, tongue, and occasional teeth, he drove her wild, the climaxes coming one after another until they blurred into one. She thrashed and bucked in the frenzy of it, the rock-hard grip of his rough hands on her hips holding her ruthlessly in place as he feasted on her indeed. She pressed her cheek against the stones, the gritty caress of them on her tender nipples yet another tease.

At last, when she was wrung out, sobbing for breath, voice hoarse from screaming her pleasure, wilted and boneless, he sat up, carrying her with him as he pivoted to sit on the side of the bed, her straddling his lap so his erection pressed against her belly. Though he still wore his pants, the leather erotic against her nakedness, spreading her thighs wide, he'd undone the fastening at some point. He kissed her deeply, tasting of her and oddly like the sea and flowers, as she curled languidly around him. A kiss she'd remember for the rest of her life. His hands poured through her hair and over her skin, gripping her bottom to rock her against him, his cock hot and huge against her.

Then he broke the kiss and gazed into her face, searching her eyes. "Shall we stop here?"

The words took a moment to penetrate. "No. I want it all."

"You've had plenty."

"Not enough." She kissed him, drawing on those sensual lips. "I want all of you. Please, Isyn."

He chuckled, deep in his chest, holding her close against him. "I've discovered an odd quirk in myself." His hands tightened in her hair, his expression fierce in arousal. "I seem to love to hear you begging me."

"Please, Isyn," she whispered hoarsely, adding a whimper that made his cock spasm against her. "I'm begging you. I need you inside me." She rose up on her knees to take the pressure off his leg, bringing her sopping sex to hover over the head of his cock. "Please, Isyn, please…"

Transferring his grip to encircle her waist with one bracing arm, he used the other hand to position himself, the thick head of his cock pressing just inside her. "This?"

"Yes, please." She rained kisses on his upturned face, so

gorgeous with his lambent green eyes and ravenous expression.

He lowered her a bit, her body easily sliding over him, then stopping, holding her easily as she attempted to take more of him. "Like this?"

"More," she begged wildly. "More more more."

"Look at me, Gendra," he murmured, catching and holding her gaze. With both hands on her hips, he slowly lowered her, her body enclosing his with dreamy intensity. He filled her, stretching with a pleasure that became almost agonizing. She shuddered at the intimacy, his eyes marking it. "I've got you," he told her firmly. "I love you."

She almost wept with the keen immediacy of the moment, her heart and body thrumming in one need, a single, core knowing. She took him fully inside her, their bodies sealed together, their spirits intertwining, the sheer delight of their joining a delirious pleasure that simply hadn't been possible with anyone else.

His eyes flared green fire, face set in a rictus of arousal, his hips flexing into her, the penetration so deep she cried out, then pressed down. Gazes locked, they found their rhythm, rocking together, the shivers of impending orgasm gathering, drawing tight into her groin, her belly, her breasts and heart. He pressed the flat of his hand against her lower back, pressing her even tighter against him. "Gendra, I—"

"Let go," she urged, even as she held on tighter. "I've got you. I love you."

Throwing back his head, he released a guttural cry, hoarse as the howl of a wolf, his hands vising on her as he thrust repeatedly, deep into her core. And she rode the wild waves of his climax, her own need feeding off his until she burst, following after with her own higher melody of inarticulate desire. And love.

~ 19 ~

At some point in time, he regained his senses. Gradually his desire-fogged brain cleared, and he became aware of Gendra collapsed over him, their bodies still joined, her limbs tangled stickily with his. The fire had died down too much, so he needed to get up and put on more logs or she'd get chilled. He also needed to move his aching leg, awkwardly pinched between them.

He didn't move, fully intending to stay that way forever, if only his Briar Rose would remain in his arms. She stirred, murmuring something he couldn't make out, and nuzzling kisses under his ear that made his cock, still buried in her tight, velvet-hot sheath, stir to life. He should probably move. Really, he should.

He didn't.

But she did. Slowly sitting up, she kept his hardening cock inside her, her glorious hair falling in a gilded, tumbling cloak of rich brown silk around her slender golden body. Her perfectly shaped breasts stood out, her tight nipples reddened and mouthwatering. She pushed back her hair with one hand, giving him a slumberous smile, feline in its satisfaction, and she rocked her hips, making him gasp.

Setting both hands on his chest, she raked her soft, round nails over his skin, adding to the increasing build of tension as she lifted her hips and sank again, an ancient rhythm like the ocean distantly surging beneath the ice that held it captive. He lifted his hands to her breasts, marveling anew at how perfectly they fit into his palms. All of her, made exactly to fit him, mind, heart, and body. She arched into his touch, expression dreamy, nipples hard points in his palms, and she worked his body like a goddess come to claim him. He gave himself over to her, his personal goddess, the magical fish he'd pulled from the sea. He could die happy this way, ending his miserable existence drowning in the miracle of her love.

She arched her entire body, a slim golden bow of a woman, drawing back in a perfect curve from her narrow hips and concave belly, up the continuous line of her breast, throat, and jaw. The cry of pleasure she released sounded like the guttural purr of a big cat, and he threw himself up into her, filling her with his seed, wondering for the first time if they could make a child.

Through the wrenching orgasm, his emotions tossed wildly—horror at his utter carelessness that he hadn't thought of it before, agonizing hope that there might be life to come out of this sterile world; terror that he'd bring a child into it only for them to be condemned to a crushing fate of ice and loneliness; a sweet, heart-twisting wish that Gendra wouldn't be alone; an even more bitter wish that he wouldn't miss it all. Closing his eyes against the onslaught of visions, he finished, her body milking him of all he had to give.

She tapped a finger between his eyes, so he opened them,

finding her bending close, hair a fire-riddled veil all around them, eyes a smoky violet, lips curved in sensual satiation. "I suppose it's not practical for us to simply stay like this always, making love over and over," she murmured.

With a low laugh, he ran his hands up her long back, fingertips rippling over the delicate bones of her spine up to her neck. Clasping her there, he pulled her down for a long, rapturous kiss, then let her go. "I don't know that we'd freeze, exactly, but the room is getting decidedly chilly—and I know you wouldn't choose to be anything but practical."

She canted her head at him, eyes sparkling, her expression soft and mischievous. "I've discovered an odd quirk in myself. I seem to love being impractical, too, at least where you're concerned."

He flushed at the memory of confessing what her begging did to him—and at the even more vividly arousing image of her thrashing wildly against him, her salted-blossom flavor heady in his mouth, her silken body his to possess. He, impossibly, hardened inside her, and she cocked a sultry brow. "Again?" she purred.

"No." A third time so soon might truly kill him. "Give an old man a chance to rest."

She laughed, a melodious peal of sound, and clambered off of him, lifting her hair to perform an enchanting pirouette before letting it fall to veil her exquisite body again. "No old man could make me feel the way I feel now. Any more vigorous and I'd never walk again." She pointed a coquettish finger at him. "No, don't get up. I can handle the fire."

It was a joy to see her happy. Until this invisible sadness

had fallen away from her, he hadn't realized how much her sorrows had been weighing down what turned out to be an effervescent personality. "It's good to hear you laugh," he commented, easing his aching leg fully onto the bed and stretching it out. Ah yes—he'd be paying the price for acting like a young man in love. Though any price would be worth it.

"I laugh all the time." She had a puzzled frown as she returned to him, the fire crackling into greedy vigor, her hands full of washing cloths and her warmed oil.

"Not that laugh," he explained. "A fully happy laugh."

She began washing the residue of sex from his body, something he sort of regretted as he loved having her scent all over him. Still, she was determined, cleansing him and using the opportunity to discreetly check his injuries. He should've known she wouldn't skip treating him, and he smiled in vindication as she palmed warm oil and began working her magic hands into the exact spot where his hip felt the most strained.

"That's how we knew Stella had truly fallen in love with Jak," Gendra confided after a long enough silence—excepting his grunts of pain and groans of sighing release—that he'd lost track of the conversation. "She giggled at breakfast, the morning after they finally consummated the affair, and it was this sound…" She trailed off wistfully, her eyes rising to meet his. "We dubbed it the love giggle, and Jak took great pride in it, saying it was all for him."

He coiled a long lock of her hair around his finger. "You miss them."

"Yes." She let out a heavy sigh. "I mean, of course I miss

them, but I miss them now more than ever. I want you to meet them, and for them to meet you."

"Briar Rose...." he sighed. "We have to face that I likely can't ever leave this place."

"This again? I'm not facing any such dire, gloomy, and morose sort of pessimism."

He smiled despite himself. "I feel like the descriptors of my unsunny outlook are multiplying."

"As well they should." She paused in her ministrations, pinning him with a fierce indigo glare. "I'm not leaving you, Isyn. Either you're coming with me or I'm staying here with you."

"I want you to—"

"What?" she snapped, cutting him off, her fingers digging painfully into his muscles. "You want me to be the sort of person who abandons the man she loves? Because I can't be that. I might not be hero material—I know I can be dreadfully self-absorbed—but my parents are both heroic, with the greatest of hearts, and they raised me better than that. I won't change who I am, not even for you, Isyn, not even if you ask me to—because then I'd no longer be the person you fell in love with. At least, I hope you know who you fell in love with."

He stared at her a moment, a bit taken aback by the sudden ferocity of his gentle Gendra. Opening his arms, he beckoned for her to come to him. "Come, lie beside me under the covers. You can pummel my poor body into submission in the morning."

She looked aghast at her death grip on his thigh. "Oh, Isyn,

I'm sorry. I didn't—"

"No, you didn't. I'm fine. But come lie down. Sleep beside me." Once she'd complied, her slim body tucked perfectly against his, the furs cozily piled around them, he kissed her on the forehead. "I know who I fell in love with, Gendra," he murmured. Because she didn't reply, already asleep with the easy speed of youth, he added, "and because of that, you can't stop me from doing everything in my power to save you from going down with me."

THEY HEADED OUT on the ice again in the morning—the folk happily speculating about an excellent catch as they towed the sled along—Isyn feeling every moment of the wild night before in the least jolt or jostle of his aching bones. Moving the storm away, even from a narrow alley, and holding it clear felt like opening a vein, too, the drain almost nauseating. Gendra guessed it, too, throwing him assessing and concerned looks with almost irritating regularity. He deserved it, of course. *This is what you get for cavorting with a nubile young woman like the last fifty years never transpired,* he chided himself. But for her he produced a warm smile and squeezed her hand under the furs.

"Maybe today isn't the best—" she began, and he interrupted, knowing exactly what she'd say, as she'd already said it several times.

"We're not wasting a single day in looking for that rift. I'll be fine."

"Says the man with a fever and who couldn't put weight on his injured leg this morning," she muttered unhappily.

That was true. He'd made one attempt, and it had felt like he'd applied a red-hot poker to the inside of his thigh bone. The leg was getting worse. He knew it, and by the dark worry in Gendra's eyes, she knew it, too. The difference between them was that he knew he was done for and she still clung to a foolishly optimistic hope that he could somehow be saved. He knew better. Even if by some miracle they managed to escape the Winter Isles, and an additional miracle let them find Stella and she was able to heal him, he'd still be fifty years too old for his Briar Rose. He was no valiant prince to give her a happily ever after. She'd be tied to a dried-up old man, spooning food into his toothless mouth while his mind wandered in forgetfulness.

She deserved so much better than that. Though he might already have burdened her with a possibly unwanted child. Yet another consequence of a series of bad decisions he'd made the night before. He cleared his throat, drawing her immediate attention. "We haven't talked," he said hoarsely, "about the possibility that you could be, ah, as a result of last night. I wasn't thinking—unforgivable of me, really—and we must confront the fact that my carelessness could have resulted in a, ah..." He trailed off in the face of her bland stare.

She raised an eyebrow. "Do you need help choosing a term? Child? Baby? Pregnancy? Bun in the oven?"

He choked a little. "Bun in the oven?"

She waved that off with a mittened hand. "My father's

family uses that euphemism. A bit yeasty for my taste. Regardless, you needn't be concerned about this. You weren't careless—as I recall, I was there, too, and I'm not an idiot—and there's nothing to worry about."

"I see." They were quiet for a bit, the wind soughing over the ice and the folk chattering away. For several long minutes, he attempted to not worry. Couldn't stop himself. "Do you mean to say that a pregnancy isn't possible?"

"You seem virile enough." She slid him a knowing smile, full of cat-in-the-cream satisfaction, blissfully unaware of how his balls ached from overuse after such a long, very dry period of disuse. "And I'm living proof that Tala and non-Tala can interbreed, with my mother as pure shapeshifter as it gets and my father stolidly mossback, little as I like to use that word. Although Dafne's research shows that the people of the Wild Lands foothills around Ordnung, like my father's family, probably have ancestral overlap with the Tala, which increases the likelihood of compatibility, procreation-wise. In fact, outbreeding—another of Dafne's terms—seems to improve the odds of bearing healthy children, given the Tala history of insularity and the interbreeding that led to all sorts of problems, from infertility to fatal birth defects. Anyway, the Tala don't worry about preventing pregnancy because even a generation after my mother was able to stabilize healthy pregnancies, we'd still much rather have babies than not."

He'd vaguely known some of that, but the barrage of information made his head whirl. She was rattling on, very unlike herself, so he squeezed her hand, stopping her. "What's wrong?"

She caught her breath, pressing her lips together, her eyes suddenly luminous with tears. "It's really unlikely that I'm pregnant."

"All right," he said slowly, waiting. She looked away, using the mitten to swipe under her eyes. "Gendra, talk to me. Are you hoping you are or that you aren't?"

She looked back at him, tears freezing on her lashes like crystals, and gave a watery laugh. "I have no idea. Just thinking about it, I...." Her voice broke, and she clamped her lips together.

He extracted an arm to put around her shoulders, pulling her close against him. "It's a lot to think about."

She sniffled and nodded against his shoulder. "More than I realized until this moment."

"The thought of making a child between us," he said, thinking it through as he spoke the words, "makes the future seem real in a way it didn't before."

The stark, gut-hollowing vision of her standing alone, holding a child by the hand returned with biting vengeance. And that was the best-case scenario. If she was trapped in the Winter Isles and the folk decided to kill her—or if the alter-realm creatures attacked again and she had no way to defend herself and their child...

"Maybe that's it," she agreed quietly, then abruptly sat up, staring fiercely into his face. "I hope I *am* pregnant. I want a child—your child—but I don't want to do it alone. I want you with me."

"Gendra." He fought the overwhelming emotion elicited by her declaration and the crushing despair of having to face reality. "Even if we somehow escape this place, even if this wound doesn't kill me, I don't have many years left."

"I refuse to accept that—" Her eyes widened, face going pale.

"What is it?" he demanded, sweeping the area with his mage senses for danger. There was *something*... An inconsistency he'd detected before when the alter-realm creatures attacked. Could it be...

"A rift," she replied in hushed tone, her gaze going to the folk and back to his. "It's here."

"Are you sure of it?" Before she could reply, he grimaced. Of course she was as sure as she could be. "Bad question. Never mind."

"How do we proceed?" She asked the question with trusting expectation, as he'd assured her he was working on a plan.

Unfortunately, exhausting himself cavorting in ill-advised sex with a much-younger woman had swept most rational thinking from his mind. He had yet to develop this amazing plan. The wages of despair: a large part of him hadn't believed they'd ever find a rift. "It's under the ice?" he asked, stalling.

She nodded. All right, then. First things first. She'd said that the rifts tended to behave unpredictably without stabilization, so he'd have to try to set his magic to stabilizing it while the folk cut a hole in the ice. He called out instructions for them to stop, explaining to their dubious expressions that his magery had determined this would be a good place. Gendra listened quietly, not interfering, but still clearly awaiting an explanation.

He also took a few moments to handle the weather, including clearing a path back to land. If he did somehow manage to exit this realm—or died trying—the least he could do was make sure the folk could get back to shelter. The weather magic wouldn't hold long in his absence, but they were canny survivors, and it should be enough. If nothing else, he and Gendra would've helped the folk with one last fishing haul.

Once the folk had started unpacking their supplies, he agreed to being carried in his chair to where they'd make a hole in the ice. He hadn't used the chair the day before, his pride greater than the pain, so he'd managed to avoid having Gendra witness his invalid status. But today he needed to conserve all his magery to create a new fishing hole—and to handle anything else that might occur. Also, as she'd ruthlessly pointed out, his leg wouldn't bear any weight today. With the storm as stable as he could get it, he turned his attention to the rift submerged far below.

The shape and size of the phenomenon wasn't easy to encompass with his conscious mind or with his more intuitive mage senses. It seemed to shift and billow, not unlike the colored lights that danced in the skies on clear winter nights. It didn't feel like a doorway to him—which was perhaps how he'd missed it all these years—but seemed more like a… fold, almost as if reality had doubled over, creating a place of greater intensity. Definitely magic.

"Do you have a dagger I can use?" Gendra asked, walking beside him as his bearers carried his chair to the spot more or less over where they agreed they felt the rift was strongest.

"Why a dagger?" he replied absently, still focused on the rift and bemused by the question.

"Because, strong as I am, your sword is too unwieldy for me," she retorted, then lowered her voice, though the folk couldn't understand their conversation. "I'd prefer to be armed. If I can't have claws, I'd like to at least have some kind of blade."

"Ah, thoughtless of me." He gave her his favorite blade, figuring she needed it more, and he could give her that much. "It's not Silversteel, unfortunately."

She tested the grip, nodding appreciatively. "It's a good blade. And Silversteel is unnecessary, as I'm not planning to defend us against the intelligence today—I hope—just anything else that might cause us problems."

Us. She was determined that they would both go, and probably had it in her head that she'd defend him to the death. The folk had begun chipping at the ice, so he added judicious amounts of magery to begin the melt that would make it easier. They didn't need a large hole this time—but it did need to be big enough for Gendra to go through.

"Should I be touching the net?" she asked, shifting from foot to foot restlessly. It bothered her more than she'd said, he knew, that she had to depend on him to make her shapeshift. He'd suggested they practice, but she'd demurred, using the excuse of not wanting to drain his magic unnecessarily. He suspected she didn't want to endure his manipulation more than needed. Since his own desire to practice was derived equally from an eroding doubt over whether he could perform the same trick again—and under pressure—and the almost salacious desire to see some of her other forms, he'd given in without further protest. Now, with the moment upon them, and his doubt taking the lead, he wished he'd insisted.

"No, don't touch it until I give you the word." They were near enough to the widening circle of black water for her to make the leap from where she stood. "What form will you take—fish?"

"Osprey," she replied. "That way I ensure I can fly fast into the hole and then—Moranu take me, no, that won't work because once I'm away from you I won't be able to shift again. Has to be a penguin, then." She slanted him a crooked smile. "Not my sexiest form, but I can toddle over the ice and stay under for quite a long time in that form. Just give me a kick if I'm not going fast enough."

"I am *not* kicking you," he informed her decisively.

"Not hard." She grinned, indigo eyes sparkling. "Just a nudge. A good belly slide will get me there. How do you think the folk will react to seeing me shapeshift?"

A fine question. One with no good answer. Even after all these years, communicating with the folk was complicated and frequently muddled. "They respect magic. I'll do my part and take responsibility. They'll take it better if they believe it's all my magery at work."

"Which, in point of fact, it will be," she noted blandly, staring into the distance and not fooling him at all.

He took her mittened hand, wishing he could touch her skin, tugging so she looked down at him in the chair. "I can't push just anyone into shapeshifting. The magic is all you. I'm only a catalyst that helps you over the threshold," he reminded her. "It will be both of our magics, working together."

She smiled warmly. "I like the sound of that. And—" She

broke off, an odd expression crossing her lovely face.

"What is it?"

"I'm having two thoughts at once, about entirely different things. Or are they? They're tangled up in my mind." She shook her head slightly. "A catalyst that helps cross a shapeshifting threshold—that gives me an idea. Also, I'm thinking about the intelligence and what it's trying to do."

"Besides isolating populations of magical creatures"—he swept a hand at the diligently working folk—"and tormenting us?"

She wrinkled her nose at him, then continued seriously. "What if those things are just side effects of whatever it is that it's trying to do? Lena has observed that it seems to be experimenting. It's clearly drawn to magic, thus its obsession with Stella and possessing her. It wanted to isolate her in that tower in the poppy alter-realm, much as you've been isolated here among the folk, where your magery has grown in power. I'm also thinking about how shapeshifting is somehow prevented in the alter-realms even though, as you've pointed out, the magic is still in me, manifesting in other ways. So it's more like I'm being blocked. And the intelligence is interested in making new shapes—mashing the people and animals together at Gieneke and trying its own version of shapeshift-ing..." She trailed off, chewing her lip in thought, staring at the black hole in the ice as if it might hold answers.

"That sounds like more than two thoughts," he suggested wryly.

She flashed him a rueful smile. "I said they were tangled up. I wish I could—" She stopped, but he knew what she'd been thinking, that she wished she could talk the problem out with her friends. Well, she would be back with them soon enough. He would see to it. His best and last gift to her. Goddesses knew, he had nothing else to give her.

"It's time," he said, careful not to let any emotion show in his face or voice. The folk, satisfied with the hole's size, had all turned their attention to preparing their fishing lines and net. "Ready?"

She nodded, a determined look on her face. "I'll go down, pinpoint the rift, then come up. You throw yourself into the hole." Fretting, she studied the distance. "Is it too far?"

"The folk won't like me too close," he explained yet again. "Even in thick ice, the edge can crack, and they won't risk me. Don't worry. I'm not helpless. I can get there." He ruthlessly played on her sympathy. Anything so long as she bought the lie.

"I know you can." She smiled, meaning it so sincerely that guilt gripped him. "Once you're in the water, push me back into orca form, and I'll take you through the rift as fast as possible. It doesn't feel to me like the rift is very far down, so you won't have to hold your breath for long. Just hold on to my dorsal fin and you'll be fine. On the other side, it's not far at all to the surface. Mostly the cold will be shocking."

"I've felt it before," he reminded her. Then squeezed her hand. "I love you, Briar Rose." He wanted to say more but was afraid anything else would sound like goodbye.

She bent to kiss him, lingering over it. "I love you, too," she murmured against his lips, then straightened. "More important: Do you trust me?"

"Until the end of time," he replied, hoping those words would stay with her, that she'd understand what he was telling her. "Better go now."

Nodding, she pulled off her mitten and held out her bare hand. Draping the net over it, he reached for the magery, finding what felt like another sort of doorway. Portals within portals, wanting to pull him down to other worlds and bodies. He pulled himself from the rabbit hole of vision to see Gendra as a penguin, moving swiftly to the edge of the fishing hole. He'd never seen a penguin, and her toddling gait would've been funny if he wasn't holding his breath, gripping the arms of the chair and willing her to go faster. If he'd been close enough, he might've given her a swift kick into the water. Especially when Gizena spotted the penguin and yelped in surprise, diving for the bird.

He opened his mouth to halt the hunter, but Gendra neatly dodged and was gone into the water. The folk shouted at each other to get the nets into place while Jasperina gave him a long, accusing look. She was no fool—none of them were—and they'd soon put together Gendra's appearance and disappearance with the unusual animal sightings.

It didn't matter, because she would be free, and the folk could accept his explanations or not, which also didn't matter, as his life among them was coming to an end. Maybe, just maybe, a child of his would be going home with Gendra, a piece of him that would live on. *I love you,* he thought to both of them.

"*And I love you,*" Gendra replied in his mind, startling him, the shape of her thoughts slightly different than they'd been as an orca. He'd forgotten she could mind-speak with him while in animal form. Why then and not as a human? It didn't matter.

"*Can you sense the rift?*" he asked, diverting her from seeing too much into his head.

"*Yes. No. Sort of. It's not as clear to me as when I was in human form.*"

"*Explains why you had trouble as the orca. Let me show you.*"

"*Please.*"

Taking her mental hand, he pulled her toward where the rift loomed in his mind, a folded double layer shimmering with the time and space of multiple realms at once. It made more sense to him all the time, the magic so similar to that of the Isles of Remus and his ancestral skills that it began to reveal itself to him. Multiple portals in one. Sifting through them, he found the portal to home, his and Gendra's.

"*I see it!*" she exclaimed in his mind. "*You be ready. I'll surface and—*"

With his magery, he seized the currents of water around her, pushing her through the portal to home, her mind-voice silencing as she went beyond his reach forever.

Goodbye, my love.

~ 20 ~

"**I**'VE GOT HER!" a voice shouted as a net settled around her, fouling her wings and bringing back that sharp panic of capture.

"Are you sure it's her?" another voice called back anxiously.

"It's her." This voice more confident. Gen made her penguin self stop thrashing, recognizing those voices. Stella. Lena.

And Jak, leaning over the side of a small boat tossing in the rough water, drawing in the net. "I've got her," he said again, pulling her into the boat and removing the net. "She's not fighting me now. Gen, you're safe. You're back. Shift to human."

The disoriented panic evaporated, replaced by white-hot fury. She shifted to human form, warm and dry, only briefly savoring the delicious ability to do so. Isyn had lied to her. He'd sacrificed himself, pushing her through the rift without him. "I have to go back."

"You're home. You're safe," Jak repeated as if she were a child or mind-addled.

"You don't understand." Her voice rose with hysteria. Isyn. Isyn was still back in the Winter Isles, and time was flying there. She had to get back to him. "I'll explain later."

She was fast, Jak was faster. Anticipating her, he seized her wrist in a fierce grip. "You will *not* shift. That's an order."

"You don't order me," she spat, fighting him. Isyn's blade was in her cache—she'd taken it with her into penguin form—but she'd have to shift to get to it. Which would also break Jak's hold. Claws would work, too, and she didn't have to completely shift to make those.

"Don't do it," Jak warned. "You're not in your right mind. Give it a minute."

A minute. A minute was how long—a day? "I can't," she nearly shrieked.

"Rhy, help me!" Jak shouted.

A raven that had been circling above dive-bombed her, becoming Rhy holding her in an unbreakable bear hug. Unbreakable unless she became a bear herself. Anticipating her, Rhy nipped her ear. "Want to play I Eat You?" he taunted. "I'll win."

That penetrated her frantic thoughts. "Wrong. I always win. I have more forms."

He laughed. "You won't win anything if you capsize this dinghy and drown Jak."

Oh. How thoughtless of her. Just then, the little boat bumped against the bigger sailboat with a startling grind. Zeph, in porpoise form, popped her head up and grinned around the rope in her mouth, cackling happily at her. Above, Stella and Lena leaned over the rail, cheering and clapping. Astar hung from the rope ladder, holding a hand out to her.

"Take it," Jak ordered. "Or I'll have Stella fly over and

knock you out so we can haul you aboard like cargo."

"I forgot what a tyrant you are," she snarled.

Jak only raised a brow. "In just an hour? You're definitely mind-addled."

"I'm not. It's been—" Realizing this would take explaining—and the faster she convinced them she was rational, the sooner she could go rescue Isyn—she stopped herself. She had to convince them to let her go back, and for Stella to return with her. If the rift remained. If it would take her to the Winter Isles again.

If nothing happened to Isyn before she could get back to him.

She took Astar's hand, attempting to return his broad grin. He pulled her against him in a real bear hug, this one full of love and relief, sandwiching her between his body and the side of the ship. Kissing her forehead, he squeezed her tight. "You gave us a real scare, Gen. You truly did. Climb on up. I've got you."

The words reminded her agonizingly of Isyn—and gave her renewed determination. Climbing the rope ladder swiftly, she found herself embraced by Lena and Stella, who were both laughing and crying at once. Funny, as many times as she'd dreamed of this reunion, she had to force herself to return their hugs and not immediately extricate herself. "Nilly," she said, interrupting their gushing questions. "I need you to—"

"Gendra!" Zeph screeched, practically in Gen's ear. Back in human form, she pulled Gen into a fierce hug, talking nonstop of her relief and how Gen had better never disappear like that again. Then Rhy and Jak were aboard, pulling her into hugs also, everyone talking at once.

"Everyone, quiet!" Gen yelled over them all, stunning them into silence. Zeph gave her a wide-eyed and astonished look that might've been approval. "Thank you for pulling me from the water," Gen said more quietly, now that she had their attention. Calm and rational was the way to go. "But I have to go back."

"You are not—" Jak began, dark eyes hard and face set, but Astar held up a hand.

"I know we're on your ship, Captain Konyngrr," he said mildly, "but we're still anchored. I'm going to reassert my rank as crown prince and leader of this mission for the moment. What happened, Gen?"

"Yes, where did you go?" Zeph demanded. "We've been taking turns searching for you for an hour, and you were nowhere. And then suddenly Stella knows where you are."

Gen glanced at Stella, who smiled gravely, gray eyes sparkling with sorcery. How much did she know? "I found Isyn," Gen told them, counting on that news to shut them all up. "I fell through a rift and ended up in an alter-realm where Isyn has been trapped for fifty years."

For a long moment, the only sound was the slap of waves, growls of wind, and the creak of lines as the ship strained against the anchors, yearning to move on, even with its sails tightly furled. Gen struggled against her own furled wings, feeling the rush of every minute lost.

"Sweetheart," Stella said gently, reaching for her, "I think you should—"

"I'm fine, Nilly," Gen snapped, yanking her hand away.

JEFFE KENNEDY

Stella needed to save every drop of healing magic for Isyn. Her friend blinked at her consideringly, silver sparking brighter in her gaze as the sorceress looked *through* her. "Look all you like," Gen told her. "Isyn has been trapped in an alter-realm called the Winter Isles. Fifty years have passed for him. He's injured and he needs to be rescued. Ask Falada! She'll know we need to go get him."

Stella shook her head sadly. "Falada disappeared when you did. I rather thought she'd gone with you."

Had she? Neither she nor Isyn had known, if so. "Regardless, I have to go after him right now because every minute that passes here is like *hours* there that could—" Her voice caught on an hysterical sob—so much for calm and rational explanation—though she had run out of breath to speak anyway.

Astar put a heavy hand on her shoulder. "Take a breath. In. Out. In. Out. Better. Now, tell us the story from the beginning."

"But, Isyn—"

"From the beginning," Astar commanded, summer-sky eyes hard and jaw firm, every inch the high king, even drenched with rain and seawater. "I'm not budging on this, so soonest begun, soonest done."

They all smiled or chuckled a little at Astar's familiar personal motto. With Astar's hand grounding her, Gen took another breath and told them the story of what had happened. Leaving out the sex and falling-in-love part, though her three female friends eyed her keenly, clearly guessing there was more to it. They could drag the details out of her later. Unless they weren't able to rescue Isyn, in which case she'd refuse to speak of him ever again. Their few days together would be sealed away with her sense memories of him, safe from anyone else's prying questions. Only for her.

She stifled another sob at the thought. "So you see," she finished, "I have to go back for him. Immediately."

No one nodded, or even smiled. Instead they all regarded her somberly. Astar squeezed her shoulder. She hadn't realized he'd kept his hand there for the whole recitation. Keeping her from fleeing overboard? Perhaps.

"Gendra." He used her full name, drawing it out, sympathy in it. "He sent you back alone."

"I know! That's why I—"

"He sent you back *alone*," Astar spoke over her, gently but firmly, "in order to save your life. He knew he couldn't make it and that your chance of freedom lay with his pushing you through the rift without him."

"He sacrificed himself for you," Lena said, a reverent hush in her voice, her face full of sorrow. Beside her, Rhy turned his head to study her, some realization rippling through him.

Zeph was nodding. "Don't let that sacrifice be in vain, Gen. Isyn knew what he was doing. And he succeeded. He sent you back. You're safe with us now."

Now everyone nodded, murmuring agreement. Gen stared at them, fighting the sting of betrayal, the eroding sense of losing ground. "He only did that because he's convinced he's dying," she insisted, willing them to understand. "He thinks he's too old for me and that even if we can get him back here and Nilly heals him that he'll only weigh me down."

Stella watched her knowingly, her empath senses no doubt showing her everything in Gen's heart. Let her.

"Gen." Astar finally removed his hand, scrubbing it through his wet hair. "You have to realize you're not really making any sense."

"She's in love with him," Stella told her twin. "It all makes sense when you know that."

Five heads snapped around, everyone but Stella staring at Gen as if she'd grown scales and a second head, with googly eyes.

Zeph nodded to herself, as if confirming something, then shook her head. "Gen, I've told you over and over, you can't keep imagining yourself in love with every—"

"This is different," Gen interrupted. "This is the real thing."

Zeph snapped her teeth, an echo of her impatient gríobhth beak-clacking in it. "Love at first sight is a myth. You don't meet someone and an hour later—"

"Remember it's been much longer than an hour for Gen," Lena put in. "It sounds like at least a week in that alter-realm?"

"At least," Gen agreed, taking the rope Lena tossed her with relief. "I don't know how long I was an orca, and the time differential is confusing, I know. I'm sure you could do the calculations much better than I can."

Astar had fisted his hands on his hips, head tipped back to study the swaying mast against the turbulent sky, expression grim. "You're not going back for him."

Her stomach sank to the bottom of the sea. "Astar, I have to—"

His eyes snapped to hers, the blue as sharp as Silversteel, a glint of his aunt Ursula's determination in them. "*You* have to obey your high king, is what you have to do. And you are *not* going back through that rift, Gendra. No one is. We have this debate every time we lose someone in an alter-realm, and every time I have to weigh the potential cost of losing more people to rescue one or a few. The cost is too high. Jak, pull up anchor. We're sailing on. Stella, you sit on Gen, and if she makes any move at all to shift, knock her out."

Gen gaped at him, a thousand thoughts flying through her mind. "If it were one of us stuck on the other side, you'd choose differently."

He inclined his head, neither confirming nor denying. "He isn't one of us, so I won't waste mental energy worrying about it."

"He *is* one of us," Gen insisted, curling her fingers into her palms. "He's mine. If it were Zeph, you'd want any of us to do whatever it takes to save her."

Astar met her gaze steadily, unflinching. "My decision stands. Do I need to have Nilly knock you out right now? Because I will, Gendra. I won't risk you. And I won't risk another hour like the one we just spent searching for you."

They were all exhausted, Gen realized. Soaked, chilled, bedraggled. She could see it in all of them except Stella, who'd no doubt been kept in reserve in case Gen needed to be healed. They'd been through hell worrying about her, taking turns shifting to aquatic forms and running search patterns. And she'd been ungrateful. "I'm sorry," she told them, catching and holding each of her friend's gazes. "I am grateful beyond measure that you stayed here to search for me. I didn't know if you would."

Six different expressions of incredulity and puzzlement reflected back at her. "How could you think that, even for a moment?" Lena asked plaintively.

"I thought maybe days had gone by, and you would've given up," she explained, feeling the weakness of her argument.

"And you think you don't matter to us," Zeph snapped, invisible gríobhth tail lashing in the misty air. "You think because you're the only one in our group not paired up with their true love that you aren't worthwhile."

"*I* am not paired up with my true love," Lena gritted out.

Rhy flashed her a dark look but said nothing.

"What I mean is," Zeph said hotly, turning on Lena, "that Gen—"

"Zephyr," Astar said, not loudly, but his tone was sufficient to shut her up instantly.

"You're right, Zeph," Gen told her cousin as she glared mutinously at Astar. "I've felt like the seventh horse in a team of six on this trip. I've been wallowing in feeling sorry for myself, and if I learned anything at all in my misadventure, it's how very much each of you means to me. I've been searching for true love and overlooking the real, enduring love every one of you has given me. I've taken you all for granted, and I vow to change. But I'm asking you, each one of you, as your friend: please help me rescue Isyn."

They all looked at Astar, even Jak, and though Astar looked pained, he shook his head, all resolute grizzly bear. "I'm sorry, Gen. I know you care for the man, but the risk is too great. I can't allow it. The mission must take precedence over our personal feelings."

Gen nearly retorted that he'd risked the mission due to his own personal feelings more than once, but some newfound maturity had her biting down on the unfair and callous words.

"Willy," Stella said quietly, waiting for him to look at her. "Why are we sailing to the Isles of Remus?"

Astar huffed at her. "Not now, Nilly."

"I'm perfectly serious," she insisted gravely. "Shall I ask someone else? Jak, why are we sailing to the Isles of Remus?"

He cocked his head at her, expression changing with grudging realization. "To find King Isyn, who can help avert the catastrophe, as Queen Andromeda foresaw."

A desperate, keen-edged hope leapt from Gen's belly to lodge in the back of her throat, and she turned to Astar. Waited.

He was glowering at his twin. "Gen found him. Mission accomplished."

"And she lost him again," Stella returned equably. "It stands to reason that 'finding' Isyn so that he could assist with averting the future catastrophe involves more than we've achieved so far."

Astar's fists only tightened, his jaw dipping toward his chest in ursine obstinacy. He turned to Gen. "I know you have no reason to tell me the truth—and, indeed, very good ones to prevaricate—but perhaps you learned something from Isyn during your time there that provides the key to solving the problem?"

Wouldn't that neatly solve Astar's dilemma? A nice little

shortcut, whereby Gen visits an alter-realm, obtains the vital clue from the mage of the Winter Isles, then leaves him there to die while they go on to save the world. A stirring, tragic love affair made extra bittersweet with the sublime self-sacrifice. Worthy of one of Jak's Dasnarian ballads. In fact, Jak lifted one dark brow at her as if thinking the same thing.

She drew herself up with all the dignity she possessed, facing Astar fully. "First of all, I'd like to lodge a protest, Your Majesty—a respect I'll accord you even though you are not yet the high king, and even when you are, we denizens of Annfwn don't recognize the high throne of the Thirteen Kingdoms as the ultimate authority, something that you, as a partblood child of Annfwn yourself, know well."

Behind Astar, Rhy pumped a fist in the air in political agreement, grinning at her with flashing eyes. Even Stella passed a hand over her lips to disguise a smile, and Zeph rolled her eyes at Astar's back. Despite everything, it was good to be back.

"I would not lie to you, for any reason," she continued. "Not because of the crown you don't yet wear, but because you are my friend. I also wouldn't do anything to jeopardize this mission, and I'm frankly insulted that you imply that I would."

Astar set his teeth. "You have to understand that you've been very emotional, behaving unlike yourself since—"

She held up a hand to stop him. "I'm behaving exactly like myself. If that doesn't match who you assumed I am, that's not my problem."

Now Lena and Zeph bumped hips, doing a shimmying

dance of female solidarity that Stella joined from her side of the circle. Moranu, how she loved her friends. She wasn't sure when they'd converted to her cause, but she was immensely grateful for it.

"Finally," she said, before Astar could reply, "no, I don't know the answer to staving off this catastrophe. If Isyn gave me the vital clue, I don't know what it is. I can tell you, however, that he is a powerful mage, one able to control the weather, recognize and stabilize rifts, and trigger shapeshifting in an alter-realm that I wasn't able to do on my own. We could use his skills."

"I've said numerous times that my own weather magic isn't enough," Lena piped up. "If I had another mage to work with who understands manipulating atmospheric conditions that might make all the difference, I'm for rescuing Isyn." She gave Gen a smile and a nod.

"Three is a magic number," Stella observed, speaking directly to Astar. "A third magic worker could turn the tide for us. Another vote for rescuing Isyn."

Astar growled low in his throat. "This is not a democracy."

"Gen does have a point that you are not yet the high king and technically have no actual authority," Stella pointed out placidly, impervious to her twin's growing outrage.

"And many cultures around the world have implemented successful democracies," Lena replied. "That system of government is superior to our monarchies in many ways, not least because it prevents one person from having absolute power."

"Besides which," Zeph put in, slipping her arm through

Astar's and turning the full power of her charm and beauty upon him, "Nix and Cavan were our hosts. Wim and Marjie became friends. Will we want to face them someday and say we were in a position to rescue Isyn but decided to leave him to die? Lesser insults have led a kingdom to rebel against the high throne, which is not how you'd want to begin your reign, I'm thinking."

Astar tore his unhappy gaze from her, looking to Jak and Rhy. "Guys, what do you say?"

The girls all traded exasperated glances. As if the "more-rational menfolk" would weigh in differently.

Rhy, somehow managing a relaxed slouch against the mast despite the pitching of the little boat, shrugged nonchalantly. "Here or there, the mission is the same to me. I do recall Queen Andromeda tasking me to find Isyn, so I'm all for following the orders of the queen of Annfwn." He added a mischievous smile and a wink for Gen. "If that also aids the pursuit of true love, then I'm the last to refuse." Lena made a quiet snorting sound but for once restrained a cutting remark. "And," Rhy continued, gaze lingering on the back of Lena's head, "I love the sound of a democracy, which falls neatly within the Tala method of choosing rulers, by merit rather than the chance of birth. I vote for rescue."

Without acknowledging Rhy, Astar pinned Jak with a desperate look. "Captain Konyngrr, this is your ship. It's your right to overrule us all and make the call that we sail on. In fact, you already made that decision, and I support you in it."

Jak considered him, tumbling a dagger between his fingers as another person might flip a coin to decide by chance. He slid a look to Stella, who smiled at him, all warmth and love. Sheathing the blade, he slipped a hand behind Stella's neck and kissed her, hard and fast, then snugged her against his side. "I trust my lady's vision. If my star says that's where I need to go, then that's how I'll navigate. Besides, we all know Gen is the most sensible of all of us. I vote rescue also. And," he added, giving Astar a cheeky grin, "as the local tyrant, I'll make it a fiat. Off we go to the Winter Isles." He tossed Gen a salute.

Astar fumed only a moment, then sagged and nodded, turning back to Gen. "All right then, what's your plan?"

Um. Her "plan" had consisted of flinging herself back through the rift immediately and dragging Isyn back with her. Or taking Stella to heal him and then dragging him back. Time was ticking by. How long had it been for him since she'd left? A day, at least, maybe more. He'd be back on the island. In pain. His health worsening. She couldn't think about that.

Looking around the circle of expectant faces, she realized she didn't need to make the plan alone. Here were all these bright and courageous people. "Can you all help me figure one out?"

~ 21 ~

I SYN HAD KNOWN that the light and warmth his Briar Rose had brought into his life would make it seem all that darker and colder in her absence, but he hadn't expected the despair to dig its claws in quite so sharply. *Dire, gloomy, and morose sort of pessimism.* Gen's teasing words no longer amused him; they haunted his thoughts, circling like the scavengers that would no doubt be feasting on his bones before long.

Sending her back alone had been the right thing to do, but being the one to make the romantic sacrifice wasn't romantic at all. No wonder none of the ballads dwelled on the person left behind. Well, usually that person immediately died and the tale continued with everyone grieving for them and singing their praises, literally. Would Gendra go tell his parents about his life and—by then—death? Yes, she would. She was exactly the sort of person to take that upon herself. They'd all sit around and weep for him, and his parents would no doubt erect a statue in his honor, and they'd tell the tale of the lost prince of Erie.

Dire, morose, and gloomy pessimism, that was him. All that was left of him anyway, with Gendra gone from him forever. Limping around his small room, which felt like an empty cave without her sparkling presence, he picked up the drawing he'd made of her. It seemed like a faraway fantasy that she'd been there at all. Perhaps it had been a dream, brewed up by fever and unsatisfied longing. But for the drawing of an ideal woman who arguably could be a product of his imagination, it would be more rational to conclude she'd never visited. Jasperina certainly refused to speak of the shapeshifter that had come and gone, she and the folk giving him only betrayed glares as lingering punishment for the whole escapade.

Maybe if he tossed the drawing in the fire, he'd be able to better resign himself to his dismal fate. Holding it in one hand, he hobbled to the fireplace, leaning heavily on the staff. He'd been better off before without the reminder. He hadn't been happier, but at least he'd been dully reconciled to this twilight existence where beautiful lovers didn't exist.

He held out the drawing, the heat licking against his skin, the flames making her wild eyes seem to shift, watching him knowingly, when a distant roaring caught his ear. Another attack? Interesting—all he felt was dull interest, no fear or anger. Perhaps today would be a good day to die. At least he'd go quick. Buckling on his sword, he pulled on his alpaca wool cloak.

A knock on his door had him turning, pocketing the drawing. Removing the wards, he called to Jasperina that he was coming. The door flung open to reveal not Jasperina, not a monster, but a man in a fighting stance—sword in one hand, dagger in the other in a throwing hold. Dark eyes, dark hair, and a gold earring in one ear. Bizarrely, a small nighthawk sat on his shoulder, head cocked, one bright eye fastened on him.

Isyn gaped in shock, then remembered himself and reached for his sword.

"Don't do it, Isyn," the man said in Common Tongue, his body alert. "I'm here to rescue you."

"Excuse me?" Isyn managed, kicking himself for not thinking faster. He kept his hand near his sword hilt. This guy looked fast, so Isyn doubted he could outdraw him, but he'd hate to go down empty-handed.

"I'm a friend," the man said. "Well, a friend of a friend, and—"

"Oh, for the sake of the Three, Jak," a woman said with exasperation. "Lead with words, not blades." She wedged herself around the bladesman, who side-stepped but kept the throwing dagger trained on Isyn, a warning glint in his eye. With her dark blond hair in a long braid down her back, she wore fighting leathers like he did, daggers sheathed on her hips. "I am Princess Salena Nakoa KauPo. Call me Lena. And *we* are here to rescue you." She glared at the man—the Jak of Gendra's many tales, no doubt—and he grinned back, undaunted.

Isyn's heart had taken a painful leap, thudding mercilessly in wretched hope and jubilant terror. "Gendra, is she—?" He couldn't finish the sentence, overwhelmed by the possibilities. She was here. She was dead. She was missing.

"She's here," Lena said with a warm smile. "She's with the shapeshifters rounding up the folk so we can make a clean escape. Once you're healed enough, that is. Jak, is the room secure enough, or do you want to check under the bed?"

Jak relaxed slightly and checked behind the door. "Hey,

anything happens to you or Stella, my ass is dinner for a wolf *and* a grizzly. I'm good, but I'm not *that* good." Apparently satisfied, he shut the door, glancing at Isyn. "Better to ward it again. Just to be safe. Work fast, my star."

The nighthawk launched from his shoulder, landed on the bed, and chirped expectantly at him.

"You have to shift her back to human," Lena explained. "Gen said you can."

"I... what?" His frozen brain felt about six leagues behind the events.

"If you can't," Jak said over his shoulder, as he pulled the stool over and perched on it to watch the door, now with a dagger in each hand, "we go to plan B. I don't like it as much, but we can do it."

"The nighthawk is Stella," Lena explained patiently, turning her back on Jak. "She's a healer, but she can't heal you while in animal form. Gen said you're able to use your magery to initiate shapeshifting in this alter-realm. If you can, do it now. She'll heal you, and we'll all get out of here."

Oh. He looked about for the golden net, wondering what he'd done with it. He'd considered pitching it into the sea after Gendra, another dramatic gesture, but—even though his memory of that day was fogged with grief—he kind of thought he hadn't.

"Is that it?" Lena asked, moving to a pile of things in the corner. "Can I touch it or—"

"Don't touch it," Jak barked without looking.

Lena stuck out her tongue at his back, surprising a laugh from Isyn—and finally snapping him out of his stunned state.

"It won't affect you," he assured Lena, "but I can—"

"*You* can sit on the bed," she informed him firmly. "You don't need to be on that leg more than necessary."

"I understand why you and Gendra are friends," he muttered, obediently sitting.

She gave him a radiant smile as she brought him the net. "Gen said we'd like you, and I do."

"Some of us are reserving judgment," Jak said, attention on the door. "Hurt my woman—and touching her hurts her, just so you know—and I'll be gutting you. Gen would forgive me."

"In your dreams," Lena retorted. "Now quit distracting us."

Jak glanced over his shoulder, pointing a dagger at Isyn. "You've been warned."

Lena moved between them to block the sightline. "I don't want to rush you, Isyn," she said gently, "but the longer we're here, the more chance for something to go wrong."

"Right." He looked at Stella. "You're all right with this?"

She chirped, dipping her beak, and Jak muttered something in the background. Laying the net on the bed between them, Isyn nodded to her. "As soon as you touch it, you'll feel my magic, but you control the shape you take, not me."

Without hesitation, the nighthawk grasped a cord of the net with a taloned foot, and a young woman appeared in its place, rusty-black hair spilling in a loose veil around her. Wide and solemn gray eyes dominated her delicate face, her serene smile warming them.

"Hello, Prince Isyn. I'm Stella," she said in dulcet voice that immediately put him at ease. "Gen has told us a great deal about you, as has your family. It's a pleasure to finally meet you."

He managed to stammer some sort of reply, his memory of how he was meant to greet a quasi-princess and sorceress of her status murky.

Her smile stayed steady, so he must've gotten through it all right. "Lie back, and let's get to work, shall we?" She helped to ease him onto his back, running her hands over him as she did, a thoughtful line between her brows. He flinched, and she raised those brows. "Painful?"

"Ah, no—I thought… no touching," he whispered, jerking his head in Jak's direction.

"Jak worries about me excessively," she said, loudly and clearly. "Me touching you isn't a problem, so long as I'm using healing magic, which I am, and which Jak knows. He's just being protective of all of us."

"All of you?" Isyn echoed.

"We all came along," Lena told him, leaning against the post at the end of the bed. "Gen insisted on coming back for you, and we weren't about to let our group get separated again, so all seven of us are here."

"All of us in one boat, for good or ill," Jak put in from his guard post. "Metaphorically speaking, naturally, as it meant abandoning our actual boat."

"What about Falada?" he asked. "Gendra said she'd come with you to help find me."

"She did." Stella gave him a solemn look. "But Falada disappeared when Gen went through the rift the first time. We haven't seen her since.

They hadn't? But…

"Be still now," Stella counseled calmly. "First things first."

Heat emanated from Stella's hands, disturbing and painful, so Isyn looked to Lena for answers. "And Gendra is doing what?"

"Jak and I are the only ones who aren't shapeshifters in the group, so we're pleased to add you to our number," Lena answered.

Jak muttered something in a harsh language that didn't sound pleased at all, but both women ignored him, so Isyn did likewise.

"Since they can't shapeshift on their own once in the alter-realm," Lena continued, "the others all chose forms good for fighting here—and that could withstand the swim."

"Fuck me, that water is cold," Jak inserted, and Lena grimaced ruefully.

"Stella was able to use her sorcery to keep us warm and dry as we went into the rift on the other side," Lena continued, "but once she shifted, she couldn't do that anymore. Fortunately, her healing and empathy work here. So it was up to me—I have some weather magic, which works here, like yours does—to warm up the air once we surfaced. It was only partially successful."

Surfaced. "How did you get through the ice?"

Lena's eyes lit up. "Zeph went first, in gríobhth form. Not much stands in her way. She cracked through, and we followed. The two of us who still had thumbs and words volunteered to get Stella to you. So, Gen, Willy, Rhy, and Zeph—as saber cat, grizzly, wolf, and gríobhth, respectively—

are all downstairs making sure the folk don't interfere with your rescue. Gen seemed concerned that they might."

"She's not wrong," he conceded, understanding the logic, but still slightly hurt that she hadn't rushed to his side. Perhaps her feelings had changed once she was no longer trapped with him. He considered mentally reaching out to her. If she was in animal form, they should be able to talk that way. But she knew that, too, and yet she'd said nothing. There must be a reason for that.

"Soooo..." Lena purred, eyes bright in her high-cheekboned Nahanaun face. "Are you in love with our Gen?"

He choked a little on some spit he'd suddenly inhaled.

"Yes," Jak called. "Tell us about that." He sounded considerably less friendly, if that was possible.

"Gossip will have to wait," Stella declared. "Gen is correct that the bone was set wrong. I've cleared out the infection and the inflammation, but Jak, it turns out I *will* need your manly hands to break and reset it."

"Happy to assist," Jak declared, much too jauntily. The stool scraped, and he was beside the bed, grinning at Isyn as he stuck both daggers in the bedpost beside Isyn's head.

"Be nice, Jak," Stella warned.

"I'm always nice," he returned, kissing her temple.

"Be nice to *Isyn*."

"That was not in the mission instructions. I'd remember."

Isyn was really feeling substantially better. What a difference it made to have the infection and inflammation gone. "Maybe we don't need to—" Isyn began.

"We *do* need to," Jak replied seriously. "You can't put

weight on this leg. Your muscles have gone to shit. You can't run. You won't be able to kick to swim. I saw you—you can barely even stand on your own. And if you're not in the best condition we can get you into, you'll jeopardize getting everyone back safely."

"Especially Gen," Lena added. "We are grateful—more than we can convey—that you sacrificed yourself to get her home again, but she won't fall for the same trick twice."

"We don't care so much about you," Jak said with a sly grin, "but we love Gen. We're doing this for her."

"And the mission," Stella reminded him.

"Either way," Jak agreed amiably, smoothing a hand down her hair. "Gimpy here isn't going to be the one to screw things up. Not on my watch. What do you want me to do?"

Isyn only half listened to Stella's explanation, staring steadfastly at the low ceiling, managing not to flinch when Jak plucked a dagger from the bedpost, used it to slit Isyn's pants leg from cuff to thigh, then casually tossed it back to *thunk* again into the wood.

Lena grabbed the stool and sat by Isyn's head. "Jak is deft with his hands," she told him. "Don't be fooled by his attitude—that's just how he deals with pressure. He'll do right by you, if only because Stella would have his head if he didn't. Want to hold my hand? No shame."

Recalling Gendra's comments about the powerful reassurance of human contact, he accepted the offer. "Thank you."

"Gen would want me to," she replied with an easy smile. "She'd be up here if she could, but we all have our assignments, as coming here at all required extensive compromise.

Also, she was doubtful she'd even fit through the door in saber-cat form."

He nodded, though he still wondered. *Saber-cat form.* She'd never mentioned that to him.

"I should put you unconscious for this," Stella said, standing next to Lena. Jak was sliding a flat brick under Isyn's thigh, the edge of it under the break. Isyn could just guess what was coming next. "It's going to be excruciating."

"What will you do, exactly?" he asked.

Stella raised a winged brow. "Are you sure you want to know?"

"Yes," he said firmly, and when Jak glanced at him, Isyn fancied he saw the first glimmer of respect in the man's face.

"All right," Stella replied evenly. "Jak will use the brick as a fulcrum." She drew a line across his thigh with a light finger, crossing the worst of the tangled scar tissue, which looked considerably less angry. Not for long, apparently. "At my signal, he'll crack your femur at that point. It will be weak, as it's barely knitted together now," she told Jak, who nodded decisively in acknowledgment. At least he was taking *this* seriously. "As soon as he cracks it, he'll pull down." She framed Jak's hands around Isyn's leg in demonstration, then met Isyn's gaze. "I want him to pull hard, to detach as many of the bone fragments as possible. Your muscles and ligaments are atrophied, but they're also tight and brittle, so they're going to tear. I'll be in there with my healing magic, and I can quiet the nerves somewhat, but it's more important for me to focus on keeping blood clots, bone fragments, and—most concerning— any bone marrow from reaching your brain or heart, where they'll kill you. I'll also have to prioritize knitting the blood vessels back together so you don't internally hemorrhage. Only then can I start pulling the bone and other tissues together again. It won't be fast, and it's going to be agonizing. No one will blame you if you prefer to be unconscious."

Jak gave him a long look, shaking his head minutely.

"If I'm unconscious, the wards drop, and you'll be vulnerable," he noted, and Jak grimaced.

"Our people have things well in hand," Lena reassured him.

"And it takes healing energy to knock me out," he guessed, Jak giving a flicker of confirmation. "I'll stay awake."

Stella gave Jak an accusing look, and he smiled winningly, the picture of innocence. Moving with agile speed, he plucked a dagger from the bedpost and offered the hilt to Isyn. "Put it between your teeth and bite down," he suggested. "Helps to keep the screaming down."

Isyn glared at him, unamused. "I'll go for something cleaner, thanks all the same." Grabbing a fold of blanket, he rolled it and stuck that between his teeth.

"Have it your way," Jak replied cheerfully, getting back into position, laying the sharp edge of his forearm against the fulcrum point. "Don't crush Lena's hand, or Rhy will be all over you," Jak cautioned as Stella minutely adjusted the position of his arm.

"Me and my hands are not Rhy's business," Lena told him, then smiled at Isyn. "Squeeze as hard as you need to. I promised Gen."

That made him feel better, that Gen had worried about

him enduring this.

"Ready?" Stella asked, and Isyn nodded, focusing on the ceiling. She laid her hands on his thigh above the break. "Go."

Jak twisted his shoulder, snapping down with his weight, the bone splitting in an excruciating wave. Isyn had promised himself he wouldn't scream, and indeed he didn't because no more than a guttural choking sound made it out. Before Isyn had begun to assimilate the growing wave of agony, Jak pulled down, the tissues tearing and hot blood pulsing in a black wave through Isyn's vision. Healing magic seared in its wake, like an internal cauterization. He chewed on the blanket between his teeth, throwing his head back to contain the screams climbing up his throat.

"You're through the worst of it," Lena murmured. "You're doing so well. I understand what Gen sees in you. It takes a lot to impress her, and you've done it."

Stella gave quiet instructions to Jak, each time resulting in an adjustment that sent new waves of pain up through his spine. Gradually the excruciating disruption eased into a more basically nauseating agony, Jak finally releasing his vising grip from Isyn's leg. Stella had him go to Isyn's feet and grasp Isyn's ankles, aligning them as she checked the position of his hips, giving him an absentminded smile. "We don't want to go to this much trouble only to have one leg be shorter than the other. Bite down." She signaled to his tormentor, and Jak did something that sent a fresh wave of agony through him.

After that, the pain gradually subsided, the healing magic less unbearable and more comforting with every passing moment. The warmth made him sleepy... and Lena squeezed his hand. "Don't sleep," she ordered. "This is my other job, and the other reason it was better to keep you awake for this. Normally it's best to sleep off the healing, and your body will want to, but we don't have time for that. Nilly is going to give you a wake-up jolt in a moment, then we're out of here as fast as possible."

"You'll still be gimpy," Jak said, coming to retrieve his blades, "because there's only so much Stella can do about those weak-ass leg muscles of yours. But you should be reasonably mobile. Once we get you out of here, I can help whip you back into shape." He grinned with lethal anticipation.

"Jak," Lena huffed his name in exasperation. "Do you *have* to?"

"It's a guy thing," he replied. "Isyn gets it."

She glared at him. "Dick-swinging, here and now, *really?*"

Jak tugged a wisp of her hair that had escaped the braid. "There's never a wrong time for dick-swinging, darling Lena."

"That takes care of it," Stella said, straightening, Jak immediately steadying her as she swayed, none of the irreverent mischief in evidence as he embraced her, murmuring a question in her ear. She nodded, pushing at him enough to look past his shoulder at Isyn. "Go ahead and try the leg."

"*Isyn,*" Gen's voice sounded in his head, heightened by the pitch of a raging battle. "*Tell Jak we need help. We're under attack, not the folk. Tentacle monster and monkey lizards. Tell Stella to call Astar. I can't reach him.*"

Tersely, he relayed the message, Jak springing for his blades and Stella closing her eyes, presumably to call her twin.

"You three stay here," Jak said, heading to the door.

"I'm coming," Isyn replied, making it clear he wouldn't be dissuaded.

"You sure?" Jak cocked an eye at Isyn's leg, which felt whole, though cursed weak.

"I can wield a blade," he replied, making for his sword.

"Use this one." Jak tossed him his own sword. "Silversteel works best, Astar's in no form to wield it, and I prefer my daggers."

"Astar and Zeph are outside and under attack, also," Stella informed them. "You have the Star?" she asked Jak.

He patted his chest. "Right over my heart."

"Good. I'm coming, too." She held out a hand to Isyn. "Shift me."

"Stella," Jak began, "you're tired from—"

"I'm tired from healing, yes. I can still fight," she snapped at him. "And if we lose all of you, Lena and I are dead along with you." She turned a silver-bright stare on Isyn. "Shift me."

Pulling the rope from the pocket of his cloak, he laid the piece across her palm and sent the magery through her. A black jaguar stood in her place briefly before bounding to the door. Isyn hastily dropped the wards, Jak unbarred it, and they ran through. "Bar the door behind me," he told Lena, and she nodded. No argument from her.

"We're on our way," Isyn belatedly replied to Gen as he ran—all right, quick-hobbled—out the door.

~ 22 ~

THEY WERE TAKING too long.

Gen paced up one side of the hall and down the other, lashing her tail and flexing her claws. The slight click of them with every step made her feel ever so slightly better. She'd be happier to be slashing something with them, but that was the saber cat thinking. Isyn wouldn't want them to actually harm any of the folk, and so far they'd managed to simply terrify them into barricading themselves into the alpaca enclosure.

Every once in a while, a straggler or five showed up and attempted a bold attack, but the four shapeshifters had managed to herd those valiant but misguided warriors into various attached rooms where an eye could be kept on them. Other than that, after their arrival and the initial roundup and containment of the folk, there hadn't been that much to do. Which gave her too much time to worry.

Stella had said that if Isyn's injury was as bad as Gen had guessed, then it would require breaking and resetting the bone to get him in good-enough shape to withstand an escape, especially if they ended up fighting their way out, and that it would take time.

But wasn't it taking way too long?

She paced back up the hall, cocking her keen ears for sounds from Isyn's room, gleaning nothing more than she had in the past while. However long it had been. Saber-cat brains weren't great at time either. She considered yet again attempting to talk to Isyn mentally—it should work with her in animal form—and she discarded the idea yet again. He could've spoken to her, and he hadn't. There must be a reason for that.

Hopefully it wasn't because something had gone terribly wrong, and that was why it was taking so long. She growled deep in her chest. From his guard rounds on the other side of the room, Rhy cocked his head at her. An enormous black wolf with blue eyes, he'd been quite effective in sending the folk running for cover. Conversely, Zeph had been *too* terrifying. The folk had frozen at the sight of the gríobhth, so Zeph had removed herself from their vicinity and was outside patrolling the skies while Astar did likewise on the ground in grizzly form. All they needed was an alter-realm attack, so both were on the alert for trouble besides from the folk. The folk themselves couldn't be discounted either. They would have to be plotting their own escape and overthrow of their monstrous guards. The longer this dragged on, the more likely the folk would come up with something clever.

Really, it shouldn't be taking this long to heal Isyn. Should it?

Stella had been concerned about the prospect of breaking and resetting the bone. She hadn't said so, but her eyes had gone dark and thoughtful, a silver glimmer hinting that she might be checking the potential future outcomes. Gen hadn't needed Stella to explain everything that could go wrong. Bone splinters. Blood clots. Marrow poisoning the bloodstream. Magical healing was miraculous, but it wasn't a panacea. So much could still go wrong, especially for a man in Isyn's weakened condition.

She eyed the narrow staircase that led to the upper hall where Isyn's room was located. No way she could fit through that. Maybe she *should* try to mentally speak to—

The doors to the alpaca enclosure flew open precisely when she was at the farthest point of her patrol and Rhy midway through his, both of them too far to respond effectively. Careless of them—she could just hear her father's sour review of their strategy—and deviously clever of the folk. Especially as a dozen of them had *mounted* the alpacas and were yodeling with high-pitched cries of war as they galloped in a phalanx bristling with makeshift spears. Taking advantage of their guards' distraction, the stragglers poured out of their alcoves, attacking from the sides.

Rhy wheeled and charged the flank of the main force, leaving Gen at the point of the *V*—and with spears pointed straight at her as they closed with startling speed. Moranu take her, she was *not* going to harm the alpacas. Losing even one could jeopardize the survival of the folk. Letting out a roar to summon Zeph and Astar, she took a vicious glee in scattering the alpacas, too. *That's right, I'm the apex predator,* she thought at them. *Fear me.*

She roared again, swiping a paw through the air, making a display of her lethal claws. The phalanx dissolved into a melee of panicking alpacas and screaming folk, furry bodies tumbling across the floor as they were flung from their wildly bucking steeds—only to right themselves with surprising agility given their stocky appearance, recovering and regrouping.

Rhy had one group of folk separated, snapping and dodging like a sheepherding dog sending armed sheep back to the fold, but the lion's share—or, rather, the saber cat's share, apparently—remained her problem. Where in Moranu were Zeph and Astar?

The folk had divided themselves into two forces, one on either side of the hall, with her in the middle, and they began advancing on her, spears leveled. She recognized their leaders, too, unfortunately, Jasperina at the fore of one and Gizena— where had she gotten her harpoon?—leading the other.

An arrow *whizzed* through the air and _thunked_ into her hindquarter. Moranu take them, that stung! Gen had zero intention of discovering how the harpoon felt hitting a smaller body with no water resistance to lessen its force. She might not want to injure any of Isyn's folk, but she was running out of options. A single saber cat couldn't do much herding, and Rhy was still occupied with the other group. From the fierce expression on Jasperina's furry face, she had a pretty good idea who Gen was, and she wasn't taking any prisoners.

Another *whizz-thunk*, and an arrow embedded itself in her shoulder. *Roar*, that hurts! Gizena leveled the harpoon at her as they steadily advanced.

Where were Zeph and Astar??? For the first time, she became concerned. What if they had—

A slit opened in the air above, as if an unseen hand had sliced a dagger through it, a disconcerting shimmer of several realms kaleidoscoping by on the other side of it... until it stopped and a tentacle monster fell through, landing on the floor with a mighty plop. A black-fleshed blob made enormous by its cloud of thousands of stinging tentacles, it waved them furiously—and a hail of monkey lizards stormed through the rift, shrieking and falling on the folk and Gen with equal hatred.

No time to think. Gen whirled into a fury of claws and saber-sharp fangs. At least these creatures she could kill or maim with impunity. Unfortunately, contending with a tentacle monster along with an entire herd of monkey lizards—and two arrows embedded in her sides!—was more than even a saber cat could handle. At least it was only one tentacle monster? But it had several folk wrapped up in its waving tentacles as it rolled in that disconcerting octopus style straight toward Gen.

With a snarl, Rhy leapt through the air, gripping a tentacle that had one of the folk tightly wound up in his jaws and ripping it clean through with his momentum. The tentacle relaxed, allowing the member of the folk to roll clear, and they immediately charged back into the fray, howling in high-pitched fury.

Gen clawed and bit at the monkey lizards mobbing her, trying to make her way to help Rhy with the tentacle monster. There had to be a way to kill it. The monkey lizards hung all over her, pointed teeth chewing through her thick fur, not inducing great harm—yet—but distracting as a cloud of stinging flies. Rhy yipped in pain, a tentacle wrapped around his midsection slicing deep so that blood flew, his huge teeth wreaking havoc on another as a third snaked around his throat. The folk were in disarray, and a white-eyed alpaca galloped into a wall trying to flee the several monkey lizards hanging off of it.

That was it. They needed reinforcements. Hopefully Isyn would—*could*—answer.

"*Isyn,*" she called mentally. "*Tell Jak we need help. We're under attack, not the folk. Tentacle monster and monkey lizards. Tell Stella to call Astar. I can't reach him.*" She held her breath, afraid there'd be no reply, biting a monkey lizard in half to relieve her anxiety. *Ugh*, they tasted like bitter algae. No answer. No answer. Was he dead?

"*We're on our way,*" Isyn replied tersely.

Relief flooded her, followed by immediate concern. "*You shouldn't—*"

"*Fight. Don't talk.*"

Hi. Nice to hear from you. You're welcome for the rescue. I love you, too, she thought grumpily to herself, but a monkey lizard chomped on her ear, and she roared, sending it, along with a chunk of her ear, flying.

"*This is why you should be fighting, not talking,*" Isyn said in her mind with grim amusement. "*And I do love you, and we'll talk about you coming back for me, but this would be a saliently more effective rescue if we all survive to leave this place.*"

He did have a point. As rescues went, this one was pretty weak. She forced her way toward the howling and snapping Rhy. It seemed hopeless.

"*While we're alive, everything is possible,*" he reminded her. "*Stay alive.*"

JEFFE KENNEDY

"You too." In a way, that exchange felt every bit as powerful as trading I love yous.

Then a dagger flew through the air, severing the tentacle around Rhy's midsection. A black jaguar leapt into the other tentacles lashing at Rhy, Stella swiping with claws to free him. A voice called loudly over the fray—Isyn, at the top of the stairs, glowing with health and gloriously steady on two legs as he held the Silversteel sword before him. His ivory hair waved around his fierce visage, his eyes green bright even from a distance as they unerringly fell on her. He called out again in the language of the folk, and they paused, hesitating only briefly before converging on Gen.

Only her utter trust in Isyn kept her from defending herself—and good thing, too, as the folk began removing her monkey-lizard barnacles, using knives, spears, and teeth to rid her of the unwelcome burden. Isyn fought his way toward her, the Silversteel sword cleaving through the monkey lizards, and he seemed like a hero of old, invincible and shining with nobility.

She did her part, rendering and severing the fallen monkey lizards with fang and claw, permanently removing them from the battle. Isyn made it to her, placing a hand on her shoulder as he smiled at her. "Magnificent," he said, then pointed the sword at the tentacle monster, where the jaguar, Jak, and a profusely bleeding Rhy were desperately severing tentacles as fast as they could. "How do we kill it?"

"We haven't succeeded yet. How did you kill the one before?"

He shook his head. "We didn't. The folk say it went the way it came."

328

"*Stella can vanish it—but she needs to be back in human form, and she needs the Star of Annfwn.*"

"We can arrange that." He set his jaw. "To me!" he called in Common Tongue, Stella and Rhy immediately following the command in his voice, Jak following a beat after.

Isyn pulled a severed piece of the golden net from his cloak pocket. "Stella, use your sorcery to remove that beast."

She took the rope in her teeth, transforming to human, Jak handing her the Star with one hand as he fended off a monkey lizard with the other. "I can't do sorcery inside the alter-realms, but I do have an idea. Keep the folk clear."

Jak guarded her flank as she faced the quickly approaching tentacle monster. Isyn spun to Gen, holding out the rope. "Shift. Heal."

"*Rhy first,*" she told him. Before he could argue, she turned her head to snap at the arrow protruding from her flank. Catching it in her fangs without breaking it off wasn't easy, but fortunately it wasn't barbed and slid out with a sharp tug. A bright pain in her shoulder alerted her, and she swiveled to find Jasperina there, a scowl on her furry face—and the arrow in her hand that she'd pulled out for Gen. Jasperina clucked something, then dashed off.

Isyn held out the rope. "She wished you luck," he said, sounding as bemused as Gen felt. Nearby, Rhy—a healthy wolf again—grinned at her in canine amusement, tongue lolling, then charged to help Jak keep the tentacle monster off Stella while she concentrated on whatever she planned to do. "Hurry," Isyn advised.

She clamped her teeth on the rope, shifted to human,

and—even though they couldn't afford the time—seized Isyn's face in her hands and kissed him hard. Then she was back to saber-cat form and leaping to join Rhy in worrying at the tentacles reaching past Jak's guard.

"When I have time, you'll pay for that," Isyn promised, his mental voice so firm and full of sensual mischief that it brought joy to her heart. He stepped up beside her, his still weaker leg brushing her flank, and she realized he trusted her to guard that side. He was good with the sword, too, the Silversteel flashing in arcs timed perfectly with her own slashing claws and slicing fangs. They worked well together in way she hadn't even known to dream.

"Stand back!" Jak shouted, sweeping Stella into his arms and jogging back. Isyn repeated the command to the folk, who all scrambled away, one tugging a recalcitrant and terrified alpaca along. Rhy, Isyn, and Gen also all turned their tails and ran—just as a rift opened in the floor beneath the tentacle monster. It fell through, the rift closing again. The complete cessation of fighting was almost disorienting.

"Astar and Zeph need us," Stella said. "It's the intelligence."

"Let's go," Jak snapped, taking off at a run, still carrying her.

Rhy cocked an ear at the upstairs, whining.

"He's wondering about Lena," Gen told Isyn, understanding Rhy all too well. *"We shouldn't leave her behind."*

"Lena is up there, in my room," Isyn told him, and Rhy took off running. "Can he find her?" he asked Gen.

"Wolf nose," she replied, and he nodded.

"Let's go to the aid of Astar and Zeph, then."

"Want a ride?"

He gazed at her in such consternation that she felt a little shy. Was he revolted? Afraid? Then he grinned. "Briar Rose, you never cease to amaze me." Gingerly, sheathing his sword, he clambered onto her wide back, lying low against her and winding his fingers through the fur at her ruff. "Too tight?" he asked, his mouth near her thankfully now-intact ear.

"Squeeze with your knees. There, like that."

He huffed a breath of surprise as she leapt into an easy lope out of the hall. *"I won't let you fall,"* she promised. *"I've got you."*

"I love you, too," he replied, proving that he hadn't forgotten. Not that she'd expected him to, but... "I didn't expect white."

"?" She sent the wordless question as a cold blizzard wind hit her the moment they made it outside. Lifting her muzzle, she sniffed for the others.

"Saber cat," he explained, letting out a yelp as she took off toward the beach. *"When Lena said you were in saber-cat form, I didn't expect white with shadow patterns. You're beautiful."* His fingers massaged through the fur at her ruff. *"Soft, like your inner thighs."*

"You're distracting me, Isyn."

"Sorry. I don't know why I'm thinking about sex with you under these circumstances."

"Side effect of the healing." Which she knew, so she shouldn't read into it too much, but she loved that he still wanted her, that he could want her even when she was big, furry, and lethal.

"Side effect of that kiss. I missed you, Briar Rose."

She was on the verge of saying the same, when he continued.

"But I wish you hadn't come back for me."

~ 23 ~

ISYN WAS SAVED hearing Gendra's reply to that—and the argument that would inevitably follow—by the astounding sight of a golden gryphon shooting up into the wintry sky.

He thought he'd been prepared for the sight of the shapeshifters after listening to Gendra's many stories about them. But he somehow hadn't expected them to be so… larger than life. First there was Stella becoming a glossy black jaguar—a shock after her relatively unprepossessing nighthawk form. Then Gendra herself, looking like something out of a book of tales, her incisors easily the length of his forearm, her snow-shadowed fur-covered body more than large enough to carry a man his size. And Rhy as the biggest black wolf Isyn had ever seen.

But seeing a real, live gryphon with his own eyes was something else entirely *"Is that…"*

"Zeph, yes," Gendra mentally snapped, and he quickly recalled what he'd said only moments before. *"There's Nilly,"* she added before he could muster a soothing reply.

Her sharp eyes had spotted the sorceress first, but Isyn made her out now, standing on the rocks, the Star of Annfwn glowing like a small sun in her hands, echoing the larger star that was the gold-furred and feathered gríobhth.

"Hold on," Gendra said. *"I'm making the jump."*

Jump? He tore his gaze from the gryphon, glittering as if made from gold even in the snow-laden air, who wheeled about on a wing tip then dive-bombed something. Leaning out to look ahead to the rock promontory towering over the frozen sea below, he saw it was a drop of at least four times his height. Surely Gendra didn't mean to... *"It's too high! You'll hurt yourself."*

"I'm bouncy," she replied, her forbidding tone making a mockery of the term. *"Trust me."*

Which he did. But he still closed his eyes, hanging on to her warm fur and lying as tight to her lithe body as possible. Her muscles bunched... She leapt. They were falling through the air, his stomach somewhere far behind... And they landed with a jarring thud that became a scrambling slide across the ice. He opened his eyes and lifted his head just in time to see a massive grizzly bear, the brown form standing out amidst the gray, rearing on his hind legs and battling...

There his brain stopped making sense of anything at all. *"What in the Three is that??"*

"Nothing to do with our goddesses, that's for sure," Gen answered grimly. *"That's the intelligence I told you about, in the flesh, or rather, ice. It makes itself out of whatever is available."*

That helped his lagging brain resolve what he was seeing. A creature, manlike in shape but unrefined, towered over the grizzly by several times, and was formed entirely of ice. Semitranslucent and collecting snow by the moment, it looked like an animated snow monster from a child's tale—if not for the blood spattered everywhere. The grizzly roared, swiping a chunk of ice and snow from the thing's thigh, while the gríobhth dove, ripping at the thing's head with beak and talons. It laughed, taking a step toward Stella and kicking the grizzly out of its path as if the enormous bear was a child's toy.

"Stella!" it howled. "You are mine. I love you!"

Zeph flew into its face, forcing it back as it batted at her. One massive ice paw caught her hard and sent her tumbling through the air—but she recovered, circling back immediately.

Gendra slowed in her headlong race across the frozen sea, catching up to Jak, who was still running and had made it amazingly far. Reading Gendra's intention, Isyn held out a hand to Jak. Catching sight of them, Jak reached across with his far hand, grasped Isyn's forearm, and used the leverage to vault onto the saber cat's back behind Isyn. Gendra took off at top speed again, Jak wrapping a viselike arm around Isyn's waist to hold on.

"Use the Silversteel sword against it!" he yelled in Isyn's ear. "Get to the head if you can. Between that and my Silversteel daggers, we should be able to take it down—or at least hold it off until Stella can open a portal for us."

Isyn nodded. Not like he could argue, but...

The ice giant slammed down a great fist, just missing the prone Astar, who barely scrambled out of the way in time. But that gave Isyn an idea. Drawing the magery to him, he fed it into the ice at the giant's feet. The healing had replenished him in more than physical health, the magic swelling in him as it hadn't since his youthful early days in the Winter Isles. Without needing to hold the weather back, he poured melting magery beneath the giant as Gendra skidded to a stop and roared at the monster, drawing its attention from Astar.

"Be careful of the ice," he told her. *"I'm melting a hole beneath it."*

"Smart." As soon as Jak leapt away with agile grace and Isyn followed more slowly, she took off again. Gendra dodged another fist, slamming into the ice, cracks radiating outward as Isyn's magery weakened it. The ocean wasn't deep here, but if he could drop the giant into a hole and quickly refreeze it... His mind half on the melting ice, half worrying about Gendra as she played her cat's game with the ice giant, he blindly followed Jak.

The guy was insane, fearless, or both. Using his daggers as handheld crampons, he leapt onto the back of one leg, climbing rapidly. Isyn didn't notice any particular effect from the Silversteel. As he looked up at the towering giant, however, he felt puny, even the large and beautifully crafted Silversteel sword like a toothpick in his hands. How was he supposed to attack it—hack at its ankles like a small rodent?

"Nilly destroyed its last incarnation by slamming both daggers into its ear holes, so that's probably Jak's plan," Gendra filled in for him, clearly aware of his thoughts. Zeph screamed an eagle's cry and dove for the giant's head, pulling its attention from Gendra. *"That's why he said get to the head if you can. It's more vulnerable."*

"If it's self-made of ice, why would the head be any different?"

"Good question with no good answer. But that seems to be the case, no matter its shape. Especially if you can get inside its head. Can you tell when the ice will give?"

He mentally tested the rapidly thinning ice. Between the cracks the giant had created and Isyn's magery, a hole could open at any moment. *"It's weak enough now. But the others—"*

"Have been in the water once today already." The giant roared, batted Zeph away, and grabbed for Gendra. She ducked, drawing it back to the thinnest spot. *"Do it."*

If he couldn't climb to the head, he could bring the giant down to his own level. Driving his magery into the ice directly beneath the giant's feet, he melted it fast. With a massive *crack*, the ice gave, a black hole of arctic water opening up, taking the giant down in a huge splash of water. Astar's hind end fell in, but he held on with his front paws, claws digging in for purchase. Zeph landed and held out a taloned paw to him, which he grabbed—an unreal sight. Gendra scrambled away in the other direction, a shadowy white blur in the whirl of snow. Jak, momentarily dislodged by the sudden fall, dangled by one hand from the dagger embedded in the back of the giant's neck, until he caught himself and swung up with gymnastic grace to resume his climb.

All of which left Isyn face-to-face with the giant, now armpit deep in the rapidly reforming ice. Isyn froze it as fast as he dared, especially immediately around the giant, keeping one eye on Zeph's lashing tail and bunched haunches as the gryphon slowly towed the grizzly out of the icy water.

The giant swiped at him with a massive hand—one that looked more like a bear's paw than a human appendage—and Isyn ducked, bringing the sword around with his momentum. A solid, powerful strike, weakened somewhat by the lack of muscle in his newly healed leg. Much as Isyn hated to admit it,

Jak was right about him needing to build up strength again. Still, the blow should've sliced deeply into the giant's wrist—but it bounced off, jarring Isyn to the bone, the Silversteel chiming with a clean, sweet note of purest silver.

The giant struggled, tossing its head to shake off Jak, who'd reached one ear. "Stella! You are mine! I love you," the giant yelled, imploring and furious in one.

"Wrong," Jak snarled. "She's mine." The head was far too massive for Jak to stick both daggers in simultaneously. Gendra roared and sprang, leaping to one shoulder and climbing to the giant's head. The ice cracked and snapped like breaking boulders around the giant as it tried to free itself, and Isyn poured more magic into solidifying the ice's hold, melting and melding the surrounding ice into the giant's body.

The chiming note of the Silversteel sword seemed to hang in the air still, a haunting song telling him something... It tugged at him, calling to his magery. The magic and the Silversteel pulling at each other. Following instinct, he poured magery into the sword. Gendra had suggested that, using objects to focus his power, and now he found the path as easily as the well-worn trail he'd paced around the island for so many years alone.

He was no longer alone, and these people needed him. With a two-handed grip, he swung the sword in time with the giant's next swipe at him, focusing his magery into the Silversteel... and lopped off the entire hand like a hot knife through butter. Animal voices roared in approval, Jak flashing a grin from his precarious perch.

"*Nice,*" Gendra said, the single word worth a world of

eloquent praises.

The giant focused on him, its features literally sharpening as its eyes studied him with an uncanny expression of dawning recognition. "You," it said, its voice clearer now. "I killed you. You drowned. You should be dead."

"Not quite yet," Isyn bit out. Though it had been a near thing and growing nearer all the time.

Its features sharpening further, the face became something Isyn *almost* recognized. The familiarity tugged at his attention, in what turned out to be an unfortunate lapse.

"You are mine," it growled.

"What, no declaration of love?" Isyn sneered.

"*Isyn!*" Gendra screamed in his mind, eerily echoed by the saber cat's roar, and the giant's other hand clamped onto him, trapping his sword arm against his body. Stupid of him. Too stupid, too old, too slow. The giant brought him closer, the mouth gaining definition, cracking, then opening with slow and horrific majesty.

"This time you will not survive. Your magic will be mine."

The Silversteel sword was still in his hand, though hanging at a useless angle, a silver toothpick he couldn't even swing. He could lift the point, though, and infuse it with his magery. *Especially if you can get inside its head.* Here was his opportunity. He only needed to wait for the perfect moment. The mouth opened wider.

"Stella has opened a portal," Jak shouted. "Retreat! Everyone to the rocks!"

Zeph stooped from above, landing near Jak just long enough for him to clamber onto her back. Below, Astar began to lope toward the rocks, pausing to look over his shoulder to roar at Gendra, still on the giant's shoulder.

Gendra growled a protest. *"Can you get free?"*

No, he couldn't, but even if he could, he wouldn't try. The giant dragged him closer. If nothing else, he could buy them time. *"One more strike,"* he told her. *"I'll be right behind you."*

"Liar," she spat, a big cat's cough in her mental voice. *"You're not tricking me again."*

"I'm not tricking you," he lied as earnestly as he knew how. The stories always said you couldn't lie mind to mind, but he figured people lied to each other in all sorts of ways. Spoken words were just the surface. *"I'm buying you time."*

"When we get out of here, you and I are going to have a long conversation about your obsession with being a martyr," she snarled. The giant paused, looking to the side and waving its handless arm. Gendra appeared around its neck, claws dug in as she balanced with feline grace.

"Go!" he yelled at her, audibly and mentally. Her deep-blue gaze fastened on him, whiskered muzzle lifting in a snarl of disdain.

The giant shrugged, irritated, and a long icy tail rose in the air behind it. With a whiplike snap, it hit Gendra, sending her tumbling from its shoulder.

"Nooo!" Isyn shouted. And was enclosed in the giant's gaping maw.

~ 24 ~

T HE PRECIPITOUS FALL—AND the double blows of the whipping tail and the harsh landing on the jagged ice—stunned Gen. It wasn't true that cats always landed on their feet. If only.

She recovered just in time to see Isyn disappear into the giant's mouth. Zeph swooped low, Jak shouting at Gen to retreat. Astar was roaring at her, too. On the promontory, a portal shimmered, Lena, Stella, and Rhy, still in wolf form, silhouetted by the light of it.

She'd promised Astar, promised all of them, that she'd retreat when ordered to. That had been a condition of the entire rescue. It had been an easy promise to make, because she'd been so certain any retreat would include Isyn—or would mean he was lost to her forever.

She refused to believe he was lost.

The ice beneath her paws shuddered, icy water soaking the fur between her toe pads. The giant was melting, losing shape, seawater pouring off of it in buckets as the ocean reclaimed itself and the animating intelligence fled. Where was Isyn? He couldn't melt. He had to be there still. They hadn't come all this way, gone to such lengths to heal him, only to lose him again.

"*Isyn!*" she called as she clambered over the shards of ice that had broken, refrozen, broken again—and now were melting into a soup. Her back paw slipped, briefly dunking her in the shockingly cold water. At least the saber-cat form handled the icy water well.

"*Isyn!*" she called again, ignoring Zeph and Astar's strident calls and Jak's increasingly foul Dasnarian curses. She didn't care what they'd do to her. Nothing could be worse than losing Isyn.

"*Isyn!*" she called a third time, the ice beneath her giving way and submerging her entirely before she kicked to the surface, striking out with her paws for purchase—but only bobbing chunks of ice met her efforts, sliding away. If only she could change form. She tried, doing her utmost to find orca form. Isyn had to be in the water, drowning even as she wasted time, the intelligence finally completing its task. She'd heard what it said to Isyn. *I killed you. You drowned. You should be dead.*

And now it was finishing the job.

Not while she had breath in her body.

Letting herself sink, she tried again to shift and failed. She needed to find Isyn. He could trigger her shift. The water was dark, almost lightless and bone-numbingly cold. She could barely see, couldn't scent Isyn at all.

You've been searching for him your whole life, she told herself fiercely. *Are you going to just let him go now?* No. No, she wasn't. But she *would* trade her life for his.

Moranu! She prayed with all the intensity she could muster, seeking help from the goddess as she almost never did. Zynda's devotion to the goddess had gotten her literally killed. *Her favors are not guaranteed. Our lives and efforts aren't coin we pay to obtain something in return.* Nevertheless, Gen had to try. Perhaps her mother's devotion would weigh on Gen's side of the equation.

Moranu, please, she prayed as fervently as she knew how. *Let Isyn live. He's barely had a life, and he deserves so much more. Take mine instead.*

The water swirled around her, black and multifaceted at once, filled with living shadows. Forms and shapes emerged and hid again, reminding her of Isyn's painting. Then the many-faced goddess of shadows spoke. *I don't want your life, dragon's daughter.*

Then what do You want? she asked desperately. *Whatever the price, I'll pay.*

The goddess tsked. *One doesn't pay for favors. They must be freely given. Gifts offered with no thought of receiving anything in return, not even gratitude. There is nothing more precious than the gift given freely.*

I have nothing to give.

Ah, but that's not true.

Gen thought frantically. Moranu didn't want her life, but She did want something freely given. Something precious. Something equivalent to all Gen wished for Isyn: the opportunity to build the life that had been stolen from him. In that moment, her quest for true love seemed childish and shallow. She'd been searching for someone to fill a fantasy role, not really thinking about what it meant to truly love another person. They'd had their moments together, their nest away from the world, and they'd loved in that so-short time, loved passionately and intimately. And she'd saved up those memories. Nothing could take that away from her.

I'll give up Isyn, she offered. *Isyn doesn't have to be mine.*

Done. You'll need a better form to save him, though.

The water suddenly cleared, no longer numbingly cold, but refreshing. She could see, and she sensed Isyn immediately. Diving for him, she moved through the water like flying, the fluid parting for her like air. Seizing Isyn's limp form in her forepaws, she carefully caged him—still holding the Silversteel sword in a death grip—in her talons, then shot upward.

She burst through the ice like it was nothing, soaring into the air, her wings catching with ease despite her burden. Zeph, looking surprisingly small, circled her with a cry of triumph, relief, and joy all combined. The pair of them struck out for the rock promontory where the others all stood, pointing at them, Lena jumping up and down.

Backwinging to land on her hind legs a short distance away—a good thing she'd observed her mother's dragon-form skills many times—Gen carefully deposited Isyn on the rocks. He stirred, stared up at her. "Magnificent," he whispered, and passed out again.

Then Jak and Astar were there, Jak helping to scoop Isyn up into Astar's strong grizzly arms.

"You'll never fit through the portal like that," Jak told Gen, halting Astar so he could dig through Isyn's pocket for the sodden piece of net. He held it out to Gen as Astar carried Isyn to the portal and stepped through. Lena and Rhy were already gone. "You might blend into the landscape, but I don't think you want to be the Dragon of the Winter Isles forever, so figure it out. And hurry. Stella can't hold the portal open much longer."

Dragon form.

Dragon *form.*

Dragon form.

She'd finally gotten it. Or rather, Moranu had given it to her. Looking down at her own hands—taloned feet—she understood Jak's remark. She was snow white, with vague silver-gray markings. And she was enormous. Powerful, invincible, and extraordinary, as she'd always imagined dragon form would be. The one thing she'd always wanted, and it was hers.

Well, one of two things: dragon form and true love. And she'd given up the latter.

Now she at least had dragon form. One of two. But what if this was the only time for her? Astar had achieved dragon form only that once and never again. He seemed cheerfully unconcerned about it, but she could imagine her life stretching before her, empty of love, with no chance of feeling this way again. No, worse—she still loved Isyn with everything in her. The goddess hadn't taken that away, so it must be that Isyn wouldn't return her love.

That would be true agony.

Or, she could stay here in the Winter Isles, in dragon form. She'd be immortal. And forever heartbroken.

"Gen," Jak said, still holding out the rope. "You have to shift. We're waiting on you."

All the others had disappeared through the portal. Gen

spread her wings, longing to stretch them, to discover what this form could do. Better that than to live without love.

"Gen," Stella called, her expression abstract with concentration, her eyes alight with silver magic as she read Gen's emotions. Or her future. "Remember what you said on the sailboat. Don't overlook the very real and enduring love we all have for you. Don't leave us."

Chagrined, Gen dipped her chin in acknowledgment. She'd offered up Isyn's love to save him, but her life would not be an empty one, not if she filled it with love. And she already had so much of it. Look at Stella with her shining eyes, holding the portal open. Jak, utterly serious for once, offering the bit of rope and looking as if he'd stick it to her with a dagger if she refused. Reaching out a long ivory talon—the same shade as Isyn's hair—she touched the rope.

And nothing happened.

Jak swore viciously. "We need Isyn's magery. Call him back."

"I can't," Stella said. "I could only make a portal that goes in one direction."

Something shifted inside Gen, and she realized the power indeed lay within her. Moranu had given the gift, the thing Gen had sought all her life, and She hadn't asked for anything, not even gratitude.

Nevertheless, Gen sent the surge of gratitude, and yes, love.

And gave up dragon form.

Jak blinked at her sudden collapse back to human form only a moment before seizing her wrist and hauling her to the portal. Taking Stella's hand in his other one, he pulled them both through, and Gen braced for whatever they'd find on the other side.

Whatever life brought, she would be grateful.

~ 25 ~

ISYN COUGHED UP ice water. Someone thumped his back vigorously—with perhaps more power than necessary—landing a sound blow between his shoulder blades that made him hack up one more wave of it. The folk never had gotten a good grasp of the physiological differences between them. But they had managed to keep him alive. Gasping, he held up a hand. "I'm good. Enough already."

"What was that?" a man asked from behind him.

"Chittering and squeaking," a woman replied authoritatively.

"That's the language of the furry mini-bears," another man replied. "Isyn used it in the hall to get the vicious creatures to quit attacking *us* and focus on our common enemy. Finally."

"They're called the folk," another woman replied. Isyn knew that voice: Lena. "Have a modicum of respect, Rhyian." Lena crouched beside Isyn. "How are you feel—oh, Danu!"

She fell back on her behind, eyes huge in her face, and Rhy moved with lightning speed, putting himself between her and Isyn. No longer in wolf form, he looked like the classic Tala man from the stories, tall and long-limbed, black hair streaming wild away from a face dominated by savage deep-blue eyes.

"What did you do?" he barked.

"Nothing," Lena protested. "I was startled is all." She aimed a decent knuckle punch at the back of Rhy's knee, which buckled slightly, though he didn't lose his stance.

He did soften, however, glancing over his shoulder. "Ow." He offered her a hand up.

"Save it for Isyn," she snapped, pushing to her feet on her own.

With a shrug, Rhy swung the hand around to Isyn, who accepted the help cautiously, glad he'd managed to hang onto the Silversteel sword. "Hello, Your Highness. I'm Rhy," he said, baring his teeth in a decidedly wolfish smile and squeezing Isyn's hand a little too hard. "We met over a tentacle monster but haven't been properly introduced."

Lena was still staring at him, a very odd look on her face.

"Call me Isyn, and thanks for the rescue."

Rhy snorted disparagingly. "If you can call that disaster by such a grandiose term."

A tall blond man—bleeding from multiple lacerations, fresh bruises forming, and favoring one side—edged Rhy aside, giving him an exasperated look, holding out his hand to shake Isyn's. "I'm Astar, and this is Zephyr." He put his arm around the other woman, letting her support him. Tall like Gendra, she was striking and fierce in the same Tala way as Rhy. The grizzly bear and the gríobhth. Amazing. "And you met Lena already. Nice work with the sword," Astar added.

Crown Prince Astar, heir to the high throne, Isyn reminded himself, and bowed. "Your Highness, it's an—wait, where is Gendra?"

They all exchanged looks. "She was a bit... *big* to fit through the portal," Zeph replied first, arching her brows significantly.

An image flooded his mind of an enormous ivory dragon gazing down at him. "The ... dragon?" he said weakly.

"Yeah, how about that?" Rhy said to the others. "She did it."

"We always knew she would," Zeph agreed.

"Jak stayed back with your piece of net to help her shapeshift back," Astar explained.

"And Stella with him, obviously," Lena said, looking concerned, "to hold the portal open. They've done this before, so you don't have to worry."

He was shaking his head, grip so hard on the sword's hilt that it cut into his palm. "The net won't work without me. Gendra won't be able to shift without my magery to fuel the object."

The look they exchanged this time was more concerned. "I can go back for them," Zeph said.

"No," Astar replied in a forbidding tone before she even finished. "No one is going back through. Those three can figure it out without us. We'll wait."

Isyn wasn't waiting. Gendra had risked her life to save him, multiple times, and he'd rather die a slow death in the Winter Isles than condemn her to a lonely existence there. "Begging your pardon, Crown Prince Astar, but I'm going."

"You two really are made for each other," Astar said, though without much heat. "Rhy?"

Wiry arms encircled him in an unbreakable grip. "Even Jak

can't escape this hold, and he says you're weak still," Rhy taunted. "Though you don't look old to me."

"Rhyian!" Lena scolded, clapping a hand to her face. "I said he looked old-*er*."

Isyn relaxed, no longer fighting Rhy's hold. Maybe the Tala prince would drop his guard and Isyn could slip his grip. Preparing to bolt the moment he could, he looked around for the portal, unable to sense it. They stood on a rocky promontory, very like the one they'd left, but delightfully unfrozen. He was soaking wet and not cold at all, which felt like a miracle. Actual green grass cushioned his feet, and moss coated the rocks. Surf roared nearby, invisible behind the thick mist. Birds sang in a verdant forest he could just see in the close distance, and the scent of soil and fresh leaves filled the air. He'd forgotten how rich a living world could be.

"Where are we?" he asked.

"We don't know," Astar answered. "But we think it must be our own world since we were all able to shapeshift back on our own. Nilly's been practicing opening portals of her own— and choosing the destination—so she might know. We'll ask her."

"Nilly can't come too soon," Zeph said, sliding Astar a concerned look. "You need healing."

"It's nothing fatal, just inconvenient," he assured her with a fond smile. "Our Nilly will be drained."

"Can't you heal by shapeshifting?" Isyn asked. So far Rhy's grip hadn't softened by even the teensiest amount.

Astar grimaced ruefully. "Not all shapeshifters are able to, just like not all shapeshifters have more than one form. I have my First Form only and—"

"And dragon form," Zeph reminded him with a proud smile.

"Just the one time, when I needed it most." He kissed her nose, then looked back to Isyn. "But I can't heal. Or cache extra outfits like Zephyr and Gen can." He gestured to his decidedly unprincely outfit of a simple white tunic and blue pants. "Otherwise I'd shift back in something useful like fighting leathers."

"Let the girls play with changing outfits," Rhy replied, tightening his grip as if Isyn had made an offensive comment.

"Manly men don't care about clothes?" Lena inquired silkily.

"Only so far as what it takes to keep the maidens from blushing," Rhy retorted.

"Good thing there are no maidens in sight." Her pleased, sly expression confirmed that she'd annoyed Rhy, though Isyn couldn't see his face. How could they be engaging in banter when three of their group were missing?

"They should have come through by now," Isyn ground out.

"Give it time," Astar said, Zeph nodding.

"They can do it," Rhy and Lena said at the same time.

And Isyn realized they were all worried and distracting themselves. A tightly knit group, Gendra's friends—and one he wasn't a part of.

"I really think Rhy can let Isyn go," Zeph said to Astar after a long, fraught silence. "The portal doesn't even seem to be open on this side."

Lena shook her head. "I can't sense it either."

Astar sagged, worry creasing his brow, but he nodded at Rhy. "Let him go."

"Aw, and I was having fun." Rhy's death grip relaxed, allowing Isyn to draw a deep breath. Isyn braced, prepared for a shove or some other callous treatment, but Rhy kept stabilizing hands on him, surprisingly gentle given his sharp tongue. "Steady on your feet? Yeah, you got it. We'll have you back in shape in no time." He patted Isyn on the back and stepped to the side.

"Is there a plan," Isyn asked the group, "for what we do if they don't come through? I feel I should point out that, if this is our world, it's been a longer time there."

They all looked at Astar, who grimaced and scrubbed a hand over his face, wincing at the forming bruise there. "I apologize, Prince Isyn, but we are not long on planning. The entire excursion to rescue you was constructed on the fly. I'm afraid we're playing this by ear."

"Say that we're following instinct and intuition," Zeph said, nudging him. "It sounds better."

He smiled, wearily. "Look at you, becoming the diplomat."

She pretended to buff her nails. "I've been practicing. But I do have a backup plan—if people don't like my sweet words, I become the gríobhth and eviscerate them."

Astar belly laughed, and Zeph beamed, clearly pleased to have relieved his worry at least for a moment. "Ordnung will never be the same," he told her.

"It could stand to change," Rhy commented sourly.

There must be other ways to get back to the Winter Isles.

Perhaps Isyn could find that rift in the ocean he and Gendra had both come through. Even if the others came through Stella's portal, Isyn would have to find a way to liberate the folk from their icy prison. Otherwise they'd eventually die out. He owed them too much to let that happen. And then there was Falada, and wherever she'd gone.

Zeph's head whipped around. "Someone's coming." She stepped away from Astar, and the gríobhth stood in her place, defending him and Lena.

Isyn lifted the Silversteel sword, finding himself side by side with Rhy, also brandishing a sword. Rhy slid him a wicked grin. "Sometimes unfriendly beasties come through the rifts," he explained.

"Believe me," Isyn replied, gaze focused on the empty air that held Zeph's keen attention, "I've had experience. That's how I broke the leg—fighting one of those tentacle monsters."

"And you lived to tell the tale?" Rhy actually sounded impressed. "If we have to be saddled with another mossback, I'm glad it's someone useful."

Isyn didn't have a chance to absorb that statement, which was astonishing on several levels, because Jak, Stella, and Gendra stepped through empty air onto the lush green grass. Gendra had transformed yet again, from dragon back to her vividly lovely human form, once again his Briar Rose, wearing a blue gown under her white fur cloak, the shadow-fox hat he'd given her perched jauntily on the long chestnut curls that spiraled around her in glossy waves.

Her indigo eyes, shifting with shades of violet like a calm sea at twilight, met his—and welled with tears.

~ 26 ~

"OH, ISYN," GEN breathed, unable to believe her eyes. Not only had he been restored to health, standing on two strong legs again, thanks to Stella's magic—but somehow he'd also regained his youth, looking no older than he must have when he fell into the Winter Isles. This was the gift from Moranu, she realized. The goddess had answered her prayer that Isyn be given the life that had been stolen from him.

He reached her in two strides, sheathing the Silversteel sword in a smooth movement, taking her carefully by the arms. No, of course he wouldn't kiss or embrace her, because she'd given up his love. The sacrifice had been worth it. Seeing him whole again, his whole life ahead of him—it was absolutely worth it. So why was she crying?

"What's wrong, Briar Rose?" he asked. "Are you hurt?"

Yes, but not in the way he meant. "I'm fine," she assured him. "Look at you. You're young again."

"I'm... what?" He looked stunned.

"I *said* he didn't look old," Rhy complained.

"Stella's healing must've helped?" Lena ventured.

Stella stepped closer, reaching up to lay a hand on Isyn's cheek, turning his head to face her. "This wasn't my work. But you're all correct. Your body is not quite thirty years old."

Isyn's face lit with wonder. "I feel good," he ventured.

"Maybe it's an effect of traveling back through the rift," Lena mused. "Which would be useful if any of us get stuck again in one where time moves faster."

But Gen knew that wasn't it. This was the work of Moranu. She couldn't seem to stop crying. She didn't know why. She'd given him up, knowing the price and willing to pay it… but, oh, how it sliced at her that he didn't love her anymore. If he ever truly had.

"Briar Rose," Isyn said softly, turning his attention back to her. Lifting his hands to cup her face, he brushed away her tears with his thumbs. "Why the tears? You know you can talk to me."

She caught her breath on a sob. She *couldn't* talk to him, not about this. If she told him about her bargain with the goddess, he'd pretend to love her anyway. He was just that noble, and he'd feel obligated to stay with her, feeling that he owed her. Tempting as it was to trap him that way, she wouldn't be able to live with herself. No, she'd let him go, as she'd promised Moranu she would, just as she'd let dragon form go. "I'm just so happy," she said, willing her face to show him. She *was* happy for him, so it wasn't a lie. "It's all right."

He frowned, searching her face, clearly unconvinced, and she recalled that he'd commented before that she said that when she wasn't convinced but was determined to please him. "No," he said slowly. "It's not all right. Something is very wrong."

"We can talk about it later," she pleaded. "When everyone

isn't listening in. Please... I need you to let go of me. Don't touch me."

His expression froze, clear green eyes icing over. Releasing her, he stepped back and bowed formally. "As my lady wishes."

"Prince Isyn?" a voice called, filled with incredulous hope, and Isyn spun away from her, hand going to his sword hilt.

The rest of the group, who'd drawn discreetly back while she and Isyn talked, formed an instinctive defensive ring around him. "Who is that, Isyn?" Astar asked on a growl.

"I don't... Commander Siebold?" Isyn's voice rose with his astonishment.

A big man strode out of the mist, grinning ear to ear, a heavy broadsword swinging casually from one hand before he sheathed it on his back. He went right up to Isyn, their group all tensing, then dropped to one knee and bowed his head. "I should say, King Isyn," the man corrected in a tone of reverence. He raised his head. "We've been waiting for you for a long time, Your Highness. Welcome home."

"BUT HOW DID you manage to create a portal to bring us directly to the Isles of Remus?" Lena asked Stella yet again. They were trailing in a short parade behind Isyn, who was in the midst of a hugely enthusiastic group of people, more arriving by the moment as they made their way to what would apparently be Isyn's palace. Gen only caught a glimpse of his ivory hair and tall form on occasion as they crowded around, all wanting to talk to and touch him.

"I'm trying to think of a way to explain," Stella replied patiently. "I thought about the problem a lot while we were sailing, how each of us seems to influence which alter-realm we end up in. It's a kind of … picturing where I want to go."

"But you'd never been here before," Lena argued, "so how did you picture it?"

"I just… did." Stella sighed heavily. "I can't put it into words."

Jak, on her other side from Lena, Stella's arm firmly looped through his, gave Lena a warning look. Stella was exhausted— especially since she'd insisted on healing Astar enough for him to walk on his own, even though Zeph, Rhy, and Gen had all volunteered to become a horse to carry him. Astar had, surprisingly, allowed the healing instead, reminding them all that the people of the Isles were largely unfamiliar with shapeshifters, and it was better to remain discreet. He and Zeph followed immediately behind Isyn's group, Astar having graciously yielded to local royalty, meaning Isyn, and Gen walked beside Rhy, bringing up the rear.

Isyn had beckoned her forward, but she'd waved him off, and he'd been immediately distracted by the many questions his people were hurling at him. She had to make it clear to him that she'd make no demands on his heart. A clean break so he could live the life he was meant to.

"'Briar Rose,' huh?" Rhy commented.

Gen blushed, cursing shapeshifter hearing. "It's from a

mossback tale," she told him. "A term of affection."

"Oh, I figured out that much," Rhy replied cheerfully, sliding her a mischievous look. "What I can't figure out is why you're not up there with him."

"I don't think I could fit through the mob." As the forest track from the shoreline widened into a proper road, well-maintained and smooth, people had begun to line the sides of it, making their procession feel more formal and more festive all the time. They were shouting Isyn's name and cheering, throwing flower petals.

"You saved his life," Rhy pointed out remorselessly. "He's only here because you talked us all into rescuing him. He could show a little gratitude."

"I don't *want* his gratitude," she ground out, perilously close to tears again.

Rhy cocked his head, studying her. "I misspoke. He could demonstrate his love for you by acknowledging you in front of his people."

There was no getting around this very awkward conversation. "I'm giving him up," she whispered, willing the others not to overhear, though she'd no doubt have to tell every one of them exactly this. "Look at him. He's king of the Isles of Remus, and I'm not fit to be a queen."

Rhy snorted. "And Zeph is? She's going to be *high* queen."

"That's different."

"Why?" he demanded. "Thrones and crowns are mossback things. They aren't what matters."

"They *do* matter. And I made such a big deal about Zeph leaving Astar alone so he could do his duty and make his marriage of state. I'd be a hypocrite if I changed my mind now."

"Ah, well." Rhy sighed and thrust his hands in his pockets, tipping his head back to contemplate the sky. "It seems we all end up eating our own words and convictions at some point. The question is: Do you want to be right or do you want to be happy?"

She didn't tell him that she'd traded her chance for happiness so that Isyn could have his. "This is Isyn's destiny, what he fought for so hard, for so long to gain."

"If you love this man, *you* should be fighting for him. True love, as you've said so often, doesn't happen often. It's a rare and precious gift—and you shouldn't take it for granted."

Lena glanced over her shoulder, her expression opaque, making it clear she could hear every word. She dropped back to Gen's other side. Wonderful.

"What's going on? Why does Gen have to fight for Isyn? They're in love."

"As you're well aware, Salena," Rhy replied sardonically, "love doesn't last forever."

"It can if it's not treated carelessly," she snapped with considerable heat as Rhy winced. She slipped her hand into Gen's. "Why do you say you have to give him up, honey?"

"I won't force him to be with me," Gen answered, giving Rhy a narrow glare. "Sometimes a love affair is meant to last only a short time. It can be a product of the intensity of the moment. I'll savor what we had, but that was a very particular set of circumstances, and Isyn needs to move on now. I won't be so selfish as to be forever running after him because of something we once had."

"Ouch," Rhy breathed, and Gen immediately felt bad.

She looped her arm through his. "I'm sorry. I didn't mean to be harsh."

"It's a fair point," Rhy allowed.

"Is it, though?" Lena asked, surprising them both. She wasn't looking at them, gaze fixed firmly in the distance. "It seems to me that you should talk to him. Give Isyn the opportunity to tell you what *he* wants, instead of you deciding for both of you."

"What if he won't talk to her, though?" Rhy asked. For once he didn't sound angry or demanding. His eyes were on Lena, and he sounded like he genuinely didn't know the answer and was beseeching her for an answer.

Lena slowly turned her head and met his gaze. "Then she needs to *listen.*"

Gen sighed internally, knowing they weren't talking about her and Isyn at all. The last thing she was going to do was anything that might impede Isyn breaking free of her and the past that had claimed him for far too long.

~ 27 ~

EVERYTHING WAS MOVING too fast for Isyn to keep up. After decades of living in a frozen, nearly silent world, the barrage of scents and sounds was nearly overwhelming. And the people, all talking at once about a myriad of things he hadn't thought about in years. Politics and land squabbles and trade routes with other nations. He'd never imagined he'd miss the starkness and scarcity of the Winter Isles, but as he tried to assimilate the sheer quantity of the outside world, he found himself longing for a small room and a few moments of quiet.

And Gendra there, too, cuddling close to him.

But she'd asked him not to touch her, and she'd been lying to him. She wasn't all right at all. Something was very wrong, and she'd been avoiding him so deftly that he hadn't been able to corner her long enough to find out what. They'd reached the palace, an astoundingly lovely work of architecture, all in white with red-tiled roofs. It rambled along a peaceful bay, protected from the harsher waters of the strait, with a wide sandy beach that stretched for leagues in both directions. Though it had a few towers topped with cone-shaped red roofs flying colorful pennants, the place looked more like a country house, with its many wings and balconies, than any kind of fortress. Nothing at all like the confines of Castle Marcellum.

He'd been taken to a suite of rooms on the top floor, with doors that opened onto a vast rooftop garden, verdant in the cool mist of the gathering evening, and no doubt vistas of the bay and surrounding forest when the sun shone. His people—so odd to think of them as his people—had assured him the sun typically banished the mist by mid-morning. They also promised that the crown prince and his fiancée had been given the best rooms other than his own, and his other traveling companions all housed according to their specific requests. Every effort had been made to accommodate the wishes of the heroic team that had brought the king of the Isles of Remus safely home.

Which meant that Gendra hadn't expressed the wish to see him, much less share his rooms. And why should she? They'd been thrown together by circumstance, and she'd made it clear by her words and repeatedly avoiding him that she didn't wish to renew their love affair.

Still, when she'd transformed back to human when they were fighting the tentacle monster, she'd kissed him. A real kiss that had set his loins on fire and turned his heart over. What had changed?

He wouldn't know until he asked her, which was why he'd flexed his newfound authority and summoned her. It might be an unfair move, but his other option was to wait for the welcome reception and ball and chase her around it like a lovelorn puppy. Though, if that was what it took, he'd do that, too.

"Lady Gendra of Annfwn," a stentorian voice announced.

Isyn had no idea who the man was. So far he'd placed about ten names to faces and stations, and that much had made his head hurt.

"Plain Gendra is fine," he heard her say from the other room. "I'm no lady."

"The king is through there, my lady," the voice replied.

Frozen in place, suddenly full of pure nerves at confronting her, Isyn stood where he was, waiting for her to find him. She did, after a few moments, stepping into the rooftop garden, her face composed in a serene mask that didn't fool him for a moment. She was upset and trying to hide it from him. The question was, what was upsetting her—being summoned to face him or whatever was causing her to avoid him in the first place?

Possibly both.

"Your Highness," she said smoothly, curtseying low so her silk skirts billowed around her like a flower blossom. She'd dressed for the upcoming ball, her gown a gorgeous indigo with a hint of violet sheen. When she lifted her gaze, she confirmed his guess that the color exactly matched her eyes. It also dipped low over her creamy bosom, leaving her arms bare and hugging her narrow waist, flattering her extraordinary beauty. His people had dressed him in deep blue velvet, the colors of the royal family of the Isles, and he wondered if Gendra had noticed they matched. He nearly commented on it, then noted that she wasn't smiling.

He wanted to seize her in his arms and crush his lips to hers and make her smile at him as she used to, wanted to carry her to the bed so she'd gasp and moan his name, and tell him she loved him still. Though… maybe she didn't.

"Don't do that," he snapped, far too harshly, and she raised one brow as she stood.

"Curtsey?"

"That. And calling me 'Your Highness.' I'm still Isyn."

"King Isyn," she corrected coolly. "King of all you survey." She gestured to the twilit sea of fog shrouding the landscape below.

"A keen irony that that I can't actually *see* any of it," he observed wryly, rejoicing that he'd managed to tease a hint of a smile from her.

"I can promise it's not the land of the blind," she said, smiling a bit more.

It was almost like they'd been before, but it seemed a vast gulf divided them, and he didn't know how to cross it.

"I have something for you," she said, her smile fading. She withdrew something from her pocket and handed it to him. "I'm returning it to you. I had it in my cache all this time."

He turned it over in his hands, feeling the disconnect of time and place as he studied the book and its title. *Tales of the Fae*, scrolled in gold leaf over a rose in full bloom. "Briar Rose," he breathed in recognition, "I—"

"I don't think you should call me that anymore," she interrupted, color flushing her cheeks.

That gave him pause. "Why not?"

"It's embarrassing," she said, sounding defensive. "And silly." Her gaze slid away, and she fidgeted with a fold of her silk skirts. Another lie.

"I didn't make you for a coward," he said, rather pleased to see her eyes flash indignant fire as they met his again. "Where is the white saber cat who scaled a giant to save me? Where is the fire-breathing dragon who fished me out of the sea?" He risked taking a step closer to her, and she inhaled sharply. Not fleeing, but a pulse beat frantically in the tender hollow under her jaw as she set her chin stubbornly.

"Isyn," she breathed, an uneven hitch in it. "Please don't do this to me. I'm trying to be brave, but doing the right thing is… It's not easy."

"What right thing?" he coaxed, coming close enough to her to take her hand and enclose it in both of his.

"Letting you go," she said firmly, but her lips wobbled, eyes growing luminous with tears.

He caught his breath at the sudden pain. "Don't you love me anymore? Was none of it real?"

She softened, gazing back at him with memories in her eyes of all they'd been to each other in those few short, intensely intimate days. "I'll love you for the rest of my life," she answered with her artless and earnest honesty. Then she rushed on before he could savor the joy of hearing those words. "But I can't be with you. We both have to face that."

"Why can't you?" he asked, utterly bewildered, holding onto her hand when she tried to tug it away. "I don't understand what I'm supposed to be facing."

She took a ragged breath. "I don't want you to pretend to love me out of obligation. You don't owe me anything, Isyn. I don't want your gratitude. We saved each other. We're even."

He'd have given a great deal to be having this conversation when he felt less overwhelmed by the sudden change in his life and world, but he'd summoned her to force this, and he wouldn't give up now. "But I do love you," he protested.

She shook her head. "No, you don't."

"I do," he insisted, squeezing her hand as if that might somehow prove it.

"You said you wished I hadn't come back for you," she accused, not meeting his gaze but staring steadfastly at some point on his chest.

"Because I wanted you to live! I was terrified you'd die saving me. Or that you'd succeed and you'd be stuck with a doddering old man."

"You are not old, Isyn! And I love you no matter how you look, aged or young, injured or whole. None of that matters to me."

That did it. Releasing her hand, he took her face in his and kissed her. She stiffened, then melted, making a small despairing sound, then dug her fingers into the velvet of his coat, sagging against him as he drank of her sweet lips. Seaside sunshine and tropical flowers. This was right. Them, together. This was meant.

He broke the kiss, holding her close as she stared up at him, the careful mask of indifference finally shattered. Instead she looked tortured and furious, changing her grip to fists, she pounded them against his chest. "Stop *doing* that to me!"

"Doing what—kissing you?"

"Making me feel this way." Her face crumpled, and she once again curled her fingers into his jacket. "You have to let me go."

"If that's what you truly want, I will," he vowed, willing

her to believe him. "But I love you, Gendra. Briar Rose. Hummingbird, orca, saber cat, penguin, or dragon—I see you no matter what form you wear, and I will love you for the rest of my life. I've got my life back, and I want nothing more than to spend it with you."

She stilled, searching his face. "You truly mean that?"

"Of course I mean that! I know my own heart, Gendra—and I know yours."

"But I…" She shook her head, as if trying to clear it. "I don't understand," she whispered almost to herself, then pierced him with a fierce and possessive gaze. "But I'm taking the gift as offered. Would you—would you wait for me a moment?"

"I'll wait for you forever."

She giggled—a love giggle, he was sure of it—and kissed him. "This should be somewhat less than forever." Lifting her skirts so she could run, she dashed a short distance away. She folded her hands and bowed her head, seeming to be praying.

And, with a billow, a white dragon stood in her place, wreathed in the mists of the Isles, flames sparking as she breathed and extended her massive wings. He fell in love with her all over again.

When she shifted back to human form, she walked toward him, eyes shining. And when he opened his arms to her, she stepped into them, unhesitating, laying her cheek against his. "I have dragon form," she whispered, as if telling him a secret.

"I know you do. Was this a surprise?"

"A gift unasked for."

"Turns out your name is more prophetic than you made it

out to be."

"I wonder." She pulled back just enough to kiss him. "What happens now?"

"You marry me, be my queen, and we live happily ever after," he told her very seriously. "That's how all romantic fairy tales end."

"Isyn…" She searched his face. "I have to finish what we started. I can't abandon my friends."

"Of course not," he agreed. "You found me in order to obtain my assistance, and my assistance you all shall have."

Happiness lit her eyes, and she smiled, a sweet curve of her lovely mouth. "But what about being king?"

"They've waited this long," he said, kissing her, lingering over it. "Also, I can't abandon the folk. Your group is the key to liberating them from the alter-realm their world has become."

"We have to find a way to defeat the intelligence," she agreed.

"Besides, the final catastrophe is to happen here, yes?"

"We'll have to ask Stella if that's changed, but it hadn't the last time she looked."

"We'll ask, but not tonight. All I want tonight," he murmured, fitting her close against him, "is to dance with my faerie princess at the ball, and show her off in her beautiful gown. Would that be all right?"

She caught his teasing tone. "It would be more than all right. It would be wonderful."

"And then afterward…" He kissed her, long and lingering, seeking the immediate and passionate reply before releasing her and offering his arm. "Afterward, I plan to strip you out of that beautiful gown and show you what a *young* man can accomplish in bed."

"Just mind the claws," she simpered, her nails on his arm surprising him by curving into actual long, curved, and very sharp claws.

He lifted her hands to his mouth and kissed them. "I don't mind at all. I've got you. I love you."

"Yes," she sighed happily. "You absolutely do."

The story continues in
The Storm Princess and the Raven King
Coming February 22, 2022

TITLES BY JEFFE KENNEDY

FANTASY ROMANCES

BONDS OF MAGIC
Dark Wizard
Bright Familiar
Grey Magic (December 2021)

HEIRS OF MAGIC
The Long Night of the Crystalline Moon
(also available in *Under a Winter Sky*)
The Golden Gryphon and the Bear Prince
The Sorceress Queen and the Pirate Rogue
The Dragon's Daughter and the Winter Mage
The Storm Princess and the Raven King (February 2022)

THE FORGOTTEN EMPIRES
The Orchid Throne
The Fiery Crown
The Promised Queen

EROTIC PARANORMAL

MASTER OF THE OPERA E-SERIAL
Master of the Opera, Act 1: Passionate Overture
Master of the Opera, Act 2: Ghost Aria
Master of the Opera, Act 3: Phantom Serenade
Master of the Opera, Act 4: Dark Interlude
Master of the Opera, Act 5: A Haunting Duet
Master of the Opera, Act 6: Crescendo
Master of the Opera

BLOOD CURRENCY
Blood Currency

BDSM FAIRYTALE ROMANCE

Petals and Thorns

Thank you for reading!

About Jeffe Kennedy

Jeffe Kennedy is a multi-award-winning and best-selling author of romantic fantasy. She is the current President of the Science Fiction and Fantasy Writers of America (SFWA) and is a member of Romance Writers of America (RWA), and Novelists, Inc. (NINC). She is best known for her RITA® Award-winning novel, *The Pages of the Mind*, the recent trilogy, *The Forgotten Empires*, and the wildly popular, *Dark Wizard*. Jeffe lives in Santa Fe, New Mexico.

Jeffe can be found online at her website: JeffeKennedy.com, on her podcast First Cup of Coffee, every Sunday at the popular SFF Seven blog, on Facebook, on Goodreads, on BookBub, and pretty much constantly on Twitter @jeffekennedy. She is represented by Sarah Younger of Nancy Yost Literary Agency.

jeffekennedy.com

facebook.com/Author.Jeffe.Kennedy

twitter.com/jeffekennedy

goodreads.com/author/show/1014374.Jeffe_Kennedy

bookbub.com/profile/jeffe-kennedy

Sign up for her newsletter here.

jeffekennedy.com/sign-up-for-my-newsletter

Made in the USA
Las Vegas, NV
23 September 2021